DAUGHTER
OF GOD

DAUGHTER OF GOD

LEWIS PERDUE

A TOM DOHERTY ASSOCIATES BOOK
NEW YORK

DAUGHTER OF GOD

Copyright © 2000 by Lewis Perdue

This book is printed on acid-free paper.

Design by Lisa Pifher

A Forge Book
Published by Tom Doherty Associates, LLC
175 Fifth Avenue
New York, NY 10010

www.tor.com

Forge® is a registered trademark of Tom Doherty Associates, LLC.

ISBN 0-312-89074-5

First Edition: January 2000

Printed in the United States of America

0 9 8 7 6 5 4 3 2 1

To Katherine and William
My son and daughter,
without whose help this book would have been completed long ago
and without whom life would be vastly emptier. Every passing day,
I am astonished at how your love expands the boundaries of my heart
and your eyes reveal to me miraculous wonders of a world
that I have never seen before.

To Megan
My wife, friend, partner, soul mate.
I'm the kite, you're the string. Neither soars without the other.
We didn't meet by accident.

Thanks to God our Creator
Her strength and His inspiration are behind these words.

ACKNOWLEDGMENTS

To my editor, Natalia Aponte, who helped me to see this book through new eyes and guided my writing and my faith exploration to places I never before imagined. Being this well edited is an all-too-rare experience for an author.

Also to my agent, Natasha Kern, who never lost her faith in me or my writing. I have never been blessed before with such a relentless and unflagging advocate.

Many thanks to Kathleen Caldwell of Readers Books in Sonoma whose sharp eye on the final proofs caught so many things I had missed. Kathleen, I'm glad you enjoyed it so much.

So teach us to number our days, that
we may apply our hearts unto wisdom.
Psalm 90:12

(The Greek word for wisdom is *Sophia*.)

ONE

Zoe Ridgeway smelled it, felt it the instant she crossed the threshold of the imposing Swiss mansion. She tried to convince herself that she was imagining things. But even the long-lost Rembrandt hanging casually in the entryway couldn't distract her thoughts from the conviction that death lived here.

"Herr Max is eager to see you," said a tall, formal man in accented English as he gave her a short, stiff bow from the waist. "Please follow me."

She followed the muscularly broad man through elegantly appointed rooms with high ceilings and white walls covered with masterpieces. Zoe knew he was more than just a butler when he bent over to pick up a fallen piece of paper and revealed the straps of a shoulder holster pressing against the fabric of his coat. She was married to a man who used to wear one and had learned to spot concealed firearms almost unerringly.

As Zoe followed the bodyguard through the house, she struggled to conceal her excitement. As a fine art appraiser and broker, she was used to having the priceless art treasures of the world pass through her hands with an almost banal regularity. Masterpieces were her daily bread. But now she struggled to keep the awe from her face as she recognized the paintings of one great master after another hanging casually about the drawing room as they passed through. On the wall above a gilded harpsichord, she spotted a Tintoretto that she knew had been missing since the early years of World War II. And next to that a Chagall thought to have been burned during the Nazis' campaign against decadent art. Music, a string symphony of joy, filled her head as her eyes took in one astounding work after another.

They reached a sitting room and the bodyguard motioned her to wait. At the far side of the room, Willi Max slumped in his faux-Bauhaus wheelchair, looking more dead than alive.

In a silence broken only by Max's ragged breathing, the bodyguard went to the wheelchair. He bent over and whispered. Willi Max sat up, suddenly animated like a puppet jerked to life. The bodyguard turned the wheelchair around to face her.

"Welcome to my home," Max said warmly, his voice surprisingly strong. The bodyguard wheeled him toward Zoe. As he drew nearer, she made out a wizened old man with eyes the icy luminous blue of glaciers backlit by the sun. He held out a shaky hand. "I am so glad you could come on such short notice."

Zoe took his hand. It felt dry, light, insubstantial, as if the life had already left this part of the man's body.

"It's my privilege," Zoe said sincerely.

Max's face was nearly immobile but his eyes flashed his approval.

"But come now!" Max said with a nod to his bodyguard. "I have little time left and there is much to accomplish." The bodyguard turned the wheelchair and pushed it across the dark-wood-paneled drawing room toward a wall of bookshelves. Zoe followed, then stood a respectful distance behind them, absolutely still on the hand-knotted Persian carpet as the guard slid aside a hinged section of bookshelves to reveal a hidden door. The bodyguard knelt on one knee before a wheelchair-height security keypad and paused as if to reassure himself that he remembered the proper sequence.

Soft tones filled the room as the guard punched in the security alarm combination. Zoe's palms were damp with the tension. She spread her fingers and, as casually as she could, made as if she were smoothing out the wrinkles in her long gray pleated skirt. She looked about her and listened, the music in her head changing as she gazed first at one painting and then another.

She tried to fix in her mind what she had seen so far. Notes were not allowed at this stage. Max was keenly aware of the effect his art had on people and he had expressed his desire that she experience the art first without the prosaic intrusion of work. It was not the first time a client had tried to influence her appraisals this way and, as usual, she had prepared herself for this contingency. With the guard occupied with the keypad and Max facing away from her, she slipped one hand inside her blazer to make sure the minicassette recorder was still running. It was not the first time someone had tried to dazzle away her objectivity. It was, however, the first time someone had succeeded.

Zoe had loved art all her life with a passion that had driven her to make it her profession. But despite the satisfaction of spending her life surrounded by the world's most beautiful objects and historical antiquities, she had always dreamed of discovering buried treasure: unearthing a hitherto-unknown trove of priceless art that would be nearly impossible to value.

Instead, it had discovered her.

Less than forty-eight hours ago, Willi Max had phoned her, apologizing when she told him that it was still the middle of the night in Los Angeles, something he seemed well aware of.

"I am dying," he had said without any trace of emotion. "Faster than most people. I have little time remaining and I needed to call you before I changed my mind or . . ." He left the obvious unstated.

Zoe had never heard of the man and had nearly hung up on him, half convinced it was a prank call. But his precise English, the imperious German accent, and his obvious sincerity kept her listening despite the sleep that clouded her thoughts.

"I wish personally to make the arrangements for the care of my legacy," Max had said. Legacy. Not collection. Zoe remembered his words now, finally starting to grasp their true meaning.

The sleep had cleared instantly that night when Max offered her nearly ten times her normal fee to drop everything and fly to Zurich.

"I have heard that you are the best art historian and broker in the world," Max had said. "And honest . . . honest. I want my collection handled honestly . . . morally." There had been a long silence. Zoe wondered if the man had suffered a stroke and died, but then he broke into a spasm of coughing. Finally, "I have read all of your published works," he said, "even the books . . . and"—he coughed again, briefly—"and all of the articles about you. . . . I believe that you will understand. It is vital to understand."

As if Max had sensed her continuing reluctance, he had sealed her commitment that night by mentioning that there was a substantial consulting fee in it for her husband as well, since his collection included items that needed the attention of a scholar versed in the ways of religious manuscripts and reliquaries—things Max's research would have told him were not her strong points. As a result, she often worked with her husband, Seth Ridgeway, who was a professor of philosophy/comparative religion at UCLA. He specialized in a particularly fertile period of religious development from about 500 B.C. to A.D. 700.

A long, low tone sounded from the alarm system and interrupted her reverie. Zoe watched as the bodyguard opened the door. Max seemed energized by the opening and with a great effort sat nearly upright in the wheelchair. "After you, my dear," he said chivalrously. Zoe looked at the bodyguard who beckoned her forward with a slight bow and a nod of his head.

Instants later, Zoe stepped through the door and looked about. The room had a ceiling that had to be forty feet high, walls painted off-white in order to focus on the room's objects. Like almost every room she had seen in the vast mansion, this one was almost a cross between a gallery and a warehouse—too filled with art to have a clear focus. Then, as Zoe began to look closely at the art around her, her skin came alive with great electrical coils of astonishment. Here was a legendary Vermeer that had been written about in the artist's letters but never seen.

Music like the most exquisite orchestral strings filled her heart and demolished the last wisps of the her scholarly objectivity. Instead she opened her soul to the beauty of the art and the music it created in her.

She approached the Vermeer and let its remarkable shadows speak to her. The incredible depth and perspective invited her to step bodily into the scene. Zoe tore her eyes away from the Vermeer and found herself looking at a case containing a Leonardo codex that, as far as she could tell, was not among any previously described or known. Zoe turned slowly, her eyes finding in rapid succession a previously unknown van Gogh, a Picasso thought to have been destroyed, a Gutenberg Bible, and the Torah from King Solomon's Temple.

Zoe dream-walked her way around the great room. Rare books lined mahogany bookshelves; priceless manuscripts and scrolls from antiquity jammed a glass case. Religious writings gathered from caves and ruins in secrecy by night-prowling Bedouins who peddled them on the underground market hundreds of years before the Dead Sea Scrolls were revealed.

Zoe knew that any single item by itself could be the centerpiece of a great museum. But all of them together? Her head spun. A symphony filled her every thought.

Her circumnavigation brought her back face-to-face with Max, and when she looked at him Zoe saw his face shine at the awe that his art had inspired in an expert who was widely acknowledged as unimpressible.

"I'm not sure what to say." Zoe searched for words. She felt her cheeks burn as she struggled to resurrect her composure.

"I believe that words are mostly inadequate," Max said. His head doddered as he looked up at her. To make it easier for him, Zoe Ridgeway seated herself on a nearby Mies van der Rohe sofa and struggled to assimilate the overload.

Max glanced up and with a nod dismissed the guard, who closed the security door behind himself.

"As you are beginning to grasp, this is a legacy, not a mere collection," Max began, his words coming in small bursts between deep rattling breaths. "I wish for you to help me atone for my legacy."

Zoe looked at him questioningly.

Max closed his eyes for a long moment and then continued. "More than half a century ago, I was a conscript in the Wehrmacht—the army of the Third Reich. I was one of many who were pressed into service in the Austrian mountains south of Munich, in the region known for its salt mines.

"Hitler had looted many of the great collections and it was here in the mines that the art was brought for safekeeping. I saw many awesome things and one thing in particular which has been a burdensome secret for me since those days."

A coughing fit racked the man's frail body, bringing the guard back into the room. Max took a deep breath and waved the man away.

"When the Allies came, I—and many of my comrades—fled, taking with us each as much of the art, gold coins, manuscripts, religious reliquaries as we could carry.

"I made my way to Zurich and with the help of a network of those who had preceded me set up a new life. I sold some of the art I had brought with me. But instead of simply living on it, I used the proceeds to buy the art and rare objects from those who came after me.

"It was a desperate time," Max explained. "The market was flooded; cash was scarce; survival was paramount. What you see around you was acquired for pitifully little for someone like me who was prepared to take a chance. I kept what I could and disposed of what I needed to in order to obtain the funds for my own survival . . . and to acquire more."

Max's eyes were moist as he scanned the room. "I had to, you see. I fell in love with the art. It has always owned me and not the other way around."

Zoe nodded, feeling the irresistible gravity that pulled her toward the magnificence gathered in the room.

Again, deep coughing racked his chest.

"It is a sin, I know, for me to have had all of this for so long, and I wish for you to help me atone."

Zoe raised her eyebrows.

"Most of the art is stolen. I wish for you to return as much of it as possible to the rightful owners—or to their heirs. I have already transferred to an account in Zurich . . ." He fumbled under the blanket that covered his lap and knees and produced an envelope. Zoe got up and took it from him. She looked cautiously at it and then sat back down.

"The account is in your name and that of your husband; either of you can draw upon it. It represents an amount that would be several times your normal commission if the art were sold."

Zoe's head spun. That had to be tens of millions of dollars.

"If you cannot locate the rightful owners, then I wish for you to make a decision as to which public museum—or museums—should receive the art as a donation. There is a separate provision in my last will and testament that provides for all the expenses associated with this."

Zoe opened her mouth, but words would not follow.

Max shook his head. "Don't," he said. "Think about this; sleep on it. Talk to your husband. For there is an even more awesome responsibility that I would like the two of you to assume, larger, more important, more awesome than all of the art. An ancient secret; a religious truth; knowledge that can change the entire course of human affairs."

"What . . . ?"

Again, Max shook his head. "On the table beside you . . ."

Zoe looked over and saw, for the first time, a leather briefcase.

"Take it to your husband. My research indicates that he reads ancient Greek fluently."

Zoe nodded dumbly.

"He will want to read this as soon as possible." Max coughed violently for a moment. When he recovered, he continued. "I will also be sending you something via courier, something I must retrieve from a more secure location."

More secure than this? Zoe wondered. What on earth could be more important than all this?

He blinked at her. "I have just now—this moment—decided to send this item to you."

"Why?"

"Because I see truth in your eyes," Max said. "When it arrives, examine this thing. Talk to your husband. You and he must be truthful with each other about your decision. Then come back to see me tomorrow and give me your answer and we will begin our work here."

TWO

The last golden rays of sunset bathed Seth Ridgeway in warm Gauguin colors as he sat on the hotel room sofa and bent over the ancient manuscript spread out on the coffee table. Finally, he straightened up and looked across the room at Zoe.

"So where's the rest of it?" he asked anxiously, then bent over and carefully set the last page of ancient paper on the pile. Seth wore running shoes, shorts, and a faded navy-blue LAPD T-shirt. Salt from his long run airbrushed faint white semicircles around his neck and armpits.

Zoe pulled the minicassette recorder's earplug from her ear, set down the pen she was using to transcribe notes, then turned to face him.

"He said he would send us the rest of it tomorrow." She sat at an antique secretary's desk in the far corner of the Eden au Lac's largest room.

Her heart softened when she looked at his face. It wore a worried expression that belonged more on the face of a five-year-old with a broken toy than it did on a forty-year-old ex-cop with a half a dozen gunshot scars and a Ph.D. in philosophy. The world saw Seth as a tough guy. To crooks and cops, he had been a legend who could shrug off the incoming rounds and still make the bust. And even scarier (at least to the UCLA athletic department, which had once mistakenly enrolled a basketball star in his class), he gave the toughest grades in the department. But Zoe knew that inside the tough shell and behind the myth was a wide-eyed little boy with an insatiable curiosity and a deep soft heart capable of intense love and immense faith. The love had made her life a steady procession of days each more enjoyable than the one before.

But Zoe had never understood Seth's faith. He was a scholar of religion and he knew the deceit and lies that underpinned every religion. Still he believed. Where somehow he found a reason to sustain his faith, she saw a sham. She didn't—couldn't—believe in God. Seth did. It was a mystery that their years together had done little to illuminate.

"Tomorr . . . ?" He let the word trail off as he gave her a frustrated, eyes-closed grimace.

Zoe nodded as she stood and walked over to him. The powerful aroma of his strenuous workout had nearly faded, but the intense masculine fragrance he gave off triggered a long series of sensual memories. She remembered the taste of his salt on her tongue, and the slick hardness of his bare muscles. For an instant, she thought of slipping quickly out of the flowered sundress under which she wore only the bottom of her bikini. Instead, she said, "Max is a very strange man, but very sincere—at least I believe so. He said that if he thought we truly understood the piece you have now, the importance of it, then you could have the rest."

"Have?" Seth responded. "Just *have* . . . not buy, read, borrow. Have?"

Again Zoe nodded as she put her hand on his shoulder. "All this stuff doesn't matter to him anymore, he said. He wants to atone."

Seth nodded. "It's certainly the right thing to do, even if it does come from looking at death in the mirror."

Zoe glanced at her watch.

"Something wrong?" Seth asked.

"Max." She frowned. "He said there was something he was going to have a courier deliver here. I thought it would be here by now."

"Something?"

"I said he's an odd bird." Zoe shrugged, then shook her head as she sat down next to him. She looked first at the manuscript pile and then back to Seth. "So what's there to understand in all that Greek, professor?"

"First of all, it's a passion—"

"Another nifty torture tale, right? Maiming martyrs for fun and profit."

Seth nodded. "First part, this"—he tapped the pages with his index finger—"is the narrative. The second part—the stuff we don't have yet—is supposed to be the actual word-for-word transcription of the trial."

"I'm amazed every time I think about how much paperwork the Romans stashed away in their archives."

"They practically invented bureaucratic paperwork," Seth agreed.

"So what's so special about this one?" Zoe asked. "I thought passions were usually embellished by the good church fathers beyond any connection with reality—you know, good propaganda for the faithful."

"Usually are." He raised his eyebrows and lifted his face to the ceiling for a moment. Then: "The first thing to understand is that if this document is authentic, this will turn out to be one of the many lost writings of Constantine's biographer, Eusebius. It's the story of a young woman named Sophia, and according to what's written here, she lived in a tiny, remote mountain village near the Anatolian city of Smyrna. The place is called Izmir today—in Turkey—but back then it was right in the hotbed of the early Christian church, not a long way from some better known New Testament cities such as Ephesus and Philadelphia—"

"I know that, sweetheart," she said warmly. "I'm not your student anymore."

"Sorry." He gave her one of the quick lopsided smiles that had captivated her so thoroughly the first day she had seen him at the podium. It was a smile that had launched her on a campaign of seduction, lust, and love that led her from being student to lover and, finally, wife.

"Okay. Anyway, Sophia's little village near Smyrna was a pastoral, herding-type settlement, more like a medium-term resting place for nomads, and from what I can tell here, it probably never had more than two or three hundred people, tops. There was little commerce with the outside world—no temple, no church, synagogue, pagan altar—nothing. That in itself is unusual because at the time this was written—A.D. 325, just a few months after the Nicean Conference—religion was the hot topic everywhere. People talked religion like sports scores or Beltway scandals today. Back then there were scores of different sects and variations of Christianity, and all of them were scouring the earth for converts in between bare-knuckle bouts over who was the"—he used his index and middle fingers to form quotation marks—"One True Church."

"Gee, they sure started early." Zoe frowned. "Worship our true god of love and kindness or we'll rip your babies apart." She shook her head disdainfully and settled herself into the far end of the sofa, facing him.

Seth shrugged and gave her a faint smile. "So here we have a little girl growing up in a sheep pasture with no religious training or tradition at all, and then suddenly, a few days after menarche, she starts to have visions, starts to hear the word of God."

"Well that's certainly enough to get her martyred right then and there," Zoe said.

Seth frowned. "I'd just as soon not start in on that tonight if that's okay with you." He opened his mouth to speak, then thought better of it.

Zoe scanned his face slowly, her gaze returning to the limitless intensity of his eyes. Her face softened toward him, but when she spoke, her words carried the steel of her own convictions.

"Seth, you know by now that I'm not on your case, not personally anyway. But you know as well as I do that organized religion is *not* spiritual," Zoe continued. "Religion kills, it divides people. It lies and cheats and steals and spends a lot of time covering up its crimes. Just look everywhere: Jews and Arabs, Orthodox rabbis setting themselves up as Hebrew ayatollahs to excommunicate other Jews, Sunni Muslims who kill Shiites, Catholics and Protestants killing each other and every damned one of them is as racist and sexist as a pickup loaded with Klanners. If there were a God and if God looked like any of the cartoons that these guys have created, then we're in a lot worse trouble than anybody can possibly imagine."

"Yeah, well . . ." Seth grumbled. "It's an old story . . . in history, not to mention you and me." He got up and walked over to the room service cart by the door and fiddled with the cork of an already opened bottle of Château La Gaffelière.

Zoe refused to let the issue drop. "And I *really* love that damned psalm about being beside the Rivers of Babylon that Joni Mitchell turned into a sweet little ballad," Zoe continued as she got up and paced. "Only nobody remembers that at the end of the very same psalm it says 'Blessed are they that dasheth the heads of thy little ones against the rocks.' This was vicious. It's genocide. If I believed in God, I sure couldn't believe in one that tells me to kill babies."

Seth quietly poured the wine into two glasses as she continued. Then, he walked over and handed her a glass. The intensity fled from her face as she looked at his open, concerned face.

"I'm so sorry," Zoe said as she took the glass. "I got carried away. The headlines have been so upsetting lately . . . all those smug, self-righteous people. . . ." She let the thought dangle. They both understood.

"Peace," he said. "At least for us."

Zoe smiled and held out her glass for a toast.

"To you," she said.

"You," Seth said, and clinked his glass against hers. They both sipped at the wine and stood quietly together for a long moment.

"You want to go back to the manuscript?" Seth asked finally.

"Of course," Zoe said. "I'm really sorry. The excitement of this whole thing's got my nerves on edge."

They walked back to the sofa and sat down. Seth scanned the pages. Then: " 'Apparently one day in this settlement without a church or synagogue,' " he continued, " 'Sophia got up on an oxcart parked in what passed for the center of town and started preaching. Miracles followed: healing—' " He waited for reaction. She gave him an indulgent look but said nothing.

" 'Sophia went about casting out demons, and one time when the villagers' oil supply had run out for their lamps . . .' " He held up a finger as he put down his wineglass, bent over the manuscript and carefully sorted through the pages.

Zoe sat down beside him and placed her hand on his thigh, feeling the hard, lean muscles under her fingers. Her eyes searched his face and watched the muscles shift and focus as he concentrated on the manuscript.

"Here it is," Seth said as he pulled a page of the manuscript from the pile and began to read from the handwritten Greek. " 'Thereupon the whole multitude being dismayed, Sophia directed those who attended to the lights to draw water and bring it to her. This being immediately done, she prayed over the water and with firm faith in the Lord commanded them to pour it into the lamps. And when they had done so, contrary to all expectation, by a wonderful and divine power, the nature of the water was changed into that of oil.'

"It says here that the people referred to her as 'Zaddik,' which is translated either as 'the Righteous One' or 'the Teacher of Righteousness.' "

Seth stopped and pointed to the page. "Now, see that? It's a circle around her name . . . and here." He pointed to another place. "That's the word for 'she.' "

Zoe nodded. "And?"

"And remember I told you this is a preliminary draft—not the finished work?" he began eagerly. "Well, this is the same story that I have read before from the works of Eusebius. But in the final version, it's the story of the martyr Narcissus—a 'he' in the final version. This manuscript is probably the true version, but it was edited to change the sex."

"Now *there's* a big surprise," Zoe said.

They looked at each other silently for a moment before Seth continued.

"Yeah. Well, it wasn't very long after she started performing miracles that word got out. Eusebius, who was a bishop in the Christian Church as it has become and as it was recognized by Emperor Constantine, paid a visit to Sophia's little hamlet. It wasn't all that far from Constantinople or from the palace in Nicomedia. I figure that this had to turn into a major event that had the full attention of the emperor himself."

"How come?" Zoe took a sip of her wine. In her mind she visualized the Byzantine art and the architecture she had studied while he populated her vision with the people of the time.

"Constantine was paranoid about unity," Seth said. "He came up in a time when the Roman empire had four Caesars who fought among themselves. He spent most of his career in wars and campaigns to reunite the Roman empire—something he saw as vital for survival against the barbarians who were hammering on every gate and against internal dissent. When he finally became the undisputed emperor, he was determined to rule a united empire no matter whom he had to remove to do it."

"But Constantine is known as the first Christian emperor," Zoe said.

"Only on his deathbed," Seth said. "Sol Invictus, the Sun God, was his main deity until the last hours of his life. For most of his life, Christianity was a political power tactic for Constantine, a method of governing rather than a religion."

"Not very original."

"No, but I think he was the first true master at shaping religion to help consolidate governmental power. He saw that this new religion wasn't going away, and that over the previous three centuries it had been a destabilizing influence on the rule of the empire. He saw it as clearly a growing force, so instead of fighting it he co-opted it. He controlled the church for his own purposes and shaped theology for the sake of political expediency. So many things that people today think are divinely inspired were actually Constantine's political edicts enforced by the power of the sword."

"Such as?"

Seth thought for a moment. He sipped at his wine and turned toward the window to gaze at the setting sun. Finally, he turned back toward Zoe and said: "How about something that is about as fundamental to the Christian church as you can get: the Trinity."

Zoe frowned.

"There was absolutely no unanimous agreement in the Christian church that Jesus was to be worshiped on a basis equal to God. Indeed, you could find a lot of solid evidence that Jesus himself would not be happy with this.

"But back in 324 or so A.D. the issue came to a head with a bishop named Arius, the presbyter of Alexandria, who was preaching that Jesus 'the Son' had been created, begotten by God 'the Father' and, therefore, was not quite as divine. Others disagreed and there were riots in the streets all over the empire caused by this and maybe another half dozen major theological issues. This doctrine spread like wildfire and with it more riots and bloodshed.

"Riots in the streets are not something an emperor likes to see. The whole thing baffled him. He called the issue 'truly insignificant' and was astounded when all the feuding parties ignored his directive to stop arguing. That's when he called the Nicean Conference. Church theologians today put a spin on the conference as a divinely inspired gathering of holy men guided to a common decision by the Holy Spirit. In reality, it was Constantine's way of calling them all to a meeting behind the woodshed."

As Seth spoke, sunset faded, filling up the room with deeper and deeper shadows. Neither of them moved to turn on a light.

"Constantine had the steel swords of his army to back him up," Seth continued. His story of the past played in Zoe's mind brighter and brighter as the gathering darkness gradually erased the detail from the present.

Zoe broke the silence. "As far as I can remember, this wouldn't be the first time theology was written with the sharp point of a sword."

"And not the last." Seth smiled. "So when all the bishops got to arguing again during the conference, Constantine had had enough. He was still an unbaptized pagan but he stepped in and declared that Jesus and God were 'consubstantial' and of 'one substance with the Father.' And what's more, anybody at the conference who didn't sign the declaration attesting that this was the word and will of God wouldn't leave the conference . . . at least not alive. Not surprisingly, all but two signed and those two were excommunicated and their writings ordered to be burned." He paused for a moment. "And so it is that the Trinity—the undisputed centerpiece of the Christian religion—was legislated at the point of a sword by a fellow who wasn't even a Christian at the time and it was not for the faith but to restore civil order."

Zoe gave him a wry smile and shook her head slowly. "So, the Nicean Creed was just Constantine's way of having everybody get their stories straight, to spin things the same way."

"Just that."

"Hmmph," Zoe said as she got to her feet and walked over to the window and looked down at the lights around the lake. "That old saying . . . the one about there are two things the public should never see being made: sausage and a law?" She turned to face him. "I guess there ought to be three. Theology."

"It's not pretty." Seth agreed as he got up and went to her side. Together they looked out over the lake.

"I just don't understand why you keep on believing when you know this stuff."

Seth sighed loudly. "Sometimes I wonder myself, but I keep thinking that underneath all the theological lies and church bureaucracy there are still some bits and shreds of truth to believe in."

"But what good are the shreds if the whole remains a mystery?"

"Maybe the mystery is the point." He shrugged. "Maybe the mystery has to remain because we're looking at the infinite through finite eyes. Maybe what God really wants is not blind acceptance of dogma but a lifetime of searching . . . discarding what is obviously false, testing the rest. That's why this manuscript that Max gave you is so important. It shows once again how the truth was edited to create a supposedly divine authority for what these people wanted to do. In this case, they wanted to suppress any sort of contention that women had a place in the church. So they did a sex change on Sophia."

"Oh, please," Zoe said.

She frowned for a moment, then her face recomposed itself as she sipped at her wine. Seth watched as her eyes changed ever so subtly, reflecting the shifting thoughts behind them. When she spoke again it was clear her mind had come about on a decidedly different tack. "The transcript of the trial?"

"Yeah?"

"If it really exists—the real translation, not just the summary or whatever Eusebius put in the manuscript—then wouldn't that be some sort of secular confirmation that the story of Sophia is true? That she worked miracles?"

"The power to heal exists in many people's minds."

"But wouldn't the trial transcript offer some sort of proof? After all, the authorities are obviously hostile to her. If they confirmed the miracles and the healing, wouldn't that be a level of credibility lacking from accounts written by those who believed in her?"

"Could be. Could also be that some clever Christian revisionist could have created the transcripts and attributed them to the trial authorities in order to make it look that way. But regardless of that, this is by far the most important thing I have ever come across in my entire career," he said. "And it just kills me to have only half the story."

Zoe nodded. "I know how you feel. That house . . . the art . . ." She let her words drift off into the darkness for a moment.

"It's like everything I have ever done, everything I've ever studied was just practice for this," Seth said.

Zoe murmured her assent.

"I think that sometimes God takes a hand and shoves us into the breach," Seth continued. We just have to think a little to recognize the push for what it is. I've been praying for this all my adult life."

"Seth, c'mon." Zoe shook her head and turned toward him. "I'm as overwhelmed by all this as you are. This is the event of a lifetime for me as well. But this isn't divine intervention. You *earned* this; and you were in the right place at the right time."

Seth turned away from her and folded his arms across his chest. Zoe gave a big sigh. They stood like that in the darkness for several minutes.

We're looking at the same scene, Zoe thought as she watched headlights move along the lakeshore roads. But how can it be that when we look at the very same things, we can reach such contradictory conclusions?

"Seth," Zoe said finally. "We just see things . . . differently."

Seth turned slowly toward her. He gazed for a moment at the shadowy outlines of her face, then smiled.

"Ain't that the truth." He leaned over to hug her and she made a loud sniffing sound. "Say, maybe you'd like to take a shower so I could get really close to you." She ran her hands over his shoulders and down his belly, brushing over the front of his running shorts with a light fluttering of fingers.

"Now that sounds like a good idea," Seth said as he turned toward her and started to give her an embrace. Zoe put her hands on his chest and gave him a gentle push.

"First the shower." She gave him a peck on his cheek.

"Oh, dang," he said with mock disappointment as he turned for the bathroom. "But I expect a better kiss than that afterwards."

"Count on it!" Zoe said as she turned on a lamp next to the window and gathered up some of the papers on the desk and stacked them atop a thick padded envelope. "I'll be right back after I drop these off at the hotel's safe deposit box and check to see if Max's package has arrived." She gave him a lascivious look. "Then you'd better be prepared, mister."

Seth went into the bathroom and turned on the hot water. He heard the room door close as Zoe left, then stepped into the shower.

There was no doubt that Zoe was right about the widespread spiritual corruption that underlay organized religion, he thought as he stood under the water. There was no doubt that both early Judaism and Christianity saw God as incorporating both male and female. The first chapter of Genesis clearly described an androgynous God where men and women were equal. Then at a much later date, some creative church official added the Adam and Eve story in Genesis 2, obviously to support the doctrine of male domination.

As he shampooed, Seth ran through in his mind the indisputable historical research that proved that what people viewed as Judaism or Christianity today represented only a tiny fraction of the religious diversity that had existed in the early days of their development. But church officials shaped religion to fit their culture and political needs, all the while telling the faithful that it was the other way around. To make this work, church officials winnowed through texts and scriptures and rejected those that failed to support the god they wanted to worship. Equally authoritative scriptures were burned as heresy because they didn't support orthodox dogma.

He rinsed his hair and began to soap up, conscious of the soreness that still edged the puckered bullet scars.

The Christian Bible of the year 1300 contained more books than the same Bible of 1700 because the church revised history as dogma changed. Were people who worshiped according to the older Bible and believed the now-missing chapters going to get kicked out of heaven?

He rinsed off the soap, turned off the water, and reached for a towel.

How could anyone possibly overlook the fact that the selection of writings for inclusion in scripture was a political act and that all of the books had been extensively rewritten to conform to dogma as it changed from era to era? Many books of the Torah could not have been written by Moses as alleged because they contained historical references that occurred after the prophet's death. Similar problems afflict the books in the Christian New Testament, where there was scant or no evidence to conclude that the books were written by those who were supposedly the authors.

Seth toweled off and finger-combed his hair as guilt sat like a stone on his heart. Raised as a strict Presbyterian, he could never shake the feeling that he was going to hell because he questioned the absolute perfection and holiness of the New Testament.

Preoccupied with the thought, he stepped back into the bedroom, still toweling at his hair, when the scene struck him like a fist.

The Greek manuscript was missing along with Zoe's notes and the mini-cassette recorder. Her purse lay on the floor, the contents scattered around it. Zoe was nowhere to be found.

Seth lunged for the telephone.

THREE

The tall, fair-haired American strode from the side-street shadows into the withering brightness of the Piazza Venezia. A brutal September sun welded the square's snarled traffic into a lava field of gas fumes and scorching metal. Stepping off the curb, he tacked a ragged diagonal across the square toward the Via del Corso.

The American was a lean young man in his thirties with the sort of New England skin that burned too easily in the Roman sun. As he waded through the swamp of Fiats and Vespas, he held one hand on his new summer hat while the other securely gripped his thin shiny aluminum briefcase. He wore cordovan loafers with tassels, a khaki poplin suit, a blue pinpoint oxford cloth button-down, and a Yale school tie.

Gaining the far curb, he checked his Rolex and cursed silently as he headed toward the Piazza Colonna. Damn! It just would not do to be late for his appointment with the Holy Inquisition.

He had assumed that the man who had summoned him would be found at the Vatican. But no, it was in some out-of-the-way location way the hell on the other side of the Tiber.

The Holy Inquisition had never died, he had learned to his surprise, it just changed its name: Vatican spin doctors changed it to "the Holy Office" in 1542 and then, in 1965 to "the Congregation for the Doctrine of the Faith."

A business associate, a man who had once been a Jesuit priest, had told the American, "The CDF is indisputably the most powerful department of the Curia and carries far more weight and wields more power within the Vatican than the KGB ever did in the Kremlin even at the peak of Soviet power."

The American stopped now at the intersection of a small street that had no sign. This has to be it, he thought as he turned right and followed the narrow way, remembering the former Jesuit's comments: "The KGB metaphor is apt, particularly for you. Because today the CDF operates more like an intelligence agency than an army of God and prefers to destroy lives and careers behind the scenes rather than in the light of critical public scrutiny. The head of the CDF is always the reigning Pope, but the inquisitorial apparatus is run by an executive simply known as 'the Secretary.' This job title, like the agency itself, dates back to the thirteenth century; back then it was called 'Grand Inquisitor.'

"The CDF has its own investigators and a network of snitches that puts the former East German Stasi to shame. You need to remember this and never let down your guard. These folks ain't Friar Tuck; they're dangerous and deadly serious. They gather incriminating evidence, then present it to a four-person tribunal consisting of the chief judge, known as 'the Assessor,' who is assisted by two Dominican monks and a 'Commissar.'"

As the tall, thin American neared his destination, he remembered the way the former Jesuit had leaned across the table of the small Arlington, Virginia, bar and said quietly, "You'll be meeting with the Assessor. He is powerful, very powerful; some say he will be the next Pope. Do what he says, do it for the sake of your life and your career if not for your faith."

The American mounted the steps to the building and noted that all the windows were covered by ornate—and very serious—wrought-iron grillwork. He pressed the doorbell. From within came a shuffling.

As he waited, the American remembered the rest of the former Jesuit's briefing. Most cases heard by the Assessor and the other judges never get beyond the walls of the Vatican, but when the veil of total secrecy is parted a bit, the public usually sees the persecution of church theologians—such as Hans Kung, when he questioned the doctrine of papal infallibility. Kung pointed out, among other things, that the infallibility doctrine had no biblical basis and had not existed before 1870. The CDF's punishment of Kung illustrated that—loyal to its Holy Inquisition roots—the suppression of truth is a virtue in pursuit of Church orthodoxy.

In a published decree, approved by the Pope, the CDF stated unequivocally that "the freedom of the act of faith cannot justify a right to dissent."

An eye appeared at an old fashioned peephole in the door. The American focused on the eye and gave it a smile. The eye quickly disappeared.

For the Catholic Church, questioning dogma even in the pursuit of religious truth had, until recently, been a sin punishable by death. One of the CDF's most active subdepartments is the Pontifical Bible Commission, which is charged with doing whatever is necessary to protect the church's official dogmas from attacks—truthful or otherwise. In this regard it is charged with repressing, destroying, or hiding in the Vatican Archives historical documents or objects that would cast doubt on the official interpretation of Scripture or theology.

The door opened.

The American stopped breathing when he found before him the Assessor himself in ordinary street clothes instead of the scarlet of the Cardinal that he was. Two large men, obviously bodyguards, loomed behind him.

"Thanks for coming," the Assessor said, extending his hand. Cardinal Neils Braun, former Archbishop of Vienna, head of the Papal Secretariat for Non-Believers and Assessor for the CDF, was a formidable man. He was very tall, sturdy, with a photogenic chiseled face that looked hewn straight from the Austrian mountains he loved so much. He had the moves and phenomenal wiry strength found only in successful rock climbers who prefer not to use ropes, pitons, or other mechanical devices. He would turn sixty on Christmas Day and he intended to spend the time alone, hiking in the hills near his Innsbruck home or tackling a new face of rock that no one had ever scaled.

"Welcome," Braun said again with the graciousness of a man who knows of and enjoys the effect he has on ordinary people.

The American swallowed hard and then shook the Assessor's proffered hand. "Good afternoon, Your Eminence."

"Please call me Neils," Braun said, knowing how Americans loved familiarity. "After all we're just colleagues working on the same problem here."

Braun saw the stress lines ease from the American's face, watched the shoulders relax and the rigidness fade from his chest and knees. Good, good, the Assessor thought to himself. Setting people at ease was the first step to controlling them.

"If you say so . . . Neils." The American smiled awkwardly in the face of a man who might well become Pope.

"Then come on in out of this heat." The two bodyguards merged with the darkness behind them as Braun stood to one side and motioned the American to come in.

After a short walk up two flights of stairs and down a plain, dimly lit hallway, the American found himself settled into a brocade armchair, sitting across an elegant mahogany desk from Braun. The American squinted against the bright light flooding through the window behind the cardinal. Bars guarded the window even here on the third floor.

"Please tell me what you learned in Zurich," Braun said without further preamble.

"Well—" The American cleared his throat. "To be very concise: Max is dead, the woman art broker is missing, and so are all of the paintings from Kreuzlingen."

"The Stahl painting?"

The American shook his head. "Nowhere to be found."

Braun frowned. "Your investigations have indicated who is responsible."

"Not definitively."

"But you have a . . . best guess?"

The American nodded. "It has all the footprints of the Russian mob, most likely with the cooperation of some of their people inside the KGB." He thought about this for a moment. "Or it could be the other way around. The extensiveness of the corruption makes it hard to determine who is actually in command."

"And for what reason?"

"For the money, the foreign exchange. The collection is priceless. I wouldn't be surprised if it had the sanction of the Kremlin. Hard currency is hard currency."

The cardinal nodded. "We have seen much of this since the collapse of the old Soviet Union and the monetary crises that have followed on its heels. Many of those who tried to assassinate me during that bad old time are still trying."

The American wanted to ask the obvious follow-up question, but he held his tongue instead.

"Zhirinovsky," Braun answered the American's unspoken question. "He and his ultranationalist thugs would like to see me out of the way for the same reasons that Khruschev and Andropov did."

Again, the American held his silence, waiting for an answer that did not come this time. Instead, the cardinal swiveled his chair a quarter turn and gazed upward for a long moment at a carved ivory crucifix on the wall. After a long sigh, he turned back to face the American.

"There are things that you must know in order to help us further," Braun said. "These are things you may find deeply unsettling in your own spiritual life. They are unpleasant and troubling, but if you are willing to shoulder the responsibility of the truth I will tell you, you will be in a position to perform enormous service to your church."

The American nodded. "I will do whatever I can."

The cardinal gave him a smile that seemed to penetrate the American's soul. "Thank you. First of all, I'd like to tell you that you have been selected over our other personnel because of your deep faith and because you are American, like the woman and her husband. Also because you have already established a certain credibility in this matter by your previous successes."

"Thank you."

"It is I and the church which will thank you," said the cardinal. "Now let me tell you that just as the Holy Father is the heir of St. Peter, we at the CDF are the heirs of Constantine."

The American looked puzzled.

"Like Constantine, we guard the unity of the church," Braun explained.

"But the strongest and most comforting faith is that which is united, unequivocal, unreserved: in other words, faith must be black and white with no shades of gray. But like Constantine, we know very well that our holy Scriptures and the history of our faith and religion have been rewritten, edited, and altered to fit the exigencies of many different times. In reality, there may be many different interpretations of the truth. There are authorities which seem equal and yet disagree; there are relics and Scriptures and historical proofs that we find compelling and yet, if known, would shatter the unanimity of the church's theology and create uncertainty. Without unanimity the church would never have survived. It would have splintered into a million little footnotes in the history of faith.

"What's more, uncertainty offers little solace in a tumultuous world. For ordinary people to receive hope, they must have a certainty to believe in. If there are doubts about matters of faith or religion, it is our duty at the CDF to wrestle with the devil so they don't have to. If there seem to be two roads to faith, it is our duty to travel them both and then to blockade the wrong path so that the faithful do not have to wander. We fight with the doubts and then create an answer for the church, to be sure that answer is consistent with all other decisions and then with the prayers and blessing of the Holy Father, to declare those answers the unassailable word of God. Unified belief is far more important than the contradictory truths that must remain secret because most people cannot cope with them without falling victim to Satan's influence."

He fixed the American with a silent gaze. "Do you understand me?"

"If I hear you correctly," the American began tentatively, "you're saying that it is not so much *what* people believe as that they all believe precisely the same creeds—those created and approved by your office—with no reservations whatsoever. Unified faith means unified strength."

Braun smiled broadly and nodded. "You are very perceptive. You were wise not to neglect your religious studies."

The American looked surprised.

The cardinal laughed. "Of course we have your college transcripts. We know more about your past than your current employer." Braun's voice was then suddenly serious. "Do you believe this goal is a worthy one? Would you die for it?"

The American frowned. He was practiced at deception, but quickly ruled out anything but honesty when God was involved. "Begging your pardon, Your Eminence, but I would have to think about that," he said finally. He chewed on a corner of his lower lip and gazed out the window for a moment at the brilliant sunshine. His heart pounded; he swallowed against the dryness in his mouth. Behind him a clock ticked.

The cardinal waited patiently. Then the American looked at him and spoke. "The first is possible, even probable. The second . . . ?" He shook his head in doubt. "I don't know. I'm not sure that any man could make that decision until the time came to die."

The American looked apprehensively at Braun.

"Excellent!" the cardinal said.

Relief flooded through the American.

"An honest answer and that gives me confidence," Braun continued. Then the smile vanished from his face, replaced by the stern countenance of the Assessor. "The Almighty Father accepts your best efforts. But I accept only your best results. Do you understand that?" The American nodded. "Will you agree to accept me as your guide and your only Confessor? " Again the American nodded his assent. "Will you agree to follow my directions to the letter, the penalty for disobedience being excommunication and eternal damnation?"

The American gave him a long stunned look, then nodded. "Yes, Your Eminence."

"Good," the cardinal said.

"You've heard, of course, of the Shroud of Turin?"

The American nodded. "Of course. Who hasn't? Reportedly the burial shroud of Jesus Christ. It's a long roll of linen with the image of a crucified man on it. All of the wounds and marks, all of the physical characteristics of the man are consistent with the accounts of Christ's death. I remember there was quite a controversy over whether to recognize it as a true relic."

Braun paused to take a sip of tea. He used his napkin to dab at the light perspiration that had formed on his upper lip, then continued.

"That is a very concise synopsis, at least, the public version." Braun leaned back in his chair, his voice slower now. "As you are probably aware, the Vatican has never sanctified the authenticity of the Shroud of Turin. If you gathered together every blessed fragment of the True Cross that the Vatican has blessed, you'd fill up a lumberyard. Yet the Vatican refuses to bless the Shroud of Turin. Why?" Braun's question was purely rhetorical. "Because we are afraid to, that's why. Because we know there is a second shroud out there—in better condition, with an indisputable provenance and indisputable documentation, attested to by the most unimpeachable of sources. And if we bless the Shroud of Turin, with its obscure history, I fear that one day we will be called upon to do the same with the second shroud."

The American looked confused. "But I don't understand, Are you saying a second shroud has been found that has been verified as belonging to Christ? If that is the case, why isn't it made public, why isn't it—"

Braun cut in. "No, you misunderstand me. This second shroud, the one that remains a secret, did not belong to the first Messiah at all. Rather, it belonged to the second."

The American sat stunned.

"A second . . . but how . . . how could—" He struggled to gather his thoughts. "Do you mean to say that all these years the church has been covering up the proof of Christ's divinity? Why keep it secret?"

Braun considered a moment before replying.

"Remember, please, my comments just a moment ago about the paramount need for unity and certainty in belief. Faith is fragile. This is the reason that we at the CDF—and our predecessors for centuries—have worked so hard to maintain the consistency of papal decrees and to defend the absolute truth of doctrine. If one small thing is admitted to be false, then ordinary people will begin to think that something else is to be doubted. The unraveling of a single thread is all that is needed to destroy an entire garment. Larger things?" He shrugged. "I can only say larger things will cause larger breaches of faith through which Satan is ever ready to leap."

"Oh, man . . ." the American mumbled.

"I said you would experience much that was unsettling," Braun said. "But have faith and trust in me, for the task that you have been elected to perform can affect the very future of Christianity."

"Wow," the American said quietly.

"This second Messiah—redeemer, if you will—lived during the time of Constantine, a ruler who found himself elected by the Almighty Father as the instrument by which Christianity would be unified and heresy eliminated. To this end, Emperor Constantine had this second Messiah brought to Byzantium and . . . eliminated."

The American felt the bedrock of his convictions shift beneath him. He grabbed at the desk for support.

"If this information were to leak out, Christianity and all that it stands for would be called into question. There would be chaos. Complete, utter chaos. A crisis of faith such as has not been seen in two thousand years. What's more, it will rock Judaism as well. After all, Jesus was a Jew and no one awaits the arrival of the Messiah more than the original people of the Bible. And even more importantly, there exists for this second Messiah historical verification that far exceeds the documentation that exists for our Lord. This verification could lead millions to dismiss Jesus Christ as our strength and redeemer and shift their allegiance to this secret Messiah."

The American noticed that the cardinal crossed himself when he said the name. "Millions would leave the church; the institution and its worldwide influence would be left in ruins."

"It'll be dismissed as a clever forgery," the American said. "A conspiracy."

"Perhaps," Braun countered. "But your holy mission is to keep the secret of this Messiah. Recover the proof, the verification. And if you cannot do this, you must make sure that no one else can." The cardinal fell silent, his face portraying an inner uncertainty for just an instant. "It seems . . ." His eyes looked inward. "That this secret Messiah is evidence that perhaps God sends us messiahs all the time. Our salvation rests on following them. But we fail to recognize them. Or worse, we kill them."

The American looked at the cardinal, tilted his head, and said: "So God tests us to see if we are ready for redemption? When finally we recognize the Messiah in our midst . . . without killing him, we are all redeemed?"

Braun nodded. "Her."

"Pardon?"

"Young man, the second shroud contains on its surface an image as well. It is the image of the second redeemer . . . a female image."

The American gasped.

FOUR

The mid-December storm rolled in off the Pacific, driving before it angry sheets of rain that pounded the waters of Marina Del Rey and the decks of the boats huddled there against the fury of the Pacific Ocean. The wind made hungry slicing noises in the rigging of the marina's sailboats and breathed life into ambitious little harbor waves that slapped like applause against their hulls. It was nearly 8 A.M.

A hundred yards east of the marina's easternmost edge, commuters struggled to get to work. Streets and storm gutters overflowed the curbs and ran across the sidewalks. At almost every intersection stalled cars rested like the carcasses of drowned animals, their soaked owners standing disconsolately nearby waiting for a tow truck or an ark. The few pedestrians out that early leaned into the gusts and wrestled the storm for possession of raincoats and umbrellas. The storm was winning.

In the main cabin of the forty-four-foot sloop *Valkyrie,* Seth Ridgeway twisted fitfully among his tangled sweat-soaked sheets and waited for the dream to come. It usually came to him on the soft padded feet of a half sleep between waking and dreaming, between reality and fantasy. It was always the same and it always ended badly just as it had in real life, but as much as the dream hurt, it was his only link with her and it was better he remember the pain than forget her.

The dream began as it always did in their hotel room at the Eden au Lac in Zurich; he felt the excitement and the anticipation. Unconsciously Ridgeway's right hand fumbled through the sheets and touched the wedding ring he still wore on his left hand. Six wonderful years, a marriage of infinite variety: she, the ethereal art history expert and he, the wounded, down-to-earth former policeman who taught philosophy. Everyone liked to wink at the way they met. Everyone except UCLA's administrators, who usually acted like people congenitally lacking a sense of joy. They frowned. And the deeper they frowned, the deeper Ridgeway and Zoe laughed. Their parties were a clash of cultures: SWAT team commanders and art gallery owners, beefy squad commanders who thought Dada was the second word uttered by an infant, and disheveled art critics who had never before met a cop unless they were arrested during a demonstration in the sixties.

It was everything but boring.

As the December storm raged now, Ridgeway moaned in his sleep; the dream ran faster and faster. He wanted to catch sight of her, to hold her, to look at her once again. But like a piece of film out of control, the dream raced by. She came into the room, exhilarated by the afternoon.

"*I did it! He's agreed to sell me everything!*" she said breathlessly. "*But that's not the half of it. I've got one helluva surprise for the art world and for you.*"

Then she pulled out the Greek manuscript.

He didn't care about the manuscript now or the art world or any other surprises either one of them might have. Having her back was the only thing that mattered now. The nightmare raced past the manuscript.

"*Say, maybe you'd like to take a shower so I could get really close to you.*" Her words sped up and raced by as she kissed him on the lips and stood back and looked at him lasciviously. He felt the way she ran her hands over his shoulders and down his belly, brushing over the front of his running shorts with a light fluttering of fingers. The dream accelerated. Seth Ridgeway watched himself in the dream turn slowly toward the shower. No! He wanted to shout. Don't let her go. Don't let her out of your sight. But the dream slammed downhill out of his control, a nightmare luge racing to the end.

"*First the shower.*" He heard her voice racing along with the dream.

"*Then you'd better be prepared, mister. You'dbetterbepreparedmister. You'dbetterbeprepared.*"

But when he was done with his shower she was gone.

Seth Ridgeway woke up to realize he was crying.

He cursed as he slammed his fist into the pillow. He felt like a sucker for not waking himself. But somewhere in the back of his mind he always clung to the hope that the dream would turn out differently and he'd wake up beside her again and they'd make love like they had that morning in Zurich five months before.

He lay there for a moment, emotionally sucker-punched, breathing heavily into his knotted-up pillow, tasting the saltiness of his sorrow.

"Damn you, God," he whispered. "Damn you, damn you!" He slammed his fist against the mattress, then instantly regretted his words as guilt settled heavily on his chest.

"Please forgive me for that, God," he said. "I didn't mean that. Help me find her; help me, please. Oh, please." He fought against the rising tears that had filled his eyes every morning for almost half a year. *My faith has been tested enough, God,* he thought. *Haven't I passed the test? Can't you bring us together again?* And again he apologized. *I'm sorry, God. I know you have your own plans; please bring Zoe back, but if that is not your will, then give me the strength to cope with that.*

Slowly he turned, unwinding the sheets that had wrapped themselves around his legs. He tore them away from his sweaty body and lay on top, listening to the rain thudding against the deck above him. It was a sad, soothing sound and he let it wash over him as he thought about Zoe and ran over in his mind what he could have overlooked back in Switzerland.

While he waited for the police to arrive, he ran down the steps to the front lobby. He checked the hotel's restaurants and shops, and finally her rental car. It rested in the same spot the valet had put it when Zoe had turned it over to him. The engine was still warm from her trip to Kreuzlingen.

Old reflexes returned to the former homicide detective. Ridgeway searched the car, the room. He took notes. He questioned the front desk, the bellhops, and the thin balding man who had parked the rental car.

The Zurich police were unimpressed that Ridgeway had once been a policeman, and more than a little annoyed that he had already interviewed many of the logical people.

Later, they sat in the comfortable chairs in the room overlooking the lake and discussed the case.

"There is no sign of foul play, Herr Ridgeway," the ranking officer had reminded him. "Perhaps there has been a misunderstanding?"

It took Ridgeway a moment to grasp the man's meaning. Had they had an argument that caused Zoe to disappear? Ridgeway controlled his frustration. Back when he was a cop he had reached similar conclusions and said similar words to men and women whose spouses had taken sudden leave. He could hear his own voice as the official continued. "Perhaps there was something she was upset about and that you were unaware of? It happens. Perhaps in a few hours . . ." He shrugged. "In any event without any indication of foul play there is nothing we can do. There is no law against running away."

Ridgeway wanted to tell the policeman about their love, about how Zoe would never do such a thing. But the words of others who had told him similar things in his own years as a cop came to his ear and he held his tongue.

The police left as discreetly as they had come. But he still received dour frowns from the front desk every time he passed. It was his punishment, no doubt, for performing such a tasteless act as summoning common policemen to the lobby of such a fine establishment.

Ridgeway got no sleep that night. He paced the room, pausing each time to gaze at the lake as if it had something it could tell him about Zoe. But through it all the pulsing void inside of him grew. Never had he ever felt so alone. Horrible visions from his police days replayed themselves over and over.

He was exhausted and nearly ready for sleep the next morning when the breakfast he ordered arrived with a Zurich newspaper. He had intended to eat and then catch a few hours' sleep before continuing his investigation. But he got not farther than the bottom of the first page. A headline on the right-hand side leaped out at him and chased the fatigue from his thoughts:

KREUZLINGEN ESTATE BURNS; OWNER SUFFERS HEART ATTACK

He read the story. Just hours after Zoe had concluded her negotiations with the estate's owner it had been destroyed by a massive fire. According to the story, the contents of the estate—including its priceless paintings—had been consumed by the flames. The owner, the story continued, had suffered a crippling heart attack and serious burns trying to save his collection.

With the newspaper on the seat beside him, Ridgeway had pushed the rented car to its mechanical limits during his crazed drive to Kreuzlingen. But all he found there was another frustrating dead end.

Local police and fire officials insisted there was no sign of arson or other foul play. Faulty wiring in the centuries-old structure had been the cause, they said. And the American should realize that the gentleman was advanced in age. Heart attacks are common among such men, they pointed out.

He fared no better at the hospital. Willi Max was unconscious and had been so since being brought to the hospital. And even had he been conscious, the doctors had no intention of letting him be interrogated. The man died three days later with his secrets and—Ridgeway was convinced—Zoe's fate unrevealed.

Ridgeway shook his head now, trying to clear away the memory. He listened as the December rain drummed steadily on the *Valkyrie*'s deck. He pushed himself to his feet and stumbled into the head. As he urinated he caught a glimpse of himself in the mirror above the sink. He didn't particularly like what he saw. In the nearly six months since Zoe had disappeared, deep plum-colored bruises had smudged themselves beneath both eyes. A layer of fat had crept around his waist for the first time in his life. Although the 185 pounds still looked taut and firm on his six-foot frame, Ridgeway knew that unless he started exercising again, he'd start to look sloppy in another six months. Worse than that, the old wounds might start acting up. The doctors said they did that sometimes. But, somehow, it just didn't seem important anymore. So what?

Ridgeway spat as he pumped the marine toilet empty and leaned over to examine himself more closely in the mirror. All his life he had appeared younger than his age. The other police officers called him the Kid. The last time a bartender had asked him for proof of his age had been just a month after he had gotten out of the hospital. He was twenty-nine years old then and recovering from the slugs that had torn through his chest and back and kidneys, but he still looked like a kid. Twenty-nine years old and the department had put him on permanent disability. The doctors had told him he probably wouldn't walk normally the rest of his life. But a year later he was fitter than the best recruit turned out by the academy. Yet bureaucratic rules were inviolable. They wouldn't give him his old job back.

But even in the worst of those days, alone, in pain, lost without the police life—even with all that he still looked like a kid. Then the years all seemed to catch up with him at once when Zoe disappeared. Now every one of his thirty-seven years seemed tattooed in the lines of his face.

Ridgeway went back to the *Valkyrie*'s galley and pulled open the refrigerator. He stood there for a long sleepy moment staring intently at the refrigerator's contents without seeing them. What he saw instead was the way he had spent the rest of the summer. He stayed on in Zurich, arriving back in Los Angeles just in time to start teaching fall classes. But despite more than two more months of investigating he had little to show for his time other than an outrageous hotel bill at the Eden au Lac, a proficiency in speaking German, a close friendship with a number of Swiss law enforcement officers, and a working friendship with an American attached to the U.S. consulate in Zurich.

The American, George Stratton, had proved invaluable in leading Ridgeway through the diplomatic and bureaucratic jungles that surrounded an American making unofficial and therefore irregular inquiries about his missing wife in a foreign country. Stratton also turned out to be a regular, if somewhat unchallenging, tennis partner.

At first, Ridgeway had been put off by Stratton's solicitous manner, thinking perhaps the man was gay or maybe a consulate baby-sitter assigned to make sure the former cop didn't do anything rash. But over the course of the summer Ridgeway realized that Stratton was just another lonely American, unmarried and more than a little homesick for the good old USA.

Through Stratton's help Ridgeway got permission to look over the ruins of the Kreuzlingen estate before the cleanup crews moved in. For three weeks he sifted through the ashes and rubble, growing more convinced by the day that the local police had been right.

But at the end of every day something about the ruins had still nagged at him. Finally, the day before the bulldozers were ready to clean up the blackened mess, it came to him: the estate's owner had been a wealthy German art collector with one of the most precious collections in Switzerland, yet there were no picture frames in the ashes, no glass, no charred bits of pictures or frames, no evidence of hanging wires or brackets. Fire, Ridgeway knew from investigating arson homicides, rarely consumed everything. But at the Kreuzlingen estate there were none of the bits and pieces—a corner of a frame here, a scrap of hanging wire there. It was as if all the art had been removed from the estate before it burned.

The local authorities discounted Ridgeway's newfound proof that the fire must have been arson and refused to halt the bulldozers and their cleanup operation. Their patience had run thin and their sympathy for the bereaved American no longer restrained their annoyance. They told him they were sure all of his questions would be answered and would he please stop second-guessing them and poking his nose into matters that didn't concern him.

There was nothing else he could do. He watched the bulldozers raze the only clues he had to Zoe's disappearance, paid his bills, told Stratton good-bye, and then came home to teach his classes.

Ridgeway dumped the cold grounds from the coffeemaker basket and poured beans into the grinder. His classes were going poorly. Before Zurich he had been highly praised for his classroom work; by his students and by other faculty members. He never missed classes, always prepared fresh, interesting materials, never delivered boring lectures.

Zurich had changed that. This year he was delivering halfhearted lectures using the previous year's notes . . . when he managed to make it to class at all. Tony Bradford, the department head who had originally hired him eight years before, had taken to asking him if he had a drinking problem.

But it was worse than a drinking problem. It was the wondering. The wondering had made him old. If he only knew if she was dead or alive he could get on with his life.

Ridgeway slid the basket with new grounds into the coffeemaker, poured in a pot of water, and turned the machine on. He stood there, blankly staring at the machine. Finally the coffeemaker's burps and gurgles cut through his reverie and he turned his attention to the gray and white storm lashing by just beyond the portholes. One minute he could see the boat in the slip next to his and the next only a wash of static like a bad black-and-white TV image.

He stared at the storm several minutes, then turned to the table where the binder containing his lecture materials had lain untouched since his last class. He approached the binder as one approaches a deformed child who ought to be loved but who inspires only disgust, sat down in front of the lesson plans, and opened the thick loose-leaf binder. He glanced cursorily at one page and then another before he realized he didn't care about them any more this morning than he had any other morning since he returned from Zurich.

He continued dumbly to thumb through the yellow-ruled pages covered with clippings, scrawled notes, and citations. He had planned to talk about the origins of anti-Semitism in Christian dogma this morning. But he had no energy left for dogma or anti-Semitism or for the students who seemed to tear at his mind, wanting to strip it bare of knowledge. He had no patience to face them.

The coffeemaker popped and gurgled its last drops and hissed a cloud of vapor that condensed on the portholes. Weary after a night's half sleep, Ridgeway slammed the lecture notes closed, shoved himself away from the table, and went to the telephone hanging by the galley. He punched in the number of the philosophy department. The phone buzzed in his ear.

"Philosophy, Mrs. Bradford speaking," he heard the departmental secretary answer. Karen Bradford was a delightful woman in her forties with long elegant features and graceful movements.

"Good morning, Karen," Ridgeway replied in his cheeriest voice. "Is David around?"

"Good morning, Seth," Karen replied, her concern apparent even over the telephone. "How are you this morning?"

"Oh . . . not bad, not bad, all things considered."

"That's good. I believe Professor Davis is in his office. I'll ring him for you."

But instead of the dull clicking of the antique GTE telephone switching system, Ridgeway heard only silence. She had put him on hold. Cradling the receiver between his shoulder and chin, Ridgeway leaned over to pour a cup of the fresh coffee into the chipped and beloved mug his first squad car partner had given him for a birthday gift. On one side it had his name and rank, sergeant at the time, and on the other a cartoon of two buzzards sitting on a desolate tree limb. The caption under the cartoon read: "Patience, hell! I'm going out and kill something." Another time, another life, Ridgeway thought as the memory almost coaxed a smile from him.

The telephone began to ring again as Ridgeway sipped from the cup. He swallowed quickly as he prepared to ask Dave Davis to take yet another class for him. He tried to think of what excuse to use this time.

"Seth?" It was Tony Bradford's voice Ridgeway heard, not that of Associate Professor Dave Davis. Ridgeway felt his mood plummet through the deck.

"Ah, yes, Tony, this is Seth Ridgeway."

"Sorry for intercepting your call but I happened to be walking past Karen's desk when you phoned."

An awkward silence hung over the phone as Ridgeway tried to think of a reply. When he didn't his department head continued.

"I don't suppose you were calling young Davis to ask him to take another of your classes, were you?" Bradford said, his voice heavy with accusation.

"Well, I—I haven't felt—"

"I thought so," Bradford interrupted, his voice growing angrier. "Seth, I've talked to you about this before and it can't continue."

"I know that, but—"

"No more buts, Seth. Either you get in here this morning and teach your class and the rest of them for this quarter or I'm going to have to consider terminating you."

Ridgeway listened numbly, mostly feeling guilty for disappointing the man who had offered him a career after the force had retired him.

"I've never seen you like this before," Bradford said more calmly. "You've always been the fighter, the instigator, the troublemaker. When the doctors said you'd never fully recover from the shooting you didn't give up, and you didn't give up when the force refused to take you off disability.

"I watched you attack the books after that final disability hearing, Seth. You always did have a good mind for philosophy—I saw that in you as an undergraduate—but the way you went after that doctorate was astounding. You took your rage, harnessed it, and transformed yourself into a first-rate scholar. That's why I offered you the teaching position. You're a scholar with experience out in the real world. That's a rare and valuable thing and I don't want to have to suspend you. But you've got to get hold of yourself!"

"It's different now," Ridgeway protested. "I'm not the same man any-more."

"Damn right, you're not!" Bradford exclaimed. "You're turning your rage in on yourself instead of channeling it into your work."

"If I just knew about Zoe—"

"Damn it, man, she's dead! You've got to accept that and move on. Because if you don't there'll be two murders. Even if you haven't noticed, it's clear to the rest of us that you're right now among the walking dead. I'd say it was time that you put your faith to work for you and pull yourself out of the mire."

Ridgeway had no answer. Bradford was right.

"The bank called yesterday. They asked me as your employer whether or not you're planning to sell the house or what. You're six mortgage payments behind."

Ridgeway vaguely remembered the envelopes. He had ignored them, along with the rest of the mail that was still being forwarded to his office at the philosophy department. He had never gotten around to notifying the post office that he had returned from Switzerland.

There was plenty of money. He had intended to pay all the bills, especially the mortgage, for as long as it took to sell the house. He had to sell; the house was haunted with Zoe's spirit. He had lain for hours in the boat, staring out at the harbor, visualizing the visits to real estate brokers. But he had never gone through with it because he knew if he did he'd have to face the house and what it held.

The house was alive with the evidence of the years he and Zoe had spent together. And to sell the house was to admit that those years were over. But he had to do something. The unoccupied house had become a target for vandals. There had been three incidents so far.

"Yes," Ridgeway's voice cracked. "I'm trying to sell it now. I'll call them. Tony . . ."

"Yes?"

"I'm sorry they called you. I'm sorry you had to get caught up in my problems. I—" Ridgeway felt the sloop sway. A good sailor knows all the motions and sounds of his craft, knows the ways it moves in the wind and waves, recognizes the movements that could only come from other human beings. Someone, he was sure, had just stepped lightly aboard the *Valkyrie*.

"Can I call you right back, Tony?"

"No, Seth, I want you to get things straightened out now. I want to—"

Knuckles rapped politely at the companionway hatch. "Tony, there's someone at the door, I have to—"

The polite rap turned into a more urgent tattoo.

"Look, Tony, can't you hang on for a minute?"

"No, goddamnit. I'm not going to let you run away anymore. You hang up on me and you're damn well fired."

The knocking grew louder. Ridgeway set down the receiver and turned toward the stern of the boat. He made his way toward the companionway, the main entrance to the boat, stopped at the navigator's station to pull a Smith & Wesson .357 Magnum from a drawer. He didn't get many visitors, especially at 8 A.M. in the middle of a December rainstorm. He'd be prepared; they wouldn't get him as easily as they had Zoe. He slipped the revolver into the deep right-hand pocket of his robe, pulled the sash cord tighter around his waist.

A rapid pounding sounded against the companionway hatch. "All right, all right," he yelled as he climbed the steps of the companionway.

He reached the top of the steps, grabbed the hatch handle, and pulled it back a crack. Waves of icy wind howled through the crack, carrying with them a sneeze of rain. Outside, standing under the protective awning that covered the cockpit, Ridgeway saw a woman about his age with brilliant blue eyes that seemed old—like they had seen too much or maybe belonged to a woman twice her age. He and the woman looked at each other solemnly.

The wind whipped her short blond hair about her perfectly oval face and tugged at the fabric of a camel-hair coat spotted dark with the rain. Behind her stood a massive fellow in a chauffeur's uniform stolidly holding an umbrella. In his other hand he held a stubby machine pistol. He held the gun casually by its handgrip, the barrel pointing at the deck, at no one in particular.

Ridgeway felt his mouth go suddenly dry. He froze for an instant as his eyes took in the scene. His thoughts of Zoe, Tony Bradford, and religious dogma vanished in a surge of fear.

With his body mostly hidden from them by the companionway hatch, Ridgeway held their gaze and slowly reached for the Magnum. Trying to keep his movements as unobtrusive as possible, he pulled the Smith & Wesson out of his robe pocket and held it out of sight at his side ready to shoot through the wood of the boards. The .357 would easily go through the boards, the chauffeur, and the transom of the *Valkyrie* and still have enough power to kill.

"Mr. Ridgeway?" The woman's voice was cultured, soothing, unthreatening.

"Yes?" Who the hell would show up on his boat with a machine gun? Someone he had arrested? Ridgeway tried unsuccessfully to match the woman or her chauffeur with a face from a bust, from a courtroom. But revenge had a longer memory than a street cop. And people didn't always do their own dirty work.

"I'm Rebecca Weinstock," the woman said, extending a long bony hand with a pencil-thin wrist behind it. "May I come in? It's rather inhospitable out here." She saw Ridgeway looking intently at his chauffeur.

"This is my chauffeur and bodyguard, Benjamin." Benjamin nodded toward Ridgeway, gave a little half bow that looked comical performed by such a huge man. "My life has been threatened on a number of occasions," the woman said. "Benjamin is here to make sure I come to no harm, not to harm you."

Unconvinced, Ridgeway glanced suspiciously from Rebecca to Benjamin and back again. "I'm not used to seeing machine guns this early in the morning."

An annoyed look passed briefly across Rebecca's face. Then she shivered as a blast of wind howled through the rigging.

"Could I trouble you for a bit of shelter?" she persisted. "The sort of proposition I have for you should not be discussed in a doorway."

"Only if your man Benjamin gets off my boat with that portable cannon."

She turned and nodded to the chauffeur. "Go wait in the car. It's unlikely they're prepared to launch an attack from the water."

Benjamin looked angrily at Ridgeway and worriedly at his employer.

"Go on," Rebecca insisted. "Mr. Ridgeway here isn't going to hurt me." The chauffeur, still dubious, slipped the machine pistol into a holster inside his coat and climbed onto the dock. He stood there for a moment, and with the hand that had held the gun, reached inside his coat and pulled out a portable walkie-talkie.

"Please take this, Miss Weinstock. I'll listen on the radio in the limo. Call me if you need me." He leaned over to hand the radio to the woman, then walked off in the direction of the limousine. Ridgeway watched him climb the steep incline the gangplank made when the tide was out, then stand for a moment on the land looking back at them. Rebecca waved, and Benjamin, who still looked larger than life across the distance, opened the limo door, got in, and firmly closed it.

Ridgeway's eyes lingered on the limo, hesitant to return to the blond woman. He listened to the beat of the rain on the cockpit awning, felt himself growing angry and tried to fight the emotion. Fear to anger. It happened to every street cop ten thousand times in a career. The fear of a life-threatening situation turned into an emotional hangover of anger as the body tried to figure out what to do with all the adrenaline. Ridgeway had learned early to recognize it, to deal with it so he wouldn't take it out on other people.

He took a deep breath, held it, and let it out slowly, then another. He closed his eyes and thought of sailing. The whole process took less than half a minute, and when he heard her voice, he was calm again.

"Mr. Ridgeway?" Rebecca Weinstock's aristocratic voice was now faintly plaintive. "I would appreciate a warm place to sit for a minute or two."

"Sure." Ridgeway said as he replaced the Smith & Wesson in his robe pocket and began to remove the polished teak companionway hatch.

He placed the last of the hatch boards below and offered his hand to help her navigate the short but steep steps down into the main cabin.

After showing her to a seat beside the table, Ridgeway turned toward the galley. The sight of the phone still lying off the hook reminded him that he had left Tony Bradford on the line.

"Tony?" he said, bringing the handset to his ear. "Tony?"

"Seth?" It was Karen Bradford again. "Professor Bradford had to leave for an appointment. He told me . . . he said I should tell you that—oh, I get so mad when he makes me do his dirty work. He said if you didn't teach class today he'd fire you."

In the embarrassed silence that followed, Ridgeway closed his eyes, tried to think. He opened his eyes and glanced at his watch. He was due in the classroom in less than ten minutes. In the rain he'd be hard pressed to make it if he left immediately. He glanced over at Rebecca.

"I'm sorry, Seth," Karen Bradford's voice broke the silence. "I really am."

"Don't apologize, Karen," Ridgeway said. "I'm the one who should be apologizing. I'll try to make it."

They hung up.

"I'm afraid I have very little time," Ridgeway said. "I have to get dressed and teach a class." Ridgeway looked at his notes on the table next to Rebecca. The woman's eyes lingered on the notebook for a moment, then returned to Ridgeway.

"But—"

"Talk to me while I get dressed," Ridgeway said, moving toward his cabin. "I'll leave the door open so I can hear you." But before Ridgeway could reach the door of his cabin, strong hands gripped the backs of his arms.

"Mr. Ridgeway, I have come a long way to see you," she said. "Don't brush me off like this." Seth turned.

"You must give it to me," she half shouted, hands held up in a sort of supplication. "Please give it to me. I've come prepared to compensate you handsomely."

Ridgeway backed up, surprised by her outburst.

"Here," Rebecca said, reaching into one pocket of her coat and drawing out a banded stack of currency that she thrust at Ridgeway. They were American thousand-dollar bills. No wonder the woman traveled with an armed chauffeur. In Ridgeway's experience the only people he had ever seen with stacks of thousand-dollar bills were Colombian cocaine dealers.

"Go ahead," she insisted, shaking the stack of bills at him. "It's honest money from good people . . . and there's more." To prove her point, she reached into her other pocket and pulled out a matching stack. She moved closer, shoved one stack of bills into Ridgeway's robe pocket on top of the Smith & Wesson. "Take it. All you have to do is give it to me and the rest is yours too."

Ridgeway slowly withdrew the stack of bills from his pocket and looked at it. There were at least fifty bills. He looked at Rebecca and tucked the money back into his robe pocket. Along with the other stack, the woman had walked onto his boat with at least a hundred grand in cash.

"Miss Weinstock," Ridgeway began slowly, "just what is it that you want from me?"

"Please don't play tiring games with me," Rebecca said. "I know she must have gotten it from him."

"She?"

"Your wife."

"My wife? What about her? What are you talking about?" Ridgeway's voice rose. "What the hell about my wife? Where is she?" He grabbed her and lifted her off her feet. "Where is she? Tell me or I'll take you apart piece by fucking piece—"

"Stop, please," she yelled in pain as Ridgeway shook her. "Stop, I . . . we— we tried to stop them. Please, Mr. Ridgeway, stop . . ."

Seth put her down on the settee. God, what was happening to him? His head hurt. He put his face in his hands and rubbed away at the pain. The insanity of all this was causing him to lose his bearings. He looked down at the woman he had begun to abuse. He had to get control of his life again.

Rebecca looked up warily at Ridgeway and ran her fingers through her hair.

"I know what you're thinking," Ridgeway said. "I'm sorry, but I thought—"

"There's no need to apologize. This thing has made people insane for centuries." Rebecca said this in an oddly calm way. "The important thing for you to remember, Mr. Ridgeway, is that we are prepared to pay you a lot of money for the painting."

"I don't know about any painting," Ridgeway said, "and I don't care that much about money. I'd rather have Zoe back."

"Of course you would, and if you cooperate with us I believe we may be able to locate her."

"She's still alive?"

"I didn't say that. I said we'd help you try to locate her. We don't know what those madmen might have done to her. But I do suspect she's still alive, since she knows what was on the back of the picture, and they don't . . ."

"Picture?" Ridgeway took his coffee and sat down at the table across from Rebecca. "I don't understand. What's a picture got to do with all this? And who the hell are you?"

"I told you. Rebecca Weinstock. I—"

"No, I mean who are you with? Who sent you? How do you know about Zoe?" Ridgeway's hand trembled as he lifted his mug to his lips. Coffee sloshed on the table. He took a sip and set the mug down in the spill. "Why would—"

"Why is always the hardest to understand," she said. "We can understand the hows and the wheres and the whos, but the whys provide jobs for philosophers and priests."

Ridgeway just looked at her, waited.

The woman seemed to consider a moment, then slipped one thin hand inside her coat, drew out a small black-and-white snapshot, and passed it across the table, careful to avoid the spilled coffee. Reluctantly Ridgeway picked up the photo and looked at it.

The photograph was of a painting of an alpine meadow, with mountains rising above a broad grassy open area ringed by conifers. Rebecca Weinstock searched Ridgeway's face for signs of recognition, found none.

"So?" Ridgeway said as he passed the photograph back.

"The painting is oil on wood, about six inches high and five inches wide," Weinstock said. "It was painted between 1936 and 1938 by Frederick Stahl, a German painter. Stahl painted it in warm tones, much like the Italian Renaissance masters whose style he tried to emulate." Rebecca paused, looked expectantly at Ridgeway.

"So?" Ridgeway said again. "What's the point of all this? What's it got to do with Zoe?"

"The point is, do you recognize the painting?"

Ridgeway shook his head. "Should I?"

She studied Ridgeway's face. Finally Rebecca sighed and nodded her head like a woman who has just made a momentous decision. "Mr. Ridgeway, I don't know exactly why, but I believe you. I don't think you've ever seen the picture. But, yes, you should have; we have every reason to believe that your wife had it in her possession when she left Kreuzlingen.

"*There was something he was going to have a courier deliver here. I thought it would be here by now.*" Ridgeway's head spun as he heard Zoe's voice. There it was, the clue that had hovered just beyond the edge of his consciousness for six months, the known but overlooked missing piece.

What could she have found? Something important enough to be kidnapped . . . killed?

"*I've got one helluva surprise for the art world.*" Seth found himself swept back into his nightmare, watching the dream gather speed, watching Zoe move away from him. "*I'lldroptheseoffatthehotel'ssafedepositboxandberightback . . .*"

A picture. Was that what Max was having delivered by courier? Did it ever arrive? If it did, where the hell was it?

"Mr. Ridgeway? Mr. Ridgeway, are you all right?"

The room at the Eden au Lac faded away and once again Ridgeway was looking across the table at the blond woman with the wise compelling eyes.

"You turned almost white there for a moment," Rebecca said. "It looked like you had some kind of attack."

"Just nerves." He set the mug down. "These last few months have been tough and your visit this morning just sort of shot my nerves the rest of the way to hell."

"I'm sorry," she said. "I know this is a strain but it's necessary to find the painting, and for you, to find out what happened to your wife."

"Tell me more about the picture," Ridgeway said.

"You're still sure you know nothing of this picture?" She held the photo up again. "Or its whereabouts?"

Ridgeway shook his head. "No," he lied, "I don't have a clue."

Rebecca looked at him, then went on.

"Stahl, the artist, was a favorite of the SS. Hitler, they say, loved the man and his work. In fact when Stahl died in 1940 Hitler wrote the epitaph that rests over Stahl's grave, wrote and delivered the eulogy himself."

Ridgeway took another look at the photograph. "Why the fascination? This Stahl doesn't seem to be that much of an artist."

She smiled. "There are many who share your feelings, Mr. Ridgeway. The Fuhrer, though, wasn't one of them. Hitler, you may know, wanted more than anything else in the world to be an artist, a painter. He was turned away from the best art academies and spent years in near poverty trying to peddle his works among the patrons of cafés and bistros in Vienna."

Rebecca Weinstock stood, stretched her legs. Ridgeway toyed with his coffee mug, spinning it in half turns as he watched his strange morning visitor.

"The world might well have never suffered through its bloodiest epoch so far in history," she resumed after she sat down again, "if someone had just let little Adolf into art school."

"That's fairly well known," Ridgeway said, impatience in his voice. "What does it have to do with Zoe and this . . . Stahl painting?"

"Patience. I haven't come all this way to waste your time. That period in Hitler's life had two specific consequences for you, and your wife.

"First, it drew Hitler's sympathy to another struggling Aryan artist—Stahl—and it made him determined to prove his artistic merit to the world, by whatever means it took. He saw in Stahl someone like himself, a struggling artist of skill but no particular genius."

"Are you saying Hitler was a good artist?"

"He was a competent craftsman who probably could have made a good career today as a commercial or graphic artist. But another Rembrandt? Hardly. And neither was Stahl. Hitler adopted Stahl, introduced him to Nazi society. They were pleased that not all of the artists in Germany were Jews or exiles. . . .

"The second consequence for you of Hitler's failed art career," Rebecca continued, "concerns his passion for building the world's largest and finest museum. The Fuhrermuseum, as it was to be called, would be built in his hometown of Linz, Austria. To fill this museum's collection, Hitler created a special task force in the SS called the Sonderauftrag Linz. The task force had to make sure the best art, antiques, statuary, relics, icons, coins—whatever—were taken from public and private collections in occupied countries. The art came from all over Europe by the boxcarload to Munich to a central collecting point. Later in the war the art was moved out of Munich to old castles and salt mines where it would be safe from Allied bombardment."

She paused and leaned toward Ridgeway. "The estate near Kreuzlingen that your wife visited was filled with pieces of art that had disappeared into the Nazi art machine. Most of it made its way across the border from Germany with SS officers who used the art to buy silence, food, lodging, and transportation away from the Allied tribunals."

"Jesus!" Ridgeway didn't believe in the old Ludlum fantasies of geriatric Nazis stalking the world, but he did believe that millions of dollars' worth of art could make murder seem inconsequential.

"But with all of the priceless masters there, what's the significance of a mediocre painting by a second-rate Nazi?"

Rebecca's voice speeded up. "I was just getting to that. Sometimes before the invasion of Poland, Stahl visited Hitler at Berchtesgaden and the two went for a long ride into the hills. Nobody knows exactly where they went. But when they returned, Stahl had the sketches from which he painted this picture." She tapped the photo with a well-manicured fingernail. "The painting supposedly hung in Hitler's private quarters at a top secret military installation in Austria. Probably located near the scene depicted in the painting."

Ridgeway reached over and picked up the snapshot again. He studied it more carefully this time. "What's that in the corner over here?" He leaned across the table and pointed to the corner of the photo.

"We believe that's the entrance to an old salt mine," Weinstock said. "It's not significant. Austria and Bavaria are riddled with them."

"What's the name of the picture?"

"The Home of the Lady Our Redeemer."

"Strange. I'd expect to see saints and halos and maybe the Virgin Mary—that's who the name refers to, isn't it? The *Lady Redeemer*?"

"Remember a moment ago," Rebecca began cautiously, "I told you they looted more than just art? That they also took antiques, reliquaries, religious objects? Well, very early in Hitler's searches for art and valuable objects his agents managed to obtain by bribery and coercion—and murder—a religious object of great value. It was valuable enough for Hitler to actually use it against the Catholic Church to all but silence its leadership—the Pope himself—on the Nazi treatment of the Jews. Before you say nonsense, remember how little comment on the subject came from the Vatican during those years. Some have directly attacked the Vatican for this, calling it a scandal."

Ridgeway looked at her, shaking his head. "Yes, I know that. But how? I mean, what could have that kind of influence?"

"Something, Mr. Ridgeway, that would undermine one of the church's strongest foundations. That's what Hitler and Stahl went to see that day they took their ride." Rebecca's voice was rising. "Somewhere in that painting"— she tapped the photograph agitatedly—"is the key to finding it, and I believe your wife knows what the key—"

"But what's the painting a key to?"

"Knowing that would be very unhealthy for you," she said. "There are men who have devoted their lives to making sure the world never finds out."

"But if my wife's involved . . . if there's still a chance to find her, I've got to know everything." He looked at her suspiciously. "What's your role in all this? Why is it so important for you to get to the painting first?"

She chose her words carefully. "Those men I just mentioned—the ones who will stop at nothing to preserve the secret—my father was once one of them. It took many years before he realized that it was not the church they were trying to protect but themselves. Because of this, he left the priesthood and married. But he couldn't forget what he had seen, so he made contact with a small but growing group of men in the Vatican who are trying to prune away the politically motivated dogma and lead the church back to its spiritual roots."

"Lots of luck."

She looked at him for a long moment. "I believe it can happen," she said. "I believe that good people can make the Catholic Church speak to its congregation's true spirit if only they can strip away the rules of man and return to the word of God."

Her words electrified him. Their meaning resonated in his heart. Finally, Seth asked, "What happened to your father? And why are you here?"

"My father died," she said without emotion. "I inherited his duty."

Ridgeway looked into her eyes for a long time and then got up. "I may know where the painting is. Then again, I may not. But you'll never find out unless I know more . . . a lot more." He turned around to see what effect his words might have had.

While they measured each other, a nondescript rented sedan glided slowly into the parking lot at the end of the pier and nosed into a space some twenty yards west of Weinstock's limousine. A cinder-block building containing public rest rooms sheltered the sedan and its occupants from bodyguard Benjamin, who had been watching the *Valkyrie* intently.

Unseen by Benjamin, two men dressed in yellow rain slickers got out of the rear of the car. Two others, similarly dressed, stayed in the front with a clear view of the *Valkyrie*.

"It's your life," Rebecca told Ridgeway again.

"It's my life, yes. So?"

As she nodded, all hell broke loose. First the telephone rang. Its buzz cut through the tense silence of the *Valkyrie*'s cabin and startled both individuals. Ridgeway reached over and grabbed the telephone from the cradle. "Yes?"

"Seth? This is Tony Bradford."

The voice pulled Ridgeway back to his mundane reality. He looked at the brass clock on the cabin wall. His philosophy class should have started seven minutes ago.

"Seth? I hoped you wouldn't answer. Then at least I could assume you were on your way here, that maybe you'd hit on a legitimate delay."

"Tony, I—"

"Forget it, man. I hate to do this, but as of right now you've been suspended. I want your office cleaned out by the end of the day and I want that huge box of your personal mail out of our storeroom. We're not a goddamned post office box for your convenience. If it's not out of here this afternoon I will personally go down there and throw the stuff away." The line went dead before he could answer.

Ridgeway was still looking at the dead instrument in his hand when the portable radio crackled in Rebecca's pocket. She fumbled to get it out. "Hello, Benjamin?" Panic was in her voice. "Benjamin, are you there?"

There was no answer.

Seth turned. Distant movement caught his eye. He looked out the porthole and through the tangled sheets of rain he saw a man in a yellow storm slicker close the door to Rebecca's limousine. The man turned and spoke to a second man, also in a yellow slicker, who had walked around from the rear of the car. The second man leaned over to look through the window of the door for a moment and nodded. The two men exchanged words, then started toward Ridgeway's dock.

"Were you expecting someone?" Ridgeway asked without looking at Rebecca. He pointed toward the limo. The two figures in yellow slickers were making their way quickly down the dock, looking neither left nor right but directly toward the *Valkyrie*.

"Benjamin?" she called into the walkie-talkie. Static was the only reply. Rebecca stared at the instrument in her hand as if it had personally betrayed her.

Ridgeway drew the .357 Magnum from his robe pocket, felt it slide past the wad of thousand-dollar bills Rebecca had forced on him earlier. He thought briefly about handing them back but the footsteps sounding on the dock seemed more serious business.

"I think you'd better sit this one out a minute," Ridgeway said. "Go into the forward cabin, and keep quiet."

She seemed to shrink as Ridgeway led her quickly forward and eased her down onto a bunk.

Ridgeway spotted his khaki trousers hanging on the hook behind the cabin door. The realization that he was naked under his bathrobe did nothing for his confidence. Quickly, he laid the Smith & Wesson on the bed and reached for his pants, hearing above him the sound of one man and then another stepping aboard the *Valkyrie*. He had just snapped the catch on his trousers and pulled the zipper shut when the inch-thick teak companionway boards above his head exploded inward, torn by a silenced machine gun into a maelstrom of long twisted splinters.

"Back in the corner!" Ridgeway shouted, grabbing the Smith & Wesson and throwing himself against Rebecca. She groaned in pain as they tumbled into the corner of the cabin, just forward of the head. Instants later, Ridgeway watched in awe as the teak door and bulkhead wall on the other side of the cabin erupted with tiny brown geysers, spraying the area with a deadly pattern of slugs. He felt Weinstock shaking. But what he noticed most as he lay there with his cheek mashed against the forward wall of the head was the dull thud-ding vibration of slugs as they embedded themselves in the wood less than an inch from his head. Luck had tossed them at least one miracle; without silencers to rob them of their muzzle velocity the slugs would have sliced right through the two walls of the head, killing them both.

As suddenly as it had started, the firing stopped. Wind whistled through the bullet holes and Rebecca started to move.

"Be still," Ridgeway whispered. They lay there some time, listening for a sound that was not part of the storm overhead. Eventually it came, the faintest of scraping noises, the sound of street grit grinding between a hard-sole shoe and the *Valkyrie*'s deck. The sound grew louder until it was directly overhead.

Whirling onto his back, Ridgeway fired twice through the ceiling. In the confined space the pistol sounded like a cannon. Though his ears were ringing, Ridgeway heard a surprised grunt of pain. Moments later, there was a heavy thud followed immediately by a metallic sound of a gun skittering across the deck.

"Quickly now," Ridgeway urged as he helped Rebecca to her feet.

She followed Ridgeway uncertainly through the galley and into the main cabin.

"You'd better crawl under that table," Ridgeway said, pointing to the massive teak slab that afforded the cabin's only ballistic protection.

As soon as she was safely under the table, Ridgeway spun and made for the after cabin. The hatch there would afford him a clear shot at anyone on deck.

Seth had barely started toward the after cabin when the roof once again exploded inward with another burst of automatic weapons fire. Ridgeway fell to the floor and crouched in the darkened passageway.

Slugs continued to slam through the deck. Through one of the many ragged bullet holes above him Ridgeway saw what he thought was the figure of a man. He sighted along the barrel of his Smith & Wesson and began to squeeze, when suddenly he heard a muffled cry of pain from Rebecca. Ridgeway glanced under the table. She had not pulled her right leg completely underneath the heavy teak slab. A dark red stain spread across her trousers.

Ridgeway fired upward and then clambered over to her side. Behind him, an answering burst of slugs stitched a tight crosshatch in the foam beneath the fire extinguisher. Ridgeway raised the leaf of the teak table and gently shifted Rebecca's leg until it was entirely shielded.

"Don't worry," Ridgeway said. "We'll get you out of this and to a hospital." Ridgeway started to crawl out from under the table when a furious blast of slugs shredded the carpeting less than an inch from his face.

"Damnit!" Ridgeway shouted, "that's fucking enough!" He rolled out from under the table and fired three quick shots. One of the bullets evidently found its mark . . . a long shriek of pain cut through the roaring of the storm.

Wearily Rebecca pushed herself up on one elbow. She craned her neck and looked at Ridgeway. Her pants leg was now soaked with blood.

"Mr. Ridgeway—"

"Quiet!" he snapped. Getting to his feet he cautiously mounted the steps to the companionway. In one swift movement he cleared away the debris and, with a single shot remaining in his gun, stepped warily out onto the deck. Directly in front of him lay a dead man, two blood-red eyes staring up from a yellow rain suit. On the bow of the boat, thirty feet away, lay another corpse, also in a yellow slicker. Ridgeway heard the slam of a car door and pivoted around to spot two more rain-suited figures running from a dark sedan parked next to the rest rooms.

Feeling the knot in his gut ratchet tighter, Ridgeway barreled down the companionway into the main cabin and bent over Rebecca.

"We've got to get out of here . . . more coming." She took hold of Ridgeway's hand and crawled painfully out from under the table.

"But . . . how?" Rebecca stuttered. "I can't swim . . . there's only one way off the dock."

"My tender," Ridgeway said. "Skiff with an outboard." Making their way onto the deck, Ridgeway guided the limping Rebecca to the dock finger that ran alongside the *Valkyrie*. There, nuzzled into the space between the finger and the *Valkyrie*'s stern section, was a small white fiberglass skiff. Ignoring the shouts behind him, Seth fell to his knees, and pulled the skiff closer to the dock. So engrossed was he in his task that he did not hear the muted reports of silenced weapons.

When he turned toward Rebecca, Ridgeway froze at the sight of the woman's throat or rather what was left of it. Automatic weapons fire had replaced skin with a gaping red hole.

Rebecca Weinstock's face wore a puzzled expression. Her lips moved, but no words came from them, just a raspy liquid sound. Almost nonchalantly she closed her eyes and pitched forward onto the dock.

Then shouts: "There! Next to the woman." A volley of gunfire followed the shouts. Ridgeway looked over just in time to see a line of slugs cratering their way along the dock toward him. Reflexively he dived into the dark cold waters of the harbor.

FIVE

Zoe sat on the edge of the sagging metal bed and screwed plugs of toilet paper into her ears. Beneath her, the rusty bedsprings screeched in concert with the metal grid that supported her thin lumpy mattress. Their protests were lost beneath the rattling of the ventilator fan welded into the metal door. Across the room from her, an obsolete PC sat on a scarred metal desk, its fan wheezing like an old hair dryer. The monitor made erratic arcing sounds in the saturated dampness that reeked of mold and spilled industrial fluids. In the corner, an electric heater hummed and buzzed against the damp winter chill with little effect. Zoe wore a heavy ski sweater with a snowflake design, wool twill pants with panty hose underneath, and two pairs of thick wool socks.

Moments later, the sound ricocheting off the bare concrete walls began to fade as the toilet paper plugs, moistened with hand lotion, began to swell.

The noise receded. Zoe allowed herself a small satisfied smile. Yet another improvisation had allowed her to prevail in a situation she once thought she'd never survive. She thought of her father, the welder, mechanic, and gifted would-be sculptor who had taught her how to use all his tools despite her mother's insistence that tools weren't for girls. Zoe shook her head slowly and gave her own hands a faint frown.

Then, as she did every night before her dinner arrived, Zoe closed her eyes and tried to remember. The days had become weeks had become months. She remembered in vivid detail all but the early days when the Russians came from Moscow with their bag full of drugs.

They had ransacked her mind in search of the painting, using drugs that had left her memory scattered like pages spilled from a file. Every night she focused on recovering another page, placing it back in its rightful order.

The first hypodermic had brought her unwanted sleep as she waited for the elevator at the Eden au Lac. In the swift dimness that followed, she felt hands supporting her, and voices, some Russian, most German.

"Let's get the professor while we're here," said a German voice. Zoe tried to scream, but the nightmare had taken away her voice.

"No," said another German speaker, this one with authority. "He's excess baggage right now; two bodies means twice as many headaches. If the woman tells us he knows something, we can always pick him up later."

Then even the sound faded to black.

Zoe awakened in an old industrial storage room, which became her cell. First, there was no food and plenty of cold. Then plenty of warm food and blankets. Days of deprivation alternated with comfort, desperation followed hope, her moods and fortune rotating with the interrogators. She told them all she knew but they still thought she knew about the painting. That's when they vandalized her mind. The drugs turned time into a crazy taffy dream of half-lit, half-sentient, half-remembered unreality.

Zoe's brow furrowed as she struggled to recover the days they had stolen, but they remained tantalizingly out of reach. She felt the misty emotional gravity of the memories pulling at her, but in her mind's eye the scenes remained unfocused.

"Damn." She muttered under her breath. Nothing came into focus until the vague first memories of Thalia's voice telling them that she could use experienced help organizing, cataloging, assessing the art they had taken from Willi Max's estate.

"Give her a chance." Thalia's low, soothing voice sounded in that gray dimness of first awakening. "Look—if she doesn't work out, you can still ship her off to Riga in an oil drum. But for right now, her hands and her head are more use to me still attached to her torso."

Dear Thalia.

Alone now in her improvised silence, Zoe rocked on the bed as she worked again at the lost memories.

But she got Seth's face instead. Already her mind's portrait of him had started to fade like a photo left in the sun. The months had washed away his details. She had cried about it the first time she realized his image was fading from her memory. But then an odd thing happened. As quickly as the image of Seth's face faded, her vision of his eyes grew more vivid. Now she could see in his eyes the tiniest threads of color and structure, but only the vaguest outlines of his face. It was as if an artist had sketched out a face on the canvas but had painted only the eyes.

The eyes were enough, though. As she sat there thinking about him, she realized they had always been enough, for they truly mirrored the man behind them. She had learned to watch Seth's eyes as others watch the sky to predict the weather. His eyes had as many moods as the sky. They were deep blue when he was lost in thought, gray when he had worked himself to the dropping point, turquoise when he was sad or melancholy, and a deep, almost pure green after they made love.

The memories came flooding back now, carrying with them a sense of loss that very nearly equaled the pain of the past months. She tried to remember his voice or the feel of his hands against her breasts, but he had disappeared, all but his eyes. She fought against the tears swelling in her own eyes. She wanted him so.

Zoe fought the sadness and tears as she craned her head back; with both hands she massaged at the tension in the back of her neck. She opened her eyes. Above her, the joists and the rusty iron pipes and the fire sprinkler heads made precise geometric shadow paintings on the age-yellowed floorboards of the office above.

Just then, movement caught her eye. Zoe turned her head and saw the door swing slowly open. Quickly pulling the tissue from her ears, Zoe stood up as her hulking jailor stood for a moment in the doorway. The giant stumplike man whose arms and legs did not seem long enough to match his oversized torso filled up the opening; almost engulfed in his huge fist was the usual paper Movenpick take-away sack filled with her dinner.

"Welcome to Chez Bastille. I'm Andre, your maître d'," Zoe said in English, knowing the man spoke only Russian. "Will this be a table for one?" As he had done every evening, he raised one woolly eyebrow at her, then set about scrutinizing the room. He motioned to her with his head; Zoe acknowledged his nod by stepping over to the far corner of her cell. She stood by the chamber pot at the foot of her bed while he placed the bag on the battered desk next to the old PC. He then made a circuit of the room, studying every surface for signs of an escape attempt. The Hulk gave her a brief victorious look and walked to the door. But instead of immediately exiting as usual, he stood to one side and nodded.

A moment later Thalia Yastrubinetsky appeared at the door holding a silver tray with a bone china tea service. Incongruously, a Movenpick bag sat next to the ornately enameled teapot.

"I thought we could discuss the progress of your reports," Thalia nodded at the old PC as she walked into the room. She gave Zoe a wink as she set the tray down on a two-drawer filing cabinet next to the desk.

Zoe frowned. True, in the absence of books and magazines, she passed much of her incarcerated time at the keyboard of the old 486 PC allowing the comforting familiarity and beauty of art to transport her from her dingy cell. Zoe spent hours transcribing her notes of the previous day's examinations, documenting her findings, and creating the best records of provenance possible—

a task simplified by the anal-retentive Nazi mentality that saw the path to Val-halla paved with both the bodies of inferior races and the proper documentation of their stolen treasures.

But anxiety turned uneasily in Zoe's chest. Thalia had made only infrequent visits here and it was always to drop off a book or records. She had never lingered. Something was wrong.

"Well," Zoe said tentatively, "I don't have much more than earlier today, since I usually do the work after I eat."

"Well then, let's eat!" Thalia said with a genuine enthusiasm she reserved for great art and food of almost any class. She was an impressively tall, ample woman in her mid-forties with long curly red hair and a beatific face. She was the daughter of an elderly Minsk art dealer who had fallen behind on his pay-ments to a Moscow Mafia loan shark. Instead of beating the old man as they ordinarily would, the bosses forced him into business with them, using his once legitimate business to dispose of stolen artworks and antiquities, a task that had led to the treasures at Kreuzlingen. As her father's assistant, the actual work had fallen into Thalia's hands.

The jailor stepped into the hallway, closing the door behind him. The dead bolt slammed into its secured position with enough force to make a point.

"Such an attitude," Thalia said, staring briefly at the door. Her accent was more New York than Minsk. Then, she turned in a slow full circle to take in the room. "You really ought to do something with this place." Most of Thalia's family had been among the Russian Jews granted exit visas during the admin-istration of President Jimmy Carter. Only her widowed father remained behind. He was frail and in love with his art business. To leave, he would have been required to liquidate himself into poverty in order to pay the punitive immi-gration taxes assessed by the Soviets. Instead, he remained and sent her to live with her aunts and cousins in New York City and paid her tuition through Columbia. She later learned he had borrowed the tuition money from Moscow loan sharks, confident that he would be dead before time came to collect.

"You didn't come down here tonight to talk about the interior design," Zoe said as she walked over to the desk.

Thalia shrugged as she grabbed Zoe's Movenpick bag and thrust it at her. "Here. Put some meat on your bones." She turned abruptly to grab her own bag. "Go! Sit! Sit!" Thalia pulled out the room's only chair for Zoe and then concentrated on unloading her own dinner. After a long moment, Zoe moved the chair back where she could see Thalia better and pulled a cold-cut sandwich from the bag along with a tall plastic cup of vegetable soup. She set them on the desk and opened the soup and took a sip.

Thalia stood by the silver platter and mounted an athletic assault on an identical sandwich. The room's mechanical cacophony filled the silence. Thalia looked at the door, then set her sandwich down and moved closer to Zoe.

"This is the only place we can talk," Thalia said quietly. "They monitor us everywhere else." Zoe nodded. "They're pushing me to wrap things up," Thalia said. "Something's jerked their chain and they want to close up shop as quickly as possible."

"But what?"

"Who knows? Maybe the police are on to them? Maybe your husband if he's as good a detective as you say."

Zoe's heart lifted at the thought of Seth searching for her. She had dreams about him appearing at the door to her cell.

"How long do we have?" Zoe asked.

"A week at the outside."

"But we still have all those Goddess figures to examine!" Unexpectedly, the take from Kreuzlingen included a massive packing case jammed with hundreds of statuettes, figurines, and other representations of the Great Goddess—some called them Venus figures—that spanned more than ten thousand years, starting with the paleolithic and neolithic. It was the most incredible find among an unbelievable collection.

"Those will take months to do properly," Zoe protested.

"We don't have months," Thalia said. "What's more, all the fakes you've pulled out of the other parts of the collection have priority. They're pretty upset that you think so many of them are counterfeit."

"BFD," Zoe replied. "They can learn to live with it." She took a long swallow of the soup, which cooled quickly in her cell. "So what do they really care?" Zoe dabbed at her lips with a paper napkin. "They're selling stolen art to people who know it's stolen. What are the buyers going to do? Complain to the police?"

"Remember that some of them *are* the police," Thalia cautioned.

Zoe shook her head ruefully and finished her soup.

"They may be thieves," Thalia continued, "but they want to continue selling art to these same collectors and curators. I understand that they have a pipeline into some of the back rooms of the Hermitage that contain a lot of art the Soviets looted but won't acknowledge."

"Figures," Zoe said darkly, then took a bite from her sandwich. She chewed slowly for a long time as the room's sonic drizzle filled the audible space around them. She swallowed and then said, "Well, the good news is that there don't seem to be any fakes among the Impressionists and the other 'decadent' works." She paused. "But then, you wouldn't expect that the leading counterfeiters would turn out a lot of pieces the Nazis had outlawed. On the other hand, I'd say a good twenty-five percent of everything from the medieval through early nineteenth century is either a total fake or has been so extensively restored as to make it brand-new for all practical purposes."

"They'll flip," Thalia said.

"Not if we don't tell them." Zoe smiled.

Thalia gave her a long puzzled look.

"I've let most of them through," Zoe said. "I marked the fakes with a very tiny 'f' in the lower right-hand corner for paintings and on various places on the sculpture and reliquary. It's in the database as well; just a solitary 'f' in the description field."

"You're wicked," Thalia said as recognition dawned on her face. "If they become known for peddling fakes, then nobody buys from them anymore."

"Bingo!" Zoe said. "Plus, they can't blame you because *I'm* the fakebuster. All I have to do is survive and these guys are toast."

Thalia's face fell as Zoe raised the dark unspoken certainty that she would not live to see her plan executed. Gloom settled between them for a long moment.

Thalia stayed in a nearby commercial hotel, escorted there and back by their captors, a walking prisoner held hostage and frozen into inaction by the threats against her father. They had been clear that Thalia and her father would suffer long and terribly before they died should anything unusual happen— Zoe's escape, the arrival of the police, a smuggled message—even if it were not her fault.

"Well! I'm sure looking forward to learning how you spot the fakes." Thalia's forced enthusiasm broke the deepening silence. She cleared a space and filled two teacups with the steaming liquid. "We'll need to start that tomorrow so we can get those items out of the way."

"It'll be a good trade," Zoe replied as she splashed milk into her tea and sipped at it. "I really don't know that much about the paleolithic and neolithic periods, and you know so much."

Thalia shrugged modestly.

The women sipped at their tea in silence, each caught by reluctant thoughts of an uncertain future that neither wanted to acknowledge.

"I'd still be a lot happier the sooner we can get to the Goddess figures," Zoe said finally.

"Me too," Thalia agreed. "Unfortunately, the geniuses in charge don't care much for . . . what did they call them? 'A bunch of fat broad pottery.' "

Zoe drank the last of her tea. "Figures," she grumbled.

"We could do it tonight," Zoe suggested.

"The fakes?"

"I was thinking Goddess."

Thalia shook her head. "They're adamant. All the recent stuff first. Then the Goddesses."

"So, can we get the fakes out of the way tonight? Will they give us permission to work late?"

"I don't see why not," Thalia replied. "They're anxious to get things wrapped up. They wanted to punt on the Goddess figures entirely. I got us an extra week by convincing them that the 'fat broad pottery' would bring them millions. They told me they might even have to move on less than a day's notice and that they would have to be prepared to tie up all the loose ends in a matter of hours."

Fear closed Zoe's throat then. She was a loose end. Thalia had saved her life once, and for months now had protected her, shielded her from the extremes of confinement, had even been able to civilize things with a rose here, good tea there. But Zoe knew that Thalia was just as much a prisoner. She had no keys and no freedom to come and go. With her father held hostage there was now nothing more that Thalia could do to protect her.

Zoe struggled to chase away the dark unspoken presence that was nearly palpable now. Thalia's face hung long with the thought.

Zoe rallied them both.

"Look, if we were out there working in a big Bahnhofstrasse gallery, we could get hit by a Mercedes or something crossing the street. Nobody really knows how much time they really have, so let's just use all the time we have . . . whatever that is. Beats the shit out of sitting around feeling bad."

SIX

The pale winter day had long since faded into Roman darkness by the time the American had finished briefing the Cardinal Assessor. Cardinal Neils Braun sat with his back to his visitor, staring at the window, seeing the images of both their faces more and more clearly as the darkness beyond deepened.

The American was thinner now, Braun thought. The man's face was carved deeply in lines that had suddenly appeared over the past six months.

"I just don't understand how they could still elude us," the American said wearily. The man has not complained, has not made excuses, the cardinal thought. That was good. After all, the bags under the American's eyes spoke far more eloquently about his unrelenting efforts than words possibly could.

"You are sure you have the resources you need?" Braun said as he turned away from the window to face the American.

The American nodded. "You have been most generous. I have also made substantial use of my own employer's resources as well."

The cardinal nodded. Unexpectedly, he smiled. "God will reward us in his own time."

The American tried, unsuccessfully, to keep his sigh of relief to himself.

After a moment, the cardinal continued. "You have been good about not asking questions, about not probing too deeply."

"Thank you. I really don't want to pry into things that aren't my business. Actually, I'm better off not knowing most things. . . ."

Braun nodded. "But I have been thinking that knowing more about the substance may help you in your quest, may spark some creative thoughts."

"If that is your judgment," the American replied tentatively. "By all means."

"Have you wondered all these months what is inside the box you seek?" The cardinal asked. "How its contents could possibly prove the authenticity of Sophia's shroud and her genuineness as Messiah? After all, we're talking about something that's nearly seventeen hundred years old. . . . Wars, the Crusades, the disruptions . . . how can you prove something of this import beyond even a reasonable doubt?"

The American nodded. "I have wondered and I have also decided that perhaps I was better off not knowing," he said.

Braun smiled. "Perhaps as a member of the church and as a faithful man, you are better off not knowing. But as a soldier of God, I think perhaps the details may help you in your search."

The American's eyes held the cardinal's gaze for a long moment and then he nodded reluctantly.

"The history is entwined with the proof," Braun began, "so let me start in 310 A.D., when Sophia was born in a small Anatolian hamlet into a family of merchants, apparently as the illegitimate offspring of the merchant's eldest daughter. The circumstances surrounding the birth are not clear. The family tried to keep the birth of the illegitimate daughter a secret, and succeeded for more than thirteen years. The girl was never allowed outside of the fairly comfortable family residence, and never brought in contact with any of the household workers. The obvious explanation for the secrecy was to avoid the shame of the unmarried birth. But from a diary kept by the girl's mother, we know the real reason had to do with paranormal occurrences that had taken place as early as the middle of the gestation period.

"The girl's mother, apparently, had begun a series of prophecies during her pregnancy, all of which dealt with mundane workaday life situations, and some of which involved her father's business. All of the prophecies came true.

"Then after the birth of Sophia, people who bathed or held the infant were given fleeting powers of prophecy. The fact that Sophia was not put to death for being not only illegitimate but also possessed by demons is an indication that the family may have known more about Sophia's birth than they dared to put into writing."

"More?" the American asked. "Such as?"

"Perhaps they had some message or indication of the baby girl's divine origins." He looked hesitantly at the American. "But that's just speculation. I'd like to stick here with what can be proven." The American nodded.

"Superstitions then, even more than now, were powerful instigators of violence. To be possessed by demons was to die quickly at the hands of one's superstitious neighbors. So, to make sure the word didn't spread about their daughter, and thus endanger her and the rest of the family, they raised the baby in total isolation.

"But locks and barriers were no match for the developing Sophia. At the age of thirteen, the girl appeared at her grandfather's side at a trade negotiation. The incident was confirmed by the accounts of nearly a dozen men. According to those accounts, she mesmerized them, speaking as an adult and somehow finding the words to preach to them. They were stunned and captivated by her. Her terrified grandfather rushed her away, fearing for his life, his business . . . for the lives of his daughter and the rest of the family. But the violent actions he expected never materialized. In fact, just the opposite happened. Afterwards, the men who had been present reported feeling totally serene and at peace. They were fond of Sophia and demanded to see her again and again. Soon she became a fixture in the village and began to develop a following. Then she started healing people."

"You actually believe this?" the American asked incredulously.

Braun nodded. "I have no choice. The documentation is too overwhelming not to . . . as you will see. Consider Valerius Daia—her first miracle, for example. Pressed into the service of the Roman army in 285 A.D., Daia's legion was sent to Mesopotamia by Emperor Diocletian in 295. A year later, Narses of Persia routed the Roman legions and their leader Galerius. The extensive military records were plain in the case of Valerius Daia. His right leg had been maimed and was paralyzed, rendering him unfit for further military service.

"The trail picks up again in the small village near Smyrna where Sophia lived. Under a general order from the emperor, the village diverted a small portion of the taxes it had to pay to Rome into a fund that provided small stipends for honorably wounded soldiers of the empire. It was the first simple attempt at veterans' benefits. At any rate, Valerius Daia's name first appeared on these village rolls in 297 A.D. Then in 323 A.D., there is an unusual entry in the village records calling for a cessation of those payments due to 'extraordinary circumstances resulting in the healing of the palsied leg of Valerius Daia.' "

Braun paused to let his words sink in. He fixed the American's eyes with his own and leaned forward. "She touched his leg, you see. She touched his leg and he was healed. We have an account of the miracle as recorded by the village scribe, but we also have military and financial records to corroborate the event." He paused.

"There are other records as well. The Romans were fastidious record keepers. And then there are the relics and artifacts that were meticulously recorded and documented by civil authorities and come to us now with an impeccable provenance. There is no way to deny these."

The room had grown cold, and for the first time since Braun had begun his extraordinary soliloquy, the American noticed that the room had also grown dim. In the west, the sun appeared low on the horizon. The American shivered.

"But all these records. How could they be preserved for more than sixteen hundred years?"

"There is a building on the grounds of the Vatican whose basement contains forty miles of shelves filled with books, parchments, stone tablets, dossiers, and manuscripts of the most remarkable significance. Here, for example, the church has stored court records of sorcery trials, the letters of Joan of Arc, the original handwritten records of the trial of Galileo, a petition from seventy-five lords of England pleading for the annulment of Henry VIII's marriage, documents concerning the Crusades, details of the scandalous lives led by the nuns of Monza, reports of prophecy fulfilled and prophecy yet to come. Millions of items of the most secret nature are guarded here in L'Archivo Segreto Vaticano—the Secret Archives of the Vatican," Braun said. "The records that irrefutably confirm the resurrection of Sophia are stored here." He paused as if his thoughts pained him too much to translate into words. "And until Emperor Heinrich IV sacked Rome in 1084, Sophia's shroud, her passion tale, and other records of impeccable credibility also rested in L'Archivo. We think that Constantine's biographer, Eusebius, secretly gathered all these items and had them sealed into a jewel-encrusted gold box."

"But why him? He was Constantine's main bishop."

"Revenge, most certainly."

"Pardon?"

"It's well documented now that Eusebius was a secret follower of Arius, the bishop who wound up on the losing end of the Nicean Conference. Eusebius was a spiritual guerrilla in Constantine's court. That box that Eusebius put together—an item we refer to as the Sophia Passion—contains very credible evidence that the Nicean Conference had more to do with covering up Sophia's divinity than it did hammering out a creed to guide the faithful on a single path."

He looked silently at the veins on the backs of his hands for a long moment, as if seeing there a reenactment of the battle that had set the truth loose on the world.

"When the reports of Sophia's miracles and teachings reached Rome," Braun continued, "they were regarded as extremely serious by both Pope Sylvester I and Emperor Constantine. To the history books, the Reformation period was the most unsettled in our history. But there have been greater ones, ones more threatening to the survival of the church. Think of what Constantine and Sylvester I must have thought when they learned of Sophia. There they were: Constantine, the first Roman emperor to grant Christianity the official protection of the empire; Sylvester, the first Pope to rule legitimately in the eyes of civil authority after nearly three hundred years of persecution.

"By all rights, this should have been a glorious era for the church," Braun said, "but it was anything but that. As part of an official, protected religion, members of the church started to lose the bonds of mutual dependence they had needed for survival. It had been easy to stifle heresy and maintain spiritual unity when the faithful had to depend on other church members for survival from roving bands of Roman legionnaires bent on eradicating them. Unity was survival. But the church, once officially sanctioned by Constantine, quickly lost that coherence. Encouraged by its connections to official Rome, the church quickly developed the bureaucracy that the Vatican is now so famous for. And as the bureaucracy gained a life of its own, it found itself frequently in conflicts.

"To assure its survival, the church quickly transformed itself from a religious movement founded around a charismatic leader into a bureaucratic institution. To begin with, they had to contend with hundreds of spiritual splinter groups—chief among them the Gnostic movement—that had continued to challenge the basic tenets of the church chief. Among these challenges is the fact that Jesus accepted women as equals, allowed them as disciples and spiritual leaders, and said that God was both male and female."

"This is fact?"

Braun nodded.

"Dear God," the American said softly.

"Yes," Braun said kindly. "Now you have a wider glimpse at what we wrestle with in secret." He paused. Then, "So where were we? Constantine. Well, Constantine recognized the advantages of ruling with the blessings of a spiritual leader," Braun continued, "and Sylvester certainly knew how hard it would be to rule as an outlaw from civil authority. So when they heard of this young girl in a distant village who performed miracles and preached to her elders, they knew they had to act quickly to avert yet another challenge to their authority.

"Emissaries representing both Constantine and Sylvester journeyed to visit this remarkable girl," said Braun. "When they got there, they found the situation even more serious than they had initially heard. Sophia, even though only fifteen by this time, had become the focus of a splinter religion that had captivated her native village and had started to spread to the countryside." Braun pushed his chair back and continued.

"The church was being torn apart by these spiritual splinter groups whose beliefs were based on interpretations of scripture. They shuddered to think of the power and attraction of a group organized around someone with the power and charisma that Sophia exercised. The parallels that could be drawn between her and Jesus Christ were not lost on them."

Braun reseated himself. "Besides," he said, resting his elbows on the table, "she was female. None of the Apostles recognized by the orthodoxy were women. Women—"

"Pardon me, Your Eminence—"

"Neils."

The American hesitated. "Neils."

"Yes?"

"You sounded like a lawyer when you talked about no women apostles as *recognized by the orthodoxy*. Does this mean there were women in this position, just not recognized?"

"Most certainly," Braun said. "Chief amongst them was Mary Magdalene. She and Peter got into some pretty hot arguments."

"And you know this because of the Gnostic Gospels?"

Braun nodded. "Those and other holy scriptures."

"And they are just as valid as the books that were included?"

"Just as valid, but terribly inconvenient to Constantine and the man who defined the institution we have today. Peter, you see, won his power struggle with Mary Magdalene, which is why women are relegated as adjuncts, secondary worshipers in every church. Christianity had borrowed from Judaism and institutionalized the doctrine of male dominance in its new religion, rationalizing the authority to do so on spiritual grounds. 'Our *Father* who art in heaven.' To them, God was clearly a man, as was his son. To admit now that the church had been wrong on this would open the Pope to criticism on other matters."

The American sat stunned.

"Understand," the Assessor said, "that the men in charge of the church at the time were very adept and pragmatic. They realized that survival for the church meant converting the greatest number of people to a single orthodoxy to reduce the endless disturbances and thus help Constantine govern more efficiently. That is why they stripped down and simplified the requirements to be a Christian: recite the creed, be baptized, and faithfully follow the edicts of the hierarchy. Internal self-knowledge and examination were discouraged, outlawed because they could raise questions. The Gnostic way was a tough one, requiring great spiritual effort on behalf of the believer.

"For the church to prevail, it also needed to reach an accommodation with the pagan Romans. This is why the day set aside for worshipping Sol, the sun god became our Sunday. And why the birth date of the Roman god Mithra—December 25—became the birth date of our Savior. There are scores and scores of such incorporation of pagan practices."

A pained expression showed on the American's face.

"I realize this is painful to you, my son, but you must be strong."

The American nodded.

"But let me get back to Sophia. Clearly, quick, decisive action was called for," Braun continued, "but the emissaries had no time to send a messenger to Constantine or Sylvester, so they made a historic decision."

Braun paused to take a sip of his tea.

"The oldest volume in L'Archivo Segreto Vaticano is a thick ledger filled with the fine handwriting of a scribe of Constantine's court, recording the interviews with the villagers. They were questioned about Sophia and her life and their remarks recorded and compared to the testimony of those who had preceded them. The interview with Sophia was saved for last, and when they had finished, they reviewed the transcripts of the interviews and found them in agreement. I have a copy of the interviews for you to read . . . translated into English from the original Latin."

The American nodded.

"And then what happened?"

"Roman troops killed them all."

"All of them! All of the villagers?"

Braun nodded solemnly. "All of them. The scribe, one hundred fifty villagers, and Sophia.

"They were buried," Braun continued, his voice wavering. "And a week later, when the shrouded bodies were inspected in the cave that served as a mass tomb, one of the shrouds was empty. It contained the image of a fifteen-year-old girl." Braun slowly got up from his chair and walked to the American's side. He put his hand on the younger man's shoulder and looked down at him. "We are the guardians of this secret Messiah," Braun told him. "We must find the Sophia Passion and make sure the world never learns the secret of Sophia—or the possibility that she and our Lord Jesus Christ may be two of many Messiahs that God has sent to teach and to test us. Revealing this secret would tear our institutions apart and in the end open the door for the enemies of the faith. For, once people begin to question even one part, they will question every part. If they believe they have been deceived before, the trust can never be recovered. It would create only misery and death."

The American looked up at him. "I . . . I'm sorry that I asked about this. I had . . . had no idea. I think maybe I really didn't want to know."

"The truth doesn't always make you free," Braun said, "especially when you're the one charged with keeping its power from disturbing the faith of hundreds of millions of your fellow Christians."

SEVEN

Ridgeway shook uncontrollably as he clung to a concrete piling under the pier. Through the narrow slits between the boats, he had watched the two men carry the bodies of their comrades back up the dock. The tide was out. The marina's seawalls loomed about him like giant cliffs.

Fighting the cold-induced haze in his head, Ridgeway weighed his chances of swimming farther. He knew it was no use. He had only been able to make it three docks down toward the main channel, diving deep to cross the spaces between piers, pausing to catch his breath in the relative seclusion of the boats.

Now the cold had permeated the deepest parts of his body, driving out even the heat generated by exercise. It was all he could do to cling to the piling and he knew that he either had to climb out and face his assailants or die in the water.

Ridgeway had heard stories about hypothermia, how pleasurable it felt to slip into unconsciousness. It was so comfortable that those who were later revived showed anger toward their rescuers for returning them to the world. He closed his eyes and felt the tension vanish.

The water was warm and Zoe was at the wheel. They had the large genoa foresail up, and through the slim space between the sail's foot and the deck they could see the island of Salt Cay sliding past on the horizon. Ridgeway took a glance at the compass and the chart draped over his knees. The island of Jost Van Dyke lay ahead in the distance. He leaned his face into the sun and thought of the fresh lobsters and piña coladas at Foxies. He closed his eyes and let the sun's rays bleed through his eyelids. He felt Zoe's hand in his hair and . . .

Suddenly salt water was choking him. His eyes clouded with muck. He had let go of the pilings! He was sinking. His arms seemed frozen and his legs were stiff, lifeless, but he told his legs to kick and they obeyed. His head broke the surface and he breathed greedily, trying not to make noise, though it was hard to hear anything above the storm. To his right, a rope arced down from the dock and then back up again out of sight. Ridgeway kicked desperately and stretched out for the lowest point of the arc. The tips of his fingers brushed the rope but failed to catch it. Again he went under, but this time when his legs propelled him to the surface his hands found the rope easily. He pulled himself upward on the rope and as he did found it was a slack mooring line between the dock and a small powerboat.

Ridgeway continued pulling until his hands grasped the dock cleat to which the rope was made fast. He remained there for a moment, looking about. The awkward flying bridges and superstructure of a powerboat blocked his view of the near dock.

Ridgeway leveraged himself against the mooring line with one leg and threw the other over the edge of the dock. For one long moment, his body seemed frozen in space, spread-eagled and perfectly taut, and then the next instant he was supine on the dock with the rain pounding at his face. He turned his head and gulped at the sharp wet air, coughing softly.

Slowly he levered himself up on his elbows and struggled into a sitting position. To his left, on the other side of the basin, one of the men continued his march away from him. Seth rose cautiously to his feet and waited for the numbness to fade. Then he moved slowly toward the main part of the pier. Reflexively, his right hand fumbled in the pocket of his robe for his revolver, but all his fingers closed around was a thick wad of thousand-dollar bills. He put the thought of the money and the gun out of his mind and continued ahead.

When he had first climbed onto the dock, a large powerboat had hidden him from view. But now as he made his way up to the bow of the boat and reached the main dock, he could clearly see the fence at the top of the seawall and the buildings beyond it. And just as clearly as he could see, others could see him.

Move! He urged himself on. Then, breaking into a run, he made his way rapidly up the dock toward the steep ramp that led to the land. He looked for the other man. What had happened to him? Where was he hiding? As he neared the ramp, he paused by the bowsprit of a large ketch and scanned the top of the seawall. No sign of anyone in a yellow rain slicker.

Had the man seen him? Was he up there, just out of sight, waiting for him to walk up the ramp? Ridgeway knew only that he had to move; he had to go up that ramp no matter what was waiting for him. To stay on the dock was to die. He took a long, shuddering breath, then started up the ramp's steep incline.

He was almost at the top of the ramp when he caught a glimpse of yellow out of the corner of his left eye. He fell quickly to the ramp and lay on his stomach. Options. What were his options? To go up the ramp was to face the man with the gun, to go back down was to face certain death by exposure. He began to crawl upward.

Just short of the top Ridgeway summoned the last reserves of his strength, pushed up, and raced toward the cars. He passed the killers' black sedan, then the public rest rooms. He felt his bare feet slapping against the asphalt, and for one instant thought that it was a good sign that feeling had returned to them,

The storm blew at his back. He breezed past his own car—its keys were somewhere aboard the *Valkyrie*—and made for the limousine. No matter what they did to Benjamin the Hulk, the keys were probably still there, he hoped.

Splashing through an ankle-deep puddle of water, Ridgeway crossed a narrow gutter and cut through a line of anemic shrubbery to the limousine. The sounds of his desperate breathing came to him over the storm as he leaned against the hood of the limo, urging his knees not to collapse.

He raised his head to look behind him. Across the basin, one of the men ran for a moment, then slowed. The other agent still stood against the fence some forty to fifty yards away.

With a deep breath of decision, Ridgeway pushed away from the hood, stood up shakily, and walked to the driver's door and opened it. The rich, warm, coppery smells of bloody death wafted out.

As a rookie, Ridgeway had worked traffic detail and seen mangled bodies—their limbs twisted away, their torsos ripped open, their internal organs exposed. As a homicide detective he had seen the perverted things human beings intentionally did to others. But never had he seen anything as hideous as the sight that greeted him when he opened the driver's door of the limousine.

Weinstock's bodyguard sprawled spread-eagled in the middle of the front seat, his hands and legs bound with a rope that led to doorposts and other parts of the car. The man was completely naked and had been slit expertly from the top of his pubic hair to his breastbone. His intestines spilled from the slit and coiled on the leather-upholstered seats.

At the sound of the door opening, the butchered body groaned. Benjamin was still alive. His face, colored slate gray, turned toward him. The eyes opened and after several long seconds filled with sad recognition. The mouth opened, but closed again wordlessly as if the exertion had been too much for him. The eyes closed and the huge man's head lolled back on his shoulders.

Ridgeway felt his skin tingle and tasted the sour acid of fear and nausea. His mouth worked like a fish out of water. Finally he willed his eyes away from the horror and with a supreme effort convinced his legs to move. He backed up a step, turned to run, and found himself staring at a young man with a knife in one hand, a silenced machine gun in the other, and a victorious smile on his face.

"We've been waiting for you," the young man said in heavily accented English. He looked toward the front seat of the limo. "Benjamin and I."

The man wore jeans, a windbreaker over a V-necked sweater, and running shoes. The clothing was soaked and plastered to his skin. His short hair was also soaked and plastered to his skull. He appeared to be in his late twenties, with the sort of lean, angular muscularity associated with a long-distance runner. A crazy glint showed in his eyes as if the light were reflecting off something fractured behind them.

Ridgeway backed away from the young man, unable to respond. He felt the cold metal of the limousine pressing against his back as he leaned against it, hoping the icy calm and old instincts that had saved him so many times as a policeman would not fail him this morning. Ridgeway looked desperately around, his eyes searching for help, for a weapon, for an exit.

The rattling of the machine gun's bolt drew his attention back to the man who stood professionally in front of him, out of Ridgeway's effective reach yet close enough to make running hopeless. "Don't try to escape," the man said as if he'd read Ridgeway's thoughts. "You and I need to have a talk."

"A talk like you had with . . . Benjamin," Ridgeway said, trying not to look at the grim butchery in the front seat.

"If necessary," the man said.

Consciously Ridgeway forced himself to focus on the man, on his words, to divorce his thoughts from the sight of the butchered man, from the cold, from the danger.

"I don't think you'll need to use that," Ridgeway said, pointing at the man's knife.

"Keep your hands to your side," the man snapped. And then, with a flourish, he folded the knife and stowed it back in the pocket from which it had come. "We'll see if you need that sort of convincing or not in just a minute. Now get inside—in the back."

The thought of getting inside the car with its warm sweet smell of death set Ridgeway's stomach churning harder, but he had no choice. The man moved around toward the rear of the car to cover Ridgeway as he opened the limo's rear door. The warm, nauseating smell billowed out.

"If you will look inside, you will see two handcuffs, one fastened to the handhold over the door on the other side and another attached to the front seat brackets. Take your seat and I'll show you how to put them on."

Ridgeway sat down on the blood-soaked upholstery.

"Look on the other side," the man said as he moved closer to keep Ridgeway covered. "You'll see that the free end of each handcuff is open. I want you to attach the upper handcuff to your left wrist, and the lower one to your left ankle." Ridgeway realized that the young man enjoyed his surgical skills and would carve him open regardless of how much he cooperated.

Benjamin chose that moment to unleash a long low groan of exquisite pain from deep inside his tortured body that grew in pitch and intensity until it expanded and blocked out every thought of Ridgeway's head save that of escape. Ridgeway flew at the door on the opposite side, preferring a bullet to slow death by dissection. The door wouldn't open. Ridgeway smashed frantically at the door, then at the window, cracking it with his fist.

Behind Ridgeway, a burst from the machine gun put a stop to Benjamin's unholy screaming. Ridgeway recoiled as a yellowish white blob of the guard's brain smeared the side of his head and splattered against the window. Then, after an instant, he heard the killer's voice.

"Put on the cuffs," the man said. His voice was all threat. Ridgeway was trying to calculate how quickly he'd die of the gunshots if he lunged at the killer when he caught a glimpse of a blur so swift that it seemed to segue into the gray morning rain.

Instants later, an arm appeared from behind the killer and jerked his head backward. Reflexively the man pulled the trigger on the silenced machine gun. Ridgeway rolled onto the floor of the limo as slugs pounded into the closed door behind him, tracking up into the roof.

Seth looked up and saw the butcher's eyes grow wide with surprise, then pain. Finally the man closed his eyes and his facial muscles went slack.

Struggling up to a sitting position, Ridgeway watched as the young man's body was tossed aside. Through the open door, Ridgeway saw two rain-splattered legs clad in gray slacks, and above them a navy-blue windbreaker. His savior's face was not visible. Ridgeway watched as one of the arms of the windbreaker pulled a long folding woodsman's knife from the young man's back. The other hand pulled a cloth handkerchief from the rear pocket of the pants and wiped the blood from the blade. The hands folded the blade, then placed it in a pocket of the windbreaker. A moment later, the man leaned down.

"Ridgeway?" came the voice. "Ridgeway, are you all right?"

Ridgeway looked up into George Stratton's clean-shaven face, and for one insane moment all he could think about was what a lousy backhand the man had shown in Zurich.

EIGHT

Zoe followed the Hulk through warehouse shadows and corridors of darkness. The handcuff binding her to his wrist rattled meekly between their hands. Thalia walked silently behind them as they made their way toward a large structure in the middle of the cavernous warehouse that resembled stage scenery and sets for an unfinished house. The roof was flat like a box and it sat without a foundation directly on the stained concrete floor. Barely visible in the darkness, cables—for power and the computer network—snaked down to the structure from the warehouse ceiling.

One hundred ninety-six, Zoe counted silently and took another step. *One hundred ninety-seven, one hundred ninety-eight.*

They stopped before a metal door set in the narrow end of the structure. One hundred and ninety eight steps from her sleeping cell to her working cell. Every day, one hundred ninety eight steps there, one hundred ninety-eight steps back. The monotony had grated on her nerves at first, but as the months went by, they turned into a comforting ritual that defined the physical limits of her life.

The Hulk inserted his key, unlocked the door, and stepped in, jerking Zoe in with him. An instant later, light flooded the room as the Hulk flipped on all the switches. The light filled a room with neutral walls that was at least twice as long as it was wide. Color-corrected lighting hung generously from the high ceilings and evenly bathed everything in near shadowless illumination.

The room was laid out with an elegantly decorated gallery and sitting area at one end complete with Bauhaus and van der Rohe furnishings plundered from Willi Max's home. At the far end were the working and staging areas for the art: workbenches with basic tools for removing canvases from frames, black lights to check for hidden restorations, alcohol, solvents and other chemicals for testing and cleaning, easels dressed with paintings, rows of tables scattered with statuary, reliquary, and the odd piece of jewelry.

Folding screens could be arranged to conceal the working area when prospective buyers were brought in to view and buy. Thalia had been coerced into overseeing the operation. To make sure she got the highest possible prices, her commissions had been earmarked to pay off her father's debts. Some of the buyers who came here were respected curators from prominent museums or representatives of wealthy collectors who checked their morals at the door for a chance at fabulous new finds. They'd sip from decades-old bottles of expensive French wine looted from Max's collection and browse the impromptu showings arranged for them. Checks would be written, greed satisfied, curatorial ambition sated. When Zoe came in the next morning, a few more pieces would be missing.

The whole thing was the stage for a drama she knew was nearing the finale. Zoe was certain that when all the art was gone, they would kill her. But tonight, her enthusiasm for the art had again banished the thoughts of death, at least until she could be alone with her thoughts again.

Zoe and Thalia made straight for a collection of easels and tables in the far corner of the room. Behind them, the door slammed shut as the Hulk made his exit. Moments later came the sounds of the double-keyed bolt being locked from the outside. It was the only door and the only opening into the room.

"I saved these for you," Zoe said as they arrived in the corner that they had begun to call Forger's Row. In front of them were a Vermeer, a very large silver tray depicting Adam and Eve's expulsion from the Garden of Eden, two almost identical Renoirs, one obviously a copy of the other, a silver reliquary in the shape of an index finger, and a collection of a dozen Corots.

"The rest are marked, sold, and shipped."

"They'll ruin some pretty famous art careers if word ever gets out," Thalia commented.

"They deserve to be ruined," Zoe said sharply.

Thalia carefully surveyed the fakes.

"So what's wrong with this?" Thalia pointed to the silver plate.

"It's a beautiful piece," Zoe said. "Exquisite, in fact, but it's not from the early fifth century as it claims."

"How can you tell?"

"The fig leaves covering their genitals."

"So?"

"That sort of prudishness wasn't common until the late Renaissance," Zoe said. "It was unheard of when this was supposedly made. Sex hadn't been turned into a dirty process until the Catholic Church really took it through the ringer after the first millennium."

"Damn!" Thalia slapped her forehead with the palm of one hand. "Of course! I knew that! Why didn't I think of it?"

"According to the documentation, a lot of pretty famous people didn't make the connection either."

"But why?"

"Blinded by the beauty, perhaps. Or maybe it's because they wanted to believe it was old. Art is in the mind and so is what we believe. You want to believe because you can get a higher price for a genuine piece."

Thalia murmured her agreement, then pointed to the two Renoirs. "It's pretty obvious to me that the one on the right is the fake. It has no finesse."

Zoe chuckled. "Actually, they're both by Renoir. When he needed some money, he'd dash off his own copy of one of his best-selling works and sell it."

"Of course," Thalia said. "I should have remembered that. It's just been so long since I handled anything so recent. Most everything I've dealt with in the past few years has been six or eight thousand years old or more."

"Don't feel bad," Zoe nodded.

"It does raise the question of legitimacy," Thalia said as she looked from one Renoir to another. "I mean, it *is* a genuine Renoir, but . . ." She thought for a moment. "I suppose there's nothing wrong with an artist copying himself."

"Nothing at all," Zoe agreed. "Some, like Renoir, did it for money. Some artists were in love with a concept, returning to the same subject time after time. But even more significantly, I think that other artists returned to the exact same pieces because they believed they had become better painters and sculptors and wanted to do justice to subjects they had fallen in love with."

Thalia nodded slowly as she thought about this. The faint rumble of a train filled the silence with bass notes. The floor vibrated beneath their feet.

"Okay then, how about the Vermeer?" Thalia said finally, pointing to a painting of *Joseph in Egypt Revealing His Identity to His Brothers.*

"The Vermeers. Plural," Zoe said as she leaned forward and pulled a second painting from behind the first. "Actually there are two."

"Zoe!" Thalia said suddenly, her face wide with surprise. "This Vermeer . . . *Miracle at Galilee*—" She pointed to the one Zoe had just revealed. "What's it doing here?"

"I added it to the collection this afternoon right before we knocked off. It was in a corner. Somehow I had overlooked it earlier."

"It's . . ."

"Uh-huh." Zoe nodded. "Without a doubt another Van Meergeren. Every Vermeer in the collection was a fake except the one which struck me so deeply that first day I visited Max."

Hans van Meergeren was perhaps the most famous *known* art forger of modern times. A Dutch painter of great skill and little inspiration or originality, he was famous for his forgeries of Delft genius Jan Vermeer. The paintings, supposedly from Vermeer's "lost years" in Italy, received widespread acceptance by many collectors and curators. His elaborate counterfeits were exposed after World War II when he was accused of being a Nazi collaborator and selling them national art treasures. To save his skin, Van Meergeren confessed that the paintings he had sold to the Nazis—including one called *Christ and the Adulteress* that Reichsmarschall Herman Goering purchased—were forgeries that he had painted himself.

"You're sure?" Thalia's face had paled.

"What's wrong, hon?" Zoe asked as she gently touched Thalia's shoulder.

Thalia took a moment to control her shallow ragged breathing, then said, "That one is mine."

"Oh, no." Zoe's voice was low and dull. "Oh, no, no."

Thalia nodded.

"How can that be?"

"I thought that since we had all these top collectors in here, that I could sell some of my father's art as well. This was his prize piece."

"I am so sorry." Zoe felt the helpless inadequacy of her words thud painfully in her heart.

Thalia shook her head and leaned close to the painting. Then she stood back. After loosing a long low sigh, she turned to Zoe.

"You're really sure?"

Zoe made a face. "I wish I weren't," she said.

"How? How can you tell? They both look like genuine Vermeers to me."

Zoe nodded.

"I'm not sure at all how I really do it," Zoe responded. "I look at a piece and it . . . affects me and I know almost immediately whether it's a fake or not."

"Affects you?"

Zoe hesitated.

"Seth is the only person alive who knows this," Zoe said tentatively. Thalia looked expectantly up at her. "I owe my life to you," Zoe said finally. "I—we've grown so like sisters. Surely I can trust you with this secret?"

Thalia nodded.

"I hear sounds when I look at paintings, at colors," Zoe began slowly.

Thalia frowned as if she had misunderstood Zoe's words. "Sounds?"

Zoe nodded. "Red is medium low like a cello; yellow very high like a piccolo."

Astonishment painted Thalia's face wide and round.

"I've always heard colors," Zoe continued. "For as long as I can remember. I thought everyone did. The older I got, the more worried my folks were. My mother thought I was possessed by demons and had the whole church praying for me Sunday after Sunday.

"My dad, on the other hand, sneaked me off to a shrink we really couldn't afford—that was the source of a running five-year quarrel. But the shrink immediately diagnosed me as having synaesthesia."

Thalia looked concerned.

"I was so relieved that I wasn't crazy."

"Uh-huh," Thalia said skeptically.

"Synaesthesia's a harmless neural crossover—a bit like cross-talk on phone wires—where the senses get mixed up. Some synaesthetics taste shapes, others smell in color. Psychedelic drugs like LSD and peyote produce the same sorts of experience, but about one of 25,000 of us experience it naturally, probably because our brains hardwired themselves differently before we were born. Most synaesthetics are left-handed women—just like me—and the most common form is having sounds that trigger colors—just the opposite of me."

"Amazing," Thalia said softly. "But I thought that fakebusting today relied on science and not intuition, you know, carbon dating, spectrographic analysis—that sort of thing."

Zoe smiled and shook her head. "For every scientific advance, the forgers just develop a way around it. Dishonesty somehow manages to keep pace with science—greed and ambition make sure that happens.

"Van Meergeren, beat technology by taking mediocre seventeenth-century paintings, scraping off the picture down to the original ground—usually a beige wash and gesso—and then starting over with hand-ground paints using pigments identical to those in an original Vermeer. If you're using a spectrograph to check for authentic pigments, it passes. Of course, the Bakelite and lilac oil base would be a giveaway, but then you'd have to know to test for these as well. The scientific window is very narrow and the forger's palette is immense."

"Hmmm," Thalia murmured knowingly.

"Besides, people involved with art are right-brained; they don't apply scientific tools and methods with any sort of rigor or consistency," Zoe emphasized. Most of the time, scientific tests are conducted to verify hunches. Intuition almost always comes first."

"But there are a lot of good fakebusters out there who don't have your synthesis—"

"Synaesthesia."

"Yeah, that," Thalia said. "But that short circuit in your brain didn't just turn you immediately into a fakebuster. As a little girl, you didn't beg to be taken to the Getty Museum so you could point out all their forged art."

"True," Zoe said. "The raw ability needed to be trained. I had no idea that this sixth sense would ever be useful, but because it was about color and music, I gravitated toward those in my education. I suppose the education was sort of like computer software programs in my head that gradually developed. I had no way of knowing that I was programming my wetware every time I looked at art, standing before a piece for hours, absorbing the brush strokes, the way light fell on a sculpture, the shape of faces, the drape of cloth—a million things I can't put into words but which my mind eventually began to set to music."

"This is too weird," Thalia said. "Not just sounds, but music?"

Zoe nodded. "Makes sense, right? Yellow piccolos, red cellos, black kettle drums—with all the colors in a painting—or the million degrees of gray in a marble sculpture—stands to reason that you've got a pretty big orchestra performing. Some simpler pieces sound like jazz or rock or R&B. The broader my music exploration was, the more ways the art had to express itself."

"Music in your head."

Zoe nodded. "In my head."

"In Russia, they lock people up for that so they won't hurt themselves." Thalia winked at her. "You don't have any little voices in there—you know, Martians or the CIA or something—telling you to kill people?" The tension faded as they both laughed.

"So what does my Vermeer sound like?" Thalia asked tentatively.

Zoe turned to face the painting and after a short moment, she said: "Like a world-class orchestra with second-rate strings."

"Second-rate strings?"

Zoe cocked her head and pursed her lips as she struggled for the correct words. "Strings are subtle," she said finally. "Look here—" She pointed at the painting. "It's got that wonderful deep luminescence, almost like frosting with light that we've all come to associate with Vermeer. The glowing highlights and deep realistic shadows are true to form as well."

"The good parts of the orchestra?"

"Right on," Zoe said. "But look at the people's faces." She pointed to the image of Christ and then moved her finger around the crowd depicted on the shoreline. "First of all they're blocky. They convey no soul or feeling. They're just faces without meaning. And look at the fishing boat on the shore—it's all squashed up and out of proportion. Vermeer was a stickler for accuracy, for precise perspective."

Thalia leaned forward. "Yes." She cocked her head and finally stood up straight and looked at Zoe. "You're right. I never noticed that before." She sighed with resignation.

"You were distracted, no doubt, by the amazing luminosity and wonderful interplay of shadows and light that he did capture," Zoe said. "No doubt your brain told you that if these were so good, then you could suspend your skepticism."

"Amazing," Thalia said. "Truly amazing. But how does your head know to make good music or noise? How did it learn to tell you which pieces were fakes and which genuine ones sound like Bartók?"

Zoe laughed. "Actually genuine Jackson Pollocks sound like Bartók doing scales badly."

Thalia laughed along with her.

When they caught their breaths, Zoe explained: "Programming again. Every reputable museum and collection has a basement or back room filled with known fakes where scholars can go to see pieces that are proven fakes. Even the best collectors get fooled. The honorable course is to take the items off public display and make them available to scholars who want to learn from their mistakes. The most disgraceful museums are those without fakes in their basements. They continue to display fakes and refuse to acknowledge their mistakes because they're too afraid of offending powerful benefactors or board members." She paused. "Anyway, I figure that collectively, I've spent a couple of years of my life nosing around the archives of fraud comparing the real with the fake."

Thalia nodded as she stared lovingly at her "Vermeer." After a long moment, she looked into Zoe's eyes and asked: "Does it really matter?"

"Does what really matter?" Zoe said at this unexpected turn of the conversation.

"If the painting gives joy . . . if even the experts can't tell, does it really matter to the owner—or the public—if it was painted by someone else?" Thalia looked back at her "Vermeer." "I've loved this painting since I was a little girl." When she turned to face Zoe again, her eyes glistened with tears, which she quickly wiped away.

"Of course it matters," Zoe said trying to ease the intensity of her own feelings. "Loving a fake painting is like . . . like loving an unfaithful man . . . or maybe a false god. It's wrong; it's . . . it's evil."

Thalia gave her a knowing smile. "Is it evil if your heart doesn't know? If it never knows?"

"You mean it's better to be ignorant?" Zoe was indignant.

"Perhaps," Thalia replied. "Perhaps."

Zoe shook her head violently. "I can't buy that. I just can't. I just believe that—" Zoe swallowed against strongly felt words that welled up in her throat, words that could not comfort, sharp truths that could only increase Thalia's pain.

Thalia touched Zoe's shoulder gently with a single finger. "I know what you believe and how strongly you believe it. I'm not suggesting that ignorance is best, but merely that people who choose to remain ignorant are often the happiest—with their God, with their mates . . ." She looked at her "Vermeer," then back to Zoe. "And with their art." She loosed a great sigh. "Well, now I know why Papa always refused my suggestions to sell it." She gave a sigh of resignation. "I suppose that makes it a little easier to sell it." She gave her fake Vermeer a good-bye look, then reached over and slid it back behind the other one.

Thalia then turned her back with a resolute determination that Zoe had come to recognize as inarguable finality. Then: "Okay." She paused. "So you have these loony tunes in your head and the world's best memories of exposed fakes. That's what makes you the champion fakebuster?"

Zoe marveled at the older woman's resilience for a moment and then replied. "Well, that's not entirely it. One of the best ways to polish off your fakebusting education is to know a forger, have him teach you his secrets," Zoe said. "You really get to know what to look for when you can watch one create a fake masterpiece."

"Pretty hard to do, I imagine."

"Pretty hard," Zoe agreed, "but not impossible."

Thalia's eyebrows arched. "So you got to know a forger?"

"Uh-huh." Zoe nodded. "Biblically."

"Oooh, girlfriend," Thalia's face brightened. "Let's take a break. I've got to hear all about this."

NINE

The single-story motel squeezed itself onto a narrow slab of earth between the patched asphalt of the Pacific Coast Highway and a gullied embankment that sloped steeply down to a fringe of beach. A VACANCY sign burned vaguely into the deepening evening, appealing in vain to customers who had mostly taken their travel to Interstate 5, some six miles inland, and their business to the newer chain motels that hugged the interchanges.

The bored desk clerk who had checked in Ridgeway, Stratton, and the rest of the party an hour before sat impassively; watching through bulletproof glass as cars straggled past, their headlights burning small temporary holes in the fabric of darkness. If this night's business was typical, he'd check in a lost traveler who took the wrong exit off I-5 and followed the road too far west, and maybe a Marine from nearby Camp Pendleton with his girlfriend or somebody's wife. Which was all fine with him. After all, he had only four rooms to rent out.

The motel looked like the sort of place local people expected to close or fall into the ocean any day. It seemed to have a steady parade of owners and desk clerks, none of whom ever stayed long enough to get to know anyone locally on a personal level. None of them realized it had had only one owner since the U.S. National Security Agency had bought it in 1963.

The clerk had given Stratton the key to a suite of rooms in the back of the motel facing the ocean. On a calm summer day, the rooms out back had a view of the Pacific from San Onofre to Oceanside, its waves dotted with surfers, fishermen, and sailboats. But tonight, the remnants of the storm tore at the motel, forcing little sighs and whistles under the door and through cracks around the windows. The curtains Stratton had drawn to keep out the wind swayed gently with each gust.

"Damn it," Ridgeway barked at Stratton, "you had no right. No right at all."

It had been hours of madness. Over and over the scene played itself just behind Ridgeway's eyes: the inside of the limousine, Rebecca Weinstock's bodyguard moaning in pain on the front seat, the killer's head being jerked backward, the muscles of his face going slack, and then the image of the blood being wiped from the glistening woodsman's knife.

Ridgeway had immediately recognized Stratton. But before words could be spoken, hands hustled him out of the limo and into a waiting sedan. Wet, shaking with cold, Ridgeway shivered in the backseat of the sedan as it careened out of the parking lot, Stratton's partner, Jordan Highgate, at the wheel, Stratton beside him.

Highgate drove the sedan south out of Marina Del Rey. They stopped at a shopping center near Long Beach where Highgate went inside and emerged half an hour later with a set of dry clothes, a paper sack filled with toiletries, and most important, hot coffee. Ridgeway's hands were shaking so badly that Stratton had to hold the coffee for him, feeding him sips as if to a small child.

The car had been silent as Highgate steered it expertly south, staying off the clogged freeways. Ridgeway drank the hot coffee and dressed himself in the dry clothes, jealously guarding his blood-soaked robe with the thousand-dollar bills in the pocket.

For the first forty-five minutes, Ridgeway was content to be alive, dry, and warming up. But as his body warmed, his gratitude turned to suspicion and, finally anger as Stratton explained that he and Highgate both worked for the National Security Agency.

"That was no accident bumping into you in Zurich," Ridgeway said.

He stared silently at Stratton as the auto's tires hissed over the wet streets. "You've been following me ever since I returned from Zurich."

Stratton nodded. "Since the day you walked into the consulate."

"You were using me as bait, hoping someone would show up," Ridgeway said. "Hoping you'd catch the people who came to my boat today."

Stratton nodded again.

"Damn it, man," Ridgeway fumed. "What gives you the right to play God with my life?"

"It's not a question of having a right." Ridgeway heard Stratton's voice behind him now in the motel room. "We've gone over all that. I wish you'd get past your anger so we could discuss things."

"There's nothing to discuss," Ridgeway snapped as he turned from the window to face Stratton, who sat on the foot of the bed. Highgate stood impassively by the door as Ridgeway regarded the doors and windows openly, sizing up his chances of escape. Stratton saw him.

"Don't even think of leaving," Stratton told him. "The building's locked up like a safe. Steel doors, bulletproof windows, filtered air. The door's got an electronic lock on it. Nobody gets out without the desk clerk throwing the right switches in the front office, and he doesn't do that until I give him the code. Nobody gets out. Nobody gets in." He shifted in his seat. "There's really no reason we can't talk about all this . . . about cooperating. . . ."

Shaking his head, Ridgeway walked over to face Stratton. "You're really something. You lock me up in what amounts to a jail cell and you expect me to sit around and have a chat?" He shook his head and turned away. "Other people may work like that, *Mister* Stratton, but not this one. I have nothing to discuss with you, not anymore."

"But we can be a great deal of help to you," Stratton persisted. "You need us to find your wife."

"You could have told me in Zurich," Ridgeway growled. "We could have worked together then."

"We've been over all this before," Stratton interrupted patiently. "We didn't know then what we know now."

"You could have told me what you knew."

"I couldn't . . ."

"You could have," Ridgeway said angrily. "By every moral principle, you should have."

Stratton stared off into the middle distance of his thoughts. Finally he sighed. "There was the matter of security," Stratton said, almost to himself. "I had to have approval, clearances. This was—is—a classified matter. It takes time to get all the necessary approvals."

"The goddamned fire was no secret," Ridgeway flared up. "Zoe's absence was no secret! Just what was so goddamned fucking classified about things?"

"There's no reason to get blasphemous," Stratton said quietly. "It doesn't help us solve anything."

Ridgeway stared at Stratton incredulously and shook his head.

"Listen, I know you're angry," Stratton began. "You have every right to be. And upset too. But the best way to locate her is for you and me to work together."

Ridgeway shook his head violently.

"I saved your life," Stratton said. "Doesn't that count for anything?"

"You used me as bait. You only saved me from a situation you could have prevented. You invaded my privacy, tapped my telephone, followed me every-where, watched my boat so you could be there to catch them when they arrived. Whoever they are. You seem to have done such a trustworthy job that just about everybody is dead, almost including me. And for that I should trust you?"

Ridgeway shook his head and took another sip of the coffee.

Stratton got up and crossed the room to the coffee table. He reached for a plastic cup and then changed his mind. He tossed the cup on the table and then sagged wearily into a pseudo-Scandinavian chair next to the table. He wiped his face with the palm of his hand and leaned back.

"I think maybe I should have just let the man cut you open like he did the chauffeur," Stratton countered.

"Maybe you should have," Ridgeway said quickly. "Because I'm going to be no damn use to you."

Stratton shook his head.

"What will it take?" Stratton said.

"For what?"

Stratton closed his eyes for an instant and grimaced. He took a deep breath and exhaled audibly.

"What would it take to get you to work with us?"

Ridgeway shook his head ruefully as he carried his coffee over to the foot of the bed nearest Stratton and sat down facing him.

"You don't understand," Ridgeway said. "I don't trust you. I don't work with anybody I don't trust."

"Mr. Ridgeway, I admire your principles," Stratton said. "But the world can't afford them. We've gotten ourselves involved in something that may affect the stability of the Western world and you just may hold the key. But you want to sit on your cherished principles while the rest of the world goes to hell!"

Ridgeway rolled his eyes as he pushed up from the bed and walked over to the coffee table.

"You're a maniac," Ridgeway said. "You and your friend there." He filled his plastic cup with coffee. "This isn't the first time I've heard people talk like this. 'Oh, we can't afford principles now,' " Ridgeway mimicked Stratton's voice. "The criminals and crazies have got control. Extraordinary times call for extraordinary people. That's what the Nazis said and every Communist and right-wing dictator.

"I've heard it all before," Ridgeway said. "In the squad room, on the streets, at muster. I've even thought about it seriously. I've even been tempted to act outside the law in order to enforce what I thought was justice, but that would have made me a criminal, not a cop. You can be one or the other, but never both. You're a cop of sorts, Stratton. Maybe you ought to start behaving like one."

Stratton's face reflected the world-wise smile of a whore enduring a Salvation Army lecture.

"Ordinarily I'd agree with you," Stratton countered. "But the facts in this situation are unique. It's such a strange story that I have trouble believing it."

"Why don't you try out some of the facts on me for starters," Ridgeway said. "Let me see if I can give you a new perspective on things."

"I can't tell you unless you agree not to reveal anything you hear," Stratton said.

"Now, you know I'm not going to agree to that," Ridgeway said, exasperated. "So why don't you lay down your book of regulations and your threats and your secret classifications for a while and tell me something I might believe?"

A sudden blast of rain slammed against the wall of the motel room and rattled like buckshot. The men fell silent, listening to the fury outside. "I can tell you the truth," Stratton said finally, "but you may have a hard time believing it." Ridgeway searched the man's wide, open face, looking for signs of deception. If the SOB's lying, Ridgeway thought, he's a damned good actor.

"I'll settle for the truth," Ridgeway said after a pause.

Stratton's head bobbed in grateful acknowledgment. He looked at his feet and chewed on his lower lip. Suddenly Ridgeway saw, not the evil manipulator of moments before, but a thoughtful, almost professional man gathering his thoughts. "My unit of the NSA has intercepted a lot of traffic that's somehow connected with a KGB/Moscow Mafia operation involving looted Nazi art and some kind of religious artifact. Because of the steady series of financial crises, word has gone out that Mother Russia needs hard Western currency. The government's desperate and they'll take dollars, deutsche marks—whatever they can get by whatever means they can get it, no questions asked.

"Our information is sketchy, mostly what we could piece together from intercepted cables and taped telephone conversations. Our sources tell us that there are a lot of these kinds of operations going, looking for cash by any means. Well, it turns out that one of these desperation operations involves a group of KGB and its Mafia allies who are associated with Zhirinovsky's Falcons—those are the guys who almost got you this morning. Like everybody else, they're looking for money, but this group of sweethearts stumbled over old intelligence reports concerning some paintings looted by the Nazis in World War II. The paintings are worth enough to bail out Russia almost single-handedly. But more importantly, one of the paintings was somehow used by the Nazis to blackmail the Vatican during the war."

Ridgeway's frown softened. "A painting?" He shifted uncomfortably as he remembered Weinstock's words shortly before she was killed. "Tell me more."

"We don't know that much about it," Stratton replied. "It was apparently painted by some obscure artist named Stahl . . . but that's not important. What is important is the fact that there is a secret section within the Curia at the

Vatican that has been searching for this religious relic for centuries. We know this because the KGB has their telephones tapped, and we've got the KGB's phones tapped."

"The Vatican is a top priority for Zhirinovksy," volunteered Jordan High-gate. Ridgeway turned and looked at him, still standing by the door, ramrod straight and devoid of expression like a guard at Buckingham Palace. "The ultranationalist Russians want to find a way to neutralize the Vatican's influence. They figure whatever worked for Hitler might work for them." Highgate looked to Stratton. Stratton nodded.

"Not incidentally, what would work against the Vatican would also presumably work against the Russian Orthodox Church, which Zhirinovsky and his people need behind them if they are to assume the total control they're after. That, as you know, would alter the global picture in the worst possible way. Don't forget that Zhirinovsky's threatened the occupation of an oil-rich Islamic country—Azerbaijan. Zhirinovsky insists the whole country should be Russian again even if it means ethnically cleansing the entire nation. Indeed, his election platform was based on taking back all of the former Soviet Union's colonies and cleansing them to make them safe for Russians. His papers and speeches were filled with warm favorable references to Hitler."

He paused. Then, "Until Zhirinovsky's people learned of the secret Vatican task force, they, and everybody else, assumed all of the talk about the blackmail of Pius XII was just one more of the outrageous rumors connected with the Third Reich. I certainly did until I listened to the tapes, looked at the cables. And even though we've only got the faintest notion of what's going on, we know there's something there."

"So what *is* going on?" Seth asked.

Stratton shook his head. "I don't know. I really don't know what significance the painting might have."

"Humph! Thought you guys were supposed to know everything," Seth fumed. He jammed both hands in the pockets of the new pants Stratton had bought for him and leaned against the wall next to the window. "How did Zoe get caught up in all this?"

"We've been following Rebecca Weinstock for nearly a week now," Stratton said, "since we'd heard her name mentioned in one of the KGB tapes. She is—was—apparently a wealthy Austrian art collector. She had tried to buy the art collection in Kreuzlingen that the KGB thinks includes the painting they're after. The KGB, through their Zhirinovsky counterparts, got to Weinstock, and you, before we did." Stratton's voice was apologetic.

"Does . . . is there anything in your information about where Zoe might be?" Ridgeway asked.

Stratton shook his head. "No," the agent said. "But we hope she's still in Switzerland, and possibly still alive."

Ridgeway nodded faintly to himself. He pushed away from the wall, pulled a corner of the curtains aside, and stared out into the murky storm. The storm's fury mirrored his innermost thoughts. He had to cooperate with them, he decided. There was simply no other alternative. He'd never find her by himself. But he would have to be careful to use without being used. The NSA had a reputation for ruthlessness that a Borgia would be proud of.

"All right," Ridgeway said as he turned away from the window. "I'll work with you."

Stratton smiled. "I thought you'd eventually see the wisdom."

"I have a few conditions, though," Ridgeway said. "I work independently. We share information. I don't want you following me. If the Russians get on to you, I don't want them on my tail too."

Stratton tried to look unperturbed. "If that's the way you want it," he said. "I'd hoped we'd work a bit more closely."

Ridgeway shook his head. "No way"

They locked eyes for a long moment, each trying to see past the meaning of what they had told each other.

Stratton hesitated. He looked at Highgate, at the ceiling, and finally back at Ridgeway. "Okay. You have a deal."

Zoe followed Thalia into the gallery area and sank into the supple leather of the Mies van der Rohe armchair. Thalia handed her a glass of wine, then sat next to her on a chrome and leather sofa.

They had relaxed this way half a dozen times before, mostly on nights such as this one when their work took them late into the night. They purposely stayed away from the very best-known names, and for that discretion their forays into Willi Max's hijacked wine cellar earned them frowns and scowls from their captors but no real punishment.

Thalia closed her eyes and rolled the wine about in her mouth for an instant before swallowing. When she opened her eyes, she said: "One of the oddest things I ran into when I lived I New York City was the way Americans— especially some of the men—took all the fun out of drinking wine."

Zoe tilted her head. "Odd? How?"

"I think they're afraid of it," Thalia said. "They have a problem with the sensuality of wine . . . sexuality if you will." She swirled her glass and looked at the deep ruby liquid for a moment. "They want to *think* about wine, not *feel* it. The feeling is the part that scares them to death so they desensualize wine by quantifying it: they score it with numbers, dissect it into acid and sugar components; they write endlessly about the winemaker, the weather, the inches of rainfall the vineyard got. They want to collect it, not just drink it. They have self-anointed priests and holy men—sommeliers, collectors, and wine geeks—who speak a jargon that excludes the uninitiated. They have dogmas about which wines are good, which are not, which ones to drink with which food, which glasses to use—their rituals put any established religion to shame. They have books and magazines that are like holy scripture that they all memorize. They worship the concept of the wine rather than the experience of drinking it—yadda, yadda." She waved her free hand dismissively. "They're all like a bunch of Moonie cult drones. Problem is they get so wrapped up in all this left-brain, bean-counter bullshit that they never actually experience the sensuality, they never just let themselves feel the pleasure.

"What's more, I think they do this on purpose," Thalia continued. "They're afraid of what they can't quantify because quantification means control. I think this is what was at work in religion too. The fear of sensations, this abject terror over things you feel as opposed to those you can't is why male-dominated religions evicted the Great Goddess—she was sensual, sexual. The guys needed to cut God down to size just as they do with wine."

Thalia paused to take a quick sip of her wine.

"You get all of this out of how guys don't really enjoy wine?" Zoe asked in amazement.

Thalia shrugged. "It's about experiencing the indescribable, about feeling rather than thinking, and in that sense wine and the Creator of our universe are a lot alike. They are both sensual and they both must be felt, *experienced,* rather than understood or analyzed to death. Logic built Western civilization, but logic cannot properly comprehend the infinite or the sensual. The Goddess was about creation—the world, life. Procreation is sexual and from the earliest days it has been a woman's function, something men felt they had no control over. This was a problem. They needed to exert control and since they couldn't really control their own urges, they decided to control the object of the urge.

"Most sex laws control the behavior of women and not men. Men transgress with a wink and a nod; women get pilloried, shunned, or burned at the stake. Over the ages, the male-centric religious spin doctors couldn't handle the incomprehensibly sensual nature of the Great Goddess Creator, so they gradually marginalized her into a local fertility deity and turned sex from a pleasurable, spiritual experience into a dirty little act. It was about the only way their big heads could exercise any control over their little heads."

"Quite a theory." Zoe shook her head and then took another sip of the wine.

"Yeah, well I've had a few years to formulate my unified theory of *putzes,*"

Thalia said. "But that's not why I broke into the wine cellar. I want to hear about your forger friend."

"Talk about a *putz*," Zoe said.

"Too bad," Thalia said sympathetically.

"No. Extremely good, actually." Zoe smiled mischievously. She set down her wineglass and held her hands out like someone describing the fish that got away. "A *putz* about this big."

Thalia laughed so hard she spilled wine on her dress. "C'mon, seriously. Tell me."

Zoe picked up her glass and after a sip of wine, continued.

"I met Erik in Amsterdam the summer between my sophomore and junior years at UCLA," Zoe said. "I had an internship with the Stedlijk Museum and roomed with a Dutch family who had a house on the Vondelpark—like their Central Park—not far from the museum. One afternoon not very long after I had started work, one of the assistant curators asked me to accompany him on his rounds, returning paintings—rejections from aspiring artists who had hoped to be exhibited there."

Zoe shook her head slowly. "It was one of the most depressing days I have ever had. The sadness."

"Rejecting the work means rejecting the artist." Thalia nodded knowingly.

"No kidding. Well." Zoe sighed. She closed her eyes for an instant, recalling the vision of that day. "Well, the last stop of the day took us to a sprawling brick building west of the Zeedijk—the main red-light district. "We had several surrealistic paintings by a Dutchman named Erik van Broek."

"Van Broek?" Thalia said. "He's famous. His paintings go for hundreds of thousands."

Zoe nodded. "I thought his paintings were excellent myself—in fact the earliest commissions I made after I became a broker were from the first sales of his works in the U.S. But back then, the critics trashed everything he did."

"Critics!" Thalia snapped. "Vicious, talentless wannabes who fulfill their own worthlessness by tearing down the work of those who can create."

Zoe raised her eyebrows. "I see you've met some of the same ones I have." They smiled.

"Anyway, it was the last stop and I went up alone, carrying the paintings to a rambling third-floor loft in what had once been an old shipping warehouse. I was a new face to Erik so when he opened the door, his face was wide and open, covered with sweat. He had these brilliant green eyes that positively sparkled. He was very, very tall like a lot of Dutch men—over six six—and he had this wiry musculature . . . like a pro basketball player." Zoe paused and closed her eyes for a moment. "His arms bulged out of a paint-splattered sweat-shirt with the arms torn off. He had on running shorts but they covered up only a little bit of these incredibly muscular legs; he had a towel draped over his shoulders." She opened her eyes and looked at Thalia. "Inside, beyond the door, I saw a set of exercise weights on the worn wooden floor. Sweat glistened all over his body."

"From the sound of your voice, lightning struck you."

"Oh yeah," Zoe nodded with a deep faint smile. "He did. He electrified me. I felt like the rest of the world had suddenly disappeared. Maybe it was the smell of the sweat or the sight of this perfect body, but I was thunderstruck. Suddenly, I was wet. I was twenty years old and had never been so totally floored." She gazed into space.

"Then?" Thalia prompted her.

"I was so stunned that I dropped both of the paintings. The thud shattered the moment. When he looked down and realized why I had come, he bent over to gather the paintings, then slammed the door in my face."

"Obviously that didn't stop you."

"Oh no. Not even a little. I was captivated by him. I spent every moment thinking about him. Before going to work and after I got off—and almost every lunch break as well—I'd go hang out in a little bar across the canal from his studio and wait for him to come out. Pretty soon, I got a pretty good idea of the sort of people who came and went: suppliers, people in chauffeured cars, individuals in expensive sedans. I realized that he wasn't just another starving artist. That and the fact that I loved his paintings."

"Before or after your hormones took over your life?"

"Before . . . and a lot more afterwards," Zoe said. "Anyway, whenever he'd leave the building, I'd follow him."

"You stalked him."

"You could say that. But after a week, I realized that every evening about eight he'd leave to have dinner at a little Indonesian *rijstafel* restaurant over on the Rembrandtsplein. He was like clockwork."

"So you suddenly developed a yearning for Indonesian food."

"It's actually very good," Zoe said. "The first night, I was sitting there when he walked in. He scowled at me and left. The next night, he pretended not to see me and asked for a table as far away from me as the small restaurant could accommodate."

"And the third night?"

"Before then . . . that afternoon, I went down to the Kalverstraat and bought the thinnest, sheerest, lowest-cut white knit top I could find. I bought one size smaller than I usually wear and then put it on without a bra. I put on a blazer for the walk over so I wouldn't get propositioned, but when he walked into the *rijstafel* palace, I slipped out of the blazer and gave a little stretch that I had practiced all that afternoon."

"Let me guess. He sat down at your table."

"Uh-huh." Zoe nodded. "Right after he tripped on his tongue." She giggled. Thalia joined in.

"And then?" Thalia prompted.

"Well, I don't remember what we ate. I don't remember anything we talked about. But I remember the fireworks that simply ripped me apart that night."

"Your first orgasm?"

"The first without a battery."

This brought a chuckle from Thalia.

"Anyway, I saw him constantly for about a month after that, always *rijstafel* and sex. But as time went on, we spent more time talking about his art, about critics, about the art restoration business he said provided him with most of his income. The angrier he would get, the more spectacular the sex would be afterwards.

"One morning . . ." Zoe gazed into the distance for a moment. "In July I remember, I got up before Erik and wandered through his studio. I wandered into the room where he did his original work. I remember that there was some wonderful Dutch light coming through a tar-specked skylight that turned the whole room into a sort of glowing Vermeer still life of brushes and paints and cans, containers of solvents, spatulas.

"I crossed the room and through the doorway leading to his restoration studio. Half a dozen paintings lounged on easels, all of them in various stages of cleaning or restoration. I remember a Cézanne sent to him by a German gallery and a Gainsborough from America. The critics may have hated Erik, but even his enemies acknowledged his skills at cleaning and restoration."

Zoe set her wineglass down on the glass and chrome end table, then stood up and stretched. "I had never been any farther than this room, but that morning I wandered over to a doorway at the far end of the room that had always been padlocked before. But this morning, the padlock hung open on the hasp so I walked through and found myself in a room with even better natural light than Erik's studio. Like the restoration room, easels abounded, populated with a score of masterpieces I had never seen or heard of. There was a Monet, a van Gogh, a Mondrian—racks and racks of them. When I walked closer, I saw that none of the paintings was signed. The Monet was unfinished, as was the van Gogh. Just as the light went on in my head, I heard footsteps behind me. I turned and saw Erik standing in the doorway, his face playing a mixture of anger, fear, and astonishment. For a fleeting instant, I saw desperation and murder in his eyes, but that passed so quickly I still wonder if I really saw it."

"People have killed for far less than artistic ambition," Thalia said. "Not to mention the money involved."

Zoe nodded as she began to wander slowly about the room. "He was that committed. Uh-huh." She stroked the cheek of a third-century Greek marble bust with the back of her index finger, then turned back to face Thalia. "But all he said was, 'This is your secret and mine, kitten. Right?' He slipped his hand around my waist and I started to melt again. I nodded. Then from somewhere, somehow I managed to find enough strength, enough presence of mind to step away from him and cut a priceless deal. 'Agreed,' I told him. 'Our secret on one condition: I want you to teach me all your tricks.' Well, you'd've thought I had slapped him. I saw that murderous desperation for another instant and then he agreed."

Zoe went back to her chair and sat down. "That was it for the great sex. I became a student, a threat, an obligation, and for the rest of the summer his sheets were warmed by the same steady procession of artist groupies that had trekked through his bed before I had come along. I learned then how vain he really was, how he cared for nothing but his art, how I would have been discarded in a few weeks anyway."

"That must have hurt."

Zoe shook her head. "Not really. That was when I learned just how committed I was to my end of art. The sex had been good, an eye-opener for me, a coming of age, but none of that really mattered anymore because for the rest of the summer I spent hours and hours learning the most current forgery methods—a lot of which are still unknown to fakebusters."

"Remarkable," Thalia said. "Is he still forging the masters? Even now that his own work is selling so well?"

The familiar sound of a metal door slamming somewhere distant in the warehouse filled the brief pause.

"Here he comes," Thalia said as she hurried to clear away the evidence of their foray into Willi Max's collection of grand crus. Zoe took the glasses back to the work area and stashed them under a shelf.

"He doesn't do fakes anymore," Zoe said. "But the fakes are as responsible for his success as his own talent."

"How so."

"Well, first he started painting them for the money, and then for the revenge."

"Revenge?"

"He targeted the critics who had rejected him—which was most of them. As you know, they're creatures of fad and fashion rather than of any sort of discretion or good judgment. At first, he wanted to destroy them—and he did ruin a couple."

"How?"

"Well, Von Gleick in Hamburg was one of Erik's worst critics."

"Von Gleick," Thalia interrupted softly. "His reputation was ruined by a forgery case."

"Not an accident," Zoe went on. "It just so happens that Von Gleick also spent a lot of time telling the world what an expert he was on Jackson Pollock."

"Sneezing with a mouthful of paint."

"No kidding," Zoe agreed. "So Erik started knocking out 'undiscovered' Pollocks . . . took him about half an hour per painting. Erik's restoration business allowed him to 'launder' the fakes into unscrupulous hands, allowed him deniability about the actual source of the paintings. As Erik had planned, Von Gleick went gaga over the undiscovered Pollocks, praised them, authenticated them, fawned over them. Then, through a series of anonymous tips, Erik notified galleries and collectors who had purchased the paintings and tipped them off to small, hidden inconsistencies that he had deliberately painted into the works."

"He set up Von Gleick and then pushed him over the cliff," Thalia said gently. "Then, in some ways, Von Glieck's suicide was really murder."

"Erik didn't care," Zoe went on as footsteps grew louder in the warehouse beyond. "Harper-Bowles in London and LePen in Paris were emotionally stronger, but their careers were destroyed as well."

"No big losses for the art world," Thalia mumbled.

"Whatever," Zoe said as the footsteps stopped by the door. They heard keys jangling. "Well, I think Erik realized that destroying the critics wasn't as useful in the long run as putting a ring in their noses. A rumor started—by Erik I am sure—that he had created fakes that implicated a large part of the critical world, and certainly everyone who had previously trashed his work."

"He's blackmailing them."

"Only at the beginning, I think." Zoe said. "I think it was enough to stop the negative reviews so that his art could be appreciated for what it is."

A key grated into the dead bolt on the outer side of the door. An instant later, the door opened and the Hulk stepped in, one end of Zoe's handcuffs already ratcheted onto his wrist.

TEN

By the time Seth Ridgeway pulled his Volvo to a halt in the driveway of his house in Playa Del Rey, the storm clouds had parted sufficiently to catch the last rays of the setting sun. Ridgeway watched as the fading light struggled feebly to separate gray sea from gray sky. Gripping the Volvo's wheel tightly, he thought of all the times he and Zoe had stood side by side, arms around each other; enjoying this view. It had been all the reason they needed to buy the house.

It was a little white two-bedroom bungalow that had been constructed in the late 1930s in a California beach interpretation of art deco. Its original owners had built it as a vacation home and had positioned it at the very edge of a steep bluff that rose more than seventy feet above the beach. On a clear day Santa Catalina Island seemed to wait just at the end of the driveway.

Seth turned off the ignition of the Volvo and sat immobile for several minutes, listening to the complaints of the blustery wind as it swept up off the ocean, still angry from the storm. Reluctantly, he turned away from the view of the Pacific and looked at the house, their house . . . his house now. The sunset had stained the white stucco a nicotine yellow. Long deep shadows from the tall lithe cedars they had planted in front crawled across the lawn and up the sides of the house. One of the panes in the living room's bay window caught a bright moment of the sun and focused it on his eyes. The scowl on his face intensified as he squinted through the reflection.

The last two days had been insane and he didn't know whether he should be angry or frightened. He had slept the night at the NSA's motel, fighting nightmares and bizarre dreams through a thin, exhausting sleep.

He found himself particularly irritated at the liberties Stratton and his cohorts had taken. Stratton's cleanup crew had arrived at the dock just moments after they had hustled him out of the limousine. The crew had stripped his boat, taken it out to sea, and scuttled it. The items stripped from the boat, Stratton informed him, had been deposited in Ridgeway's garage.

Seth knew that such measures would save him from answering difficult questions. Still, he was miffed that Stratton's people had obviously been able to go through all his belongings on the boat in search of the painting. He wondered if Stratton's men might have had some involvement with the previous burglaries that had occurred at his house while he had been living on the boat. It was obvious now that those had been someone looking for the painting.

He allowed himself an ironic smile as he got out of the car, walked over to the garage door, and opened it. The painting wasn't here and never had been. Before this morning, he hadn't even been aware of its existence, much less where it might be. But he knew now, and he knew it was safe. He didn't intend to let Stratton or anybody else get their hands on it.

Seth surveyed the piles of sailing gear and personal belongings Stratton's people had stacked on the garage floor. It looked like a nautical flea market. His eyes scanned the piles for a moment and came to rest on a small leather-bound volume the size of a thin volume of an encyclopedia. It was the ship's log Zoe had given him for Christmas three years before. He bent down and picked it up. Drops of rain had raised dark splatters on the cover. A snapshot fell out when he opened the log's cover. He caught it as it cartwheeled to the floor.

He closed the book slowly and stared at the photo in the half darkness. It was a picture of him and Zoe taken just before the Zurich trip. Doug Denoff, who had been the best man at their wedding, had snapped the shot as he and Zoe swabbed the *Valkyrie*'s deck following a long weekend sail to Catalina.

He felt the hollow void in his chest grow wider as he gazed at the picture. Zoe had a quiet beauty that didn't advertise itself: it was just simply there, a subtle foreshadowing of the deep beauty that lay beneath the skin. He thought of that day now, how it had been one of those ordinary occasions whose re-markable nature remained undetected until much later. It had been the last time they had gone sailing together. He wished now that he had realized then how special that sail really was. But some special moments never announce them-selves until it's too late to savor them.

He looked at the snapshot for another moment and slid it into his wind-breaker. For a second he thought he was going to cry, then suddenly he shut the *Valkyrie*'s log and tossed it back on the piles of boat gear. The *Valkyrie* was gone too. He had sailed to Hawaii and back on the *Valkyrie,* had ridden out a Pacific hurricane near Los Cabos, had spent many of his memorable times with Zoe on the *Valkyrie*. The craft was so intertwined with Zoe that it seemed almost fitting they were both gone, taken from him by insane men who would stop at nothing in their quest to possess a missing painting by a mediocre Nazi painter.

Patting the snapshot in his pocket, Seth turned away from the piles of boat gear, and headed for the door that led from the garage into the kitchen. He thought of Stratton, Weinstock, the killer on the dock. They all wanted the painting he had, wanted it badly, and that alone was reason enough for him to keep it away from them . . . for now. It was his only leverage. Zoe's fate, and his, too, for that matter, were intertwined with the painting. He'd let somebody have it only when he was sure he'd get Zoe back.

If she's still alive.

She has to be, he thought. She has to be.

Seth pushed his way past the door and into the dark kitchen. He closed the door behind him and stood in the deepening darkness for a moment. The heavy staleness of a house shut tight filled his nostrils. A feeble light filtering in from the dying sunset dusted the edges of the cabinets and counters and reflected weakly off the appliances. He looked at the Cuisinart Zoe had given him for his birthday the year they were married. He had enjoyed cooking then. Since Zoe's disappearance, he had taken to eating cold cuts and TV dinners.

Without turning on the light, he made his way from the kitchen, through the dining room, and into the living room. Zoe's touch was everywhere. There was nowhere he could look that was free from something she had done, some article she had given him, or he her. He closed his eyes as he fought back the inevitable tears. His eyes tingled for an instant and then he opened them and wiped at his face with his hand as if he could rub away the sadness. He sniffed once and then walked to the bay window. The spider plant Zoe had hung there had turned into a dried brown mop. He started to turn from the window to get the watering can when he saw it. A light-colored Toyota parked on the other side of the street, four houses down.

Keeping his eye on the Toyota and the man who sat behind the wheel, Seth slowly backed into the protective darkness of the living room. The car was familiar. He closed his eyes and tried to place it. In traffic. Definitely in traffic on the drive home from the marina. But somewhere else. Where?

He opened his eyes and stared at the car. He could see only the faintest outlines of the driver's head and shoulders. Then it hit him. He had seen the car parked in the lot at the motel Stratton had taken him to. Stratton had had him shadowed.

It made sense, Seth thought. He would have done the same thing had he been in Stratton's place. It was faintly comforting to know the surveillance was there for now. It might come in handy if he had unexpected visitors. But, he realized, he had to get rid of them for a couple of hours while he retrieved the painting. And he had to lose them without appearing to do so on purpose. He didn't want to make Stratton so suspicious that he would pull him in and question him thoroughly—an act Seth knew would mean drug-assisted inter-rogation. He was safe from that and would retain his freedom as long as Stratton believed Seth didn't know the location of the painting.

It was easy enough to lose a tail, to disappear. But most of the ways he had used before as a cop all looked suspicious. He had to lose the tail naturally. That left out wild auto chases and last-minute dashes into elevators. Seth stared into space for several long moments. He thought of slipping away from a basketball game at the Forum. According to the car radio the Lakers were playing some-body tonight. No, too uncertain, and his absence would be easy to notice. Movie theaters and concerts all had the same problems.

He sat on the foot of the bed and stared aimlessly around the room. He rejected staging some sort of emergency blackout at a department store so he could slip out with the crowds in the dark as too complicated. It had to be in character. He began listing places he normally went, and places he could be expected to go in his current circumstances.

He sat nearly motionless for the greater part of an hour before a broad smile finally spread across his face.

The University Research Library at UCLA is a massive seven-story monolith at the northern end of the campus. It was jammed with students when Seth Ridgeway arrived. The students, some of whom recognized and greeted him, scurried purposefully among the brightly lit book stacks.

Holding his briefcase in his left hand, Seth stepped off the elevator at the fifth level. The briefcase was heavy with tools, and he paused to swap it to the right hand. He walked over to the plan of the fifth floor and studied it earnestly. He looked at the catalog numbers he had scratched on a yellow pad, then back at the plan again.

Soon, he heard the whirring sounds of the other elevator approaching. It stopped at the fifth floor. Seth still pretended interest in the floor plan as he furtively watched the elevator doors part and disgorge the man from the light Toyota.

He was a tall, thin man in his mid-twenties, well over six feet, with muddy blond hair. He wore thick eyeglasses that magnified his eyes and gave him a surprised expression. He was dressed casually in morning shoes, jeans, and a windbreaker over a crew-neck sweater. They all looked newly purchased for the occasion.

The man walked two paces from the elevator and stopped. Seth returned his eyes to the floor plan, glanced at the paper in his hand one last time, and then turned away and walked toward the art history section.

The man had followed him closely but professionally from Playa Del Rey to the UCLA campus, and from the parking structure to the library. Seth had been careful to strengthen the pretense, searching the computer for topics in art history, Nazi Germany, Stahl. He was also careful to leave his search trail on the computer screen so his tail would get a good idea what he was after. He wanted the man to think he was acting like a normal academic, hitting the books before taking action.

In the next hour and a half, Seth pulled books from the shelves, marked them with slips of paper, and carried them down to the photocopy machines on the second floor to duplicate several pages. He filled page after page of his yellow pad with notes, all of which he left in plain view. The stack of photocopied pages grew as did the pile of books on the carrel. He carried his briefcase with him each time, and made a show of pulling out a container full of nickels and dimes for the copy machines. He gave the impression of a serious scholar who carried the little necessities of his profession in the battered leather briefcase.

Seth carefully built this illusion, leaving his research only long enough to locate some other document. His notes were there, his windbreaker hung over the back of the chair. He wanted Stratton's tail to get used to Seth leaving for varying lengths of time, carrying his briefcase and a stack of books.

It worked. The tail followed Seth down to the copy room three times and over to the snack bar at the North Campus Union building once. There he watched Seth drink a cup of coffee and eat a stale doughnut before returning to the stacks. After that, the man sat at a nearby carrel with a book he pretended to read. He was convinced Seth would not leave without the substantial pile of research that had accumulated.

When the tail stopped following him down to the copy room, Seth gradually began to increase the length of time he stayed away.

The words in the book swam beneath Seth's eyes now as he sat at the carrel and tried to time the moment correctly. If it didn't work, Stratton would pull him in and they'd go over him with everything they had. The drugs would make him talk, the NSA crowd would get the painting, and with it the leverage he needed to get Zoe back.

If she's still alive.

"Damn," Seth muttered under his breath. He wiped at his face and rubbed his closed eyes. The doubts, the fears, the sadness. They raged like a flood, just beneath the surface of his thoughts, washing away at the foundations of his resolve. She had to be alive, Seth thought. If she wasn't, he had to be a fool to do anything but turn over the painting to Stratton and his crew.

He opened his eyes and looked at his wristwatch. It was 9:17. The library would be closing in a little less than two hours. He had to get moving.

The tail barely raised his head when Seth got up and walked toward the elevator with his briefcase in one hand and a thick volume marked with a dozen pieces of paper in the other. From the corner of his eye, Seth saw the man look up briefly, and then return his glance to the book spread out on the carrel in front of him.

Seth got out of the elevator on the first floor, and after ditching the book in a return bin, walked out the front of the library and swiftly down the front steps. He made directly for the North Campus Union and drew another Styrofoam cupful of coffee. He sat at a table and scanned the door of the union for five full minutes. There was no sign of the tail.

Casually, Seth stood up, picked up his briefcase. Then, carrying the half-full cup of coffee, left the bright warmth of the North Campus Union and headed south along the broad concrete sidewalk decorated with animated groups of students talking excitedly about saving the world, toppling multinational corporate power elites, the nature of truth, and more prosaic obsessions and curses: papers due, loves lost, parent problems.

He felt old. The world was no longer his to make over. It never had been. Believing that was for the young. All he could do now was elbow himself some personal lifespace.

He stepped quickly now, trying not to appear urgent as he made his way among the twisted shadows of trees, their wintertime skeletons projected on the sidewalk by streetlights.

The crowds thinned as he approached the main campus quadrangle. Seth resisted the temptation to turn around to see if the tail had finally caught up with him, and turned instead to his left, walking down a short ramp into the basement level of Haines Hall. The door yielded to his push, and he walked confidently into the hallway.

The philosophy department was located one floor above. If the tail put in a sudden appearance, Seth would make for his office, pretend to search for some book or file, then return to his carrel at the library.

But despite his fallback plan, Seth felt his hands grow cold from more than just the temperature. He passed the elevator and then the stairs, and walked toward the unlit end of the corridor.

He stood at that end for several moments, buried in shadow, staring at a plain wooden door with a plain doorknob and a deadbolt. He tried his office key in the locks. It didn't work. He hadn't thought it would. The storeroom was seldom used and only Karen and Tony had keys.

Seth set the briefcase containing his lock picks and other tools unused since his days with the LAPD down on the floor and snapped open the hasps. Fumbling around in the dimness, he pulled out a set of picks that folded into a handle like a pocket knife. It had been years since he had last used the picks, so he set to work on the easiest lock—the one in the doorknob—first.

His rusty fingers manipulated the tumblers clumsily, but after a few minutes began to remember their old reflexes. In the old days he'd have picked a lock like this one in seconds. The lock and knob rattled as he worked in the dimness. Finally it yielded with a satisfying clack.

Seth paused a moment before setting to work on the dead bolt. He reached up with his right hand to sweep a strand of hair off his forehead. His fingers came back wet with perspiration, and abruptly he was aware of perspiration on his upper lip and the cold damp spots under his arms.

After taking a deep breath, Seth drew his face close to the dead bolt and studied it. He leaned down and pulled a small penlight flashlight from his briefcase. The extra light enabled him to get a look at the markings and the construction. The deadbolt was cheap, its only purpose to block entry to a room that contained old books, obsolete equipment, extra chairs, complete sets of Tony Bradford's *National Geographics* dating to 1946, Seth Ridgeway's forwarded mail and newspapers that were too voluminous to stack on his desk, and a painting of inestimable worth.

As he pondered the attack on the deadbolt, voices drifted down the stairs. Seth turned out the flashlight and froze. The voices grew louder, a man's and a woman's. Moments later, he heard the light clack of a woman's heels and then the softer, heavier tread of a man's feet as the couple started toward the basement. Seth gathered his tools and briefcase and hurried into the farthest shadow under the stairs.

The couple's words grew more distinct as they neared the bottom. Her roommate was tired of being asked to leave so they could use her apartment. Why didn't he move out of the fraternity house and get his own apartment? All they needed was a quiet, dark, comfortable place, he said, maybe there was an office open in the building. Seth thought he recognized the male voice as that of one of his students. The couple reached the bottom of the stairs and continued their discussion. She thought the idea of furtive sex in offices that had accidentally been left unlocked was degrading and unromantic. The male voice, which had sounded so much like a man's at first, gradually degenerated into an adolescent whine. Seth definitely recognized the male voice now. He had heard the same whine many times before. He identified it as belonging to a below-average student of his who was headed for academic suspension.

The couple continued their bartering at the foot of the stairs.

Go away, Seth thought, as he looked at the luminous dial on his watch. Time was creeping fast. It was already past 10 P.M. Stratton's man wouldn't wait forever.

And still they negotiated, promises for passion. From what Seth could tell she was getting the best of the bargain. She was even slipping in references to marriage. In his fever, the boy was agreeing to things he would later try unsuccessfully to deny. His concessions made her more agreeable to his suggestions.

"Over here," Seth heard him say. "There's a storage room under the stairs that they sometimes leave open. There's even a couch inside."

Seth's insides went cold. There was no way they could avoid seeing him.

"You seem to know a lot about it." Her words were frostbitten around the edges. "Do you bring your dates here often?"

"No . . . no I—it's just—the storeroom belongs to the philosophy department. I helped them carry some files down here once, that's all. I've never brought anyone here before, honest."

There was a long silence. Finally Seth heard her laugh. Beneath the girlish giggle was the carbon steel sound of victory.

And before Seth had time to think more about it, the couple stepped into the deep shadows beneath the stairs and were quickly face-to-face with him. The boy had one hand around her waist and another slipped inside her blouse.

She gave a quick high cry of surprise and jumped back as she covered her mouth. The boy's face looked like a motion picture running full ahead fast: fear, embarrassment, recognition, and back to fear. Both their faces, white and drained of blood, reflected the dim light like twin moons.

No one said anything for what seemed like aeons. Seth's insides churned. On the one hand, he was a member of the faculty and had the rank and authority. As a member of the philosophy department, he also had a valid reason to be there in the storeroom. On the other hand, he hadn't wanted to be discovered and had skulked there in the darkness listening to their very private conversation.

"Professor—" The boy spoke first but the words seemed to stick in his throat.

"Good evening," Seth said awkwardly. The words were inane but they were all he could think to say.

Suddenly the boy began to speak furiously, making excuses that compounded his embarrassment rather than easing it. His companion's cooler feline instincts prevailed. She told him quietly to shut up and pulled him back toward the lighted portion of the corridor.

"Good evening, professor," she said, all composed and polite. "It was . . . interesting bumping into you."

As their footsteps faded into the distance of the far end of the corridor and finally disappeared, Seth wondered if the boy had any idea just how far over his head he had gotten.

When he heard the door close at the end of the corridor, Seth left his briefcase in the deepest part of the shadows and set to work on the deadbolt. Despite its complexity it yielded to his ministrations in little more than a minute.

Seth replaced the lockpicks in the briefcase and opened the door. There was movement in the darkness, frantic scurrying. The light from the corridor failed to penetrate the gloom. He reached inside the door for the light switch, but it threw no light when he flicked it. The bulb had apparently burned out. That was going to make Tony angry. On occasion he liked to get away from things by coming down here, sitting on the old sofa, and eating sandwiches constructed of unusual fillings and materials. Pulling his flashlight from his windbreaker pocket, Seth stepped through the threshold of the room. He heard a pattering, a series of scratchings, and a constant rustling.

He turned on the flashlight. The first image the light revealed was remarkable chaos. Someone had scrambled the contents of the room. Furniture was overturned, the contents of shelves swept onto the floor. Over it all was strewn a layer of paper. Someone had opened every piece of his mail that Karen had so carefully stored here for him.

His heart suddenly grew so heavy that he felt as if it would rip itself from his chest. They must have found the painting. It should have been part of the large packet of materials the Eden au Lac Hotel had forwarded to him, the contents of their hotel safe deposit box that he had forgotten to empty on checking out. His leverage was gone, and with it, his hope for getting Zoe back.

He idly swept the room with the flashlight's beam as he stood there in stunned silence. A moment later the light revealed a scene so horrible that even the worst moments of his police career had left him unprepared.

Tony slumped in the far corner of the room, a single red bullet hole puckering the middle of his forehead like a third eye. On his shoulder a large brown rat was burying its snout in Tony's neck. The rat turned toward Seth and stared arrogantly back, blinking eyes that shone red in the flashlight's glare.

Seth stood there, completely paralyzed. As he watched in horror, another rat emerged from the cuff of Tony's trousers, his snout glistening with blood. Seth leaned down to pick up something to throw at the rats when something warm and furry launched itself across the side of his face.

He lost his breath in an involuntary gasp, swatting the dark furry thing in a blind panic. A second later he heard it thump against the far wall. With shaking hands, he trained his flashlight on the area, catching a glimpse of the rat as it lay stunned. It revived quickly and scurried away.

Seth fought the hysteria that rose in his chest and clutched at his neck like an unseen hand. Frantically he swept the flashlight's beam about the room until he found what he wanted. Trying to ignore the wet biting sounds made by the rats in the darkness, he made his way to the near corner of the storeroom and grabbed a wooden-handled broom.

In a frenzy of anger and frustration bordering on tears, he swung the broom at the rats, clubbing them away from Tony's body. The claustrophobic windowless room grew thick with panicked pattering and scratching and a steady high-pitched chorus of indistinguishable screeches. Seth continued to sweep at the area around the corpse long after the last of the rodents had fled into the hallway.

He dropped the broom and knelt down beside Bradford, reaching out his right hand and gingerly touching Tony's shoulder with the backs of his fingers. The body was still substantially above room temperature. He hadn't been dead long. Seth stood up and played the light around Tony's body. He hadn't been beaten by his assailants. The only damage other than the large-caliber wound in his forehead had been done by the rats.

Unconsciously, he backed his way toward the door to the hallway. The sounds of shallow, panicked breathing filled his head, and he had to look around him before he realized the sounds were his own.

Stepping from the storeroom with its sweet sickly smells of blood and death, Seth stood motionless in the darkness, his back pressed against the cool concrete wall. He willed his knees not to collapse as he struggled to organize his thoughts.

The chain of events came gradually. Someone had learned of his mail being stored here. Who? Not Stratton's people, he thought; they would have mentioned it to him. There would have been no reason to have him followed. They'd have the painting by now. It had to have been the same people who attacked his boat. But how? How had they learned? Seth thought for a moment, and the conversations he had had that morning with both Tony and Karen Bradford came back to him. They had both mentioned the mail and the storeroom. Someone must have tapped his telephone and learned where his mail had been stored. They had broken into the room just as he had. Tony had probably decided to make good on his threat to remove all the mail and had disturbed them in the act of going through it all. And they had killed him for that.

Seth felt the nausea only instants before the vomit filled his throat. He bent over and retched violently. He heaved until nothing more emerged, then wiped his mouth and lurched over to his briefcase.

Somehow, he managed to get the briefcase closed and make his way to the men's room on the second floor without being seen. He plugged a sink with a wad of paper towels and ran it full of cold water. He immersed his face. The cold wet shock gradually soaked the nausea away, and he stood there, eyes closed, trying to breathe normally while his heart experimented with a slower pounding.

Gradually, rational thoughts crept back into his mind. He had to call the police and report Tony's murder. He had to call someone before the rats returned. There was no question of getting involved now, he thought, as he turned toward the door and left the men's room. Before this, there had been a compelling reason to avoid entanglements with the law. A lengthy investigation of the murders at the boat would have cast suspicion on him, delaying his search for the painting and for Zoe.

But the painting was gone now, he thought, as he unsteadily made his way toward the philosophy department offices. The painting was gone, and with it, his only leverage. He had to turn things over to people better equipped to investigate. He leaned on the wall beside the departmental office door and fumbled for his keys. At least they'd believe him now, he thought, as he searched for the right key. There would be nothing of the skeptical chiding he had received in Zurich.

Seth unlocked the door, pushed it open, and turned on the light switch in the outer reception area. The fluorescent lights flickered for a moment before casting their bluish illumination over Karen Bradford's battered wooden desk and the scarred wooden chairs that lined the wall opposite it.

He turned quickly to the right and made his way down a short dark hallway to his office. He unlocked the door and made his way into the standard closet-sized quarters allotted to faculty members. The administrative bureaucracy in Murphy Hall comforted themselves with thick carpeting and executive trappings, but those who did the actual business of the university settled for war surplus furnishings wedged into claustrophobic corners. His eyes fell on a sampler behind his gray metal desk. Zoe had made it for him.

Those who can, do.
Those who can't, teach.
And those who can't teach become administrators.

The words were an expression of his own thoughts, and as such, had made him very unpopular with the UCLA administration. Truth was always painful.

Seth settled himself behind his desk and picked up the telephone to call the police, when an envelope with his name on it caught his attention. It bore Karen Bradford's handwriting and had been taped to the shade of his desk lamp to catch his eye.

He replaced the phone on its cradle and peeled the envelope from the lamp shade.

"Tony has been quite angry with you," the note began. "I realize how shocked you've been with Zoe's disappearance. And I know you've really not been yourself. Neither has Tony. I was afraid he might do something precipitous with your mail, so this morning after we talked I went down to the storeroom and sorted out any letters or parcels that seemed important. I've stored them in my filing cabinet, in the bottom drawer, at the very back. The key to the cabinet is enclosed."

The note was signed "K."

Ridgeway eagerly grabbed the key from the envelope. He got up so quickly that his chair tumbled over backward and clattered to the floor. With thoughts of Tony Bradford momentarily forgotten, Seth rushed to Karen Bradford's desk. The two-drawer metal filing cabinet rested behind it.

The screams began as he sat down in Karen's chair and bent over to insert the key in the filing cabinet lock.

First a female voice. It began as a high scream of surprise and quickly deepened to thick shrieks of terror. Then the male voice. More a shout than a scream. And then the female voice again, quivering now, climbing higher, each note a step closer to hysteria.

Ridgeway recognized the voices from minutes before. The couple had returned, desperate, he assumed, for a place to consummate their bargain. He had not relocked the door, and they had quickly found Tony Bradford's body.

The girl continued to scream. The volume seemed to be growing louder, either through sheer lung power, or because they were coming up the stairs.

Seth jammed the key into the lock. He had to hurry. The philosophy department office was the first one at the top of the stairs. They'd see the light and want to use the telephone to call the police; he'd never get back to the library in time. Everything still hinged on Stratton's tail suspecting nothing.

The cabinet opened easily. Seth slid the bottom drawer out and immediately spotted the pile of mail and parcels Karen had promised.

He snatched it from the drawer.

Oblivious to the screams, Seth sorted frantically through the mail. His hands quickly found what they were looking for: a parcel the size of a shirt box wrapped in brown paper with the Eden au Lac's return address. The wrapping yielded easily to Seth's determined fingers. He discarded the hardboard protector and bubbled plastic foam and found himself looking at a painting of an alpine meadow. *The Home of the Lady Our Redeemer* was printed on the back of the frame. He rewrapped the painting in its protective coverings, took it and the rest of the mail back to his office, then tucked the whole lot into his briefcase and headed for the door.

As he stepped into the corridor, Seth heard footsteps on the stairway and the sounds of the boy trying to comfort the girl whose steel-reinforced composure had finally shattered. Seth tucked the briefcase under his arm and ran from the building.

Zoe wrestled with the temptation to pray as she stood in the middle of her room and imagined a way out.

Before they had locked her in here, she hadn't believed in a god who listened to people's prayers. To begin praying now would be just the sort of hypocrisy she despised so intensely.

Her mother had tried to raise her as a strict fundamentalist Protestant. Every Sunday they went to a small brick church in Orange County, south of Los Angeles. The creed held dancing as a sin and considered most elected officials to the left of Ronald Reagan as the Antichrist. They knew that the world was created in 4004 B.C. because the Bible said that and no one disputed it because every word in the Bible was personally written by the hand of a wrathful, Zeus-like God who would send you straight to an awful eternal Hell if you didn't believe in his only begotten Son.

Her father never did attend the church and that, along with what to do about the mystery of her hearing colors, provided grist for endless argument and acrimony. In a quiet moment when Zoe was in her teens, he explained that, "with all the churches in the world and all the different ways to believe, it just seems awfully arrogant for each one to think they are the only right ones and that everybody else is going to hell. Perhaps we should sift through all religions and try to find their bits of truth."

The church had been an easy creed to rebel against. She turned her father's credo around and where he conceded that most religions probably had their own seeds of truth, Zoe decided that the vicious conflicts among them meant that they held no truth at all. When Zoe refused to attend church, her mother became even more fanatical. One Sunday after a particularly heated breakfast argument, her mother went to church and never came home. Neither, apparently, did one of the baritones in the men's choir. Zoe never heard from her mother again.

The disappearance had been all the proof Zoe needed that God was a con man and people were suckers. She concluded that this was about the only thing that Karl Marx actually got right.

So now, cramped in the bowels of a warehouse in Zurich, Zoe fought her own hypocrisy: the urge to pray. There were no atheists in foxholes, the saying went. To her that meant desperation forced people into a faith of convenience that wrapped them in the false comfort of self-deception. Her desire to pray had surprised her at first, then she recognized the urge for what it was and had resolved to maintain her own personal dignity and not surrender herself to begging for deliverance from a god that she had no faith in before.

She wished she believed in God so she could strike a deal.

Just get me out and I'll believe in you; I'll do whatever you want.

Zoe shook her head, ashamed of thinking the thoughts. What good was a god you could jerk around with the cheap deal of the moment?

"So hopeless," she said quietly to herself. Thalia kept her energized and positive, but every night when they brought her back to the room, depression seemed to leak out of the shadows.

She turned slowly around, facing one by one the three solid concrete walls and a fourth broken only with a heavy metal door with a double-key deadbolt and hinges that had been spot-welded at one end to prevent the removal of the hinges. The ventilator fan was welded to the door over a hole barely large enough to put her head through. She looked at the concrete slab beneath her feet and then the ceiling boards above her. Over the cell's ambient noise level she struggled to hear the faint tapping of footsteps from the office above.

The heavy void of hopelessness settled around her heart and became a dark pit that yawned to suck her in.

"*You always have to assume there is a way.*" Her father's words startled Zoe. "*And your task is to discover the solution, no matter how impossible it seems because there's no profit in assuming failure.*" She had not thought about the words for almost ten years. The sudden presence of his words, almost as clear as if he had just spoken them, startled her and made her skin feel as if it had caught fire.

In an instant, she vividly remembered the scene in his makeshift art studio. He had been working on a four-ton cube of steel for a sculpture that would be the centerpiece of his gallery opening. The sculpture was titled *Mind Fire* and the problem was getting a mass of steel heavier than a Chevy Suburban to look as if it were lighter than air.

Zoe continued to turn in a slow circle now, but what she saw was years beyond the concrete walls and half a world away.

"*When the logical doesn't work,*" he had said, "*look for answers in the illogical.*"

In the end, he improvised a polishing method using walnut shells and an electromagnetic suspension device.

"*When your mind fails you, seek answers from your spirit.*"

Mind Fire was purchased for more than her father had made as a mechanic over the previous seven years. And he had lived for another seven years before a mammoth bronze casting fell over and crushed him to death. She had founded her first art gallery with the inheritance.

"You must imagine your way through obstacles." His voice spoke to her. *"Turn off your mind and let your feelings loose."*

"Give me the inspiration, Dad," Zoe said softly as she fought back tears. "This needs to be a masterpiece of imagination. Help me, Dad."

ELEVEN

The Nochspitze is a ragged splinter of granite rising some eight thousand feet above sea level in the Austrian Tyrol southwest of Innsbruck. It's an inhospitable mountain: cold, steep, bereft of trees, and inaccessible to all but birds, skilled rock climbers, and those fortunate enough to ride in the private cable gondola that travels to the massive chalet perched just below the mountain's summit.

The chalet had originally been built as a guest house in 1921 by an Austrian innkeeper who had hoped to lure skiers up from the slopes. It had twenty-five guest rooms, all with their own baths and fireplaces, and a dining room situated in a soaring A-frame wing that cantilevered out over the precipitous cliffsides.

But the very isolation that made the inn attractive also served as a barrier to its success. Transporting guests to the inn required a lengthy trip up winding switchback roads from Innsbruck to the tiny cable car station at the mountain's base. In those days, unpaved roads made automobile travel impossible, so the journey had to be made by horse-drawn vehicle. In wet, frozen, or snowy weather, the trip was either impossible or so arduous as to be completely unattractive to prospective guests. The inn went bankrupt in 1924 when the gondola cable snapped, killing five people.

Two years later, a wealthy Italian industrialist bought the inn to use as a private retreat and conference center for his business, and upon his death seven years later willed it to the Catholic Church.

Behind the windowpanes of what had once been the inn's dining room, Cardinal Neils Braun, archbishop of Vienna and head of the Pope's Secretariat for Non-Believers, stood at military parade rest, his back straight, feet apart, hands clasped at the small of his back. He wore a heavy alpine sweater, twill slacks, and light hiking boots. His scarlet robes hung in the closet of his room, where they always stayed when he came here. He ran a hand through his thick shock of salt and pepper hair as he gazed absently the frost-glazed windows down at the tiny human specks gliding along the ski slopes below him.

He looked across the valley and in the distance tried to pick out a mountain face he had not yet climbed. From the front of the chalet, he could see the Olympic slalom runs of the Axamer Lizum where Jean-Claude Killy made history in 1968. He squinted now as the afternoon sun edged its way from behind a cloud and burned deep shadows into the painfully white landscape. Overhead, the clouds hurried swiftly across the sky like tall ships under full sail. They were the remnants of a storm that had dumped nearly half a foot of snow in the Austrian Tyrol the night before.

In the valley below, his eyes followed the dark serpentine meanderings of the Inn River as it flowed between snow-covered banks. It hadn't yet frozen completely, much to the dismay of the skaters. His eyes followed the river now, as it ran past the hieroglyphic shapes of the airport's runways and smack into the heart of Innsbruck. As his gaze finally came to rest on the snow-frosted roofs of the city's Gothic architecture, he thought of the man he was about to meet, Hans Morgen, a simple village priest with a most complicated past. And, perhaps, no future whatsoever.

Neils Braun turned now from the window overlooking the ski slopes and looked across the vast conference room. Large enough to feed one hundred people at a time, it had only a single oblong oaken table nearly twenty feet long resting beneath the soaring A-frame roof with its huge rough-hewn timbers. At the far end of the room, embers glowed and cracked in a huge natural stone fireplace.

Besides the table, there were twelve chairs arranged symmetrically around its perimeter. There was no other furniture in the room.

The knock at the door at the far end of the hall came at precisely 3 P.M. Braun pushed back the cuff of his sweater, glanced at his wafer-thin watch, and noted with approval the caller's punctuality.

"Come in!" Braun called. His voice boomed heartily in the silence.

Hans Morgen opened the door and pushed his way vigorously into the room. He stood in the entrance for a moment, blinking at the snow-reflected light pouring in through the windows.

He was a tall, lean man, more sinew than flesh, with bright blue eyes set in a long, ascetic face. In the sharp light, shadows cut deeply into his craggy features, accenting a prominent chin that jutted over an exposed clerical collar. He carried a walking stick, but on this day had no need to lean on its support.

Braun was surprised at how strong and unbowed the priest was despite his age and the shifting shrapnel that could transform hearty good health into instant death. But then, the cardinal thought, they were both active Austrians with good genes. From the extensive file that the CDF had compiled on Morgen, he knew that except for Morgen's time in the seminary, the man had skied and hiked the hills around the tiny village of Alt Aussee almost every day since he was a small child. He had rowed his shell on the lake in the summer and skated it in the winter. Morgen, according to the file, knew more about the region as it existed half a century ago than almost anyone else alive.

"Good afternoon, Your Eminence," Morgen said. He looked around the room, eyes cataloging the ascending A-frame roof, the stone fireplace, the hand-made table and chairs, and the obvious lack of anything else. Finally he made his way toward Braun. The hard leather heels of his shoes clopped sharply on the highly polished wooden floor.

Braun met him in the middle of the room.

"It's good of you to come," Braun said when they were face-to-face. The cardinal extended his hand. Morgen hesitated for a moment and studied the cardinal's face with a proprietary interest that briefly shook Braun's composure. Finally the two men shook hands.

"I wasn't aware that I had any choice but to comply with your summons," Morgen said evenly. The cardinal ignored the remark, an affront that would ordinarily be the subject of severe discipline coming from a lowly priest.

"I took the liberty of having tea prepared," he said as he stood up quickly and walked to the door. Morgen turned in his seat and watched as the arch-bishop of Vienna took a silver tray from someone who stood in the shadows. Braun thanked the person and returned with the tray that he then put down in the middle of the table. "Please help yourself." He indicated the tray with its silver tea urn and pitchers of hot water and milk. The tray also contained two bone china cups and saucers, two small biscuit plates, linen napkins, and an array of tea sandwiches, biscuits, and condiments.

"High tea is a custom I picked up while a student at Oxford," Braun explained as he took one of the plates and decorated it with an assortment of food. "It seems to me such a civilized way to provide some rest and contemplation for long working days."

Morgen murmured something noncommittal as he got up and approached the silver service. He stood to Braun's right and silently prepared a cup of tea with lemon.

Each man had prepared his tea and selected a plate of food.

"Shall we sit?" Braun asked. He motioned with his hand toward one end of the oblong table. Morgen nodded and took the indicated chair. Braun seated himself at the opposite end. They were silent, sizing each other up.

"You probably wonder why I've invited you here."

Morgen knew, but instead of answering, he took a sip of his tea and waited in silence. He looked down at a cassette recorder on the table and at the microphone sitting beside it.

The cardinal took a sip from the cup, set it down at his end of the table.

"I would like for you to tell me about your time in Alt Aussee," Braun said. "About the day when . . ."

"When I nearly died."

Braun nodded.

"But I have told that story before," Morgen said without any trace of annoyance. "Twice. To the men from the CDF and to . . . to the tribunal, two Assessors ago."

"I know," Braun said, "But I am hoping that perhaps there may be details that you have remembered since. Details that have . . . come back to you."

Morgen smiled. "Brain tissue does not heal well," the priest said. "Some say not at all. I have learned to live with the limitations caused by that day. I certainly am not aware of any recovery in my memory."

"Well, perhaps we can hope for a miracle," Braun said. "You do believe in those still, do you not?"

"Of course I believe in miracles," Morgen said. "Every breath I take is a miracle."

"Then let's see what you may remember today," Braun said as he leaned over to turn on the cassette recorder.

"As you wish, Your Eminence," Morgen said, suppressing the sigh he felt.

"Dawn came up all bloody red when I was only halfway across the lake," Morgen began. "I had hoped to be across the frozen surface of the lake—the Alt Aussersee before the sun came up, but the snow was very deep. I had been running from the SS for more than three hours and I knew they were gaining on me; it was like one of those nightmares where your feet are mired and you're running in slow motion as a locomotive bears down on you with this hellish mechanical roar."

Braun's face wore a compassionate look. "I understand that you no longer have that dream?"

Morgen studied his face for a moment, trying to assess the cardinal's sincerity. "I no longer wake up screaming from it."

The cardinal nodded. "What did you do that morning?"

"I ran. I prayed. I recited the Twenty-third Psalm many times." Morgen looked for a reaction, and, finding none, continued. "I had run all the way from the Salzbergwerk—the salt mine at Habersam Mountain. I saw the relic in the abandoned mine. I sneaked in. The SS guarding the entrance thought I was one of the clergy working with the Reich. They had let me see the shroud."

Morgen's face went blank and dreamy. "I held it," he looked triumphantly at the cardinal. "I actually held it, the gold box with the sparkling jewels. I looked at the things inside and I read many of the documents that had lain inside for almost two thousand years. I still can't believe that the things that I held in my hands have felled Popes, deposed governments, made and broken empires for almost twenty centuries. Every day that I think about it—and be assured, Your Eminence, that I think about this every day—I cannot understand how something so holy has inspired so much evil. Men have corrupted, murdered, lied, and stolen for it all in the name of God. And how it kept Pius XII silent on the excesses of Hitler's Reich."

"We don't talk about that," Braun snapped.

Behind his best smile of beneficence, Morgen seethed. A righteous anger rose in his chest, cut through his fear, and steadied his nerves. That someone could do this to his church, in the name of his God! Father Morgen looked about him with steadied vision, details growing sharper.

"They came for me, down from the hills above Fischerndorf," Morgen continued.

"I could see the faint dots of their electric torches. I was encouraged because it looked as if the size of the force had dwindled. Then I heard the distant static of their voices and knew that they were gaining on me."

Braun held up his hand to interrupt. "Tell me as much as you can remember of the Germans in the village—when they came, any names you might remember. I know you remember that day on the lake with the most clarity, but details leading up to that might be very helpful to us."

Morgen nodded. He took a sip of his tea and gazed thoughtfully up at the chandelier for a moment. "At first, the Nazis came to Alt Aussee in small numbers and with great secrecy. Hitler had visited Alt Aussee, had hiked the trails in the hills above the town, and eaten at the inn's table with the townspeople. He had even bought a worthless piece of land on Habersam Mountain whose only merit was an abandoned salt mine that ran deep into the earth. Then came the war and Nazis in great numbers.

"We—the townspeople—were banished from the area around the old salt mine at Habersam Mountain. The SS built quarters there for more than two hundred fifty men, all restricted to their billets and forbidden to talk with outsiders. Supplies and replacements for the soldiers came through town in covered lorries. Dignitaries flew into the airfield at Bad Aussee and sped recklessly through town in long sleek autos with curtains to hide the identities of their occupants. Just before Christmas 1941, a rumor swept the village that Hitler himself had paid a secret visit to the mine.

"All of us in the village were grateful that the SS kept to themselves. But nothing could still the endless speculation about what the Nazis were doing with the old salt mine at Habersam Mountain. Curiosity led many to the very edge of the forbidden zone, but all they ever saw was a garrison occupying an alpine meadow, guarding the entrance to an unremarkable salt mine.

"One theory guessed it was a hideout for SS officials in case the war turned against the Reich. Others ventured that it was one more underground laboratory manufacturing Hitler's promised secret weapon. On the face of it, either guess was not preposterous. The cool alabaster white corridors of Alt Aussee's Salzbergwerk were deep enough to be impervious to any known weapon. The mines were stable, not subject to cave-ins, and maintained a constant temperature and humidity that was not inimical to human comfort. They were, in short, an ideal place to hide almost anything safely."

Morgen drank the last of his tea and was satisfied to see the cardinal play gracious host and refill it for him.

"Thank you," Morgen said. Braun nodded.

"The Salzbergwerk at Habersam Mountain remained the only Nazi presence in the hills surrounding Alt Aussee until lorries and boxcars full of priceless art, statuary, rare books, manuscripts, and religious icons began arriving in 1945," Morgen continued.

"As you know, Hitler had looted the greatest public and private art collections in the occupied countries to enrich the permanent collection of der Fuhrermuseum. He envisioned this as a magnificent structure to be constructed in the grimy industrial city of Linz, Austria, his boyhood home. Hitler, the frustrated artist, wanted to build the greatest art museum of all time so that his hometown would never forget him. But Allied bombers had interrupted the Fuhrer's plans, and so he rushed his collection to the salt mines of the Salzammergut for protection against the almost daily raids.

"Unlike the icy secretive SS units guarding the Habersam mine, the Wehrmacht units accompanying the art were frightened boys, thankful to be away from the thick of the fighting, yet actually aware of their role as guardians of a fortune in stolen goods. They rushed about frantically, confiscating salt mines all over the countryside, storing much of the art in the mines near Bad Ischl and Bad Aussee, and especially in the large deep mines at Steinberg and Moosberg. Accompanying them were museum curators—many of them now prisoners of war—traveling in the back of boxcars and transport trucks over steep mountain roads lethal with winter to take up their assigned task of protecting the Fuhrer's acquisitions.

"The trucks thundered purposefully through town day and night, making the merchants happy. All of these new visitors filled my small church and kept me very busy. So busy, in fact, that I had almost forgotten the mine at Habersam

Mountain. But with the many new Wehrmacht parishioners I had, I heard confessions of such tales of anguish and horror and evil I found myself wondering if God could possibly find enough forgiveness to absolve them."

"The Heavenly Father's infinite grace can forgive all sins," the cardinal said, a bit too pompously for Morgen's liking.

"Begging Your Eminence's pardon, I am well aware of that," Morgen snapped back. "But I was only a man—I *am* only a man—and infinite patience and wisdom are not at my disposal."

"So I have learned," Braun said with a condescending smile.

"Do you really want this story or did you bring me here to needle me?"

The cardinal gave him a flat even look for a very long moment. "Please. Continue."

Morgen sighed. "A local teenager's curiosity about the mine started it all. About two months after the art started to arrive, the local boy, thirteen-year-old Johann Hoffer, had been skiing the trails above Alt Aussee one afternoon when he veered too close to the Habersam mine. He was shot and killed. About 4 A.M. the next morning, I opened my door to a young SS sergeant named Willi Max who was torn by Johann's death. The sergeant had witnessed the killing of the boy. It had been for sport, he told Morgen, two lieutenants taking target practice on a local. As the young German begged for forgiveness, he told me about the Secret Messiah. I have spent the rest of my life wishing I had never heard the boy's confession, but I knew I had to do something."

Since the SS contingent was forbidden to enter the village, Morgen had the sergeant arrange for him to hold mass and hear confessions at the garrison. The day of his arrival, news of Allied advances had brought the young soldiers to the edge of panic. They prayed with the faith of desperate men. Losers. The Allies had entered Austria already, it was rumored, and grew closer every day. More than anything, the SS seemed terrified that they would be treated as they had treated others. It was a difficult fate to accept for men who, in six years of ruthless war, had all but forgotten the meaning of mercy.

The nervous troops spoke quietly with Morgen about slipping away in the dark. More than one asked him to bring civilian clothes to make the escape easier. None of them seemed to know what they were guarding. That secret seemed restricted to a select handful, among them the sergeant who had come to Morgen for absolution.

"One night in the compound, after I said mass, Willi Max—the sergeant—and I slipped away from the main barracks and entered the mine. The great cavern had been turned into a fortress. All through its corridors were caches of arms, ammunition, explosives, and booby traps. They showed me how the entrance was mined, designed to produce a controlled cave-in to block access. Once past the entrance, the sergeant vouched for me and I was accepted without question. My request for a tour of the mine was readily granted."

Morgen struggled to control his anger and disgust at the memory. "I was able to do this, Your Eminence, because as you well know, many within the church—especially the anti-Semitic among us—had served the Reich and its aims too faithfully." Morgen ignored Braun's warning frown and continued. "I hadn't wanted to believe the sergeant's story; but when the makeshift vault was opened and the golden box with the Sophia Passion, her shroud, and the other documents was revealed, all doubt gave way to awe. After the box was returned to the vault, the sentry opened a separate compartment and displayed the written pact between Hitler and Pope Pius XII."

Morgen focused on the cardinal's eyes as he said: "When I read the text of the papal concessions, I felt an implosion of my faith that unhinged my self-control." Morgen shook his head slowly, the regret still obvious after more than half a century.

"I can still see myself, almost as if I was detached from my body. It was as if I was no longer in control of my own fist as it flew toward the smooth whiteness of the sentry's neck. My arms seemed to be controlled in that moment by a force beyond me. Again and again I struck the sentry until he slumped to the floor, bloody and unconscious."

Morgen's breathing came quickly and deep as if his body were reliving the exertion. "And then I reached for the golden box. From behind me came a shout. 'Stop!' I turned to see the young sergeant who had shown me all this facing me; he held his service Luger leveled at my chest.

" 'Shoot me!' I said. 'I'm ready to die.' The sergeant shook his head. 'No,' he told me. 'You must leave.' I turned and was amazed to see the shroud's safe closing of its own accord, actuated by the mechanical whining within the wall. I turned to reach for the box but the sergeant lunged forward, shouldering me out of the way as the safe door closed. He saved my life. Otherwise I would have been trapped inside with it."

Morgen shook his head. "Sometimes I wish I had been trapped in there." His hand shook as he sipped at his tea. "He told me that there were security devices even within the vault, booby traps so that a person would be killed trying to steal it.

"Suddenly from the distance came voices, sounds to remind me that staying alive long enough to tell the world might be harder than making the world believe what I had just seen. The sergeant created a diversion and I escaped the mine only to be hunted down as I ran."

Morgen was silent with private thoughts that he was tempted to reveal, but instead, held back once again. He was thankful that his own secret son had avoided the ravages of war and prayed that God would forgive a wayward priest for the weakness that had conceived him. He prayed also that God might overlook the pride he had felt each day as he watched the boy develop into a man.

It had been a torture back in Alt Aussee looking into the boy's eyes, listening to his son call him "father" and not being able to tell him how true that was. He wanted to tell him, but he knew it would be years before the boy could accept the reality: that his real father was not the brave Oberleutnant who died valiantly fighting Polish barbarians but a village priest who had truly loved his mother more than her husband ever had. He'd had no right to do what he'd done, but sometimes . . .

Morgen remembered the inn by the lake that Anna had operated in her husband's absence. Its steep chalet roof reached up and caught the first of the morning sun. He thought again of the fantasy that played day after day in his thoughts, of renouncing his vows, marrying Anna, raising his son.

And again he reminded himself that he was married to the church—even if certain highly placed men had compromised it for a "higher purpose." No, there was no denying that his son was a sweet sin for which he truly needed forgiveness.

He turned away from the memory of Anna's inn—and the thought of their son.

"Where were you running to, Father?" Braun prompted Morgen.

"Where?" Braun shook off the daydream. "I was running toward a small stone cottage on the lake's southern shore, where Jacob Yost was waiting."

Morgen felt his heart fall. He had been so absorbed in the thoughts of his son that he had let his guard down for an instant.

"There!" Braun said triumphantly. "You have remembered something new!" The cardinal smiled broadly. "Now, just who is Jacob Yost?"

Caught in the slip, Morgen knew he had no choice but to continue, trying to keep the details as thin as possible while sticking to the truth.

"Yost had connections to the Resistance," Morgen said. "I had talked to him not long after the Sergeant's first confession. I was hoping he could get the secret to the Americans and through them to the rest of the world. I knew he would do it, even if it killed him. I almost got to him. The SS shot me, but not badly. But it slowed me down and they were rushing toward me when Divine Providence intervened."

The cardinal raised his eyebrows as if he hadn't read this from the previous interview transcripts.

"The Americans were battling their way through the village and a round of their artillery went astray, landing on the frozen lake surface between me and the SS who chased me. The round landed closer to them. I will always remember how the explosion split the thin ice covering the lake. The explosion lifted giant slabs of ice that shed the men, flinging them into the black olive-green waters beneath. Then, almost majestically the slabs settled back like battered pieces of a jigsaw puzzle and they were gone.

"I reached the cottage where I was supposed to meet Yost. When I stepped on the porch, the door to the cottage opened, but instead of Yost I saw a tall figure wearing the unmistakable uniform of an SS officer. I turned to run."

Morgen's voice cracked. "Then he shot me in the head."

The room hung with the priest's final declaration. The brilliance of the day had started to fade with the winter sunset. They sat there for a long time, watching the sun disappear, neither man wishing to look at the other.

When Braun spoke again, his voice seemed to echo. "Father, I appreciate the enormous strain this recounting has been and I want to say how important it is, especially the recovery of a new recollection." He paused, searching for the best words. "As valuable as that memory was, the biggest question is this—of all the hundreds of salt mines in the region, do you remember which one contained the relics of the Secret Messiah?"

Morgen tried his best to give the Cardinal the impression of a man trying earnestly to remember.

"No, Your Eminence. That is one of many details that the wounds have kept from me."

He lied.

TWELVE

Seth Ridgeway lay on his back, staring blankly through the darkness at the ceiling. As usual, the sheets were coiled around him, twisted and knotted like rope, and the blanket lay in a heap at the foot of the bed. Again he swiped at his face to clear away the perspiration that beaded on his forehead and upper lip. He wiped his hand on the sheet and turned, trying to get comfortable enough to sleep.

But sleep would not come. In his dream he saw rats crawling over Tony Bradford, tearing off pieces of flesh, and then the image took the form of Rebecca Weinstock and he saw her on the dock, clutching at a throat that was no longer there.

Seth turned again and lay on his side. He closed his eyes, but every time he did, he saw the faces of death. He had gotten to sleep once that night, right after returning home with the painting. But the sleep had been shattered by a nightmare.

In the nightmare, he was sleeping. Then someone threw on a light. Seth opened his eyes and found himself lying in the philosophy department's ground floor storage room. Tony Bradford hovered over him.

"Get up, you lazy bastard!" Tony shouted at him. His face was red and bloated with anger. The veins stood out along the sides of his neck like thick ropes. "Get up and teach class!"

Tony's words grew so loud he couldn't understand them and the light on the ceiling seemed to grow brighter and brighter. He closed his eyes against the light, but it seemed to burn through his eyelids.

Then pain exploded through his chest and sides and for an instant he was back on the street. The coke dealer was ready with his Uzi. The first burst of slugs caught Ridgeway's partner full in the face. The second burst slammed into Seth's chest and twisted him around, hammering into his side and back as he turned.

Darkness had been quick in coming then, but in the nightmare there was only the light.

Seth opened his eyes against the light and saw his partner's face on Tony's body.

"You asshole, you should have warned me," his partner snarled. "It should have been you; you should be dead, not me."

Seth tried to stand up, he wanted to explain. But his legs wouldn't move, nor his arms or mouth. He was paralyzed.

"You're a disgusting mess!" The face suddenly changed to Rebecca Weinstock's, but the accusing voice was still his partner's. Seth felt the tears of frustration streaming down his cheeks; he could explain, he wanted to explain, but the words wouldn't come and finally Zoe's face replaced Weinstock's and the voice was hers.

"You let them take me," she said. "You let them take me away. Some cop you are!"

Then Seth felt himself split in two. One part floated to the ceiling and looked down on the second. He saw himself slumped in the corner with a bullet hole in his forehead and rats chewing gaping bloody holes in his body. Then he felt the grinding, searing pain, and the pressure of the clawed feet scratching at his eyes and the warm naked tails sliding across his belly and his groin. He awoke screaming.

Seth opened his eyes now and gazed at the luminous green display of the clock next to his bed. It was nearly 3 A.M. He'd had the nightmare nearly three hours before and still its vivid horror had not diminished. Sleep was clearly impossible.

He sat up on the edge of the bed and caught sight of his dim reflection in the mirror of Zoe's dressing table. The carved wooden jewelry box he had bought for her during their voyage in the British Virgin Islands anchored one end of the dresser; a collection of bottles, nail polish, and other cluttery containers that seem to gather around women sat on the other end. They all seemed to accuse him of negligence.

He shifted slowly, then got to his feet. The bedsprings complained loudly as he got up, reminding him that Zoe had wanted the springs replaced to lessen the noise they created when they made love. Something twisted in his heart as he remembered the times they had lain together in the bed, their bodies cleaving to each other, arm in arm, breath against breath. Would it ever be again?

At the bedroom window, Seth leaned against the sill and stared out at the street. The rain clouds had cleared, leaving the stars to burn tiny bright holes in the sky.

"Why, God?" He asked softly, his breath lightly frosting the window. "What did I ever do to deserve this? I've prayed; I've tried to be moral, ethical. Why did you let this happen?" Then he struggled again not to think the thoughts that were occurring to him with increasing frequency: maybe there was no God. Or maybe God didn't care.

Across the street, the Toyota had been replaced by a dark American-looking sedan with two men in it. He felt a momentary irritation at the surveillance, but quickly dismissed it. Stratton was just doing his job.

Fully awake now, he turned to his bed, reached under it, and withdrew the painting. He set the package on the bed and unwrapped it. He held it loosely in his hands in the darkness for several moments and then leaned over to switch on the lamp next to the bed. He examined the painting once again.

It was just as Weinstock had described it. A painting of an alpine meadow, done in the warm yellow tones of the Florentine masters. There was a prominent rock face at the right side of the picture, and what looked like the entrance to a mine in the distance almost at the left border. The picture itself contained no clues that he could find.

It was mounted in a plain black wooden frame and sealed with brown paper.

He turned the frame over and gazed at the oval sticker affixed to one corner of the sealing paper. "Jacob Yost and Sons, Fine Frames for Fine Art," the label read, "II Augustinergasse, Zurich."

He stared at the label. The name of the shop that had framed the picture was the only clue he had. Why, he wondered, had it been framed in Zurich and not somewhere in Germany? He looked at the sticker again. There was a notation of some sort but the ink was too faded to decipher it. He held it closer to the light. The notation was illegible, but by holding the frame at the right angle to the light he could make out a date—May 19, 1937—and a series of numbers: 16–16. Before the invasion of Poland, before the holocaust atrocities, while Hitler was still a respectable European leader and his people were free to travel without being hampered by battles or hostile borders. They had come to Zurich with the painting. And what else? he wondered.

He looked at the painting again. His thoughts wandered. Zurich was famous for its banks and for its stability. It was also infamous in his own mind as the place from which Zoe had disappeared. The Nazis too were famous for their hoarding of gold and other valuables. Was it unreasonable to speculate that they had come to Zurich before the war to open accounts and to set up banking ties? Perhaps Hitler or Stahl or some other Nazi just happened to bring the painting along with him on such a trip and just happened to drop it by Herr Yost's framing shop.

If there was anything worth praising about the Nazis, it was their methodical nature. With them, hardly anything occurred by chance. The odds of the painting "just happening" to be along were slim.

Nodding, he picked up the telephone, dialed the operator, and asked for international directory assistance. He wanted to know if Jacob Yost, or one of the sons, was still in business in Zurich.

The phone rang twice before Seth replaced the receiver on the cradle. Stratton—or somebody else—had probably tapped the telephone. There was no telling who might be listening in on the line. He could make the call from a pay phone at the airport just as well.

Quickly, Seth pulled on a pair of corduroy slacks and a sweater. He emptied the briefcase of the tools he had carried earlier and placed in it both the painting and the damp pile of thousand-dollar bills Weinstock had given him.

He walked over to Zoe's jewelry box and lifted out the top tray. From the bottom, he scooped up his passport and a healthy wad of Swiss francs he had brought back from Zurich. Absently, he opened the passport and gazed at the visas stamped in the back. Switzerland, England, Holland—every major country in western Europe and most of the minor ones, plus stamps from the little islands in the Caribbean that he and Zoe had visited. He thought fleetingly of those halcyon days cruising the Caribbean, then abruptly snapped the passport shut and began packing.

Ten minutes later he watched the two men in the black sedan come to attention as he walked briskly from the house and tossed the bags into the Volvo's trunk. He climbed into the driver's seat and started the engine. Putting the Volvo into gear, Ridgeway turned around carefully, drove slowly down the street, and stopped next to the black sedan. He rolled down his window and motioned for the men to do the same.

"Tell your boss I'm going to Amsterdam," Seth said, and with an airy salute rolled up the window and drove off.

An hour later, he smiled to himself as he hung up the pay phone in the international terminal at Los Angeles International Airport. Jacob Yost and his sons were still in business, with a new generation of sons. The old man was still alive, they had told him, retired. Seth had mentioned the painting and artist by name, but neither seemed to evoke any recognition from the present Jacob Yost. He promised to mention it to his father, who, he was sure, would want to talk to the American gentleman about it.

I'm sure he will, Seth thought, as he walked into the nearly deserted snack bar and poured himself a cup of larcenously expensive and criminally bitter coffee. But I wonder what other people would like to talk about it as well.

As he settled himself behind a plastic-laminated table to pass time before his flight, Seth felt hope stir in his heart. For the first time, he believed there was a chance to find Zoe. An answer to his prayers, he wondered, or simply the way events were playing themselves out? He looked out the window and tried to pray. But the words failed him.

Fighting the anxiety that tightened her throat, Zoe arched her back, desperate to relieve the ache and fatigue that had knotted themselves solid after an entire day on her feet. She and Thalia had spent almost twelve hours unpacking and arranging Max's extensive collection of Venus figurines, some as old as 20,000 B.C.

Finishing her stretch Zoe looked around the room, drinking in an awesome sight that had dazzled away the critical barriers she erected between her heart and her profession. They surrounded her, a small battalion of holy women— more than three hundred statuettes covered every horizontal surface, each one tagged with file numbers, descriptions, and index numbers to more extensive files. They were made of baked clay, terra-cotta, alabaster, ceramics, and cast copper. A large carved alabaster frieze cut from the wall of an Anatolian temple was crated separately and remained to be unpacked.

She looked down at a nine-thousand-year-old baked clay Venus less than a foot long. The woman's breasts, belly, and genitals were extravagantly portrayed; the figure was seated with her arms resting on carved panthers. By contemporary body images, the women portrayed in the most ancient of the statuettes would be classified as morbidly obese.

The sight transported her to a mysteriously primitive world of so very long ago; it diverted her mind from the dread that hid in her heart, raided her sleep at night, and all too often crushed her spirit in the day. Instead of the approaching consequences of the coming few days, she felt now the beauty of the long-vanished artisans and a world they had tried to interpret through these pieces of their art that had survived.

"Captivating, aren't they?"

"Oh!" Zoe exclaimed as Thalia's voice startled her and snatched her back to the present.

"Sorry." Thalia looked down at the clay figure that had held Zoe's attention. "She's one of my favorites too. So pure in her lack of artifice and decoration, made of local mud and baked in the ashes of a fire that way back then was still mystical in its own right."

"Way back then . . ." Zoe said softly as she gazed at the figure.

"I think maybe it was around just such a campfire that somebody looked deep into the flames and saw the reflections of a vast incomprehensible world that scared the bejesus out of her. And this"—she pointed a white-gloved hand at the clay statuette—"this is how she dealt with it."

"That's what makes it so fascinating. I mean, you're talking about the origin of religion." Zoe shook her head. "I know so little about their history—"

"Prehistory," Thalia said as she picked up the clay woman. "That's why there's so little to know."

"Exactly. I've never needed to know about art much before a thousand years B.C. or so. Only a few specialists in my business do, actually. This is more archaeology than art."

"All art is archaeology," Thalia said. "Art reflects culture and culture is the way people try to make sense of life. It's just that most of us are dependent upon written history to give us some hints about the art."

Zoe nodded thoughtfully. "Think of what was going on then. She"—Zoe pointed to the clay Venus—"was shaped by hands and a mind that were reeling under an incredible explosion of knowledge. This was back when the wheel was invented, when they domesticated animals, when people began painting on the walls of caves, when the first tiny groups of early people discovered that you could grow a crop by planting the seeds—"

"When God was a woman," Thalia interjected.

"Pardon?"

"Look around you. God has boobs."

Zoe frowned.

"What a world!" Thalia said. "They've got thighs as big as mine and back then those people made her God." She laughed deeply and her entire body quaked beneath a voluminous black sweater and stretch pants.

"Odd," Zoe said softly. "Because of Seth, I know a lot about modern religions." She looked around. "And almost nothing about—" She swept her arm in arc around the room. "I never really thought about what came before. I mean, I assumed that the Venus figures were just one of a lot of little idols in a vast pantheon of gods . . . animals, a bunch of cults, and so on. You know, not really legitimate religion."

"Not legitimate religion," Thalia repeated as she walked along the table gazing at the women arrayed there. "That's thanks to my people." She stopped and looked back at Zoe. "The Torah—and the Christian Old Testament are full of admonitions to destroy the pagan temples, to burn their holy texts, to obliterate them from the landscape. But let me tell you, fifteen thousand years— maybe twenty-five or thirty thousand years before Yahweh got written up in the holy scriptures, God was a woman. The Great Goddess wasn't just part of a fertility cult or one of a bunch of animistic totems; she was acknowledged as the creator of the universe, the giver of all life. And not just in one place—all over the world. Follow me."

She set off down the aisles between the tables with amazing speed. Zoe hurried after her. "Look at the tag." She pointed to a terra-cotta Venus. "She's from Sumer and they called her Nana or Innana. And next to her"—she indicated a figure carved from serpentine—"she's the great Sun Goddess of the Eskimo, the supreme creator, same as the Japanese Creatress."

Thalia kept walking. "India, Arabia, Anatolia, Australia, Egypt, Africa, all around the Mediterranean, God was a woman. They called her Isis." She pointed to an alabaster carving and marched on. "Ishtar, Asherah, Hathor, Anahita, Au Set, Ishara, and a hundred other names, but she looks the same regardless of culture and there is no doubt that they all represent the Great Goddess who created the world and everything beneath it." Thalia stopped so suddenly Zoe almost ran into her. "This was monotheism from the very beginning."

They stopped by the largest of the Venus figures, an Anatolian stone statuette almost three feet high showing the female figure giving birth to a ram's head and three bull's heads.

"This is early sixth millennium B.C.," Thalia said. "In their culture, rams and bulls represented men. This statue clearly shows man coming from woman rather than the other way around in the Adam and Eve story."

Zoe leaned close to the statue to take in the detail.

"Back then they hadn't made the connection between sex and kids. All they knew is that women and female animals gave birth, created life; only women could create new people. Women's bodies were in tune with nature, the moon, and showed all the same sorts of mysterious cycles as the world around them."

"Which, I assume, is why we still have mother earth, mother nature."

"Absolutely. You can try to cover up the Great Goddess but you can't get rid of her. Also remember, these cultures were matrilineal—inheritance and the family name passed along the mother's side of the family, since they had no idea that guys had anything to do with it. Men were still the hunters and protectors by virtue of their strength and size, but women invented agriculture because it gave them a reliable food supply close to home."

"Which is why she's holding some sort of grain?" Zoe pointed to the large statue's hands. "Looks kind of like wheat but I can tell it's not."

Thalia bent over and squinted at the image. "It's a dwarf form of barley, one of the precursors of the modern varieties." She nodded. "But, yes, you're right about why she's holding it. She's the giver of food as well as the creator of life."

"So what happened?"

Thalia raised an eyebrow.

"Why's God a guy now?"

"Part of it is because wine and God are a lot alike and I think all that started when they realized the role that intercourse played in creating children," Thalia began. "Or maybe that in combination with the beginnings of agriculture." Beyond the walls of the art studio, they heard a door slam in a distant part of the warehouse. "That's when they started to realize that they had some control over their bodies and their food supply and that it wasn't purely divine sleight of hand."

"Knowledge," Zoe said. "Eating the forbidden fruit?"

"You could say that. Until this point, these small pockets of culture lived pretty much in tune with nature, taking what it provided and making no attempt to control its course or their own lives. When men realized that they were a key ingredient, they lost some of their awe. About this time—" She beckoned with her finger and walked to an adjoining table, where the goddess figures had grown slimmer. "See this?"

Zoe looked at a cast copper figurine with lapis lazuli eyes and some sort of amber stone set in the torso in a geometric pattern. A smaller, unmistakably male figure stood next to the goddess.

"Okay, this is about four thousand years B.C.," Thalia said. "The male figure is a sort of prince consort. The Great Goddess is still supreme, but the culture has evolved to consider that God includes both male and female portions. I don't interpret this as polytheism. I think it represents the male and female rather than two separate deities."

Another door clanged in the warehouse and now they heard faint voices.

"The culture was still matrilineal, though ownership of property was joint, but this was the Bronze Age and there were real towns and they were growing so fast that they encroached on each other's hunting grounds and crops; conflicts began. Before this, security lay in worship and in finding harmony with nature. Now, the spear and sword became the main instruments of society. The importance of the male element of God grew and—"

The quick sound of a key in the art studio door was followed hard on by a thundering crash as the door flew open. A normal-sized man Zoe knew as Sergiev came through first, followed by her hulking jailor. A wave of cold air preceded them, fluttering papers and chilling more than just Zoe's feet.

"Talk about timing," Thalia said in English. Then switching to Russian, she greeted the two men who scowled back at her.

Zoe sighed as she took a last glance at the statue as the dark reality returned.

"Come on!" Sergiev barked.

As she had every evening for more days than she cared to count, Zoe turned and held out her right hand. Her hulking jailor stood in a similar position, one end of a pair of handcuffs fastened to his postlike wrist, the other end dangling free.

Sergiev fastened Zoe's wrist to the handcuff. Without another word, the Hulk headed for the door.

THIRTEEN

Halfway between Washington, D.C., and Baltimore, on one thousand acres of rolling fields and forest, sits a sprawling complex of twenty buildings surrounded by triple cyclone fences ten feet high. The fences are topped with concertina wire whose razor-blade edges have been designed with one purpose in mind: the flaying of human flesh. One of the fences is electrified. Security forces, heavily armed and accompanied by attack dogs, patrol the two strips of no-man's-land traced by the three barriers.

In the daytime, more than fifty thousand people jam the twenty buildings protected by the three strands of cyclone fence. They work in the complex's offices, buy stamps at its post office, get their hair cut at its barbershop, purchase cold medicine in its drugstore, take classes at its college, and watch programs broadcast by its television station, which is powered by the complex's own electrical generating plant.

The visitor traveling along the Baltimore-Washington Parkway who happens to take the Fort Meade exit, and who happens to take a wrong turn after entering the army base, might happen to find himself looking through the meshwork of fences at a mammoth central building faced with green chipped stone. This is the Xanadu of spying, the Taj Mahal of eavesdropping, the colossus of intelligence gathering: the headquarters building of the National Security Agency.

In this one building is more usable office space than in the CIA's Langley Headquarters and the U.S. Capitol combined. In its basement is the world's largest concentration of computers, filled with so much sophisticated hardware that it is measured in acres. The last public leak put the concentration at more than eleven acres—enough to handle the computing needs of every business, large and small, in the United States.

But the business of these computers is not business. It is spying. Some of the brute force of all this computing power is used by cryptologists to break coded material. Some is used to translate messages intercepted in a foreign language into English. But by far the lion's share of the massive computer complex is used to analyze signals and conversations picked up by the NSA's gigantic system of signal intercepts.

Like a giant combine harvesting the kernels from a field of grain, the NSA scans billions and billions of messages that travel the world's airwaves every second: spy satellites comb the earth below for telemetry signals from Russian or Chinese missile launches; airborne spy planes snare conversations between MiG fighter pilots and their ground control; even the car telephone calls made by Kremlin officials as they travel to work somehow find themselves caught in the NSA's broad net.

But more than just the conversations of America's enemies fall within the NSA's area of concern, for the agency's job is also to determine who among the citizens of the United States is an enemy previously unidentified. To this end, the NSA's antennae intercept telephone calls, cable messages, and telexes made by ordinary individuals.

An internal NSA investigation would later reveal that Seth Ridgeway's telephone call to Jacob Yost originated from a GTE pay telephone on the mezzanine level of the international terminal at the Los Angeles International Airport. The signal quality of the telephone transmission was substandard, similar to that originating from the crude telecommunications systems found in the Third World.

Ridgeway's call was switched over to long-distance ground lines leading to COMSAT's Jamesburg, California, earth station. All of the satellites' available circuits were occupied at the time, so the COMSAT switching computer connected the call to transcontinental land lines, where it eventually found an unoccupied circuit at TAT 6 (Transatlantic Cable 6) in Green Stratton, Rhode Island. From here it made the 3,400-mile trip to the coast of France, emerging near Deauville, where its care fell into the hands of the French PTT—Poste, Téléphone, et Télégraphe. From the coast, the call was beamed via microwave to a switching center east of Paris. There the PTT computer passed the call via the primary land trunk cable to Switzerland's PTT computer, which then routed it to Zurich. At Zurich a series of computer switches finally located Jacob Yost's telephone and caused it to ring.

During this intricate process, Seth only half listened to the minute or so of clicks, clacks, thunks, and echoes in the telephone's earpiece. He was thinking more about what he would say to Yost than about the static on the line.

The conversation seemed innocuous by any standards. Seth wanted to speak to the old man, who was out. What did it concern, the old man's son asked. A painting by a man named Stahl they had framed decades ago, a picture of an Austrian meadow called *The Home of the Lady Our Redeemer*. The son was not familiar with it, but he would check with his father, and, in any event, the old man would welcome a visit by Herr Ridgeway.

Besides Seth and Jacob Yost's son, the conversation had significance for other sets of ears.

At Fort Meade, Maryland, the telephone number, mention of Stahl's name, and title of the painting all connected with alerts programmed into the eleven acres of computers. Since the phone number and two names were tagged with priority alert status, the first computer that had analyzed the taped conversation alerted a second computer known as Lodestone. Just as some humans are more equal than others, so it is with Lodestone.

Lodestone analyzed the short telephone call, then checked on the identity of the person entering the intercept keys: the telephone number, Stahl's name, and the name of the painting. The computer noted that the originator was an agent code-named Byzantium and that any messages relating to the intercept key were to be classified Top Secret Umbra. The message was for the eyes of Byzantium only. Less than three minutes after Ridgeway had hung up, a coded message was on its way to NSA agent Byzantium, who at that time was on his way to the Los Angeles International Airport.

At a cramped but nonetheless efficient set of new prefabricated office build-ings east of Paris, a PTT computer absorbed all of the information beamed to it from TAT 6. The computer was smaller, slower, and in human terms, dumber than Lodestone. But it only had to handle the traffic for some two thousand telephone calls at any given time, and that was well within the capacity of the Olivetti mainframe computer that was assigned to the task. Several PTT techni-cians strolled around, caressing the computer, watching its lights, tending its needs—human acolytes before their god.

In a room next to the computer sat a man in a business suit who worked for the SDECE—the French secret service. The man was one of three who manned the room twenty-four hours a day, waiting for the computer to recog-nize any of the code words and intercept keys they had entered into the PTT computer. The PTT was never particularly happy about having to devote some of the computer's memory and computing ability to the dirty business of spying. And the SDECE men assigned to the boring task of sitting in the adjacent room waiting for something to happen manifested little enthusiasm either. But since the SDECE and the PTT were both owned by the same government, neither had any choice, and the people from the two different agencies did their best to stay out of the way of the other.

The SDECE agent in the next room on this night was named Yves LePin, and he had gotten his job with the agency as a result of his enthusiasm for the

French Socialist party, which had finally won the government. Wary of the new batch of Socialists and even Communists of dubious security value (for the French and Italians still clung to a variety of archaic ideologies), the SDECE had placed people like LePin in jobs where they could do the least amount of damage should they turn out to be spies for someone else.

So it was that just after LePin had settled down with his twelfth cup of café au lait and the crossword puzzle from *Le Monde,* the PTT manager in charge knocked timidly at his door to inform him that the Olivetti computer had printed something out in a code that he didn't understand.

Languorously, LePin followed the PTT manager into the main computer room to accept the message. What he found snapped him immediately to attention. The intercepts that his KGB control officer—still a true believer in a country with no clear political direction—had instructed him to program into the computer six months before had borne fruit. Trying to control the shaking in his hands, LePin took the message back to his office The message was in book code. Like all codes based on published books, it was decipherable only to the person who knew which book had been used, and he was that only person.

By the time he got back to his little office, his fear had transformed itself mostly into exhilaration. After a lifetime as a common trade unionist, he would now be able to truly serve the cause of socialism. He folded the paper carefully and put it into his pocket. He couldn't wait to get home and pull the book from its shelf and start translating the code. He smiled when be thought of his clever irony in using Adam Smith's *The Wealth of Nations* to encode his messages.

Less than ten minutes after Jacob Yost's son gave him the message from the American, the old man shut himself away in his office and placed a long-distance telephone call to Munich, West Germany. Yost's call sounded in the dim corridor of the Jesuitresidenz, located in an old stone baroque building that faced the Sparkassenstrasse in the old quarter of Munich.

The old quarter's hodgepodge of medieval, Renaissance, and baroque buildings crowd shoulder-to-shoulder, eaves-to-eaves with each other around the narrow winding cobblestone streets and alleys. The old quarter is barely fifteen hundred meters across, yet more than a dozen churches crowd themselves in among the beer halls, private residences, and government buildings. The most prominent of the churches is the Dom und Pfarrkirche Unserer Lieben Frau—the Cathedral and Parish Church of our Lady—known locally as the Frauenkirche. Founded in 1271 as a chapel dedicated to the Virgin Mary; the Frauenkirche has become the trademark and symbol of old Munich. The church's twin towers, which are topped with curious cupolas that resemble

skullcaps worn by Roman Catholic clergy, have appeared in more tourist bro-
chures and snapshots than any other Munich landmark save the famous glock-
enspiel.

But besides serving as a postcard landmark, the Frauenkirche serves as a
cathedral and major place of worship for Munich's faithful. Its status as both
cathedral and parish church warrant a greater than ordinary staff, many of whom
live at the Jesuitresidenz.

The telephone rang twice before being answered by the *residenz*'s most
junior novice. He answered politely and requested that the caller please be
patient while he summoned Father Morgen.

Morgen was a strange man, the young novice priest thought, as he walked
quickly to the end of the hall and up the stairs to the third floor. He had kind
blue eyes that always seemed on the verge of tears. The abbot had told him it
was due to the injuries Morgen had received at the end of World War II.

The young priest stopped before the plain wooden door with the cross,
which was located at the end of the third-floor corridor. He paused a moment
before knocking. From inside the room, he could hear Morgen humming to
himself. It sounded like a Brandenburg concerto. The young priest wondered
why the abbot didn't give Father Morgen his own telephone. He was old and
frail and received many telephone calls. Surely an exception could be made, the
young priest thought, as he raised his hand and knocked gently on the door. It
couldn't cost very much. Besides, the parish wouldn't have to pay for it for very
long. How much longer could Father Morgen live?

"Come in," Morgen called.

The young priest opened the door and found Morgen sitting at a plain desk
next to the window overlooking the Frauenkirche.

"Phone call, Father," said the young man as he walked forward and stopped
in front of Morgen's chair to offer him a hand up.

Morgen smiled and waved away the young priest's offer of assistance. He
wasn't an invalid. They never seemed to realize that.

As Morgen got up and made his way to the door, he stopped for a moment
and took a look at the picture of his son that hung on the wall. He had grown
into a fine, handsome, powerful man—a man who stood on the verge of greatness. Morgen felt his heart tear a little, as it always did when he realized that
his son would never know his true father.

That was impossible now. The mother of the man whose picture hung on
the wall—the only other person who knew the truth—had died of a stroke a
decade before. Now, only Morgen and God knew the terrible secret.

Taking one last glance at the picture, as he always did when he left the room, Morgen made his way down the stairs to the telephone, hoping that good news would take the edge off his physical pain.

The pain and weakness shifted from day to day as did Morgen's memory and vision. It was the fragments, they told him. The Oberleutnant's bullets had shattered against his skull and against his ribs that day so long ago at the cottage by the lake. There were six of them that could have been, and still might be, fatal had they gone or should they move another millimeter. He would be dead if Yost hadn't killed the Oberleutnant and hadn't gotten him to the American army doctors. He allowed himself a small smile as he carefully descended the stairs. In five decades he had learned not to make sudden movements that could encourage the fragments to shift.

Over the past sixty years, he had had days when he felt perfectly well except for the blindness in his right eye. On those days, he wanted to ski or ice-skate again, but he knew that was toying with suicide. So he walked, kept in good physical condition, but learned to treat his body like it was old nitroglycerine.

He reached the landing on the second floor and walked slowly down the long corridor toward the telephone. The young priest did not follow Morgen to the telephone. Instead he walked quickly to the abbot's room and rapped respectfully on the door.

"Father Morgen has another telephone call, Your Eminence," the young priest said after stepping into the abbot's simply furnished room.

"Thank you very much," the abbot replied. And with a nod of his head, the abbot dismissed the young priest. The young priest was tempted to tell Morgen about the order the abbot had issued. He and the other novice priests were to notify the abbot or his assistant whenever Morgen received a call. No explanation. But then, explanations weren't expected by novices; they were just to give blind obedience. Still the young priest thought, there seemed something . . . dishonest about the whole affair.

The abbot thought much the same thing as he pulled open the bottom drawer of his desk and checked to make sure that the small tape recorder the CDF men from the Vatican had given to him was functioning. The men had first arrived there two days after Easter in 1962, just after Morgen had been assigned to the parish. The abbot had been a younger man then and had protested both the tapping of the hallway telephone and the order that he be forced to spy on one of his own priests. His protests were answered first by the archbishop of the diocese and later by a cardinal from the Vatican. Finally, when he continued to object, he had been called to Rome and told in no uncertain words that further protests would not be tolerated. And in the end they had told him nothing about the reason for the telephone taps.

He tried to deduce the reasons by listening to the tapes, despite the injunctions against it. The calls had been to a wide variety of people, art dealers and collectors—particularly a Zuricher named Yost—police investigators, and government officials. The calls that initially raised the abbot's eyebrows were the ones to or from former Nazis. At first the abbot thought the Vatican suspected Morgen of being a former Nazi himself. But that didn't reconcile with the way the priest had received his injuries. Then, as now, Morgen had seemed like a frail, harmless old man, unable to handle a full cleric's load, and who instead was allowed to indulge his hobby of trying to locate pieces of art stolen by the Nazis so he could return them to their rightful owners.

He had had some minor successes, and had even been written up in the *Abend Zeitung* by a reporter, Johanna Kerschner, who had taken an interest in him and his work.

In the end the abbot prayed and meditated and concluded that God had placed a greater trust in the hands of the men above him, and that truly all that was required of him was his faith and blind obedience. So he had faithfully mailed the tapes to Rome every week since then. And over the years, other men had come and given him newer tape recorders and then gone. They had hooked up devices that automatically recorded all conversations on the telephone. But he didn't trust the device and be still liked to check on it each time to make sure it was working.

The abbot stared at the machine and saw that the cassette was turning. Then he sighed and slowly closed the drawer and went back to the paperwork. The paperwork, he thought in despair. He wondered if God's book of life were filled out in triplicate. He crossed himself and asked forgiveness for such irreverent thoughts and began to wade through the piles on his desk.

Seven thousand miles to the east, Seth Ridgeway settled into the window seat on the upper deck of the KLM 747. He always flew KLM because they were the last professional airline still flying to Europe. With a smile he remembered how the international arrivals terminal at JFK Airport had been turned over to the same people who run Schiphol Airport in Amsterdam—essentially the same people as KLM. Now, he thought American air travelers would have a really sweet time flying, if only the FAA would just turn all American air traffic over to KLM so they wouldn't have to ride the cattle cars and urine-stinking rattletraps that pass for airplanes in the United States. Dream on, he thought as he plugged in his headset, put it on his head, adjusted the volume, and curled up next to the cabin wall as comfortably as he could with his seat belt fastened.

He closed his eyes and saw Zoe's face. She was there. He knew it in his heart. He knew she was still alive and that he was going to find her this time. He drifted off into welcome sleep as the giant 747 began to pull away from the gate. He had no inkling of the chain of events he had ignited halfway around the world.

FOURTEEN

The American sat in the luxurious suite at the Nochspitze and reread the material Cardinal Neils Braun had given him upon his return from the States. The American was a troubled man.

He walked over to the door and stepped out onto the narrow balcony that overlooked the valley of the Inn River. The night was deep and the cold air cut through the pasty haze in his mind. He leaned against the railing with both arms straight, looking like a preacher braced against the pulpit ready for a sermon.

He thought again of Braun's bizarre briefing. A second Messiah, a woman, a murder—no, he thought, a mass murder by a Pope, the rewriting of scripture, the revision of history—easy enough to do those days when so little had been written to begin with, to cover up the existence of the new Messiah.

Braun had been quite sincere and very convincing in his insistence that the existence of a second shroud made little real difference to the faithful. What was important was the symbol of resurrection and salvation and the belief in God. People weren't ready . . . couldn't, wouldn't accept a second Messiah.

The revelation of her existence would shake their faith in the church, causing untold emotional suffering. The truth would not make them free, only unhappy.

And of course they talked about the sectarian violence and unrest that would follow such a revelation, how Zhirinovsky's people would use the situation to expand and consolidate his influence in Russia and beyond. Zhirinovsky's followers were madmen, more in the mold of Idi Amin than Stalin, but both had slaughtered more innocent people than Hitler. Popular dissatisfaction since the fall of official communism had made Zhirinovsky and his followers in power the perpetual runners up. And if he or his followers ever assumed control, the question would be where the first bloodbath would happen.

The American stared deeply into the darkness, searching for answers—

answers that remained as elusive as the pinpricks of light arcing their way across the night sky.

His mind, his intellect, everything he had lived for so far, told him they were right. No truth was valuable enough if it would cause the violence, death, and upheaval that this would cause.

But his heart refused to listen.

The American turned away from the darkness, walked back into his room, and closed the door. He stood there for a moment, looking at the thick volumes covering the desktop and resting on the floor. The complete history of Sophia: the transcripts of the interviews with her and the people of her village, the decrees of Emperor Constantine, and the travels of the box with its explosively credible proof as could best be reconstructed, until it disappeared from a Bavarian mansion in the mid-1930s.

He rubbed the fatigue from his eyes and looked at his watch. It was after midnight yet he was not sleepy He sat back in the desk chair, picked up the yellow legal pad, and began to review his notes.

Following the murders, Sophia's burial shroud and the documentation of its authenticity were placed in a large box made of gold and inset with precious stones. The top was placed on the golden box and its edges sealed with molten gold impressed with the imperial seal of Constantine and the holy seal of Pope Sylvester I.

The box was then placed in a vault beneath what would later be Saint Peter's Basilica. And there it and its secrets rested in peace for seven hundred years.

It was monstrous, the American thought, as he read through the notes for what seemed like the thousandth time. It was like watching an old midnight horror movie where the archaeologist and his beautiful assistant open the mummy's tomb and set the curse free on the world. Only now, it was an ancient truth about God and murder that had come back to haunt them. He read on, trying to make sense of the nightmare.

The shroud and its documentation lay in the vault as Saint Peter's Basilica was built around it. And each Pope passed on the secret of the shroud to his successor. The discovery of the box survived the sacks of Rome by the Visigoths in A.D. 410 and the Vandals in 455.

But the shroud's discovery could not survive politics and degeneration. As the end of the Christian Church's first millennium approached, the Popes and the people around them grew to resemble the intemperate and profligate early emperors of the Roman empire. Greed, sexual excess, and debauchery abounded in the Vatican, with tastes in perversion often rivaling Caligula's. The secret of Sophia's Passion began to slip past the lips of drunken and licentious Popes. And this, more than the debauchery, galvanized the church hierarchy to action.

In 1045, Gregory VI bribed his predecessor—Benedict IX—to resign from the papacy. But the abdication inflamed rather than soothed church tensions. One faction convinced Benedict IX to retract his abdication, and thus there were two Popes claiming the throne of Saint Peter. Efforts to negotiate the exit of one or the other of the Popes failed, so a third faction of the church met to select a compromise Pope—Sylvester III—to replace them both. But the choice of Sylvester was satisfactory to neither of the other two groups, so by the end of 1045 there were three Popes all battling for control of the hearts and minds of the Christian world, and not incidentally, the considerable wealth and power of the church.

While the three Popes battled one another, more levelheaded bureaucrats within the church removed the golden box with Sophia's Shroud, along with other priceless relics, to hidden places within the labyrinthine corridors of the Vatican, so that none could be stolen or used by the pretenders.

These same bureaucrats sent emissaries to Heinrich III, emperor of the Holy Roman Empire, asking him to intercede. In 1046, Heinrich III replaced all three rival Popes with a fourth, Clement II. The emperor backed up his decisions with his army.

An unsteady balance prevailed for a decade until Heinrich III's death in 1056. He was succeeded by his son, Heinrich IV, who was six years old at the time of his father's death.

The American closed his eyes and pinched the bridge of his nose between his thumb and forefinger. How in everlasting hell could any Pope ever claim infallibility? Bestiality, necrophilia, orgies that would put the Romans to shame; greed, avarice, a lust for power. There was nothing that could be done that hadn't been done by a Pope. And to believe they were infallible made it necessary to believe that God had sanctioned it all.

Opening his eyes, the American returned to his scrawled notes. The words had begun to swim beneath his eyes. Sleep would come soon.

In 1061, Pope Nicholas II died and was succeeded by Alexander II. Alexander II was unpopular with the bishops of Heinrich IV's court and through a technicality—all Popes at that time had to be approved by the emperor—the Imperial Synod at Basel declared Alexander II's election void and appointed instead its own Pope, Honorius II.

The young emperor, now eleven years old, began to differ with the clergy among his court advisers, and so to make sure that the bishops continued to get their way, Archbishop Anno of Köln kidnapped Heinrich IV in 1062 and ruled in his name.

Heinrich IV now growing into a strong-headed young emperor, was freed in 1066 and ruled his empire in harmony with the church in Rome for nearly a decade. But in 1076, the German bishops who held so much sway in Heinrich's court disagreed once again with Rome. They refused to approve the election of Gregory VII as Pope, and, in the Imperial Synod at Worms, declared him deposed.

In reaction, Gregory VII excommunicated Heinrich IV and all the German bishops. Deprived of his holy warrant to rule, Heinrich IV faced civil war, a revolt by the peasantry, and the loss of his kingdom. The chastened young emperor repented and in 1077 was forgiven by Gregory VII, who also restored his power.

But Heinrich's confession had been a false one, constructed in league with his bishops to buy time. Later that year, Heinrich IV and the bishops again declared Gregory VII deposed and elected instead Clement III as their own Pope.

Enraged, Gregory VII again excommunicated Heinrich and his bishops, and took the additional step of awarding the mantle of emperor of the Holy Roman Empire to Heinrich's rival, Rudolf of Swabia.

In 1079, Heinrich IV's forces killed Rudolf of Swabia, crushed the forces loyal to him, and invaded Italy. Four years later, Heinrich IV invaded Rome and drove Gregory VII into exile.

Once in Rome, Heinrich installed Clement III as Pope and left, taking with him a gem-studded gold box as part of the booty from his victorious battles.

The American pushed himself away from the desk and stood up. He had had enough reading for the night, and enough to think about for the rest of his life. He walked over to the bed, where the contents of his suitcase were spread from headboard to foot. But his mind wouldn't let go of the shroud.

The whereabouts of Sophia's Passion and her burial shroud in the nine centuries since Heinrich IV took it from the Vatican were mostly unknown. From the skimpy records kept by Heinrich IV and his successors, it was apparent that none of them knew the true value of the box. It received neither special mention in the royal records nor any special treatment. It was, for all practical purposes, forgotten, along with booty from other raids and spoils from previous wars. Nothing more was heard of the gold box and its priceless religious relics until they turned up in Bavaria in 1935.

As the American stripped down and pulled on his pajamas, he thought of the educated guesses made by church historians on the probable history of the box. It was likely, according to the Vatican historians, that the box was given as a gift to a valued member of the royal court. The box was probably passed from one family member to another across the centuries. But someone in the long line of heirs to whom the box was bequeathed saw fit to sell it. Perhaps this person needed money, or perhaps had simply no use for a gaudy bejeweled gold box from the distant past.

Regardless of what happened during the nine hundred years that followed Heinrich IV's possession of the box, hard facts about it reemerged in the spring of 1935.

Acting on Hitler's orders, the German government began exacting onerous taxes from Jewish citizens of the Third Reich. Those unable to pay the punitive taxes were forced to sell their homes and businesses to Reich officials or to their friends.

Of course, most Jews did not have enough cash and savings to meet the outrageous Nazi demands, so they gave the government collectors their jewelry and family heirlooms, including art, rare books, antiques, and other items of value.

The American finished buttoning his pajama top and walked across the room to turn out the lights. He stood by the switch for a moment, torn between fatigue and the remarkable discovery he had made that day. He looked at the books on the desk and then walked over to it and picked up his yellow pad of notes.

Sheldon Brucker was the man's name. Brucker had been a prosperous antique dealer in Bad Tolz, a small village south of Munich. Brucker had used a gold box inlaid with jewels to pay part of the Nazi government's tax.

Hitler had not yet formed the Sonderauftrag Linz—the organization responsible for the gathering of art for the Fuhrermuseum in Linz, Austria—but even in 1935, he was aware of the need to scrutinize carefully the objects stolen from the Jews to make sure nothing of value was melted down or destroyed.

Objects from art dealers, antiques dealers, and the truly wealthy were all examined more carefully than the rest. The art experts and historians pressed into service by the Third Reich eventually recognized the significance of the extraordinary box with the seals of Constantine and Pope Sylvester I impressed into its metal

The box had been opened carefully to avoid marring its beauty and the documentation inside was quickly translated into German. From the moment the discovery was revealed to Adolf Hitler, Sophia's Shroud became the object of the most intense security ever. Ultimately, the shroud and its flawless documentation would be used by Hitler to assure the Vatican's silence on the

Holocaust. The church would close its eyes to one evil, hoping to save the world from a second evil that might eventually prove greater.

The American got up, turned out the light, and walked through the darkness of the unfamiliar room. Hitler had hidden the shroud well, Braun had told him. So well, that in the chaos following the fall of the Third Reich, it had disappeared as completely as if it had never left its vault in the Vatican nearly a millennium ago.

He slipped between the crisp, cool sheets, but the horrors of history kept the American wide awake.

Zoe stood in the middle of her cell and let the cacophony wash around her; she hadn't inserted her makeshift earplugs because she wanted every bit of the room to sink into her mind; if there was a way out, the room would point the way, she just needed to pay attention.

She looked at the computer on the beat-up desk, the battered chair and the table lamp with the frayed cord that was death in wait for the unwary. The remains of this night's Movenpick meal sat next to the computer. She turned to the right: metal door with the vent fan and in the corner, the chamber pot. Another quarter turn and there was her bed. One more quarter turn and her eyes fell on the cardboard boxes she used to store the clothes they had provided for her. The final turn brought her back to the computer.

There was no way to go through the concrete floor and walls. There was always someone in the office above her head. She walked over to the door and gave it the usual evening inspection, hoping for some inspiration. It was still heavy-gauge metal; the hinge pins were still welded so she could not slip them out, and the double-keyed dead bolt was still locked from the outside.

Zoe's heart pounded in her chest: slow, deep and strong. There was an exit; she just needed to see it. She thought of using the electric heater to build a fire; one that might burn the wooden ceiling.

Not before it killed me first. Not before the sprinklers put it out. Not before the men in the room above discovered it and came down here to kill me for trying.

No. It was clear that she'd need to induce them somehow to open the door. Somehow and sometime when she wasn't handcuffed to the Hulk, sometime when the man Sergiev wasn't calmly waiting with his finger on the trigger. Sometime like a time that had not happened anytime in the previous months but had to happen in the next day or so. Sometime that had not come and would not arrive on its own.

It's not going to come, she thought dismally. She'd had months to think her way out and there was no reason to think that the solution that had eluded her for months would miraculously appear this close to the end.

Despair settled into her heart like evening shadows. She saw Seth's eyes, and for a moment his entire face seemed fully painted for her. She'd never see him again. Tears blinded her; darkness swelled in her chest and left little room for her heart to beat.

"Damn!" She wiped at the tears. "Stop this, Zoe Ridgeway." But the sound of her voice exerted no authority over the flood tide that swelled of frustration and anger and fear. Half blinded, Zoe stumbled over to her bed; it gave a loud, rusty complaint as she seated herself on the sagging edge and surrendered to the tears.

Zoe had no idea how long she had been crying when she felt herself again drawn to prayer.

"Don't!" She shook her head against the thought, then got up to get the roll of toilet paper that sat by the chamber pot and used it to blow her nose. She dabbed at the tears that streaked her cheeks.

"Shit!" She exhaled loudly, then wadded up the paper and sidearmed it across the room into the wastebasket.

Before she could raise her guard, the compulsion to pray washed over her, and this time she had a fleeting vision of the room full of prehistoric goddesses and heard the echoes of Thalia's words. Zoe sat back on the bed and clasped her hands together between her knees. Then she bowed her head.

"The Lord is my shepherd," she said quietly, beginning the Twenty-third Psalm, that they had memorized in Sunday school and had recited at the beginning of every class. Only now Zoe saw a woman's face on the shepherd.

"I shall not want," Zoe continued, struggling to remember, the words faded from decades of neglect.

"She maketh me to lie down in green pastures; she leadeth me beside the still waters.

". . . the paths of righteousness for her name's sake. Yea, though I walk through the valley of the shadow of death, I will fear no evil for thou art with me.

"Fear no evil."

The thought eased the knot in her heart. She stood up and paced the room, trying to exhume the words buried so deeply.

"Thy rod . . ." she struggled. "Thy rod and thy staff they comfort me." Zoe smiled wanly as she remembered how the boys snickered about this line and about how her cheeks had burned when she'd finally learned the reason why.

"Thou preparest a table before me in the presence of mine enemies. Thou anointest my head with oil. My cup runneth over . . ."

When the idea hit, it jolted her physically, halting her in mid-stride.

"*Oh my God,* she thought as she looked up. "That's *it!*" She smiled broadly as her eyes inventoried the room, seeing it as if for the first time. "That's the way out of this hole."

Zoe's whole body seemed to tingle as she struggled with the sudden epiphany. Why didn't I see that before? she wondered. "Nothing's changed. Everything's been here in plain view for months." She considered that it could have been months' worth of mental preparation, the committing to memory of every possible detail, the constant working with scenarios, combinations, and recombinations—all of that focused into action by the intensity of impending death.

Could have been, she thought. Then she thought of the biblical story of somebody-or-other who had had the scales removed from his eyes. Then she said.

"Thank you, God."

FIFTEEN

Across the trolley tracks and a little west of the main train station in Amsterdam is a bar that has been serving gin for five hundred years. Not the effete gin favored by feverish English cricket players and American tennis dilettantes, but a richly flavored Dutch gin with an integrity its makers call genever.

The bar is old and dim and filled with dark wood, stained darker still by centuries of tobacco smoke. Its wooden plank floors are worn thin by centuries of feet, and the deep spaces between the planks are filled with a grime that has come off shoes worn by the likes of Rembrandt and van Gogh. Inside, it is always hazy with talk and tobacco.

Seth Ridgeway sat at the mahogany bar nursing his genever and watching the man who had followed him for the past three days.

The man had a pale, ascetic face, wild dark eyebrows, and eyes that the old masters used to paint on the faces of the insane. The man's coat hung on a thin reedy frame. What little hair he had left on his head seemed to be a dull chestnut color.

Seth took a sip of the genever and let it roll on his tongue before swallowing it. In the image that played across the mirror behind the bar, he saw the man sitting alone at a small round table with a glass of lager in front of him, reading from a paperback novel.

Seth had first noticed the man at Schiphol Airport, standing in the corridor just past the customs area. He had been dressed in an ill-fitting suit that looked as if it came from a secondhand shop. He looked like one of the tens of thousands of bums, street people, panhandlers, and genuine homeless attracted to Holland by its liberal attitudes and its even more liberal social welfare programs.

As Seth had walked past the man at the airport, he had looked directly at Seth and taken a single tentative step. Seth had looked quickly away and picked up his pace to avoid the expected plea for spare change.

Thoughts of the man had quickly vanished on the cab ride into downtown Amsterdam, as fatigue and jet lag leeched the energy from first his body and then his mind.

But the man had been sitting in the lobby of the Hotel Victoria when Seth came down for breakfast the next morning.

Seth downed the last of his genever and signaled the bartender for another. He shifted in his seat. The .357 Magnum in his coat pocket, obtained for a small ransom the night before, bumped softly against the bar.

He had assumed the man worked for Stratton until he had called the NSA man from the Hotel Victoria to report in.

"My man?" Stratton asked with alarm. "I don't have a man in Amsterdam. At least not yet."

Seth had felt his legs go wobbly. He had let his guard down, had given the man plenty of chances to kill him, to hurt him. But the man hadn't hurt him. He told this to Stratton.

"That doesn't mean he won't do something," Stratton replied. "We've gotten some more information in the last twenty-four hours that indicates there are more players in this game than we originally thought. And they're all dangerous."

"Game?" Seth said. "Is that what all this is to you? A game? This is my life—and my wife's life, too. This is no game."

"It's all a game, Seth," Stratton replied calmly. "You really start getting into trouble when you begin to take it seriously. You lose your perspective. That's why you need to come into the fold. We can protect you. This isn't being a cop anymore, Seth. This is a different game, a very different game."

Seth had no ready reply for the agent. Maybe it was a game, maybe not. But Stratton was right: whatever this was, it wasn't about being a cop anymore. The painting that rested securely in the locker at Amsterdam's Schiphol Airport was a secret too dangerous for him to handle. There was too much to Stratton's game, and Ridgeway didn't even know all the rules.

"Stay in your room, Seth. Eat room service. Stay off the street. Wait for me to get there."

Seth remembered Stratton's words now as the bartender slid a fresh glass of genever across the bar and took the empty glass. That had been two days ago. What had happened to Stratton? There had been no answer at the number the agent had given him and no messages left at the hotel.

Seth made a show of looking at his watch, then fumbled in his pocket and withdrew a multicolored wad of guilder notes. He retrieved two of the notes, passed them across the bar to cover his drinks, then downed the rest of the genever in a single gulp. He slid off the stool and walked casually toward

the door. The thin man with the insane eyes closed his paperback and started
to rise.

Outside, the street was cluttered with traffic of every description: bicycles,
trams, buses, and a mélange of autos, from battered Fiats and Citroëns to brightly
polished Mercedeses, all dancing a delicate mechanical ballet with each other,
trying to merge from one nonexistent lane to another in search of a turn, a
parking space, or a break large enough to accelerate forward for a few lengths.
Seth passed the display window of a diamond merchant. He stopped abruptly
in front of the window, as if something extraordinary had caught his attention.
In the reflection of the window, he saw the man with the insane eyes walk
quickly out of the bar and then stop short as he caught sight of Ridgeway.

Seth turned abruptly away from the diamonds and headed toward the central train station, a plan beginning to form in his mind. The man with the insane
eyes had not hurt him. Who was he working for? If not for Stratton and not
for the KGB, then who? The crowds thickened as he drew closer to the train
station. Christmas shoppers hauled gaily wrapped packages and shopping bags.
Most of them were women, housewives from the suburbs who had taken the
train in for a morning of shopping.

Christmas, Seth thought. Shit. He looked at the date calendar on his watch.
Five days until Christmas.

The women with their shopping bags crowded tightly around him now as
he stood at the corner of the Spuisstraat and the Prins Hendrikkade waiting for
the light to change. Seth was surrounded by a million tiny rustlings of paper
and wrappings and shopping bags that crinkled. Women chatted gaily in Dutch.
Seth could only understand a few words, basically ones that resembled German.
But he understood enough to know that, other than their tired feet, the shoppers
were happy, satisfied, content, anxious to return to their homes and their families. He resented the hell out of all their happiness.

The light changed and the crowd spilled off the curb and cascaded across
the great open spaces toward the station.

Seth flexed his legs and quickly outpaced the main body of the crowd,
gaining the noisy, crowded interior of the central station far ahead of them. He
walked past the newspaper stand to the train-schedule-covered kiosks with their
yellow and white posters of arrivals and departures. He quickly found the schedule for the line to the airport. There was a train leaving in five minutes. Seth
noted the track number and turned away from the kiosk.

Out of the corner of his eye, he saw the stranger pretending to look through
the paperback novels at the newsstand.

Seth pushed his way through the crowds to the ticket window and purchased his ticket. The man with the insane eyes stood in at the rear of the next ticket line. Overhead, trains rumbled and thundered, shaking the concrete floor beneath his feet.

When Seth got to the platform, it was sparsely scattered with people, mostly accompanied by suitcases. He walked down to the end of the platform and stopped. The clock overhead said 1:20, but there was no train. Unusual. Dutch trains were almost always prompt.

Seth turned to walk back toward the other end of the platform when he saw his shadow come up the stairs. The stranger turned away quickly and tried to feign disinterest. But it didn't work. Either the man was inept or his superiors wanted Seth to know he was being followed.

Moments later, the Schiphol train rumbled into the station and groaned to a halt. It lurched once and then loosed a great steaming sigh before the doors opened. Out poured a parade of weary faces, sitting atop bodies carrying pieces of luggage. The early afternoon flights from America had arrived.

Seth stepped aboard and looked around. The man with the insane eyes had already gotten on. A professional would have waited until the last minute to get on.

The doors clunked shut and the train gathered speed. Seth glanced out the windows as the platform slowly slid away Then suddenly they were back in the brilliant sunlight, snaking along between the harbor and the Oosterdok.

The train made its way southeast through a mostly industrial quarter, then gently curved to the south. They passed the Amstel station and headed across the open polders. Seth felt the palms of his hands tingle as he thought of the slim man with the insane eyes in the next car. What connection did he have with Zoe, with the deaths in Los Angeles? A brief shadow of doubt passed behind his eyes as he wondered if he were doing the right thing. Should he have waited for Stratton? Seth had never been good at waiting.

The train slowed as it entered Amstelveen, a suburb just south of Amsterdam that was separated from the airport by a massive wooded parkland called the Amsterdamse Bos. Ridgeway got out of the car with a half dozen others who were not headed for the airport. He did not bother to look around. He knew the man with the insane eyes would be behind somewhere.

Ridgeway made good time as he walked directly east from the train station toward the Amsterdamse Bos. As he walked, he remembered the summer day he and Zoe had picnicked in a green meadow beside a sky-blue pond in the Amsterdamse Bos. She had still been a student and had come to study paintings in the non-public collection of the Van Gogh Museum. He had pried her away from her work and she had thanked him for it.

They had rented bicycles and ridden them around the park until it was nearly dark. The terrain they had covered, and the day, were still etched in his memory.

Seth made his way into the eastern boundary of the park. The ground was soft from the winter rains and carpeted with wet, pliant leaves. Among the pale gray skeletons of deciduous trees waiting for spring were stands of conifers that painted deep green smears across the winter drabness. Seth walked quickly deep into the woods.

He crossed a narrow tarmac road, then down a short embankment into a copse of young cedar trees. He could see the road clearly from within the cedars. It was a good place to wait.

Time seemed to drag by. Seth gazed at the second hand of his watch. Once, twice around, and still no one crossed the road. Had he lost his man after all?

He waited, his warm breath hanging for an instant in the cold, damp air. In the distance he heard the urgent whines of jet engines, and moments later, the exultant roar of an aircraft breaking free of the earth. There were no sounds of traffic, no signs of cars on the road, and more important, no signs of the man with the insane eyes.

Then, just when Seth had nearly decided to backtrack to see if he could find his tracker, the man emerged from the trees on the far side of the road. He stood on the edge of the woods like a small wild animal afraid of the dangers of open spaces. Then he scurried across the road and plunged into the woods again, his head bent low. Seth realized the man was following the soft clear impressions his shoes had made in the earth.

The man seemed oblivious to all but the footprints before him, and he was almost to the small grove of cedars before he looked up. He stopped and looked at Seth with wide startled eyes. Seth trained his Magnum on the man's chest, watching with interest as fear flooded his face.

"Don't, please!" the man said raising his hands. "I mean you no harm."

"Why have you been following me, then?"

"To find out . . . find out what you are after," the man answered.

"Who wants to know?"

"Many people. Surely you know that?"

Seth nodded. "I know that, and I have a pretty good idea of who's on which side. I've talked to the people on my side and they don't know you."

"Perhaps they are on the wrong side," the man said gently.

"Perhaps," Seth replied, "but I don't think so." As Seth took a step forward, the frail man took a halting step backward, tripped over the root of a large naked oak tree, and fell into a sitting position with his back against the tree's trunk.

"Why have you been following me?" Seth asked again as he stood over the man.

"The people for whom I work are interested in you and the painting."

"How do you know about the painting?" Seth asked flatly.

"We know."

Seth stepped forward quickly and raised his hand to strike the man.

"Stop!" the man said with enough force to compel Seth into obeying. It was the voice of a man used to having people follow his orders.

"Okay," Seth said. "If I stop, I want something in return. I want information."

"I will tell you what you wish, Mr. Ridgeway," the man replied. "But not at the point of a gun."

Seth looked at him for a long moment and nodded. He stepped back several paces and put the Magnum back in his coat pocket. The man slowly got back to his feet, taking a moment to brush off the dirt and leaves sticking to his coat.

"My name is Kent Smith; I'm ordained in the Catholic Church and work as an archivist for the Vatican."

"Jesus," Seth said. Smith winced almost imperceptibly at the blasphemy. "And you want the painting too."

Smith nodded. "I'm afraid the people I work for do."

"Everywhere I turn there's somebody else who wants the goddamned thing." Smith winced again.

"And more people will turn up before you rid yourself of this painting," Smith said. "We can help you with that," he said finally.

"Who is 'we'?"

"A small but powerful group within the Vatican dedicated to making sure both the painting and the priceless religious relic associated with it are not abused or used by people for their own personal gain."

"You're the good guys? Is that what you're telling me?"

"Don't trivialize things, please, Mr. Ridgeway. We're dealing with things that could alter history." Smith's voice grew strident and evangelical. "This is a far, far bigger thing than you realize, with implications that go far beyond you, me, or your wife."

"I told you I don't care about that crap," Seth said. "There's nothing more important to me than getting my wife back."

"We can help you," Smith said. "We're a small group charged with trying to root out the worst of abuses, the political struggles and power plays that inevitably result from an organization of our size. Things . . . and people, you see, are not always what they seem."

"Like Vatican archivists playing spy versus spy in Amsterdam?"

Smith smiled for the first time.

"Exactly," he said. "And likewise, there are people in high places within both your government and my church who are not what they seem."

Then, for the smallest fraction of a second, Seth saw a luminous red dot on the front of Smith's coat. Instants later, the crack of a rifle ripped through the silence of the crisp, bright afternoon. Only then did Ridgeway recognize the red dot for what it was: the business end of a sniper's laser range finder. Ridgeway heard the slug slap through Smith's chest and watched as the frail man was hammered against the oak tree behind him by the impact.

Seth fought back the panic and let the old police survival instincts take over. He grabbed the front of Smith's coat, brought the man to cover behind the cedars, then squatted down beside him as more rifle shots flailed the woods.

Where were they? He wondered, as he pulled the .357 Magnum from his coat pocket. With high-powered rifles and laser scopes, they could be far away, anywhere, even outside the range of the Magnum. The woods were silent again. Seth strained to hear his enemies, but all he heard was Smith's laborious breathing. Seth bent his head low to hear what the man was trying to tell him.

"Brow . . . brun . . ." Smith's voice faded.

Ridgeway bent low over the dying man, trying to snare his last words. But he was too late. Ridgeway felt Smith's body go limp in his arms.

Brow, brun. Ridgeway turned the ragged syllables over in his mind a few times, finally deciding that the word Smith had been trying to say was "brown." Brown? What could it mean?

But Seth had no time to ponder the priest's last words. He heard a gunshot and then, a split second later, saw splinters explode in front of his eyes as a slug embedded itself in the tree trunk just inches from his face.

Seth dropped Smith's body and rolled away from the tree as a volley of slugs smashed into the tree. Rolling to his feet, Seth raised the Magnum and whirled frantically, trying to spot the gunman. Where was he? How could you strike back at an invisible enemy? Before he could answer his own question, two more shots raised the leaves at his feet. Then he saw them: first two red dots and then three. Swarming about him, dancing about the ground and across his clothing like a flight of lethal stinging insects. There was more than one gunman. Seth's breath came fast and heavy now. He lunged away from the spots, and as he did slugs following the paths of the laser sniper sights plowed into the ground and tossed wet earth and leaves into the air.

It was then that he heard them. From behind. No. In front. They were all around him, closing in. The red dots had returned and again Seth lunged out of their paths. But the gunmen were more methodical, more deliberate, this time. Seth pointed the Magnum in the direction of the first sound and fired.

But there was no sound of pain, no cry of surprise. Just the crack of another rifle shot and the searing burning pain across his right side.

Christ! Seth thought, as his left hand touched the wound and came away red and sticky. A quick probe with his fingers assured him that the damage was slight. It was close, though. Too close. He tried to pray, to ask for help. But the words, even the thoughts would not come.

Instead, he cursed under his breath, then jammed the Magnum into his coat pocket and scrambled up the short embankment in the direction from which he had come.

He had nearly gained the shoulder of the road when he saw the man step out of the woods on the other side. Seth saw him raise a rifle to his shoulder. Reflexively, Seth fell to his face and reached for his Magnum. An instant later he saw a slug gouge pebbles and stone fragments from the road just in front of his face. Oblivious to the gunman behind him, Seth leaped to his feet and brought the Magnum to bear.

The man with the rifle saw him and tried to get off a shot. But a rifle, though more accurate from longer distances than a pistol, is an awkward weapon. Seth sighted on the man's chest and squeezed the trigger. An instant later he watched with satisfaction as the slug hammered into the man's midsection, lifting him off his feet and twisting him around in the air. The last image Seth kept in his mind before he dropped on all fours was the sight of the red gaping hole in the man's back, trailing pieces of his entrails.

Seth tucked the Magnum back in his coat pocket and rolled toward a culvert. It was his only way to escape. To cross the road would give his killers a clear, sure shot at him.

Behind him, Seth heard the crashing sounds of men running through the woods. He took a quick, doubtful look at the culvert. His shoulders were broad and the culvert was narrow. If he got stuck or took too long in transiting it, he would be a sucker's target.

But it was his only chance.

Seth took a quick roll in the muck at the mouth of the culvert with an eye to being as slippery as possible, then plunged in. Inside, the pipe seemed to act as an amplifier; his quick desperate breaths came to his ears like frantic screams. It also snared and amplified the sounds of the man behind him. Seth inched his way through the culvert, pushing with his toes, wiggling his shoulders. The sounds of the men drew closer and closer. He heard their voices now.

"I can't see him anymore!" he heard one call to the other.

"Well, he hasn't crossed the road," came a second, more distant voice. "I have that bloody well covered."

"He must have hidden in the brush along the road," suggested a third voice.

Seth had made good time, but as he reached what must have been the middle of the roadway the culvert seemed to narrow. He was stuck! Behind him, he heard footsteps crackling through the brush. He shifted his shoulders and still couldn't move. The weight of the roadway above must have crushed the culvert slightly as it settled.

"There's a pipe here that goes under the road." Seth heard the voice clearly. He felt his hands begin to shake and his breath flutter. He swallowed hard and tried to choke back the panic.

"Bring your light," he heard the voice call.

Desperately Seth twisted and turned in the pipe. He felt the edges of the metal tearing at his hands, ripping at his clothes.

"Here's the light," a voice said. "Be careful. If he's in there he'll have his gun ready."

"Maybe we should fire a couple of rounds in there just to be sure."

Straining until blue lights threatened to cover his vision, Seth felt his body move forward, slowly at first, and then more easily. He was free!

But would he be in time? Any shot fired into the culvert would surely hit him.

He crawled frantically now, oblivious to the sharp edges of the culvert joints.

The bright circle of daylight ahead of him grew larger and brighter until finally his head emerged and then the rest of his body.

Gasping for breath, he rolled away from the pipe and lay there a few seconds.

"Don't move, Mr. Ridgeway."

Seth froze. Time stopped.

"Turn over slowly and get up."

Seth rolled over slowly onto his back and then began to rise to his feet. In front of him was a man with a toothbrush mustache and a trilby hat. He held the ugly, stubby H&K MP5A machine pistol favored by the British SAS and the German commandos who had freed the Israeli hostages in Munich. It was a fast and deadly weapon at close range. The man saw him eyeing the H&K.

"Don't try anything foolish," the man said. "It will shorten your life considerably."

"Go ahead." Seth heard the voice at the other end of the culvert dimly as if through an old-fashioned megaphone. An instant later a gunshot, followed by three more.

The man in the trilby jumped and looked at the mouth of the culvert. It was all the diversion Ridgeway needed. He leaped on the man, slammed an elbow into his face, and raised his knee into the man's crotch. Seth felt the man's testicles flatten out under the impact. The man's trilby flew through the air as he doubled up in pain.

Seth grabbed the machine pistol from the man's weakened grasp and started to run. The man began to scream.

"Over here! He's over here."

Seth emptied the clip of the H&K into the man, threw the gun to the ground, and sprinted through the woods toward Amstelveen.

SIXTEEN

T he man from Moscow they knew as "the Patron" stood next to the desk in the warehouse office and frowned at the men assembled there as they stood about eating the last bits of lunch. Grease-stained Mc-Donald's bags carpeted the old wooden desk in the middle of the office.

The Patron did not like men like these. They were all KGB, all on the take from the Moscow Mafia, all loyal to Zhirinovsky's organization. They were, he thought, the same sort of mentality and the same sort of men who paved Hitler's way to power. There was Colonel Eduard Molotov. Next to him, a man called Sergiev. Towering over Sergiev was a hulking giant, the biggest human the man from Moscow had ever seen. They were the best of the lot; they were all gutter scum and he paid them well for their personal characteristics, political leanings, and considerable skills.

"We have information that that one of the many foreign intelligence services that have been looking for the Sophia Passion are getting close," said the Patron. "This operation has been going on too long to avoid leaving a trail."

He paused. Then: "How long will it take to . . . wind things up here?"

"Not long," Sergiev replied. "The warehouse is nearly empty. The crating of those fucking fat broad dolls is done, and ready to be shipped to the buyer. The two broads are down there now drooling over some weird stone panel. We can have everything done and shipped out of here by the end of tomorrow. The only piece of loose baggage is . . ." He nodded toward his feet, to Zoe's cell down below them.

"Yes," the man from Moscow said simply. "I understand the girl is quite attractive." All the men nodded.

"Good, good," said the man from Moscow. "That's very good. I want you out of here by noon tomorrow and don't leave a trace that leads back to any of us. You will telephone the consulate for a truck and then make sure that all of the files from the operation are carried safely down to the truck and the vehicle sealed. You will then dispatch the girl in an untraceable manner. I do not care what you do with her before that. Have whatever fun you wish with her. Consider her your bonus for this month."

"You are most generous," the Hulk said with a wide grin.

Thalia and Zoe crawled on their hands and knees, faces just inches from a huge piece of alabaster nearly four feet across, round like a Mayan calendar stone and covered with elegant relief carvings and inscriptions. The frieze sat alone in the middle of the impromptu art studio, its very isolation a reminder of a stage waiting for the final curtain.

Earlier that morning, Zoe had followed her captors into the studio, worried that the previous evening's epiphany might have changed her in ways that might make them suspicious or raise Thalia's intuition. But from the first the moment they had uncrated the frieze, Zoe had no thoughts for anything else, no emotions to spare.

"This is the most astounding piece of art I have ever seen in my entire life," Zoe said, her voice soft with awe.

"That has to be the hundredth time you've said that today."

Zoe did not reply, enraptured as she was by the carvings. They were a sort of history of God chiseled in stone. There at the very center was the sculptor's concept of the beginning: God was represented as a trinity of forms, androgynous, hermaphroditic, and as a trinity within the trinity, father, mother, child. From this emerged the anthropomorphic avatars that people had used for worship, spiraling out from the center, the Venus figures of the Great Goddess closest to the center and gradually sharing space with male representations that quickly subsumed the graphic narrative.

"I don't recognize the language these inscriptions are written in."

"Aramaic," Thalia said distractedly. "Which leads me to believe this was carved in, maybe, 1000 B.C. or so, just like the little tag that came with it asserts."

"Okay, follow me here." Thalia pointed to one track of carvings. "We have the Great Goddess starting to share space with a male consort, most frequently represented as her son or lover. This starts when society makes a connection between intercourse and babies. Then a little further along." She shifted her finger. "Here we find the Goddess and her God equal in size." Her finger advanced several inches along the spiral. "Things accelerate very quickly; the Goddess gets smaller and smaller until we get to the end of the story line."

Her finger followed the spiral out to its end, leading to a very large solitary male carving positioned just inside a border of snakes and leaves. A very thin line of writing followed the very outside rim.

"What's the inscription say?" Zoe asked.

"Yahweh," Thalia said.

"Fascinating," Zoe said as she stood up and rubbed at her eyes. They felt tight and ready to explode after squinting for so long at the tiny, exquisite carvings and delicate inscriptions. "And you're telling me that the changes in the form of God were a reflection of culture."

"No doubt about it," Thalia said as she extended her hand up to Zoe. "Here. Help me up." Zoe looked down at this amazing woman. A brilliant academic, snared in her father's troubles. Not once in the past months had she complained about being pressed into service in his place. Zoe felt her heart strain against the sorrow of never seeing her again. Thalia took her hand and Zoe felt strength and love—and the rare connection with a kindred soul that had grown from the months of sharing such an intense intellectual effort. Zoe had pulled strength from her and, in the past days, a better understanding of the distant echoes of human culture.

Thalia looked at her directly, her face open with concern. Zoe averted her eyes as she helped Thalia to her feet.

"You okay?" Thalia asked.

Zoe avoided looking at her. "Fine."

"I mean, if you want to talk about . . ."

The impending separation hung darkly between them. She knew that Thalia felt it was going to mean death for Zoe.

"No," Zoe lied. "I don't want to." But she did! She wanted to ease Thalia's concern by telling her how the escape would happen. But any accidental slip, any innocent, inadvertent slip would scuttle her plans. Pulling it off would be hard enough. Everything had to happen perfectly and secretly.

"If you're sure—"

"Very sure," Zoe snapped more abruptly than she intended. Thalia gave her a puzzled frown.

They stood there for a long moment, looking at each other: the pale, athletically trim American, eye to eye with the large, imposing Russian woman with the olive skin and curly red hair. Zoe thought she saw some kind of understanding settle in Thalia's dark eyes as a small smile softened her frown of concern.

"What I really want is to know more about this." Zoe pointed to the stone. "I mean, guys didn't just wake up one day and say to themselves, 'We're part of making babies too and we're stronger so let's take all the land.' "

Thalia gave her a long, incredulous stare. "I don't know what you have up your sleeve and I don't want to know. But I hope God goes with you."

"She will," Zoe said, surprised by the depth of her own conviction. Then, nodding at the stone: "So tell me."

"You're right. This transition took a while. Remember that there were six or eight millennia of change for civilization to get from the Goddess to Yahweh. I think the time of the Garden of Eden was the era when small settlements of early people lived undisturbed and for the most part out of contact with any other settlements. But women changed all that and in doing so dug a pitfall for the Great Goddess.

"Women invented agriculture because they were the ones weighed down with children. You can discover weaving and domesticate wild grains while you're feeding your babies and keeping them alive . . . you can't very well do that while hunting. So they planted and eventually society realized that you could obtain food this way. Agriculture let families get larger. Hunter–gatherer women had to space babies out like four or five years apart, since they moved frequently and the mothers couldn't physically carry a lot of kids. Plus you simply can't feed that many kids without agriculture. But when the family settled down with its fields, mobility was no longer vital for survival and the babies could come closer and closer together.

"The brute strength of men assumed greater and greater importance as settlements grew larger and began competing with each other. This is when agriculture really took off because you need farmers in order to support a standing army, government bureaucrats, and so forth—hunter-gatherer societies just don't produce enough food to make this possible. But agriculture made for its own problems, it took up space that you needed to claim for your own and keep others away from. It also started a population boom because the more fields you planted the more people your society could support, and the more it could support the more people you had.

"Conflicts had been rare in the past, but the expanding population meant that men now had to fight against other men to protect their homes and communities. In fact the need for security propelled civilization from small communal settlements into full-fledged governments."

"So, if I accept this line of reasoning," Zoe said, "then I'd assume that men took this newfound power to heart and realized that they weren't totally at the mercy of the Goddess they worshiped, so they wanted a piece of the action and that's why they introduced the male deity."

"They also wanted a cut of the earthly goodies as well. The matrilineal system passed all property down from woman to woman; children's heritage traced through the mother's side because there was no way to establish paternity.

"As a culture, the men were in a position to change things. They're big; they're strong, but society's religious beliefs were too strong for them to just take the land and the property owned by women. I don't think it was a conscious decision . . . not like some vast conscious conspiracy, but over the millennia, marital and sexual laws were introduced that had the effect of establishing paternity. Monogamy and the prohibitions against sex outside of marriage were ways of guaranteeing that a man knew whose children were his so that property could be split up according to the new laws. At first, men shared in the property little by little, and eventually of course they took it all and reduced women to the level of just another piece of property. But to enforce the laws, they needed to call on the authority of God to scare everybody into compliance."

"So you're saying people create the god they need," Zoe said uneasily as the sounds of the previous night, her first prayer in years, echoed clearly in her mind. "According to that theory, God is a human creation devised for the expediency of explaining the unknown, and they change him—her—to suit their needs."

Thalia turned her head toward the frieze and pointed. "God doesn't change," she said. "At least that's my belief. It's just that our interpretation of God changes as culture changes. That's what I think this artist is trying to tell us."

Thalia said, "Follow this." Her finger went to a small line of Aramaic writing near the large carving of the Great Goddess. "Look how the laws regarding rape were changed as the power of the Goddess diminished: in 2000 B.C. if a man raped a woman in Sumer, he was executed regardless of her marital status. A thousand years later, if a man rapes an unmarried woman, the husband or father of the woman gets to rape the rapist's wife or daughter. Alternately, we see laws that require the raped woman to marry her attacker."

"Sick."

"Uh-huh, but it's all there, written down in the Torah, and it gets worse. If the rape victim is married or betrothed, then she must be killed. Now remember, the fundamentalists in Christianity, Judaism, and Islam today think they ought to be abiding by the letter of these laws."

"This is pretty depressing," Zoe said. "Basically, as worship of the Great Goddess was suppressed, women lost their land, their property, the right to pass their family names along to their children, and they became pieces of meat—property for men to play with."

"Even today," Thalia said, "Orthodox Jewish men are taught to offer a daily prayer that goes, 'Blessed Art Thou O Lord our God, King of the Universe, who has not made me a woman.' And Muhammad said that when Eve was created, Satan rejoiced.

"It's all there." Thalia tapped at the stone frieze. "And in the Bible, the Koran, the Torah. Sexual laws and punishment were aimed at women and applied to women. It's the beginning of the old double standard. Morality and virginity are for women so that paternity of children can be established."

They were silent for a long moment, thinking, feeling the weight of the millennia weighing on them. Zoe broke the spell.

"What are the leaves and snakes on the border?"

"A gutsy statement by the artist," Thalia said. "Blasphemy if I read it correctly."

"Meaning?"

"It's the artist's statement that the powers that were couldn't entirely get rid of the Great Goddess. The serpent and leaf of the sycamore fig—that's what that is"—Thalia pointed to the stone—"are two of the most potent symbols of the Great Goddess. That's why the authors of Genesis represented Satan as a snake—they were saying the Great Goddess was evil. They had to make her look as bad as possible so that they could close her temples and forbid her worship."

"Spin control."

"More like wagging the dog," Thalia said. "The sycamore fig was her temple, which is why you see the Prophets of the Torah railing against the altars under the trees. This is where people went to worship the Great Goddess even after Yahweh was the official deity of the land. Worship and communion involved eating the fruit of the sycamore fig—fruit that was more like clusters of grapes than the figs we usually think of. When the devout ate the fruit, they were partaking of the body of the Goddess."

"Roots of the Christian communion?"

Thalia nodded. "Just one of many things that Christianity and Judaism borrowed from the past. Incorporate enough of the old, forbidden religion to satisfy people's cravings for it . . . co-opt and conquer, only the Great Goddess has had the last laugh."

"How's that?"

"She was transmuted by the Greeks into Cybele and Artemis. But even after Constantine decreed an end to Goddess worship throughout his empire, the faithful simply converted those Goddess shrines into places to worship the Virgin Mary. This is one of the things that scares the old *schnorrers* in the Vatican. They *know* without a doubt that veneration of Mary is just thinly disguised Goddess worship.

"That's also the reason the Romans and my people had to kill the man Jesus. He believed in women as equals; the Jewish and Christian Gnostics saw God as both male and female; the Essenes who wrote the Dead Sea Scrolls also believed that God was both man and woman. They couldn't even censor all the old religious scriptures to their liking. The Book of Proverbs and the Wisdom of Solomon are pretty clear when they refer to Wisdom as female. 'Sophia' is the Greek word for wisdom."

"Sophia?" Zoe felt her heart catch; a frisson of excitement electrified her skin. "I think maybe she was another Messiah."

"I *know* she was," Thalia said. "I've listened to our Mafia buddies talking about what their real goal was at Kreuzlingen."

"Oh my God," Zoe whispered softly. "It all fits."

Thalia nodded. "I think the conference at Nicea was really as much about Sophia as Christ. The orthodox Christians had changed 'Wisdom' to the male word, 'Logos.' The real fight, the real heretics were those who argued that the church should return to its roots—to Sophia and not Logos—and acknowledge that she was an original and inseparable part of the Creator. They argued that it was wrong to try and restrict God to one sex or one form or as the God of just one people. They said this set a human limit on the limitless and that was blasphemy."

"They obviously lost."

"So far," Thalia said.

"But that concept is what our artist here is saying as well," Thalia told Zoe. "That inscription that runs all around the outside? The word that contains everything else inside from God as man, woman, and child to God as Yahweh?"

Zoe got down on her knees and ran her fingers over the ancient writing.

"The Aramaic there contains one word over and over and over," Thalia said. "It's a name. It's Sophia."

Zoe snatched her fingers away as if the words had burned them.

SEVENTEEN

In the deep mean darkness of 3 A.M., Zoe Ridgeway sat before the antiquated computer in her cell and cursed.

"Damn!" She hammered the desk with her hand. "I don't need this shit! Not now." The PC's hard drive kept filling up as she transferred from the main server all of the scans they had made of photos, documents, and the detailed provenance and records that Max had meticulously kept.

Zoe pulled up Windows Explorer and looked for more files to delete; there had to be more space. She consoled herself with the blessing that they hadn't yet shut off the main server down in the art studio and carted it away as they had almost everything else. During her handcuffed walk back to her cell that evening, the activity in the warehouse had been suddenly frenetic. Dinner arrived late, McDonald's instead of Movenpick. The reliable predictability of the past months had been swept away by an urgency she swore she could smell on the men. She supposed they knew she would notice. Perhaps they thought it would frighten her.

But the prospect of freedom filled her with an intoxicating exhilaration that had exiled fear from her thoughts. Zoe started now to delete files on her PC with a vengeance, gutting the hard drive of every unneeded image, file, software application. Then she emptied the recycle bin. That recovered another 160 megabytes. Determined to take as much data as she could, Zoe resumed her copying as the minutes ticked by on the computer screen.

As the files made their way from the server to her hard drive, Zoe looked around once again at the preparations she had made to escape. She had dismantled the bed; the heater lay face down on the floor next to the desk, plugged directly into the wall socket by the door. She rubbed her cold hands and put them under her armpits for a moment. As noisy and pathetic as the heater had been, the chill had noticeably deepened once she had turned it off. Her captors had never provided her with a coat. So on this night she wore two T-shirts—all they had given her—her only heavy plaid flannel shirt and the wool twill pants.

The cheap imitation leather flats on her feet were falling apart, but they would carry her as far as she could go tonight.

A pair of fingernail clippers—the most serious tool they had allowed in her cell—lay on the desk next to the mouse. The clipper and its tiny nail file were bent and twisted from her successful attack on the hard drive's mounting screws and the heater's cover.

As the PC's hard drive clicked and whirred, her eyes went to the ceiling, to the wire grid that had once been attached to the bed frame to support her mattress. It was now suspended from the sprinkler water pipe by a length of sheet strips knotted into rope. One end of the sheet was tied at the middle of the wire grid, making it hang like a floppy upside-down "V." The sheet rope ran over the pipe and back down to floor level, where she tied it to the leg of the desk.

Zoe was so distracted by her own thoughts that she barely heard the hard drive grinding away, pulling the files over the network. Her eyes and thoughts went over the preparations once again, looking for flaws; every step had to succeed flawlessly if she were ever to see the sun again.

To see Seth again.

She had run an electrical wire from the heater's cord to the suspended wire grid. Again using the fingernail clippers, she had cut one of the "hot" wires in the heater's electrical cord and stripped the insulation away. Then she had cut the plug and prongs from the extension cord and stripped away the insulation from two of the three wires at each end. At one end of the mutilated extension cord, she attached the two wires to each of the bare wires born of the single severed wire in the heater's cord. Twisting the connections tightly she then used strips of bedsheet to wrap and bind them, more to secure the connection than to insulate. Finally, strips of bedsheets made that end fast to the desk leg so that movement would not pull the twisted connections loose.

Next, Zoe knotted the whole free end of the extension cord around several of the wires in the metal mattress grid for strength. Finally, she twisted the two bare extension-cord wires around the wire grid a couple of inches apart and bound them with bedsheet strips as well. The electricity going to the heater would take a detour: coming out of the plug, it would go up one of the spliced wires in the extension cord, through the wire grid, and back down the other extension-cord wire to the heater cord and thence to the heating element.

Or maybe the electricity moves the other way, she thought. No, she thought, if she remembered her Dad's lesson well enough, alternating current went both ways. No matter. What counted was that the mattress would complete the circuit when she turned on the heater; the standard 220 volts found in European electrical mains would charge the whole metal mattress support grid. Zoe patted her pants pocket and felt a hard bulge in the left one left by the plug end she had cut off the extension cord. She had stripped the insulation off all three wires, twisted them together, and insulated them carefully with the remaining bedsheet strips.

So absorbed was Zoe in going over her preparations that she did not hear the hard drive stop working, the file transfer complete. Then the creak of footsteps in the room above jerked her back to the moment. Fear clutched at her heart like a cold steel hand. In the past they had conducted surprise inspections of her cell at odd hours of the night.

Would they do that this close to ending everything? Would they be coming now to tie her loose ends up?

The creaks continued. Someone was walking.

Please, God, she prayed. *Let him just be going to the bathroom.*

Propelled by the thought of the Hulk and his partner Sergiev showing up at her door before she was fully ready, Zoe leaped to her feet. No longer caring if she had stripped everything she wanted out of the server, she pressed the power button and turned the PC off. For a brief hysterical instant, she thought that this was perhaps the first time she had turned off Windows 95 before it was safe. In the next few minutes, she'd be doing a lot of things before they were safe.

With the PC's power off, Zoe worked the hard drive's data and power cables off and pulled the drive out. It was the width and thickness of a paperback novel, only shorter. It fit snugly in the right back pocket of her pants.

The room above was quiet.

"The time is the time, sweetheart," Zoe said aloud. Even if the men were not coming for her, there was no reason to delay the countdown sequence she had rehearsed over and over in her head since the escape plan had sprung fully developed into her head the night before.

Stopping for just a moment, she bowed her head. "God," she prayed aloud, "this is your plan; I could never have thought of it. Please help me do it right." She opened her eyes. Then with her face tilted upward, she added, "Please."

Up above, she heard the toilet flush and the water cascading down the thick black drainpipe that ran down the corner of her room. Bathroom. That was a good sign, she thought.

Zoe ran on automatic now, taking each step just as she had planned. First she moved the computer and its monitor to the floor and swept the desk clean. Then, she folded the thin lumpy mattress in thirds and placed it at one end of the desk.

Next, she grabbed the pieces of the disassembled bed and used the last of the bedsheet strips to fasten the pieces into an ankle-high trip snare. Struggling to keep her hands steady, Zoe grabbed the remaining piece of the bed, a metal leg with a long screw welded to it that had been used to attach it to the frame

with a wing nut. She set it on the desk, then carefully untied the sheet rope
that suspended the now-electrified metal grid.

With her heart hurtling through her chest like a runaway train, Zoe wiped
her palms, then climbed up on the desk.

"Please help me," she prayed again. "I can't do this by myself."

Then with a deep breath of determination, she picked up the bed leg and
swung it at the nearest fire sprinkler head. The impact filled her cell with a
resonant metallic clanging that immediately brought shouts from the room
above. This was not what she had imagined in her head.

"Shit!" Zoe muttered. She swung again and this time, the leg glanced off
the pipe and slid out of her sweat-soaked palms. Above her, shouts of alarm
were louder and louder.

Fighting the panic that rose in a choking flood from her belly Zoe scrambled
down from the desk, making the sheet rope fast to a drawer pull while she
retrieved the bed leg. Frantically, she got back on the desk and, using two hands,
swung at the sprinkler head with all her might. She had been aiming at the
small melting fuse that heat normally triggered. But this time, the metal leg
connected with the base, snapping the whole sprinkler head off.

Her reward was a torrent of water that instantly covered the floor of the
tiny room. Then, one of the sweetest sounds that Zoe had ever heard: the
ringing of the industrial warehouse's fire bell, triggered by the drop in sprinkler
pipe pressure. Relief flooded through her body. She had had no idea if the
sprinklers were operational or if they were connected to an alarm as was the
standard in the United States.

"Thank you, God!"

Zoe wondered for an instant how long it took for Zurich firemen to get
to alarms. No matter what it was, it wouldn't be fast enough for her. Above
her, the sounds of general confusion mingled with the fire alarm—shouts, confusion.

Calmly, Zoe turned off the light and waited. In the darkness, sounds came
to her more clearly now. The sound of the broken sprinkler head took on a
deeper tone as the water level rose in the room. After what seemed like a lifetime
lived in slow motion, shouts came from the hallway outside her cell. She recognized the angry voices of the Hulk and Sergiev. An instant later the lock
rattled, the door flew open, and the two men appeared. Dim light filtered
through the door from a distant low-wattage bulb at the far end of the corridor.
The dim yellow illumination painted the scene in shadows and low-contrast
silhouettes. Water ran into the hallway.

Zoe pressed herself flat against the shadows of the wall and let go of the
rope sheet. The Hulk heard the sound. He looked up and raised a hand toward

the grid. An instant later, the big man bellowed with a pain that seemed to come from the very bowels of his soul. A loud, low electrical hum filled the room. Arcs broke the darkness like camera flashes. The big man stumbled forward, then fell as his feet tangled with the ankle snare she had set.

Behind him, Sergiev's momentum carried him forward into the water. He dropped his gun and began to convulse even before reaching his fallen comrade as the lethal current ran free in the water that had gathered on the floor. Zoe stood there for eternity, her heart caught by the low moans of pain that went so far beyond mere words in conveying the depth of their pain. Zoe was horrified as she stood up in the shadows and watched the two men writhe on the floor. Suddenly the Hulk fell silent and his twitching seemed to lose purpose. Sergiev managed to get to his knees and turned toward the door, but the electrical current was relentless and a moment later, he fell face first into the water. Like the Hulk, he lost his voice and control over his muscles.

Zoe waited. Her cell quickly filled with the stench of the men's urine and the contents of their bowels. That was when she knew they were dead. Or close enough. She threw the mattress on the floor as a path to the door. Then, fixing the scene in her memory, Zoe lay flat on the desk and unplugged the heater. From her pocket, she pulled out the plug with all the wires twisted together and plugged that into the socket. The dim light in the hall went out as her plug shorted out the circuit. Upstairs, other voices cursed about the lights.

Carrying the bed leg as a club, Zoe felt her way toward the door, trying to stay on the mattress, trying to ignore the smells of death, trying to forget the sounds of mortal anguish that she had inflicted on the men.

Once in the hallway, she heard new sounds: sirens! Her heart soared as she felt her way along the corridor wall toward the door she knew led to the main warehouse. Pushing her way through the door, she saw there were lights here. Across the cavernous space, she saw flashing lights coming from under a roll-up door. Two of the men she recognized as the Hulk's superiors were jogging toward the art studio.

Zoe ran in the other direction, toward a door beside another loading dock at the other side of the warehouse. When she lunged through the door into the crisp cleanness of the night, she said a prayer of thanksgiving. She was running down a paved alley toward the flashing lights at the front of the warehouse when two shadows shaped like men detached themselves from the darkness of the warehouse wall.

"Quickly!" One man grabbed her as the other twisted the bed leg from her hands.

Suddenly, she was hustled away from the light, toward the depths of the night.

EIGHTEEN

The flashing lights of police and fire vehicles, ambulances, and other emergency vehicles exploded through the darkness and dazzled Seth Ridgeway as he sat alone in his train compartment, cheek pressed against the cool glass. The train had slowed to a crawl as it slowly approached Zurich's main station.

Seth kept his eyes on the bright flames as he slowly got to his feet to stretch his legs. It had been a long train ride, more than ten hours. He dragged his eyes away from the lights and scanned the blackness of the night.

"Where are you?" Seth said softly to himself as he stared through his own dim, ghostlike reflection in the window's glass.

Are you out there? Can I see the light that shines on you right now?

Rubbing his eyes wearily, he sat back down, closed his eyes for a moment, and let the knotted ropes behind them unwind a bit. Once again he was thankful he had booked all six seats in the compartment for himself. He needed the time to think and he'd wanted no distractions from other passengers. He had also wanted to be sure that a killer didn't sit down next to him. It had been expensive, but worth it. Rebecca Weinstock's money had covered that and would cover many more contingencies.

The hours after the attack in the Amsterdamse Bos were as unreal as a dream. Just as the last six months or the last twenty-four hours didn't seem real. Seth wandered through Amstelveen streets until he found a men's clothing store. The clerk had been shocked at his appearance, but shock turned to dismay when Seth explained that he had been mugged.

Which was true in its own way.

"I am so ashamed," the shopkeeper kept saying. "This is not like Holland at all. We are a peaceful people." The man kept apologizing as he helped Seth select a new wardrobe, then took him by the hand down the street to a luggage shop owned by a friend. Seth had to force money on the man for the two pieces of luggage he bought. Back at the clothing store, he put his new wardrobe in the suit bag. He placed his dirty coat and clothes into the shoulder bag, all carefully wrapped to conceal the ugly but effective Smith & Wesson .357 Magnum.

He repeated the scene with a sympathetic woman at the small commercial hotel near the train station. She clucked over him like a mother hen, insisting that she press the wrinkles from his newly purchased clothes. And like the clerk, apologized for the violence because, after all, "This is not America, where things like that happen all the time."

Following a long bath and refreshing nap, he hired a taxi to take him to Schiphol Airport and wait as he retrieved the painting and the rest of Rebecca Weinstock's money from the locker where he had left them. From the international telephones at the airport, Seth managed to leave a message for George Stratton. The incident in Amstelveen convinced him that it was time to stop the solo act. Seth described the attack in the Amsterdamse Bos, and his travel plans to Zurich. He didn't mention his possession of the painting or his appointment with Jacob Yost. There had to be something left with which he could bargain.

And after that, he had drunk the hot chocolate the hotel desk clerk had brought up to him, and sunk into the crisp, clean sheets. He slept a ragged sleep, haunted by recent scenes of dead people who all eventually wore his face.

His decision the next morning to cancel his flight to Zurich and take the train instead was an easy one. He didn't want to risk a search turning up his gun. And trains were harder to watch: no security gates controlling the crowds, no single queues for boarding, no centralized boarding areas. And they were easier to get off. Which was why Seth had taken a local train with stops every twenty or thirty minutes.

Still, he felt as if he should have done more.

But what? It was hard to run from people when you didn't know who you were running from. Hard to hide from danger when you didn't know its face. How had they found him? The question continued to hammer away at him. The telephone call from the airport? He ruled that out. There was no way they could have known he would use that telephone.

Someone unseen by him or by Stratton could have shadowed him. Unlikely. His neighborhood in Playa Del Rey didn't lend itself to hiding strangers well. It was not an anonymous street.

Stratton? He had told Stratton's man—the one keeping a vigil at Seth's house in Playa Del Rey—that he was going to Amsterdam. But that would mean that—

A chill spread through his body like ice water. Suppose Stratton's man, or the man he had assumed was Stratton's, worked for someone else?

"*Brown?*"

The man in Amsterdam Seth had initially assumed worked for Stratton turned out to be a priest. A priest working for whom? Why was a priest involved?

"*A small, powerful group within the Vatican . . . far, far bigger thing than you realize . . . the blessings of the Pope . . .*"

Ridgeway heard the priest's last words, the implications staggered him.

"*Things—and people, you see, are not always what they seem. . . . There are people in high places within both your government and my church who are not what they seem.*"

The words ran like a refrain through his fear. Who were not what they seemed? Was Stratton something other than he had represented himself to be? Or was the priest? Or Rebecca Weinstock?

And who was involved? Stratton said the people who had killed Rebecca had been Zhirinovsky's people inside the KGB. So whose interests were they looking after? Just his? Russia's?

"*We're a group charged with trying to root out the worst of the abuses, the political struggles and power plays.*"

So what did they want with a painting by an obscure Nazi artist?

Seth shook his head as the thoughts twisted around each other. Every time he answered one question, two or three arose to take its place. It was as if he—

Seth was suddenly aware of a man who had stopped in the train corridor outside his compartment. The man was about six feet tall, his build hidden under a long wool coat. A long woolen coat, Seth thought, bulky enough to conceal almost any kind of weapon. The man's hair was light brown and there was nothing remarkable about his face save a nose that looked as if it had been broken badly at least once. Their eyes met for an instant. The man nodded a polite acknowledgment, then turned his back on Seth and stood in the passageway looking out the window at the rail yard.

Startled, Seth got to his feet and pulled his new shoulder bag from the overhead rack and set it on the seat. He replayed the man's look again in his mind. Was it a look of recognition, or merely the courtesy of one stranger acknowledging another? Did the man know him? Did he recognize the man? Seth tried to remember the past days, trying to single out a face from the crowds he had drifted through in airports, on the street, at the train station. But the man's face remained that of a stranger.

But that was why men like this were always selected as killers and spies. The nondescript make the best killers because they are hard to remember, hard to spot in a crowd. Was this man a killer? Was this a killer sent to finish off the jobs botched in Los Angeles and Amsterdam?

Seth was taking no chances. He unzipped the shoulder bag and worked the Magnum from its concealment in the middle of his old clothes. He placed it on the top, where he could get to it easily, and then pulled the unzipped edges of the bag together. He sat down next to it and pretended interest in the *International Herald Tribune*.

The man didn't move, but instead stood in the corridor with his hands in his pockets for a moment before taking one hand out and reaching into the open front of his coat, where Seth couldn't see. Was he reaching for a weapon? Seth's hand jerked into the shoulder bag beside him and quickly found the Magnum. His fingers closed around the wooden stock, the index finger curling on the trigger.

The man's other hand came out of his pocket. Moments later, the man started to turn sideways. Seth tensed, ready to bring the Magnum out. As the man finished turning, Seth saw he had a package of American cigarettes in one hand, a disposable lighter in the other.

The man noted Seth's gaze and smiled. He held the pack up to offer Seth one. Feeling foolish, Seth shook his head and smiled back, the courtesy of one stranger to another. The man took out a cigarette, placed it in his mouth, and lit it. He then walked through the pale blue cloud of smoke toward the end of the car.

Heart pounding, Seth slumped in his seat and closed his eyes. He felt the sweat trickling down his forehead. He opened his eyes and wiped at the sweat. The corridor was filled with pale blue cigarette smoke, like the remains of a vanished magician.

He was seeing demons where there were none, shadows where there was only light.

Christ! He was getting paranoid!

Then for an instant, he was back in a patrol car at Manchester and 89th Place and it was dark and scary and the night was filled with death and the veteran behind the wheel had only half laughed when he told Seth: "Listen, kid, just remember you've gotta be paranoid when everybody's out to get you."

Seth remembered not laughing at first.

Suddenly the train jerked and groaned as it slowed to a stop at the platform.

NINETEEN

Zoe looked at the night and its lights through half-closed lids as George Stratton drove a rented Volvo skillfully through the snowy Zurich streets. In back, sat a man introduced as Gordon Highgate.

Though her eyes were heavy with fatigue, pain, and the accumulated weight of the last six months, she was too excited to sleep. The last two hours swarmed in her head, a montage of color and emotion: fear and exhilaration, victory and pain, the desperate sprint from confinement, panic at unknown hands—dark night, freedom, relief.

They had taken her in a van to some sort of office where they had allowed her to call Seth.

Seth failed to answer her phone call. Three times, and each time she got the answering machine. Where was he, she wondered, then realized it was ten hours earlier in Los Angeles; it was only eleven in the morning there. So she called his office at UCLA. There was no answer.

"What day is today?" she had finally asked.

"Saturday"

Of course, she thought, as she tried to force her mind out of the habits of a prisoner and back into those of a normal person. He must be at the boat.

But there was no answer there either. Damn! Damn! She was desperate to talk to Seth, to hear his voice again. Instead, she swallowed her disappointment and called the house again and left him a message on the machine. "I love you," she said over and over. And finally, before the message tape ran out, she left him word to call her at the Eden au Lac Hotel.

Through it all, the anger, most of all the anger: six months! Those goons in the warehouse had stolen six months, a half a year from her life!

Stratton and Highgate wanted her to stay the night at a safe house on the outskirts of Zurich. No. She had been firm. It was the Eden au Lac, she told them, or they were no damn better than the thugs who had kidnapped her in the first place. They argued. Zoe won.

Now, as the Volvo crossed the plaza across from the train station, she leaned toward Stratton.

"Could you stop for just a few moments?" Zoe pointed toward the Bahn-hofstrasse, the main shopping street. "I've been held a prisoner for six months, and I don't have a thing to wear." She looked down at her Levi's. "I can't walk into the Eden au Lac like this."

Zoe saw his smile; he almost laughed. "Of course."

Stratton maneuvered among the Christmas shoppers in the narrow shopping street. Highgate went in with her while Stratton stayed to shuttle the car around. It took more than a moment. Nearly an hour later, half of which was spent convincing American Express that she was, indeed, alive and well, she and Highgate walked out. Zoe wore a bright red sweater dress and new Italian pumps, and over that a stylishly warm new coat. Her arms were full of expensively wrapped boxes. Highgate, hands free for weapons and killing, scrutinized the sidewalk as they returned to the car.

Stratton then headed straight for the Eden au Lac.

Zoe's head lolled gently against the car's headrest. She closed her eyes and visualized Seth's face when he'd return and check the message. She hoped he wouldn't call before she got checked in at the hotel. What a perfect place. They would begin where they had left off six months ago.

He would fly over to see her, and before he got here, she would buy more new clothes and she would make herself beautiful again, at least she would try.

Zoe's eyes were nearly closed when the Volvo pulled to a halt on the cobbled auto court in front of the Eden au Lac's lobby. She opened her eyes and sat up.

In front of them, a uniformed porter with more gold braid than a Russian general was unloading expensive leather bags from the trunk of a Mercedes. Across the entryway from him, a similarly uniformed doorman was opening the door for a gray-haired gentleman and a woman wearing a battalion of sables. Through the doors, Zoe could see the warm glow of lights and the unhurried movement of guests with no appointments to keep. She and Seth had parted here, and there was no better place to begin putting themselves back together.

A very large man detached himself from a small group of people at the door and walked toward them. Stratton waved at the man.

"That is your main bodyguard, Richard Cartiere," Stratton said as he turned off the ignition. "If anything happens, Rich will take care of you. He's 290 pounds of former SAS trouble for anyone who might try to harm you."

Zoe thought he looked like a moving mountain as he came around and opened her door.

"Good evening," Zoe greeted the large man. He smiled and returned her

greeting with a bow. She would learn that he was a man of action and not
words.

She got out and followed Cartiere into the lobby. A doorman rushed to
take custody of her new clothes.

Seth Ridgeway cursed under his breath as the taxi pulled to a halt in front of
the Eden au Lac's lobby. Of all the goddamned places he'd like to avoid, this
would be the only decent hotel in Zurich with a reservation. Damn. He'd called
hotel after hotel from the train station. "We're sorry, Mein Herr," they all told
him, but the Christmas season is upon us. Parties, visiting, people coming from
the country to shop and celebrate. I'm afraid we have no vacancies for several
weeks. Perhaps . . ."

Seth had thanked each politely and hung up to call another number. Then
he had tried visiting the hotels in person. With the same results. The Schweiz-
erhof had been more helpful than most. The clerk behind the desk called several
of his counterparts at other hotels and finally found Ridgeway a room.

"It is at the Eden au Lac," the clerk said proudly. "It is a fine hotel, but
they are a bit farther away from our main shopping area. It is for this reason I
was able to get you a room."

Seth had tried to look enthusiastic for the clerk's sake, tipped him generously, and walked back outside to his waiting taxi.

Putting off the inevitable trip to a hotel he didn't want to stay at, Seth took
his cabdriver to dinner. They left the meter running in the cab, and Seth paid
for it all. The man was a Turkish immigrant who spoke little German and no
English. His family was still back in Turkey and he sent them most of the money
he made from driving the cab. He had a wife and seven children, the oldest a
boy of twelve. He missed them all. Beyond that, the language barrier prevented
anything approaching real conversation.

So they muddled through the meal using hand signs and facial expressions
to communicate. They had toasted each other from the bottle of Château Latour
Seth had ordered. Neither understood the toast of the other, but both felt
honored. And they shared the universal language of strangers alone in a foreign
country, separated from the ones they love.

But time finally ran out. Seth had to get to the hotel before the front desk
gave his room to someone else.

Seth's taxi driver leaped out of the cab as soon as he had braked to a halt
and opened the door for him. Then he opened the trunk and signaled for a
porter. In one of the few phrases of German the driver knew, he told the porter
to be careful with the bags. Finally Seth pulled a wad of Weinstock's money

from his wallet and counted off the amount on the meter, doubled it, and gave it to the driver.

"Merry Christmas," Seth told the Turkish cabdriver. The man hugged him, kissed him on both cheeks, then got back in his cab and drove away.

Seth was unaware of the curious looks of the porters and doormen as he turned and walked toward the entrance. He hoped the money would make for a better Christmas, and maybe a better life, for a hardworking husband in Switzerland and a wife and seven children in Turkey.

A bellhop with the imperial bearing of Prussian nobility carried Seth's bags up to his room, hung up the clothes, adjusted the thermostat, turned down his bed, and demonstrated the dry bar stocked with full bottles of whiskey and cordials, and the refrigerator with its champagne, white wine, fruit juices, and bottled water. His name was Klaus and he spoke impeccable English.

Seth tipped him well enough for the man to remember him if the time ever came to ask him a favor. Seth briefly considered opening one of the bottles of orange juice and lay on the bed to think about it. He fell asleep with his clothes on.

Far to the south, the Austrian wind shrieked up off the valley of the Inn River and heaved its icy shoulders against the lodge's stout timbers. The half-century-old wood creaked and complained with the stronger gusts. It was after 2 A.M. and lights shone in only one set of windows, high on the Cardinal Nest's top floor. Behind those windows, Archbishop Cardinal Neils Braun paced his bedroom as he listened to the man on the other end of the telephone line.

"Very good." Braun smiled into the receiver. "I knew I had placed my trust well with you."

Braun held the cordless telephone to his ear and listened to the report as he walked into the darkened coolness of his personal study. Flipping on the overhead light switch, he looked about him, at the walls lined with books, at the bound copies of his own books, seven of them, all published by commercial publishers of international renown. Philosophy, theology, history. The works had accounted in large part for the spread of his influence beyond his own important, but clerically insular, niche in the Vatican hierarchy.

Still listening to the frantic man on the other end of the line, Braun walked over to the bookshelf and pulled out a copy of the book that had put his name on the lips of people around the world and elevated him from the obscurity of the Curia to a serious contender for the throne of Saint Peter.

He pulled the book from the shelf and looked at it absently. *Communism as the Antichrist*. Based on years of solid research and on his own secret experiences as head of the Secretariat of Non-Believers, the book had been written for laymen and clerics alike. During the worst days of the Cold War, it had become a text for serious scholars of the conflicts between church and state. And it had also become a popular best-seller in every country in the free world, making him a prime target for assassins.

Upon publication of the book, he became a sought-after guest on television and a popular speaker at religious and secular events. It had not hurt his climb within the Vatican's Byzantine hierarchy.

And with its success, he had no trouble recruiting the most powerful men for the ecumenical council. He replaced less powerful members with those of more influence. Those who refused to resign and allow others to take their place usually grew too ill to serve any longer. The ecumenical council's influence grew along with his own. He became an increasingly bitter focus of virulent propaganda and denouncement by the Soviets. And with each attack, and following each assassination attempt, his own support within the church had grown. Cardinal after cardinal came to him and they all said the same thing: Neils Braun would be the next Pope. It was just a matter of time.

But it hadn't been a matter of time, Braun thought, as he angrily shoved his book back into its slot on the shelf, and walked toward his desk. Damn the Soviets! Damn their bumbling incompetence! His secret, behind-the-scenes work had weakened their regimes and hastened the downfall of worldwide communism. But they fell too quickly.

He avoided looking at the portrait of the pontiff that hung behind the desk. Looking at it made him angrier. The portrait should have borne his image. But when communism imploded, sucked inward by the black hole of its own intellectual vacuum, the attention he had enjoyed turned elsewhere as did the unanimity that he would be the next Pope because only he could stand up to international communism.

Braun turned his back to the portrait and pulled the chair from the desk's kneehole. Oh, he had never let the anger show! Not even to his closest allies on the Curia had he been anything but magnanimous in defeat. He was a young man, his supporters said. There would come another time, another day, another vote.

As he sat behind his desk, Braun cursed silently as he thought of his defeat. Time was too short! Every day the faithful suffered more and more all around the world. The nonbelievers gained ground every day; the church lost it every day. The present church had lost its backbone, abandoned the discipline and ruthlessness that had made it the world's brightest light for the faithful. They were more concerned with apologia for the past than a vision for future greatness.

No one realized it. Not the present Pope, not the College of Cardinals. None of them knew how little time they really had. Only the cardinal archbishop from Vienna knew. And even the little time they had would evaporate if the unbelievers got their hands on Sophia's Shroud. Something had to be done, and Braun knew that, once again, he was the only man who could do it.

His ruminations were interrupted as the man finished his report.

"Of course," Braun replied, in his most soothing pastoral voice. "You will continue to do well and our mission will be blessed as long as we continue to hold fast to our faith in Jesus Christ."

They hung up and Braun continued the survey of his study and knew that all would change once he had the Sophia Passion, the testament of a Messiah he was determined to keep secret at all costs.

After Sophia's secrets had made him Pope, he would call a series of meetings with the heads of the world's major religions. The power of the Sophia Passion and the threat it carried would force concessions of the most historical nature, perhaps not a reunification but at the very least a profound realignment, a coming together to marshal the forces of the world's religions under his guidance.

It would work, he was sure of it. Braun knew the instincts of self-preservation so deeply rooted in the bureaucracies of the world's established churches. Sophia threatened the very structure of the Western world's organized religions. And Braun knew that the people who sat atop those structures would do anything to preserve their churches and their positions in their hierarchies.

Onward Christian soldiers! Braun's support would give them the moral authority they needed to move against their own enemies. Enemies of governments and enemies of the church would all be the same. Political dissent would die with religious dissent.

He saw nothing less than a return to the old Holy Roman Empire, where emperors and Popes appointed each other and where each ruled with the authority of the other, always in the name of God. But more significantly Braun was talking about unity, peace, and harmony through the unity of belief. It was his crusade. God is my sword! He felt the warmth well up in his breast.

The time was right, too, in the West. Politicians and military officers and even ordinary citizens were frustrated by their helplessness in the face of terrorism and decay. They were all frustrated and would seize a promising opportunity to rid themselves of their helplessness. It would start with moral authority. Slowly, carefully Braun would solidify his own moral authority. From there he would talk with those in the military and government who needed a blanket of further moral authority with which to cloak themselves.

And from there, the awesome public-opinion-molding machines would go to work: vast armies of propagandists with their sophisticated tools to manipulate the facts, and with them, public opinion. And what they couldn't manipulate they would classify as secret. These men knew what they were doing. They knew how to use God and patriotism to lead the people. They would find the right chord to strike, and within the population the sentiments would resonate. And then violence, bloodshed, religious intolerance. My country right or wrong. My God right, never wrong.

The undercurrents were already there: the Christian Right had tapped into it as had the ayatollahs and the extreme Orthodox rabbis in America and Israel. They drew their strength from a raging subterranean river and he intended to harness them all.

TWENTY

Z urich's Bahnhofstrasse runs for less than a mile from the train station to the lake. But along its length, the visitor can see almost everything that has given this small Swiss city an international reputation for the gold beneath its sidewalks.

Banks and jewelry stores jam the Bahnhofstrasse. The banks store money, precious stones, gold, and objects more valuable than gold. The jewelry stores sell gold and precious gems in exchange for money, gold, and sometimes for things more valuable than gold. Bankers and jewelers have long been allies, but nowhere are the bonds tighter than on Zurich's Bahnhofstrasse. All the big ones are here: Swiss Credit, Union Bank, J. Vontobel & Co., A. Sarasin & Cie., and more.

And between the impressive bank buildings, with their bold public facades and polished mahogany doors lined with armor plate, are private banks: small, exclusive, the most secretive among a secretive bank industry. The brass plates on their doors bear single muted names such as Bertholdier et Fils, or perhaps a string of names as in a law firm. Nowhere is there an indication that a bank may be behind the door. If a visitor does not know it is a bank, he has no business there.

The jewelry stores that separate the banks from one another operate in much the same way. The large ones have public displays designed to appeal to the bourgeoisie, and—accessible only by private elevators and authorized escorts—salons for those who in all probability have just come from a small banking establishment with an armor-plated mahogany door.

Seth paid off his taxi at the foot of the Bahnhofstrasse, where it ended at the lake. It was a brilliant day and in the cold, clear distance, a lone sailboat braved the chill waters. From Seth's vantage point the sail looked like a bleached wizard's cap sliding across the water. He paused for a moment and thought of a summer day more than six months before, when he had taken a small rental boat up the lake as far as Zollikon while he waited for Zoe to return.

He turned abruptly, from the thoughts of that day as much as from the physical sight that reminded him of it. Walking briskly now, he passed a small park and plunged into the thickening crowds of Christmas shoppers. It was December 22, two more shopping days until Christmas.

The sidewalks lining the Bahnhofstrasse were crowded with shoppers, shop-keepers, a straggling of tourists, schoolchildren out for the holidays, and a sprin-kling of immaculately groomed men and women. Most of the women were wrapped in furs, making their stately way between limousines and banks and jewelry stores.

Seth slowed his pace to match the crowds as he made his own way toward the Bahnhof, the train station. He paused briefly in a small triangular plaza next to a tram stop to consult a tourist map the front desk had given him before he left that morning. He looked about him and oriented the map to his direction of travel.

To his right was the old city of Zurich, with its serpentine cobbled streets lined with medieval and Renaissance buildings. Yost's shop was off one of the narrow lanes that intersected the Bahnhofstrasse two blocks up. As he shoved the map back in his overcoat pocket, Seth felt the lethal chill of the Magnum's metal cylinder.

Christ, he thought as he pressed on into the crowd, death followed him like a shadow. First Rebecca Weinstock on his boat, then Tony Bradford. Then the priest in the park in Amsterdam.

And Zoe.

Stop it! He told himself. She's alive. She has to be alive. Death. Death follows you. She's dead. Dead. Admit it. You're fooling yourself.

Seth burrowed his hands deeply in his coat pockets and pressed on, head down, hurrying now as if he could outrun the thoughts that haunted him. If she was dead . . . he tried to think of an *if*, but he couldn't conceive of life without her. He pressed on.

He was about to turn right on the street that led into the old section when he heard a low, arresting sound, a haunting musical note that seemed to fill the air around him and appeal to every part of his body, not just his sense of sound. He stopped and turned around, trying to find the source of the tones that came from everywhere, and from nowhere in particular. Most of the people around him stopped also.

Beside him a woman bent low and spoke to her daughter.

"There," she said in German. She pointed, and the daughter immediately pushed through the crowd ahead of her mother. Seth followed them.

Across the street, his hat lying on the sidewalk, a bearded man of perhaps twenty, dressed in traditional alpine garb, blew into the mouthpiece of an alpenhorn. The wooden instrument, a good ten feet long and shaped like a stretched-out meerschaum pipe, seemed to glow with sound as the youth played a series of notes that resonated among the buildings.

A well-dressed woman walked up to the youth's hat and tossed in a banknote and then rejoined the edge of the crowd. Soon several other people repeated her gesture as the youth played the simple melodies and messages that the isolated alpine people had used to communicate with each other from ridge to ridge before the birth of the telephone.

Seth listened with his whole body. First one note would please his ear, then another would seem to vibrate in his chest, and another in his head. Finally, he dropped an American five-dollar bill into the youth's hat and turned reluctantly toward the street that would lead him to Yost's shop and, he hoped, some answers.

Less than ten minutes later, Seth found Yost's shop at the address on the back of the painting, which now rested in a safe deposit box at the Eden au Lac. The shop had undergone several expansions in the past forty years, taking over a number of the adjoining shops, and Ridgeway found the entrance now at Number 13 Augustinergasse, just down the street from the original entrance.

Seth stood back at the edge of the sidewalk and looked at the front of the store. He had expected a cluttered and dimly lighted shop with a display window filled with elbows of framing molding that had faded in the sun. Instead, he found an establishment that looked, for all he could tell, like one of the jewelry stores down on the Bahnhofstrasse. "Jacob Yost & Sons, Fine Art," read the discreet polished brass letters set into the cut-stone walls of the first floor of a Renaissance-era structure. It was a gallery now, not just a frame shop. Set into the stone facade at window level were half a dozen glassed-in display cases containing framed works of art. There were no prices on any of them. Either they were not for sale or they were for people who knew how to bid on fine art.

Doing his best to quell his excitement, Seth stepped quickly across the sidewalk to Yost's gallery and pushed through the double glass doors.

Inside, Seth found an elegantly warm room whose high-ceilinged walls were hung from floor to ceiling with art of every description. The fact that each work looked extravagantly expensive was the only unifying characteristic that ran through the art. The floor space of the room was empty save for a collection of dark mahogany furniture: half a dozen chairs upholstered in wine-red velvet, several piecrust end tables, and a marble-top casual table in the middle to unify it all. Two of the chairs had fur coats draped over their arms like dead animals.

A cut-crystal decanter filled with what looked like sherry rested on a silver tray in the middle of the marble-top table surrounded by a circle of crystal sherry glasses. The circle of glasses had two gaps in it, and as Seth scanned the room he quickly spotted two white-haired women lifting glasses to their lips. They stood on either side of a short, fat man in his thirties who pointed at first one picture and then another, speaking in hushed, respectful tones. Both women nodded as he spoke.

"May I help you, sir?" asked a voice in English.

Startled, Seth whirled toward the voice. A younger but equally fat version of the man who guided the two women seemed to have materialized from the right. The man's formal dark suit and muted tie made him look like an undertaker. Seth stared at the man for a long moment, trying to collect his thoughts. He hadn't expected Jacob Yost and Sons to be anything as elaborate and . . . elegant as this.

"I'm sorry if I startled you," the man said, and then he paused. "You are American, aren't you?" His eyes appraised Seth's casual attire: gray wool slacks, black leather walking shoes, navy-blue crew-necked sweater under a red down ski jacket. The man's eyes said that while he didn't approve of such attire in his establishment, he respected the eccentricities of Americans who might very well be rich.

"Yes," Seth finally managed as his pulse pounded in his ears. "I mean, yes . . . I am American, but I understand German clearly, if that would be more comfortable for you."

The man shook his head and extended his hand. "I am Felix Yost," he said. "I studied for two years in the United States, at the Getty Museum in California." Seth took the man's hand and shook it. Yost's grip was fleshy but firm and warm. "I welcome every opportunity to maintain my fluency in your language."

Seth nodded. "I'm Seth Ridgeway," he said. "I called several days ago and spoke with your father about . . . about a painting." He watched the beginnings of a frown start to appear and then vanish from Yost's face. Seth reached for his wallet and pulled from it the snapshot of the painting that Weinstock had given him.

"I wish to speak to your father about this painting." He handed it to the fleshy young man, who studied the photograph with hooded eyes. There was a long silence. From across the gallery floor, Seth could hear the two white-haired women arguing. One wanted a painting because it was a valuable investment. The other called it an eyesore.

"But dear, what a remarkably *valuable* eyesore," her friend replied. They continued in this vein as the silence between Seth and Yost grew increasingly uncomfortable. The young man seemed reluctant to look up from the photo.

"When I called earlier, I was told your father would be happy to meet with me," Seth said finally.

What Felix Yost did next took Seth completely unaware.

"Here!" Yost hissed as he thrust the photograph back at Ridgeway. "Take your filth and leave us alone."

Seth took the photo and stared blankly at Yost.

"Are you deaf?" Yost asked. "We are decent people and we will not be forever haunted by one mistake forty years ago. Get out of here! Get out of here now or I'll be forced to call the authorities."

"Uh . . ." Seth searched for words that wouldn't come to mind. What had gone wrong? The name on the back of the painting was his only clue to Zoe, his only way to find out what the painting meant. What had changed Yost's mind? Had someone talked to him? About what?

Yost grabbed Seth's upper arm and tried to steer him out of the store. "Please, Mr. Ridgeway, or whomever you say you are, please leave! We don't want any trouble and we therefore want nothing to do with the painting of which you speak."

"But why?" Seth shook his arm loose from Yost's grasp and turned to face him. Yost was a full head shorter than Seth. "I don't know anything about the painting except that it's connected with the disappearance of my wife and with the deaths of at least three people."

Yost's eyes widened as Seth spoke. "That precisely is why we wish nothing with this painting to do." Yost's fluency in English degenerated into patterns of German grammar as his agitation increased. He grabbed Seth again and shoved him toward the door.

"Please not to make me call the police," Yost pleaded. "But I will if you do not leave."

Seth shook himself free of Yost a second time and stood with his back to the door, shaking with anger and frustration as he stared down at him. His mouth worked furiously, like that of a fish out of water, as he tried to clear the inarticulate rage from his head.

Finally, Seth put his right hand in the middle of Yost's soft fleshy chest and pushed him so hard the chubby man stumbled backward, arms flailing the air like a windmill, and crashed rump first into the cut-crystal glasses and decanters on the marble-topped table.

The high-pitched tinkles of breaking crystal followed Seth out into the bright sunshine and stopped only when the door slammed shut behind him.

"He's gone!"

The abbot flinched visibly as he heard the young priest's words. The abbey's shabby financial condition faded from the abbot's thoughts now as he looked from the window of his office at the twin towers of the Frauenkirche towering over the roofline of Munich's old town. He turned slowly to face the young priest.

"What do you mean, 'gone'?" the abbot asked slowly, his words carrying the edge of a razor. The young priest's face looked as if it had been dusted with flour.

"I—" The priest tried to clear his nervous throat. "We knocked at his door with his lunch. He . . . he said he wasn't feeling well. He spent the morning in bed. He's . . . he's very—"

"Sick, yes, I know his medical history," the abbot said impatiently. "I know more about his medical history than I do my own, so get on with it!"

"He asked to be left alone this morning, and we . . . we assumed he was sleeping. He's done that in the past, you know." The young priest looked hopefully for some sign of flexibility in his master. Finding none on the abbot's chilly face, he continued.

"We knocked just a few moments ago," the young priest said. "And when we got no answer we—we were afraid he had . . . died or something—we entered the room and found he had gone."

"Gone? Just like that? Gone?" the abbot asked. The young priest nodded.

The abbot's reply began low, like rumbles on the distant horizon, and rose steadily until his words thundered at the young priest, so forcefully that he flinched under their blows. "I give you and five other incompetent human beings who call themselves priests the task of looking after a feeble, half-crippled old man and you've come to tell me that he has somehow disappeared right from under your keen eyes in the middle of the day! I—" The abbot choked on his rage. His face burned red with anger and his fists trembled at his side. For a long moment, he glared at the young priest. Then: "Get out! You and your fellows are confined to your rooms. I will deal with you later."

The young priest seemed petrified.

"Out! Out now!"

The priest abruptly came to life and ran from the room.

The abbot walked to the door of his office and closed it quietly. Then he went to his desk and sagged heavily into the chair. Why me? he wondered through closed eyes that he rubbed with the heels of his hands. Why?

He reached for the telephone. As his hands neared the receiver it hesitated for a moment, almost as it the instrument were a venomous reptile. His hands shook, from fear now rather than anger, as he dialed the number for the office of the CDF. Cardinal Neils Braun was not a man who took failure with equanimity.

TWENTY-ONE

He was being followed. There was no longer any doubt about that. Seth Ridgeway brought his glass of Alsatian pinot gris to his lips and gazed over the rim at the man across the café from him. He was a tall man, six-two or more, with wavy brown hair cut almost short enough to suit a police force or a military organization. His face had the lean and angular agelessness found usually in combat officers who have devoted a lifetime of physical effort to staying in superb physical condition. Ridgeway was suddenly conscious of the fifteen pounds he had added since Zoe had disappeared, of the roll of flab that girdled his waistline.

The man carried himself with a physical precision and confidence that conveyed strength hidden beneath the bulky wool overcoat. He wore a business suit now, with a tiny precisely knotted tie and a coat that could easily conceal a firearm. And even from across the main dining room of the crowded café, the intensity of his glacier-blue eyes was apparent.

Seth set his wineglass down slowly and pretended interest in the *rosti* on his plate. The man was no professional at tailing people, Seth thought, as he chased the potatoes around his plate with a fork. He was too obvious, looking too hard, following too closely, making eye contact accidentally. Unless, Seth stopped to think, unless someone wanted him to know he was being followed. But who could that be? Someone associated with the priest who had followed him in Amsterdam? Or someone who wanted to kill him?

He rejected this last notion. If that had been the man's intention he would have done it sooner, back when Seth had walked alone through the deserted park alongside Saint Peter's Church. He had first seen the man there, just minutes after shoving Felix Yost into his sherry and crystal.

Seth had begun to regret his display of temper as he climbed the steps at the end of the In Gassen. He had just about decided to go back and apologize to Yost and offer to pay for the damage when he saw the man.

Seth had stopped, and unlike a professional tail, who would have continued on past him, the man stopped too, startled and uncertain of himself.

Continuing on up the steps, Seth dismissed the encounter as coincidence. But the man followed him across the courtyard at the top of the In Gassen, around the church, and through the courtyard on the other side. Seth took the glove off his right hand and kept a firm grasp on the Magnum as he walked along. The man might have a silenced weapon, or accomplices could be waiting around the next corner. They would suffer for whatever they might have in mind. But nothing happened.

The man had had plenty of opportunity to kill him and escape without being seen. Yet he had just continued his clumsy surveillance. Seth sneaked a look at the man across the café again. He was amateurishly trying to hide behind a copy of the *Neue Züricher Zeitung*. Ridgeway read the headlines from across the room.

Suddenly Seth knew what he had to do. Letting his fork drop abruptly on his plate, he fumbled about in his pockets for currency to cover his meal, dropped the money on the table, then swiftly got up and walked across the room. Quickly, Seth plunged his right hand into the deep pocket of his ski parka and found the grip of the Magnum. He grabbed it and slipped his index finger through the trigger guard, curling it around the lithe coldness of the trigger.

Seth heard the man's newspaper rattle loudly and saw the expression of surprise and confusion on the man's face as he caught sight of him approaching. Startled, the man knocked over the cup of tea he had been nursing as he made an effort to rise.

"Don't bother getting up," Seth said in German, as he held up his left hand in a stop gesture. The man froze, half in, half out of his seat. "Go ahead, sit back down," Seth said.

Then, in a lower voice, Seth continued. "I have a very powerful handgun in the pocket of my coat." He watched the man's look flicker down to Seth's concealed hand, and immediately his eyes widened with fear. "It's pointed at you and will tear a hole in you the size of a dinner plate if you so much as think of doing something I haven't first told you to do. Have you got that?"

The man nodded coolly. "What do you want?" His voice was calm, confident. He might be an amateur at tailing people, Seth thought, but he had an uncanny calmness when faced with danger. Only people who had faced danger and survived were capable of that.

"I should be asking you that," Seth said. "And since I have the gun, why don't you go first?" He pulled out the chair opposite the man and sat down.

The man nodded. "Hand me your wallet," Seth commanded. The man's hand moved quickly toward his coat pocket. "Slowly! Slowly," Seth said. "Don't pull any surprises from your pockets."

The man nodded calmly, his head tilted slightly to one side, and pulled a slim leather wallet from his inside coat pocket and slid it across the table. He then leaned casually back in his chair and looked appraisingly across the table as Seth, using only his left hand, opened the wallet on the table and began to sort through its contents. There was currency, the equivalent of less than one hundred dollars in Swiss francs, the card key to a parking lot, a collection of credit cards, and a Swiss driver's license in the name of Jacob Yost. Seth glanced sharply at the man across the table.

"You're Jacob Yost?" His voice betrayed his incredulity.

The man nodded. "I am the son of the man you called several days ago. I am Jacob Yost the second—or junior, as you Americans refer to it."

Searching for words, trying desperately to collect his thoughts, Seth replaced Yost's driver's license in his wallet and slid it back across the table.

"I don't understand," he stammered. "Why would you—why follow me like this?"

"Because someone who said he was you came to our house last night. He had men with him and he wanted to hurt my father. The man is not alive. Neither are his friends." Yost's voice was matter-of-fact.

"But who? Why?" Seth asked.

"They had no identification," Yost said, "and they spoke German with Russian accents. I believe they worked for the KGB."

Seth nodded knowingly. "That makes sense," he said, and then stopped himself. "No, that doesn't make any sense at all. None of this does. But at least it fits. They tried to kill me before. I thought you . . ."

"Might be one of them?" Seth nodded. Jacob Yost smiled for the first time. "No, Mr. . . . . Ridgeway?" Seth nodded. "We are both on the same side."

Yost extended his hand across the table. Ridgeway looked at it warily. Was it a trick? Identification can be faked, Seth reminded himself. And the best of killers are also the best of actors. As he looked at the proffered handshake of friendship, he thought of Weinstock, of the priest of Amsterdam, of George Stratton. They had all come to him in friendship and they had all proven they were worthy of trust. . . . Stratton had saved his life; the other two had died.

Reluctantly, Seth decided he had to trust this man. Stifling a chill that skated down his spine, he slowly relaxed his grip on the Magnum and pulled his hand from his pocket.

"All right," Seth said finally as he took Yost's warm, dry grip and shook it. "We're on the same side."

"That's good," Yost said, shaking Seth's hand and then letting it go. "Because the man at the next table"—he nodded to his left—"has a gun more powerful than your own, pointed at your head."

Ridgeway whirled to his right and saw a stocky man with long straight brown hair. The man smiled at him, looked down at his lap, then quickly back up at Seth again. Seth followed the man's eyes downward and immediately spotted the muzzle end of a silencer hidden under the folds of a paper napkin.

Seth looked back at Yost and watched as Yost nodded at the man with the long hair. The man nodded back, reached down, and plucked a forest-green knapsack from underneath the table. He then slid the silenced gun into the knapsack, placed a banknote on the table, and left without further communication.

"You don't take many chances, do you?" Seth remarked.

"I am a very, very careful man, Mr. Ridgeway," Yost said.

"But you're taking one now, aren't you?" Seth asked, as he turned his full attention to the man across the table from him. Yost's raised eyebrows described the arc of an unspoken question on his forehead.

"You're taking a chance right now with me," Seth answered Yost's unspoken question. "How do you know I'm not just a clever KGB agent?"

Yost's eyebrows knitted themselves into one long mass as he considered Ridgeway's question. The thoughts shifted behind his eyes. Finally: "The same way you knew to trust me, Mein Herr," Yost began slowly. "If you were not who you say you are, you would never have dropped your guard with me. You would have dealt with me differently. Do you agree?"

Seth nodded thoughtfully

"Good," Yost said. "We have some important arrangements to make, questions to answer, before you meet my father tonight."

Brilliant sunlight cascaded through the windows of the sitting room that separated Zoe's bedroom at the Eden au Lac from Rich Cartiere's.

The suite simplified plans for Zoe's security. Rich Cartiere had barricaded the door to her room using his prodigious strength to move a Louis XIV armoire in front of it. Except for the windows that faced a sheer drop, no ledges or fire escapes nearby, the only way to get to Zoe was through the door that connected to the sitting room. And Cartiere, the huge former paratrooper, slept in the sitting room at night along with Stratton. Strange people, she thought. Mysterious. They would explain after she had rested, Stratton promised. She let things drop. They had saved her life.

Zoe stretched lazily now and closed her eyes for a long moment savoring the inner rapture of the condemned prisoner now granted a miraculous reprieve.

Again she said a small prayer of thanksgiving, growing more comfortable each time with the notion that perhaps faith could make a difference.

And although it was only slightly past one o'clock in the afternoon, she had already run the gamut of the Eden au Lac's beauty salon. After a long luxurious bath, the hairdresser had cut and styled her hair, tsk-tsking all the while, but too discreet to actually come right out and ask madame how her hair had managed to fall into such a shabby state of repair.

While the hairdresser fussed, the manicurist labored over her nails with the fervor of a sculptor attacking a virgin block of marble.

Next had come the woman with the facials that smelled of a well-made amaretto mousse, and later, the beauty consultant, who made Zoe feel truly feminine again. And finally, the hotel's fashion consultant, who came with books of clothing designs and fabric swatches, taking her measurements and promising to scour the boutiques of Zurich to assemble madame's new wardrobe.

Zoe turned her face into the bright warm sunlight and tilted her head downward toward the lake. Through the window, she saw a lone sailboat beating its way to windward. The sight struck a blow to her heart. Where was Seth? She had called and called, even getting up in the middle of the night, but there had been no answer, only the sound of his voice on the recording. She wished there was a way to remotely listen to the messages others had left on the machine. Perhaps they would provide a clue to Seth's whereabouts.

Her impatience raced through her body and made her insides tingle.

Where was he? she wondered with a lover's longing intensity. What was he doing right now? Had he sailed out to Catalina? It was 2 A.M. there now. Was he sound asleep, the *Valkyrie* bobbing gently at anchor in the secure anchorage at Cherry Cove?

She saw his sleeping face in her mind and felt tears well up from the tender breakings in her chest. He looked like such a little boy when he slept. Respected professor, tough cop—they were all vanquished by the relaxed face of a man who she knew was still a boy at heart. She remembered how he would smile in his sleep, have little puppy twitches like a dog chasing a rabbit in its dreams, and the way the tough, lean former cop with the hard muscles and long leathery scars he didn't like to talk about would cuddle next to her and fall asleep.

Where are you, Seth?

Her longing was complete, completely coloring her thoughts and emotions. Where was he? The only thing in the world she wanted more than knowing where he was, was to be there with him.

TWENTY-TWO

T he light along the far shore of the Zurichsee painted long white and yellow shimmers on the glassy surface of the water. The wind had died at sunset. Outside the air was crystalline clear.

"Damn you, God," Seth Ridgeway raged as he gazed at a scene that looked so much like the same view that he and Zoe had enjoyed so intensely the last time he had seen her alive.

Damn you! Damn me for being such a sucker to believe in you.

He turned from the window and walked toward the door of his room at the Eden au Lac. He stopped by the door and pulled the Magnum from his parka pocket. He checked to be sure that every chamber in the revolver's cylinder had a fresh .357 in it, set the safety on, and stuck the weapon back in the pocket. Then he patted the other pocket to make sure the handful of ammunition was still there. He hesitated, going over Jacob Yost's instructions in his mind. Any deviation and he might be killed.

Once he was sure of his orders, Seth opened the door to his room, stepped across the threshold, and pulled the door shut behind him. He walked to the elevator and pressed the down button.

Zoe walked across her room dressed in a bulky sweater pulled over new Levi's. Stratton walked out of the room first, his eyes scouring the corridor for signs of danger. Zoe followed him. Behind her, Cartiere closed the door to the suite; using his saliva, he carefully placed one of his own hairs across the space between the jamb and the door. They'd know whether or not someone had entered.

The trio walked to the elevator and pushed the button. They stood silently and looked at the floor indicator as the car went past them and stopped one floor above.

•　　•　　•

In the corridor above, Ridgeway watched the elevator come to a stop at his floor. The door opened gracefully and Seth was about to step in when he heard a voice calling to him.

"Mein Herr."

The voice sounded foreign yet familiar. Friend or assassin? Seth whirled toward the voice, plunged his hand into his pocket, and found the Magnum. Near the door to his room, he saw a man coming toward him, looking vaguely familiar. Seth tensed. Where had he seen the man? Where had he heard his voice?

"I am glad to have found you before you left," the man said as he continued to walk toward Seth. He was dark, thin, plainly dressed. "The desk telephoned and there was no answer in your room. You are in great danger."

There was no danger in the man's voice or in the way he walked. Confusing signals, a stranger in his hotel corridor. How did the man know he was here? Ridgeway's heart pounded. The man seemed harmless.

And so did a young woman who appeared at the companionway on your boat.

Seth snapped the safety off the Magnum as the man stepped into a pool of light spilled into the corridor by a brass sconce.

It was the taxi driver who had brought him from the train station the previous night. Behind him, Seth heard the elevator door close.

Ridgeway flicked the safety back on the Magnum, pulled his right hand from his pocket, and extended it toward the smiling Turkish *Gastarbeiter* who had shared a meal and his dreams of a better life with Ridgeway the night before. The man took Ridgeway's hand and shook it enthusiastically. Then the smile vanished from his face.

"There are men asking questions about you," the cab driver said in his terrible German. "They say they are with the police . . . the government. But something smells with these men. I have seen their type too many times. They are arrogant and they are bad men. I believe they work for the Russian Mafia or perhaps some other evil organization just like them. They dress like bankers and they offer great sums of money to know where you are. I have told them nothing. You have been too kind to me."

Ridgeway looked at the cabdriver, and for a brief moment felt ashamed that such a small kindness such as he had shown to this man was all it had taken to win his allegiance. And then he felt grateful, thankful that there were still good people in the world, people like this simple immigrant, who were good, honest, decent people.

"How many of them were there?" Seth asked.

"Two, three, I think. They arrived at the train station this morning and began showing your picture around."

"My picture! What kind of picture? What did it look like?"

The cabdriver closed his eyes and screwed up his face as if he were searching files in his head. "A color picture," he said finally. "There was a lady in the picture with you." He opened his eyes. "A very pretty lady. You were sitting at a table, maybe a café or a nightclub. I remember there was a name in the background behind you but I don't remember the name."

"I do," Seth said quickly. "It was the Harbor Reef, wasn't it?"

"I don't know," the driver said slowly, "that could be it, but it was in English, I believe, and I don't read much of that. German is my only language other than my native tongue."

The Harbor Reef! Seth knew the photograph. It had been taken with a Polaroid camera nearly three years ago, when he and Zoe had visited the isthmus at Catalina. And for the past three years that picture—the only one of its kind—had resided in Zoe's wallet! What did it mean? Did it make it more likely or less that she was still alive? Or did it merely mean that the men who had kidnapped her had not learned what they wanted from her and had continued the search for him that had begun in Los Angeles?

". . . will be looking for you at hotels soon," the cabdriver was saying. "You must leave."

Leave? Yes, Seth thought as he looked at his watch. Both Jacob Yosts—senior and son—would soon be waiting.

"Of course, they'll look for me at the hotels later," Seth said as he started for the stairway. Or maybe right now. Maybe there's a man with a gun waiting at the bottom of the stairs. The thought made his stomach cramp.

"But I have an extremely important meeting I have to go to—an urgent one," Seth said as he began to descend the stairs. "I don't have time to worry about that right now."

"I will take you to your meeting, Mein Herr," the driver insisted. "It would not be safe for you to be seen by other drivers. They would surely turn you in for the money."

Seth glanced sideways at the man as they gained the first landing, walked half a dozen steps, and continued on down the stairs. "How much money are we talking about?"

"More than two thousand Swiss francs."

Two-thousand francs! About a thousand American dollars. Not exactly a king's ransom, but far more than street cops usually waved around at taxi stands looking for tips. They wanted him badly.

They passed the second-floor landing. Seth reached inside his coat and pulled his wallet from his hip pocket. From it he took one of Weinstock's thousand-dollar bills.

"You passed up a lot of money just to be honest," Seth said, as they reached the landing just above the lobby. He put his hand on the cabdriver's shoulder and they stopped before descending the final flight. "I want you to have this." He proffered the thousand-dollar bill. The Turkish immigrant looked first at the bill, and then fixed Seth with a hurt, insulted look.

"I can't take that," the man said. "I did not come here to ask you for money, or for a reward. I came because you are obviously a good man and you are in danger."

"But your family . . . your children," Seth stammered. "They could—you could—use this money, is that not true?"

"That has nothing at all to do with this—a matter of honor," the cabdriver replied proudly. "I am a man of honor and I must act like one." He pushed the bill away firmly but politely with the palm of his hand, looked up into Seth's eyes, and said: "Come! You have an important meeting to attend. I will drive you."

Astounded, Seth turned to the last flight of stairs and began his descent.

"Are you telling me that without telephoning or any other kind of notification, you simply emptied the safe deposit box and mailed the contents to my husband?" Zoe was outraged. She'd made her way past two layers of the Eden au Lac's internal bureaucracy and had managed to get to the manager before he left for the evening. She snared him in the middle of the hotel's main lobby near the frieze by Bernini. Stratton and Cartiere hovered about her, trying to look inconspicuous and failing to succeed, due mostly to Cartiere's bulk.

"But Madame Ridgeway, I assure you that we had no choice," the hotel manager protested in a desperate whisper. He looked about him after ever every sentence to see if any of the hotel's other guests were paying attention to the disagreement. "After a guest checks out, we have a policy that all items left behind in our boxes must be returned to them. After all, it wouldn't be fair to deprive other guests of the proper facilities in which to store their valuables."

"Policy!" Zoe snapped. "Policies are for bureaucrats and bankers and anybody else too dimwitted to make intelligent decisions on their own. Not for the management of one of the world's finest hotels."

The manager's face brightened momentarily at this unexpected compliment from the angry American woman.

"We assumed that—"

"That painting was among the world's most valuable," Zoe said. "Priceless! At the very least it merited being hand-carried by a courier. Not trusted to the vagaries of the mails!"

As Zoe said "priceless," most of the color drained from the manager's face. "But the Swiss mails are—"

"I know the Swiss mails are reliable," Zoe interrupted. "But once the package gets to America, it's in the hands of the U.S. Postal Service, and most of the people who work for that outfit need a road map to find their way to the bathroom."

Zoe's vehemence brought color back to the manager's face, but it was a wan, unenthusiastic pink blotched with pale white. He looked about him desperately. No one was staring. The lobby was nearly deserted and the staff were busy straightening out the receipts from the busy afternoon.

"I . . . A-hem!" The manager cleared his throat nervously. It was time to play his last card, to risk stepping into the middle of what might turn out to be a domestic quarrel. If so, he would either turn this woman's wrath away from him or—he swallowed hard—redouble her wrath. And perhaps incur her husband's as well. She obviously was unaware that her husband had checked in the night before and had put the same painting back into a hotel safe deposit box. The Eden au Lac prided itself on its discretion and respect for its guests' privacy. Confidences were to be respected unless the situation became so desperate that it reflected poorly on the hotel's image.

And things were getting desperate, the manager decided.

"Your husband seemed quite happy with the arrangements we made," the manager said. "I spoke to him last night when he checked in."

The anger on her face broke and scattered like the last dark clouds of a summer thunderstorm.

"In fact, I placed the painting of which you speak back in a safe deposit box. I did it myself, madame."

He watched as Zoe's face had turned from anger to amazement to relief. Her features softened, and as they did, the hotel manager noticed for the first time how beautiful she was.

Zoe felt her heart race. Seth was here! He was here!

"Seth's in this hotel?" She turned to Stratton. "That's why he didn't answer the phone last night or today!" She paused, a puzzled look occupying her features. "But how? How did he know?"

She turned back to the manager and touched his sleeve lightly.

"What room's he in?" she asked eagerly.

The manager looked at her intensely. She didn't look like an angry wife. There was no jealousy or hatred in her eyes, only relief. Still . . . he hesitated

"Well," he began reluctantly, "normally we don't give out information on our guests but . . ."

"We've both been . . . traveling. My husband and I," she said. "And we've obviously missed connections so—"

"As I said, we normally don't give our such information, but in this case, I think we can accommodate your request."

"Thank you!" Zoe said breathlessly as she followed him over to the front desk.

Seth Ridgeway stepped off the stairs and turned toward the lobby.

"Wait!" The cabdriver placed a firm hand on his shoulder. "Not that way." Seth stopped. "There are too many people who might see you. Come with me, out the side. I have parked there just for this reason."

Seth looked out on the lobby. The main doors were straight ahead, the front desk was out of sight to the left, and there was a comfortable seating area to the right near a frieze. Save for a very large man walking toward the front desk, the lobby was deserted. As he watched, the large man disappeared to the left. The man looked like a huge walking threat.

"You're right," Seth said quickly. "Lead the way." He followed the Turkish cabdriver down a narrow service corridor and finally through a plain scarred wooden door near the kitchen that led out into the crisp night air.

TWENTY-THREE

The cabdriver pulled slowly to the curb of the Limmat Quai just north of the Wasserkirche. Late-evening traffic swirled around them as the cab came to a halt. Behind them a motorist leaned angrily on his horn. The cabdriver ignored him. Moments later the car, a BMW, pulled around the cab with a screeching of tires and roared on past.

"I will take you all the way to your destination," the cabdriver offered.

"Thank you," Seth replied, "but I have directions to follow."

The cabdriver nodded.

"Can I at least pay you for the fare from the hotel?"

The cabdriver looked at him a long time, his dark brown eyes staring from his nut-brown face.

"Please," Seth said as he pulled several Swiss franc notes from his wallet. "I would have had to pay a taxi anyway."

"If it would make you feel better," the driver said. Seth nodded as he folded the notes into a wad the size of a matchbook and passed them across to the Turkish driver.

"Thank you," said the driver as he stuffed the bills into the pocket of his coat. Seth pulled on the door handle and opened the door. "Be careful, my friend," the cabdriver said.

Ridgeway turned to him. "You too." And with that, Seth got out and closed the door. Behind him, he heard the taxi's motor race and then slow as the driver let out the clutch. The horn honked once as the taxi passed him, then disappeared into the bright weavings of traffic, making its way onto and off of the Quai Brucke.

Seth stood there for a moment, smiling to himself. The driver would be home before he discovered the thousand-dollar bill wrapped inside the Swiss francs.

Pushing the thought aside, Seth looked at his watch and noted that according to Jacob Yost's instructions he still had five minutes to reach the first checkpoint. He walked slowly along the Limmat Quai, pausing in measured turns to look into the display windows of shops along the way.

The night was almost warm and Ridgeway loosened the snaps of his parka to keep from sweating. *Die Föhn* is what they called it, the cabdriver had said. Sometimes during the winter, great high-pressure systems over North Africa would muscle warm masses of Sahara air north toward the polar low-pressure systems that normally dominated Europe in the wintertime. The result was a blast of warm air that melted snow and—in the snowcapped Alps—ski slopes. The avalanche danger always soared during *die Föhn*. It was sort of like the Santa Ana winds that blew through southern California in the winter, Seth thought as he walked along. Only *die Föhn* didn't spark great grass and range fires and make people crazy. At least not yet.

Seth stopped to look through metal burglar bars into a shop window displaying racks of rings crusted with gems of all colors: red, green, white, blue, yellow. The shops weren't as fancy here as they were across the river on the Bahnhofstrasse. Neither were the prices, he thought.

Then suddenly from behind him and to his left, Seth heard a pair of footsteps scrape along the sidewalk and come to a halt. His next breath solidified in the middle of his chest as he whirled toward the noise, his hand going for the Magnum in his pocket.

Nothing! Seth felt his heart flailing in his chest like an angry fist as he turned from side to side. He was absolutely alone on the sidewalk for half a block in each direction.

Still cautious, Seth retraced his steps past several doorways. There was no one hiding in a doorway. Puzzled, Seth continued his walk, looking suspiciously in doorway after doorway. He was sure he had heard something.

Nerves, he thought, as he reached the corner of the Torgasse and stepped off the curb to cross the narrow dark alley. His nerves had been so finely sanded down by the past week that his thin veneer of sanity had almost been completely worn away. Straining his eyes to plumb the darkness of the Torgasse, he thought he saw movement in the deep shadows. He stepped quickly across the street and back up on the sidewalk as he continued his way north along the Limmat Quai.

His heart was still racing when he reached the Rami Strasse. Looking cautiously around him, he pulled his tourist map of Zurich from his coat pocket and looked at it under the glow of the corner streetlight. Yost had marked a small "x" on the left side of the Rami Strasse about a block up. Seth looked up from the map and saw a small park-like area just up the hill, right where Yost's "x" should be. A bit closer to him, on the same side, was a tobacconist's shop, just where Yost said it was.

Still smiling, Seth stuffed the map back in his pocket and pushed on, up the steep grade of the Rami Strasse.

Jacob Yost, the son, was an odd man, Seth thought, as he made his way toward the tobacconist's shop. A colonel in the Swiss army, bodyguard to his father, a taciturn, physically hard man, angular, muscular, singular of purpose. The adjectives that described the younger Jacob Yost came to mind easily. A small frown passed momentarily across Seth's face. The adjectives described Yost but did not explain him.

He seemed dedicated to his father's safety and well-being, as if he had made a lifetime occupation of it. But why had that been necessary?

And what about Yost's brothers? The two soft, round men who ran the exclusive gallery off the Augustinerstrasse? Yost's contempt for them was palpable when he spoke of them. How had he turned out to be so different from them?

Questions piled on top of questions.

Seth shook his head slowly as he checked his watch. It was precisely 7:30. Just as Yost had said it must be, Seth pushed open the door to the tobacconist's and stepped inside. The air hung warm and redolent of books and tobacco. To his left was a large stand of magazines and books of all descriptions, paperback and hardcover, new and used. To the left were racks of fragrant tobaccos and pipes. Straight ahead the proprietor sat behind his counter reading a paperback book. He looked up as Seth entered.

"Good evening," Seth greeted the man in German.

"Evening," the proprietor replied as he carefully marked his place in the book with an empty pipe tobacco pouch, and stood up. "What can I do for you?" He studied Seth's face carefully.

Seth felt his throat go dry. Had the men with his picture been here with their offers of money? Was there a telephone number for people like this tobacconist to call? Seth swallowed hard against the hard prickly ball of fear in his throat.

"This week's *Time,* magazine," Seth replied weakly.

"Over on the wall." The proprietor pointed toward the magazine rack. "At the top, nearly all the way to the left."

Seth searched for the familiar cover as he walked toward the rack. He cast an anxious glance toward the front door of the shop, fearing that at any minute the men who were looking for him would burst in to finish what they had started seven thousand miles west of here. He spotted it from halfway across the store, slotted in between *Der Spiegel* and the *International Herald Tribune.*

Moments later, having purchased a small disposable lighter along with the thin international edition of *Time,* Seth stepped back into the almost warm night. He walked a handful of paces and turned to look in the window of the tobacconist's shop. The proprietor was already dialing the telephone.

Was he cooperating with Yost? Was this part of the security arrangements? Yost had been specific about which magazine to purchase and where and when it should be purchased. The man must be a friend.

But as Seth turned away from the shop and continued his climb up the steep hill, he couldn't help but wish that he knew for certain to whom the tobacconist's call had been placed.

It would have been a pleasant night, he thought as he walked along, if there weren't men out there in the darkness looking for him, offering a bounty to the taxi driver or hotel clerk who knew where he was. He loosened his coat again as the steep climb wrung perspiration from his body. He passed first one construction site and then another as he approached the next "x" that Yost had marked on the tourist map.

Seth paused for a moment at one construction site, using the klieg lights to check his map. It was the same here as in the colder regions of the United States, he mused. Construction workers had to labor overtime at night while the weather was good to make up for delays caused by inclement conditions. Turning around in a complete circle, he could see at least six new buildings, all decked out in the bright jewelry of electric lights, their skeletons crawling with workers.

Seth now directed his attention back to the map. He found Yost's next "x" just up ahead and to his left, then pressed on, the noise of the grit under his feet drowning in the animal rumbles of heavy machinery that reverberated from the new building next to him. He quickly covered the next block and crossed the street to the Heim Platz. Half a dozen people milled about in the small concrete square, waiting for the tram that stopped here. He milled about with them, scanning the windows of nearby buildings, trying to guess which of them might be spilling light shed by Jacob Yost Senior's apartment lamps.

At precisely 7:40, Seth walked to the trash receptacle at the curb. He lit the disposable lighter and held it near the cover of the magazine as if he were trying to read the date. Then he tossed the virgin copy of *Time* into the rubbish can.

It was a good ploy, Seth thought. From a darkened window, the younger Yost would easily be able to identify Seth in the illumination shed by the lighter's flame. Following Yost's precise instructions, Ridgeway would now linger another five minutes while the Yosts observed him, and, more important, scanned the surrounding area to see if he was being followed. Plans—Yost didn't specify them—would change if there were people following.

Time oozed past. Seth tried to pray again and the thoughts turned in his heart like sharp metal. Maybe God really was dead. The thought raised the pain of guilt in his heart. Fear for his mortal soul had just begun to pluck at Seth's nerves when first one, then two candles lit up on the top floor of the building on the southwest corner of Rami Strasse and Zelt Weg.

Seth's pulse quickened as he stepped across the street and made his way toward the building. Two candles! That was Yost's signal that all was well. On the other side of the street, he had to wait as a truck carrying a load of concrete backed slowly into an adjoining construction site. As he paused behind the barrier, he watched as a huge hopper, with the dregs of a previous load of concrete slopping down its sides, was gingerly lowered from the tip of a huge cantilevered crane. Seth looked up and saw that the crane's tip nearly touched the wall of Yost's building. From the ground it looked as if it missed by only inches.

The concrete mixer truck roared with a cloud of diesel exhaust and lumbered its elephantine way through the gates of the construction site to replace a twin that had just pulled out, empty no doubt.

Finally, the barrier was lifted and Seth and one other pedestrian, a bent old woman with a wire cart full of groceries, were allowed to continue.

Seth approached the address Yost had given him and stepped up to a locked door with a row of numbered buttons, no names beside them. He pressed the button next to 874—once very quickly, then again for a full two seconds.

As soon as his hand had dropped to his side, the foyer door buzzed from its remote release. He pushed through quickly and walked toward the elevators. An empty car was waiting for him. He stepped in and pressed the button for the top floor, number eight.

The polished brass doors of the elevator slid shut. Above him the noisy old mechanisms of the conveyance carried him gracefully upward.

When the car stopped, the doors did not open. For a moment, Seth thought the elevator was stuck, but then the telephone on the wall began to ring. He picked it up.

"Ridgeway?" It was Yost's voice.

"Of course."

"Step into the middle of the car and take off your coat."

"What?" Seth replied. "Why would—"

"Look in the corner of the elevator," Yost replied. "There's a closed circuit video camera. I just want to make sure everything is as it should be."

Seth hadn't noticed it at first but there it was, a miniature video camera staring down at him. Feeling self-conscious, Ridgeway shed his coat. Moments later, the doors to the elevator slid open and he stepped into an elegant paneled entryway with marble floors. Jacob Yost stood in front of him, holding an H&K MP5A machine pistol.

TWENTY-FOUR

Down on the Rami Strasse, a dark sedan glided through the warm night. Inside, four men peered out the windows, watching for danger. Under their expensively tailored business suits, expensively crafted holsters held deadly weapons. Death passed unnoticed when it masqueraded as wealth in a wealthy city.

"There!" said the man next to the driver. He spoke Russian. The others looked as he pointed to a building at the corner of the Rami Strasse and Zelt Weg. The driver slowed the car and pulled it to a stop at the curb just beyond the entrance to a high-rise construction site.

"Up there, on the top," said the man next to the driver. The other men leaned against the windows of the car and craned their necks upward. They saw lights on the top floor of the building, and, next to the building, the lights and noise of laborers working to build while the weather held.

"Turn right here," said the man next to the driver. "We'll park the car just past the building and walk back."

The driver nodded as he stepped on the accelerator and pulled into the thin evening traffic.

"Put that away," Seth said as he stepped from the elevator. He was more annoyed than frightened. "I've had enough of people pointing guns at me."

Yost looked at him, cold calculation flickering behind his eyes. He was a computer comparing his memory with the person standing before him. Yost nodded sharply once, then lowered the muzzle of the H&K until it was pointing at the floor.

"Good evening," Yost said with a smile. "I'm sorry for the inconveniences, but they have frequently proven to be of lifesaving importance to my father."

"I'm beginning to understand why," Seth said. Yost gave him a thin, knowing smile, then turned abruptly and walked down the hall. Seth followed him, gazing as he did at the oils and watercolors on the walls. It was like passing through a very narrow but extremely well-endowed museum. As Ridgeway made his way past the procession of paintings, he recognized several of them as works described by the younger Jacob Yost the night before.

Yost had explained then that the extreme security for his father's apartment had been necessary for more than thirty years now, partly because of the value of the paintings, but mostly because of what he had seen and learned at Alt Aussee.

After the war, Yost said, his father made his way back to Zurich from the Austrian salt mines where Hitler had hidden his stolen art. He had also learned to hate the Nazis, hate them with an intensity that only people who are confronted with absolute evil can fully understand.

In the days after the war, Yost said his father sent word to the right people that he was interested in buying the art that many of the SS were using to barter their way to freedom. He also hinted that he had connections that would get former Nazis with the right amount of money to safe places. With two other friends who had been through similar experiences, the senior Yost invited the fugitive Nazis to his shop for the purpose of examining their stolen works of art. While Yost examined the works, the visitors were taken to a room and executed by Yost's two associates.

The macabre scheme had worked for nearly a decade. Secrecy had always been on their side. Nazis came to them one by one, by referral and word of mouth. And when a fugitive disappeared and was never seen again by his former associates, they all assumed that Yost had again succeeded in getting one of the Kameradren to safety.

The system broke down in July 1949 when two former SS Oberleutnants showed up at the door of the shop and demanded that they both be processed together. One of them smelled a rat and managed to escape. Since then, the younger Yost had explained, his father had been in danger from men who—though now themselves too old to kill—were wealthy and powerful enough to hire the best of killers.

Yost had returned as many of the works of art as he could to the original owners, but many of them remained unclaimed, their owners dead or untraceable. The orphan works had allowed his father to expand the business from a modest framing shop to an exclusive art gallery.

"These are his favorites," Yost said, stopping at the end of the hall and raising his arms in a motion that took in the art on the walls. "He always kept the best of the orphan pieces for himself."

Seth stopped and opened his mouth to speak, but Yost turned quickly and opened a door at the end of the hallway. "Please step in."

Seth stepped through the doorway into a book-lined study. Puddles of yellowish light illuminated a large library table carpeted with opened books and pads of notes, their pages partially covered in a small, shaky but still precise handwriting.

At the far end of the room, sitting in a wing-backed chair in front of a welcoming fire that burned in a marble-mantled fireplace, rested an old man, his blanket-covered legs propped up on an ottoman. His chair was separated from an identical one to his left by a low piecrust table cluttered with books, papers, and a decanter half filled with amber fluid. The old man was reading a thick hardcover book.

"Father?" Yost called out from the door. The old man in the chair laid the book in his lap and turned toward them.

"Yes, Jacob?"

"Your visitor. Mr. Ridgeway."

The elder Yost adjusted his glasses as he looked up at Seth and blinked several times.

"Well, come and sit down, Mr. Ridgeway," the elder Yost said impatiently. "I hope you're not planning to linger by the door there until you're as old as I."

The younger Yost nodded his head toward the matching wing-backed chair next to his father, and Ridgeway moved forward and stopped next to the old man. He was dressed in a warm-looking wool robe tied at the sash. The bottoms of pajamas protruded from beneath the hem of the robe. His feet were clad in slippers. Seth looked closely at him and found his round, fleshy face closer to that of the two sons who managed the gallery than to his eldest son, the lean Swiss army colonel. As Ridgeway leaned over to extend his hand, he heard the old man's son back quietly out of the room and shut the door behind him.

"Mr. Ridgeway." Jacob Yost took Seth's hand and shook it with a surprisingly firm grip. "Welcome to Zurich; welcome to my home. I apologize for not getting up, but the arthritis in my knees has grown savage of late."

Seth expressed his sympathy and sat down in the chair to Yost's left. As he did, he noticed Yost's hand resting on the arm of the chair. It was horribly disfigured and scarred and lacked a thumb. Seth politely averted his eyes, but not before Yost had seen his look of shock. He smiled wryly at Ridgeway.

"This," he held up his left hand, "is part of my story. But first I want to hear yours." Yost shifted in his chair to be more comfortable as he looked at Seth. "As I understand it, you are looking for your wife, the woman who is supposed to have a painting known as *The Home of the Lady Our Redeemer*?"

Seth nodded. "She disappeared six months ago, from our room at the Eden au Lac."

"I have heard," Yost said. Yost's eyes seemed to turn inward for a moment.

In the silence left by his pause, the study became filled with the pops and crackles of the wood fire and with the steady rumble of the crane just outside the window. Seth looked toward the window and through the sheer curtains saw the arm of the crane as it passed by almost at window level.

Finally Yost pulled himself from his reverie. "I shall never forget the picture," he said. "And I will never forget the men who brought it in to me." He stopped abruptly. "But that, too, is part of my story. And I want to hear yours first, so please, begin."

While Seth related his account of the past six months, Yost pulled a pouch of tobacco from under the pile of papers on the side table. Seth noticed the packet was stamped with the name of the tobacconist just down the Rami Strasse. As Seth spoke, Yost pulled a large briar pipe from the folds of his robe and carefully filled, tamped, and lit it. Fragrant plumes of smoke drifted up from the bowl of the pipe and wafted mostly toward the fireplace.

Seth told him about his search in Zurich, about Rebecca Weinstock, about the killers in Los Angeles, the killers in Amsterdam, and the men who now looked for him in Zurich. Before the story was over, Yost had refilled his pipe twice.

"I'm sorry for my outburst in your gallery yesterday," Seth said. "I'll be happy to pay for the damage."

"Don't be sorry," Yost chuckled. "It's the most exciting thing that has happened to those two spoiled idiots in their entire pampered lives." He laughed again. "Jacob"—he tilted his head toward the door of the study—"is the only one of my sons with any brains at all. And he takes things far too seriously." Yost sighed.

Yost leaned over to knock the dottle of his pipe against an enormous glass ashtray. He scraped and poked at the bowl with a pipe tool and finally sat up to face Seth again.

"Nothing you've told me is surprising," Yost said. "So I suppose I should tell you why I'm not surprised."

He paused while he refilled the bowl of the pipe again.

"It began in 1939, when a man brought the painting into my frame shop. It was summer and I was just out of the university and working for my father. I had taken a degree in art history and had intended to become an expert in restoration.

"The visitor conducted himself with the officiousness of a minor functionary employed by important people," remembered Yost. "He stepped from a black limousine and brought the unframed picture into the shop. I was unimpressed by this uninspiring little scene painted on a small piece of wood and smelling of fresh paint. It was an unexciting sort of painting, created with skill but no genius. The man wanted the picture framed by evening. It was an unusual request, but not an impossible one. I finished it before the deadline with no trouble.

"I later found out that the man worked for none other than Hermann Goering. The painting was a present for Goering's boss, Adolf Hitler.

"As the European war intensified, my family followed Goering with interest, fascinated in a black sort of way that he had actually been that close to us. But Goering was of more than academic interest to some of my relatives who had settled in Salzburg.

"My aunt, a sister on my father's side, had married an art dealer there in twenty-eight. Life deteriorated after Hitler's annexation of Austria and her husband had been drafted and killed in action. In forty-three I was sent to Salzburg by my father to see if I could get her back to Switzerland.

"But before I could leave Salzburg with my aunt, German soldiers arrived. They were canvassing art galleries, university art departments, and museums, looking, they said, for 'patriotic citizens' to help care for priceless works of art that were arriving daily in Munich from all over Europe."

Yost told Seth that he and his aunt tried to explain to the pigheaded soldiers that the true art expert, her husband, had been killed as a lowly private in the Wehrmacht. That was all right, said the soldiers who knew more about scrubbing garbage cans than fine art, certainly Yost's aunt had learned something from her husband that would be useful, and would she and her nephew stop wasting their time and please get into the trucks out front for the short drive back to Munich.

His aunt died of pneumonia in December of 1943, but Yost continued to work in Hitler's central collecting point in Munich, cataloging and caring for paintings that arrived from all over Europe by truck, train, and airplane.

"I was fairly well treated," Yost continued. "I got a ration book, and an apartment to share with three other workers from the central collecting point. They even paid me a salary. I was told by the Gestapo that they knew about my father, knew where he lived, and if I tried to escape, 'something would happen' to Father. I didn't think the Gestapo had enough people to worry about people like me, but I took no chances."

Yost grimaced as he tried to stretch a stiff leg. "Whether it was because my work was so good, or perhaps because I had written a letter to Goering to deplore the sorry state in which the art was being stored at the central collecting point, I came to the attention of the men around Hitler responsible for the art. Among them was Hans Reger, director of the central collecting point, who singled me out for more and more responsibility."

A knock at the door interrupted Yost's story.

"Come in," he called. The door opened moments later and the younger Jacob Yost entered with a tray of sandwiches, beer, and sparkling water. "I thought you might be getting hungry," he said.

Instinctively Seth looked at his watch. It was nearly 9:30. The time had vanished swiftly.

"Thank you," said the senior Yost. Seth also nodded his appreciation as the son cleared off the table between the wing-backed chairs and set the tray down on it. He poured the beer from tall brown bottles into heavy lead crystal mugs and then left the room, closing the door behind him.

The room was silent for several moments as the two men surveyed the tray and then began to help themselves. Seth felt his stomach rumble at the sight of the food and suddenly realized how hungry he had become.

After they had settled back into their chairs, Yost resumed his story.

"I was gradually given more and more responsibility," he said, washing down a mouthful of liverwurst sandwich with a swallow of beer. "I had, after all, spent my college career—all my life, in fact—learning to care for fine art. But I was lonesome for my family and constantly afraid of both the SS and the Gestapo. But I threw myself into the work. After all, I wasn't for Hitler as much as I was for the preservation of the art of the ages. I didn't care who had the art. I just knew that I would never forgive myself if I let these works of the masters deteriorate."

He looked vaguely into the fire, as if he saw the works painted with brightly dancing brushes of flame. "They were all there, you know." His voice took on a dreamy nostalgia. "Titian, Rembrandt, Leonardo, Rubens . . . all of them." Yost seemed to mourn for a bittersweet lost memory. "Only the curators at the world's most renowned museums ever have an opportunity to care for so many of the masters."

The Nazis in charge of the Sonderauftrag Linz—Hitler's art-looting task force—mistook Yost's enthusiasm for the art for enthusiasm for their cause. Yost did nothing to discourage their misapprehension, for it gave him more responsibility, privileges, luxuries, freedom. That freedom allowed him to make contact with Resistance fighters, and through them to get word to the Allies that the world's greatest concentration of art treasures was being housed in warehouse-like conditions in the center of Munich.

"As the Allied bombers grew closer and closer to Munich, I lobbied to have the artwork moved from Munich to safer quarters. I suggested the salt mines in nearby Austria. The idea appealed particularly to the SS, since it fit in with their Wagnerian notions of holding out to the last man in the rugged mountains. For the more realistic among the SS, it appealed even more, since they correctly felt it would be easier for them to loot the works of art to use for barter.

"I made trip after trip to the Salzkammergut region of Austria, and set up my headquarters in Alt Aussee so as to be convenient to the many salt mines nearby.

"I had a small cottage by the shore of the Alt Aussersee," he said, as he drained the last of the beer from his mug. "It was just off the main road which ran between Alt Aussee and Bad Aussee. There was a church nearby, a Catholic church whose priest was a man named Hans Morgen.

"Of course, in a small Austrian town," Yost continued, "the village priest is an important figure, and I quickly grew to know Morgen well."

Morgen was initially suspicious of Yost and his Nazi connections. But as their acquaintance grew into genuine friendship, Morgen began to take him increasingly into his confidence. Not long after, Yost learned that Morgen was a linchpin of the local Resistance movement. Yost, deprived of his Resistance contacts still in Munich, began to pass information through Morgen.

"He was a truly heroic figure," Yost said with admiration. "He risked his life daily, unlike so many in the Catholic Church who supported Hitler either actively or by their inaction. I was timid, yet he was graceful enough to make me feel that my role was important."

The last days of the war, Yost continued, had been insane. As the sounds of Allied artillery and bombing echoed just over the mountains, many of the Nazis in charge of the caches of art stored in the mines panicked. One of them, a half-mad colonel in charge of a mine in the hills above Bad Aussee, made plans to blow up the priceless contents of the mine rather than "have it fall into the hands of the Jews."

Feverishly, the colonel had his men drag five-hundred-pound bombs into the mine's tunnels and place them next to statuary by Leonardo da Vinci and paintings by Van Dyck. The bombs were in place when Yost met with Morgen. All the colonel was waiting for was a demolition expert to come and remove the impact fuses from the normally airborne bombs, then replace them with fuses that could be detonated on the ground.

Late one night, a team of men showed up at Yost's cottage with a knapsack full of plastic explosive and fuses. Before dawn could replace the candlelight in the room, Yost had learned how to set the charge and its timer.

"The next day," Yost related, as he tried to make himself more comfortable, "I put the charges in my briefcase and made an excuse to visit the mine. Just before I left, I set the timer and left my briefcase by the entrance of the mine just as the Resistance men had instructed me."

Yost's explosives blew up the entrance of the mine without harming any of the paintings and prevented the colonel's demolition expert, or anyone else, from reaching the bombs to install detonators.

Days later, Yost received a desperate message from Morgen, delivered by a small boy whose mother ran the inn in the village.

"Morgen had always been so calm," Yost said, "but when I read the message he had left at my cottage, I could read the hysteria in his writing, the extreme anxiety in the wildness of his penmanship. He had a terrible secret, the note said. Something about a relic stored in a salt mine near Habersam Mountain in the hills above Alt Aussee.

"I knew nothing about the mine, which naturally aroused my curiosity. I started making inquiries. The questions I asked nearly killed me and Hans." Yost's face had grown long with remembered sorrow, as if the weight of the memory had stretched his face out of shape.

Yost's questions brought him to the attention of the SS commander of the secret mine at Habersam Mountain. An SS Oberleutnant was dispatched to Yost's cottage to question him.

Yost had not yielded to the Oberleutnant's threats and finally found himself handcuffed to the heavy iron bed as they waited for Morgen to come.

Just before dawn there had been the sounds of artillery from the direction of Bad Aussee. The Allies were coming soon; Yost could read the news from the worried way the Oberleutnant paced the floor of the cottage. Then, just after the sky had turned blood red with the dawn, a thunderous explosion rumbled off Habersam Mountain and rattled the windows of Yost's cottage.

"I strained to see what was happening," Yost said. "I must have stood with my face to the window for an hour or more, staring out at the stark flat whiteness of the frozen lake."

Finally he saw people. At first, they were too far away to recognize. But as they grew closer, Yost could make out a lone figure pursued by soldiers in uniform. And to his horror, he realized the figure being pursued was Morgen.

The SS Oberleutnant walked into the bedroom, his face covered with the first smile he had worn since they had heard the Allied artillery earlier in the still dim morning. "We will have some answers soon, no?" the Oberleutnant jested.

Yost had been sure they had killed Morgen when he heard the crack of a pistol and saw the black-robed priest fall into a snowdrift. The band of killers grew closer to Morgen when he slowly staggered to his feet and turned toward them. Yost stood, his heart wound like a spring, as Morgen raised his hands above his head and staggered back toward the killers, who had stopped, momentarily stunned by their quarry's unexpected action.

Then he watched as one of the killers raised his gun and aimed it at Morgen.

"I'll never forget what I saw next," Yost told Seth. "It was a miracle, nothing but a miracle."

Before the killer could pull the trigger, he had been shot dead. From a knoll by the lake, there was gunfire, and finally a huge explosion that blew great slabs of the lake's ice up into the air. When it all settled down, Morgen was alive and his pursuers, to a man, were dead or dying.

"Your friend is lucky," the SS Oberleutnant had said to Yost. "But he won't escape this." He pulled out his 9mm Luger and brandished it before Yost's face. Then, without commenting further, he walked from the bedroom. Yost heard his boots as he crossed the living room, then the slam of the door as the Nazi walked out onto the cottage's tiny porch.

"I screamed at Morgen to go back," Yost said, "but he couldn't hear me." As Ridgeway listened to Yost's story of what followed, the sandwich he had eaten grew into a greasy knot in his gut.

"I could see Morgen coming closer and closer," Yost said. "He was staggering through the snow toward the cottage with no idea that the Oberleutnant was waiting for him.

"I suppose the Oberleutnant had originally come with the intention of interrogating the two of us, but with the approach of the Allied troops just over the hill I think he changed his mind and decided to kill us to save time."

Yost grimaced as he shifted his legs on the ottoman. "There was an insanity in those last days. It gripped all of us, caused us to do things that . . . well, I suppose it would be impossible to make you fully understand."

Yost knew that after the SS officer killed Morgen, he would probably come back into the cottage and kill him. So it was as much for his own survival as Morgen's that Yost stretched as far as his handcuffed arms would allow, and managed to smash the mirror fastened to the wall over a small wooden bureau.

"I took the largest shard of the broken mirror," Yost said now as he lifted his mutilated left hand for Ridgeway to see, "and cut away at the flesh and the tendons and the muscles of the thumb on my left hand."

Like a desperate animal chewing off a paw or limb caught in a jaw trap, Yost hacked at his left thumb until it came free and allowed his hand to slip free of the handcuffs. Then, without bothering to bind the wound, Yost charged out of the cottage after the Oberleutnant.

"I don't remember feeling any pain," Yost recalled as he looked at his scarred and twisted hand with fresh wonder in his eyes. "But I remember the frustration I felt as I ran out the front door, I still held the bloody shard of the mirror in my right hand."

Yost saw the Oberleutnant standing at the end of the porch, his Luger raised; he saw Morgen round the corner toward the door. Yost ran toward the Oberleutnant, the jagged bloody shard of glass raised over his head like a dagger.

The SS officer aimed his Luger carefully at Morgen's head. Morgen froze, his face a mask of weary resignation.

"I heard the shot just instants before the point of the glass dug into the Oberleutnant's back." Yost shook his head sadly as he spoke. "Just another second, perhaps half a second, and the Oberleutnant would never have been able to fire."

Yost pulled the glass from the Nazi's neck and stabbed him again and again. The officer went down, spurting blood from severed arteries shining bright crimson in the snow.

"I don't remember much after that," Yost said, "except that after the Nazi was down, I went to look at Hans." A pained look washed over Yost's face. "He had been horribly wounded in the head. I could see parts of the gray matter through the hole in his skull.

"I must have gone crazy then, because my memory is blacked out. I don't remember anything until an American soldier pulled me off the Oberleutnant's body. He had to slap me and knock the mirror fragment from my hand." Yost looked Ridgeway directly in the eyes. "The American soldier told me later that when he'd first seen me, I was straddling the Oberleutnant's chest with my knees and was stabbing at his eyes." Yost's voice grew faint. "He . . . the Oberleutnant . . . was still alive. The American soldier told me he could hear the screams as I continued stabbing."

Yost shook his head. "Insanity. I suppose the only thing a sane person can do in wartime is go insane."

He fell silent for a long moment. Only the sounds of popping knots in the fireplace logs and the rumbles of the crane at the construction site next door broke the silence. They did not hear the whir of the elevator motor as it leaped to life, carrying the car to its summons in the lobby, where four men in expensively tailored business suits waited.

TWENTY-FIVE

T the ceiling panels of Yost's private elevator car littered its floor. Inside were four men. Two of them attached shaped explosive charges to the closed door.

"Carefully," said the man who had been sitting next to the driver in the black sedan. He was clearly the man in charge. "After the disaster at the warehouse, this must go perfectly."

One of the men had crawled on top of the elevator car and crouched there, watching the activity below. The disconnected wires of the closed-circuit television camera dangled beside its blind electronic eye.

"Make sure the charges are attached firmly, and then pack the modeling clay around it, just as firmly," said the man in charge. "We want to make sure it explodes outward. Otherwise . . ." His voice trailed off, his meaning clear. The charges could as easily kill them as blow in the doors. Setting shaped charges was an art, not a science.

The man in charge inspected his men's work carefully and finally gave his approval.

"All right. Everybody up on top of the car."

With help from the man who had already climbed through the ceiling of the car, the men struggled up and crouched amid the machinery.

"Be careful of the counterweights," the man in charge said, pushing the button for the top floor. As the car started to climb, he unrolled the detonator wires and handed them to one of his men on top of the car. Then, with a helping hand from one of them, he climbed up to join them.

Yost's son had come in to clear away the remains of the sandwiches and to order refills of beer. Seth declined. His stomach already felt queasy enough.

"After the American slapped me," Yost continued after his son had once more left the room, "I awakened, as if from a dream. I looked at what I had done to the Nazi and suddenly got very faint, probably from the blood I had lost from the amputation of my thumb.

"Morgen and I stayed in touch over the years," Yost said. "Later, when he had recovered from much of his amnesia, Morgen told me the story of what he had seen in the secret mine at Alt Aussee. You see, he was afraid he would die, and that the secret of the mine would die with him. So he told me all of the story."

"Which was?" Seth interrupted eagerly.

"I think I'd rather Hans Morgen told you himself," Yost said.

"Morgen? Is he here in Zurich?"

Yost shook his head. "He's in Alt Aussee. Or he will be by the time you get there."

"But—"

"Listen carefully to me," Yost interrupted. "The picture you have . . . the painting?"

Seth nodded.

"It's the key to everything that's happened to you, to your wife—and to me, and to Hans, over the past forty years."

"How?" Seth asked. "I don't understand."

"You will soon enough," Yost assured him. "But right now you must pay attention to my instructions carefully. You'll only get one chance. Do you understand?" He looked sternly at Seth, who nodded his acknowledgment.

"You must take the picture to the Thule Gesellschaft Bank. It's on the Bahnhofstrasse, just north of the Paradeplatz. Ask for the officer in charge of the floor. Give him the painting and tell him you wish access to your safe deposit box. He will know what to do."

"But what does that have to do with—?"

Yost shook his head. "I don't know. I really wish I could tell you. In the forty years that Hans and I have tracked that painting, we have only been able to learn that it is the key to a safe deposit box and that the contents of that box are of paramount importance to obtaining the Passion of Sophia."

"What? How does that—"

"Morgen will explain," Yost said.

"Why do I need to wait? Please tell me now," Ridgeway persisted. "Everything I can learn might help me find Zoe. Finding her is more important to me than anything that's been buried in a mine for five decades."

Yost smiled broadly. "But you don't have to look further," he said. "Your wife is here in Zurich. I spoke with her just an hour or so before you arrived."

Seth jerked forward in his chair as if he had been jolted by high voltage.

"Zoe? In Zurich? How did . . . why—why did she call you? Why didn't you tell me sooner? Where is she?"

Yost raised his hand for silence. "One question at a time, one at a time please." He paused and moistened his dry chapped lips with his tongue.

"She called me because I am sure that Willi Max mentioned my name to her," Yost began. "She knows my connection to the art at Kreuzlingen, and not just the fact that I have framed nearly every piece that Max had . . . collected. But she called me not about art, but in hopes that I had heard from you." He smiled.

"But why didn't you tell me about her sooner?"

"Because I knew that you would hear nothing else of what I said if I had told you that first," Yost replied. "And what I have told you is extremely important to me, to your wife, and to the rest of the world."

Seth stared blankly at Yost through wide, stunned eyes.

"Where?" Seth's voice was cracked and faint with joy. "Where is she?"

"At your hotel," Yost replied. "At the Eden au Lac."

Abruptly Seth stood up. "All this time . . ." His voice was full of wonder. "We've been apart all this time, and we wind up at the same hotel."

He stood silently for a long moment, his eyes gazing past the depths of the flames in the hearth. Then he snapped out of it.

"Thank you for your time and your hospitality, Mr. Yost. I—"

"Wait." Yost's face was suddenly filled with fear. "Promise me you will go to Alt Aussee to meet with Hans. He's put himself in a great deal of danger to meet with you."

"I—"

Seth was about to say that he would have to ask Zoe about it when the floor shuddered beneath his feet, followed by the rumbling roar of an explosion.

"Damn construction crews," Yost bellowed. "They've hit the side of the building with that crane again!"

But it was not the crane. Suddenly, from beyond the stout oaken doors that led to the study, they heard the short choppy bursts of the younger Yost's H&K MP5A, then the softer coughing responses of silenced automatic weapons.

"Father!" They heard the young Yost scream. "They're here! They're here." And suddenly they knew the son was dead.

"Quick! Close the door, Mr. Ridgeway," Yost said. "It is very strong."

From the hallway Seth heard running feet and the sound of men's hushed and hurried voices.

Seth leaped to his feet and lunged toward the oaken door. Just as the door-knob rattled, his hand found the latch to the dead bolt and turned it swiftly.

Ridgeway heard curses from the other side of the door, followed by the rattle of hinges as someone threw himself against it. The door groaned, but held fast.

Suddenly Seth thought about guns, familiar-sounding guns, guns on a boat on the other side of the world. And then, just as now, a fantastic tale from a woman interrupted by unseen assailants. And as his thoughts flashed back, the memory of slugs splintering their way through the decks of the *Valkyrie* caused his adrenaline to surge.

Seth dove away and threw himself on the floor just as the interior of the door's paneling exploded in a hail of slugs and long jagged oaken splinters.

"Get down!" Seth yelled as he rolled across the floor. He came to a stop on his hands and knees and looked toward Yost's chair. The old man had rolled himself out of his chair and was crawling painfully toward a telephone that rested on a small table by the window.

Slugs continued to slam through the door—their velocity mostly spent— and fly through the room at random.

At least one of the slugs maintained its momentum after its collision with the door; or perhaps it passed through an opening left by a preceding slug. As Seth watched Yost crawling across the rich Persian carpet that covered the fine hardwood floors, the slug slapped meanly into the old man's side just below his armpit. The spot turned red almost immediately as the artery began to gush warm and red.

Yost's body stiffened and lifted under the bullet's impact. At that instant, time seemed distended, stretched to a point of infinite slowness. Then the scene speeded up and Yost's body flew through the air, crashing into the rack of brass andirons, brushes, and other fireplace paraphernalia on the hearth.

Seth scrambled on his hands and knees back to the chair where he had left his coat. He pulled out the Magnum and ducked behind the chair just as the door to the study burst open.

The first man through the door shouted something in a language Seth couldn't understand. Russian? The man took one look at Yost's body lying by the hearth and fired his gun repeatedly into the lifeless form, causing it to jerk backward like a macabre puppet.

"Bastards!" Seth yelled as he raised the Magnum and fired at the lead attacker, a thin man in a well-tailored suit. The slug caught the man in the midsection, doubling him up and lifting him off his feet. The bullet passed through the man's intestine, shattered his spinal column, and exited from the small of his back. He was dead before he hit the floor.

Other shouts filled the silence. He was sure the language was Russian. How had they found him? How had they traced him despite Yost's precautions?

But there was no time to think, only time to react and survive. He fired a second shot at the men as they moved away from the study's doorway. Their jumbled voices filled the hallway as they sought to regroup.

Anticipating their quick return, Seth scrambled past Yost's lifeless body to the telephone. It was dead.

He was cut off. Alone. Both Yosts were dead. He fought the high-voltage panic that ricocheted through him.

Damn you, God! Why me? Give me a fucking break!

Scrambling back to his coat, Seth pulled out the handful of extra ammunition he had brought along. A dozen more rounds. Four left in the cylinder. Sixteen rounds total. Against? How many men?

Moments later a withering crossfire tore through the room, ripping at the floor, the ceilings, and the walls. Seth shrank back as the slugs' deadly invisible fingers clutched at the space around him. He turned his chair on its side and huddled behind it, but it offered scant protection.

The years of training at the police academy and on the streets came back to him. Reflexes, move quickly, survive, survive.

Seth fired twice at the doorway, once toward each side, and then lunged toward the window. He flipped a heavy marble-topped table on its side and scrambled behind it as a train of slugs tracked its way across the room and took chips out of stone.

Frantic shouts came from the hallway and moments later one of the men flashed past the doorway to the other side. Seth shot at him, and then silently cursed at himself. They had suckered him into wasting a bullet. Even if they spoke Russian, they could count rounds too.

A second later, he heard a loud thunk and the sound of an object rolling across the floor. Seth scanned the room and spotted the smooth round metallic luster of a small hand grenade just inches away from the table.

Desperately, Seth dropped the Magnum and sprang for the grenade. He scooped it up in his hand, felt its heavy malevolent power, and like a small animal paralyzed by the sight of a rattler about to strike, hesitated for what seemed like an eternity. A split second later he lobbed the grenade back toward the open doorway and threw himself face first behind the table.

The concussion lifted the table and slammed it against him, pinning him to the wall. For an instant, he heard nothing but the ringing of bells, then the yawning roar he remembered from the first day of explosives training at the academy when he had forgotten to wear the protective earmuffs the department issued.

Beyond the veil of thunder, Seth heard voices. He struggled against the heavy marble table that had saved his life and managed to shove it away just as two men burst through the door, their weapons at the ready. One of them saw him move and fired a short burst at him. Seth ducked behind the table; marble shrapnel showered the room as he scrambled for his gun. Where was it?

Frantically Seth searched the area around him as he heard the footsteps of the men growing closer. Another burst of silenced automatic weapons fire chipped away at the table, sending fragments of marble flying across the room.

There! Next to the wall he spotted the Magnum. Desperately he tumbled for it, then picked it up in his hands. He turned and saw the head of the closest man appear over the top of the pockmarked tabletop. The man raised his gun.

Seth turned and fired the round in the cylinder. The left half of the man's face disappeared, exposing his sinuses and the base of his brain. He made a gargling sound before he hit the floor.

He heard the hurried footsteps of the other man exit the room. Quickly, Seth thought. He had to move quickly. They wouldn't make the same mistake with the grenade twice. Next time they'd hold it long enough to prevent him from throwing it back.

Desperately he searched the room for an exit. There were only the door and the window. Cold air poured in through the panes of glass broken by the explosion. He had seconds at most before the men in the hallway threw in another grenade.

He tucked the Magnum with its spent rounds into his belt at the small of his back and stood up. He brushed the curtain back with a swipe of his hand, and stared out at eight stories of black empty space. Directly ahead of him, twenty-five or thirty yards away, was the lighted operator's compartment of the construction crane he had seen from the street. The arm of the crane was motionless. Seth's eyes followed the arm to its end and then down. The cables from the crane's arm ran down to a metal hopper being filled with concrete from a truck that had backed into the site. The men continued to work. Men guided a hose from the truck to the hopper. Others stood by steadying the hopper. The deafening roar of the construction site had masked the firefight above.

Frantically searching for a ledge, a toehold, he watched as the concrete hopper began to climb as the crane's cables took up slack. Then the arm began to swing toward him. The arm slowly gathered speed.

What was it Yost had said right after the explosion? The crane. He had cursed, thinking the crane had hit his building again. Then, as Seth watched the arm swing ponderously toward him, he heard a familiar clink in the hallway. What was it?

The crane's arm grew closer. *Don't let it stop, God. Please don't let it stop.*

Seth crouched next to the windowsill waiting for his chance.

Then the clink in the hallway came back to him. Shit! It was the sound of a grenade pin hitting the floor.

The crane's arm moved closer; twenty feet away, fifteen, ten. Seth crawled up on the windowsill. Five feet—

He heard the grenade thud against the floor. He took one look downward at the blackness below him and then leaped at the crane's swinging latticework arm.

He felt the grenade before he heard it. Its shock wave lifted him and pushed him forward, slamming him into the arm's gridwork. Behind him he heard the explosion dimly, its blast muffled by the powerful engines of the crane and by the trucks below and the hammerings of rivet guns on an adjacent construction site.

Seth extended his arms to soften his trajectory but the explosive force of the grenade hurled him against the crane's metal girders with an unmerciful force. He felt the muscles in his arms and shoulders strain as he reached for a handhold and tried to keep his head safe at the same time. He almost succeeded.

Flailing wildly, the crook of his knee jammed itself into the angle formed by the crane arm's triangular framework. For what seemed like aeons, Seth hung upside down, carried through the night on the arm of the crane eight floors above the ground. He felt the Magnum slide out of his waistband.

Dizzily, he looked down at the darkness eighty feet blow. Then a warm thick fluid dripped into his eyes, smearing the vision. It was several moments before he realized it was his own blood draining from his nose. He reached up to wipe the blood away.

He heard shouts from below now. Men on the ground who had spotted him hanging there. The crane was slowing.

No. God, please. Don't let them stop it.

With an almost superhuman effort he reached above him and pulled himself up until he was straddling the lower beam of the crane's arm. As he did, two faces appeared at the window to Yost's apartment, less than fifty feet away. They looked down, trying to determine where the body had landed.

The crane moved another thirty feet away from them, dragged by the momentum of the hill hopper of concrete, and then stopped. Seth wiped at the blood that flowed freely from his nose and tried to clear his head. The blow to his face had thrown off his sense of balance. He tried to move forward and the world spun. For a moment he thought the crane had started up again. And then things stabilized.

Above him Seth heard someone shout. He looked at the window to Yost's apartment and saw one of the men pointing at him. Simultaneously, both men raised their weapons. Despite his shaky equilibrium, he scrambled through the framework of the arm toward the operator's compartment.

The operator must have seen what was happening. The crane's powerful engine roared and the arm began to move again, making Seth a moving target, carrying him into the darkness away from his assailants.

There was more shouting from the window, and moments later the glass enclosure of the crane operator's compartment exploded under a massive assault of gunfire. Seth watched the crane operator jerk and dance and then collapse onto the controls. A split second later, the crane engine roared. The arm's dizzying circle accelerated faster and faster, threatening to sling Seth off.

Heart pounding, muscles strained to the breaking point, Seth clambered over the girders, fighting the increasing centrifugal force and equally aware that he'd be an easy target once he moved again into range of the killers' guns. Bullets pinged off the steelwork around him as he reached the vertical support tower. He half climbed, half fell toward the ground.

At the bottom of the crane, brawny arms hustled him away as the crane arm spun wildly, sparking as the end of the boom grazed Yost's building. Cries of alarm echoed through the construction site as a concrete counterbalance weight plummeted to the ground and demolished a section of scaffolding just instants after it had been cleared of workers.

Blood from his nose covered Seth's face and neck and matted his hair as he stumbled amid the panicked mob fleeing the berserk high-rise crane, which wobbled and twisted as the boom accelerated like a wounded carnival ride. Steel support cables parted then like cannon shots. Seth watched in horror as the vertical support column buckled. Then he sprinted into the night.

TWENTY-SIX

Behind the Eden au Lac, a red panel ambulance with white crosses on its sides and doors drew up to the service entrance. In the vehicle's backseat, KGB Colonel Molotov sat somberly and for the hundredth time cursed the bad luck that had resulted in his drawing this assignment. The woman had escaped. He had been put on notice by his superiors that any further failure would not be tolerated. He was to recapture the woman, at any cost, and her husband as well. The only bit of luck he had had was the telephone call intercepted by their agent in Paris, which told them that the woman's husband was in Zurich. He looked at his watch: his other team should have captured him by now. Molotov knew that his slate would be wiped clean if he could just get his hands on the painting. And that was what he intended to do.

Molotov took another look at his copy of Seth's passport photo, then whispered to the two men in the front seat and the man sitting beside him. "You're ambulance attendants. Remember that. And remember too that we want Mr. and Mrs. Ridgeway alive. Wound them if you must, but don't kill them. They have something that we need."

In her room, Zoe hung up the telephone. "I don't understand. Where could he be?" She looked at Stratton and Cartiere as she walked back to the table in the sitting room. "I've called his room a thousand times. We've left messages on the door, in his mailbox . . . and still nothing." She stared disconsolately at her feet. "Where could he be?"

The remains of a rack of lamb rested on the table. Zoe sat down and stared morosely out the window. It was ironic, she thought. Here she was again in the real world, the world she had longed for all these months, and still there was something missing, something that made the world real for her. She realized then how much of her existence was defined by her relationship with Seth. Until they were reunited, she would continue to feel that she had not returned to the person she had once been.

Cartiere broke into the flow of her thoughts. "I'm sure he'll call soon.

Maybe he's Christmas shopping." It was the longest sentence she had heard from him since they had met.

Zoe tried to force a smile. "I hope you're right." Her voice was so quiet the two men had to lean over to catch her words. "Of course. It's Christmas." She looked at each man in turn and then directed her gaze inward.

At that moment the telephone began to ring. Zoe picked it up.

"Hello?"

"Zoe?" It was Seth Ridgeway. "Zoe, is that really you?"

"Seth!" Zoe felt her voice crack, her hands begin to tremble. "Oh, God! It's you. Seth, I'm so happy to hear your voice. Oh, God," and she began to weep softly. "I missed you so much, darling. I missed you so much."

The tears of agony she had dammed up for so long rushed forward in a flood of relief.

"Zoe . . . Zoe," Ridgeway's voice came urgently over the earpiece. "Zoe, hold on a minute, I need your help." Zoe felt her heart catch. She could hear his heavy breathing.

"Seth? Where are you?" she asked. "Are you all right?"

Seth looked around him. He stood in a telephone booth on the Gloria-strasse, just across the street from the entrance to the University Hospital. Groups of students, some of them in medical whites, others obviously under-graduates, walked past the booth in clots of two and three. None of them paid him any attention. But that wouldn't last for long. He was sure there would be alerts out for him in minutes.

In the distance, from the direction of Yost's building, he could hear the wail of sirens. "Yeah, I'm fine . . . right now," he replied. "I'm in Zurich and—"

"I know," Zoe interrupted. "But where in Zurich?"

Seth cocked his head to one side, listening intently as the sounds of a siren grew louder. It climbed the steep hill from the direction he had run just minutes ago. "Look, do you have a car?" he asked urgently.

Zoe hesitated. "Yes, I . . . we've got one." George Stratton gave her a questioning look. "It's Seth," she said to Stratton.

"What?" Seth replied.

"I was talking to George Stratton. He works for the government . . . he saved my life."

"He what?" Ridgeway asked. Just then a police car screamed into view, trailed closely by an ambulance. Together, their blinking lights reminded Ridgeway of an alien spacecraft.

"Never mind," Ridgeway said. "Honey, you have got to get me out of here as soon as you can."

"Get you out of where?" Zoe asked.

"I'm just across the street from the University Hospital . . . up on the hill above the Old Town on the east bank. I—"

A second police car rounded the corner slowly, with no flashing lights or siren. The officer in the passenger seat was working a spotlight, playing it along the walls and sidewalks. Had someone spotted him? The car was no more than a hundred yards away, the brilliant beam of the spotlight cutting through the night.

"I've got to go," Seth said. "Meet me at the Großmünster."

"The what?" Zoe asked.

The cop with the searchlight seemed to look right at Seth.

"Großmünster. It's a big church. Ask anybody." Without waiting for a reply, he hung up the receiver and slipped into the night.

TWENTY-SEVEN

The Großmünster," Zoe said as she finished tying her running shoes and started to pull on her coat. "I think that's a church down near the river."

"I know where it is," Stratton snapped. "And I don't need any help to go pick up your husband. I want you to stay here with Rich where you'll be safe." He zipped up his coat and stepped toward the door.

"Damn it," Zoe cursed as she stepped between Stratton and the door. "I'm going to see him and you're not going to stop me from that. I'm not a piece of baggage you can just order around as you like."

Stratton glanced at Cartiere, who stood waiting for directions, then returned his gaze to Zoe.

"I could have Rich detain you until I come back," he said. "But I wouldn't want to do that to him. There's no telling what you might do." He turned once again to Cartiere. "Get your coat," he said. "I'd rather tangle with the KGB than argue with her."

Stratton motioned Zoe to one side as he opened the door into the hallway and peered out.

"It's empty," Stratton said, then looked at Zoe. "This might be dangerous. I want you to promise me you'll follow my orders quickly and without questioning me."

Zoe nodded her head, knowing her assent was the price she must pay to see Seth. She stepped into the hallway, followed closely by Cartiere. She'd make up her own mind when and where to follow Stratton's orders. Cartiere had just closed the door to the suite when the telephone began ringing.

"Hurry up!" Zoe urged Cartiere, as he fumbled for his key. "It might be Seth again."

The telephone rang a third time and then a fourth. On the fifth ring, Cartiere opened the door and Zoe rushed toward the phone on the bedside table.

She snatched the receiver from its cradle. "Hello?" There was no answer.

"Hello? Is anyone there?" She slammed down the receiver. "Damn. Damn. Damn," she cursed. "Too late." She stood by the telephone for a moment.

"Let's go," Stratton called from the hall. She and Cartiere rushed to join him.

KGB Colonel Molotov smiled broadly as he replaced the receiver of the house phone quietly on its cradle. "She's there," he said to the three men standing at his side. "You." Molotov indicated the driver of the car. "Follow me up the stairway." He turned to the other two. "Take the elevator and wait for us there."

Without waiting for confirmation, Molotov bounded up the thickly carpeted stairs, the pain from his head wounds temporarily forgotten.

Rich Cartiere felt the running footsteps through the soles of his feet. "Hold it," he said in a stage whisper as he blocked Zoe and Stratton's advance with one of his massive arms. He pulled up a Mini-Uzi from his shoulder holster and flattened himself against the wall.

"What's wrong?" Stratton asked as he flattened himself against the stairwell wall and motioned to Zoe to do the same.

"Footsteps," Cartiere said. "Running . . . from below."

Stratton paused to listen.

"Maybe it's children playing?" Stratton said. "I don't hear—"

"Children play noisily," Cartiere said. "We should hear more than footsteps."

Cartiere padded silently down the steps, fanning the barrel of the Mini-Uzi before him. Stratton walked half a step behind, brandishing his automatic. Zoe brought up the rear.

Molotov pressed himself into the recess of a door to one of the hotel's rooms. Across the hall, the driver likewise tried to force himself out of sight in the narrow recess. Both had their Czech-made machine pistols at the ready, safeties off.

"Hear them?" Molotov whispered.

"How do you know it's them?" the driver whispered back.

"Instinct," Molotov said. "Why else are they whispering? Why haven't they come down the stairs yet? They've been there an awfully long time. They're being cautious. They heard our footsteps. It has to be."

Cartiere spotted the two men in the corridor just as his feet had begun to leave the last step of the stairs leading onto the second floor. He was a surprisingly fast man for someone of his size, and would have survived had he not hesitated in midstride to hold back Stratton and Zoe with his arm.

"Get back!" Cartiere yelled, as he brought the Mini-Uzi's muzzle to bear on the man standing on the right side of the hallway. He saw the man raise his own weapon, then, out of the corner of his eye, saw another gun in another recessed doorway. Fire and duck; fire and duck; he heard his old drill sergeant screaming at them.

Cartiere squeezed the trigger on the Mini-Uzi, firing a burst that caught the man full across the face and hammered his head against the door. From his position a few feet away, Molotov felt the warm wet splatter of blood against the side of his face as he stepped into the hallway and trained his Czech machine pistol on the large man's torso. Cartiere stiffened as the slugs slapped into his beefy chest and stomach. But Molotov's look of grim satisfaction faded as the large man continued to turn toward him, seemingly unaffected by the gaping wound that turned his shirt bright red.

"Die, damn you," Molotov muttered as his clip ran out. The large man faltered; the muzzle of his gun wavered. But still he stood, and shook his head violently, like a bull waiting for the matador to finish off what the picadors had started.

In horror, Molotov watched the muzzle of the man's gun steady on a line of sight that included Molotov's chest. The KGB colonel–cum–Mafia mobster dropped the Czech machine pistol and leaped to one side just as slugs filled the air where he had been standing. Molotov whipped out his automatic and squeezed off three quick rounds at the huge man's head.

Oh my God! Oh my God! Rich's been shot! Zoe stood rooted in horror, her hand closed tight around the banister. She watched as Stratton moved forward against the wall, trying to reach Cartiere. She watched Cartiere quiver under the impact of the slugs, waver for a moment, then aim his gun and fire.

The next instant she saw two bullets take out the left side of Cartiere's face, leaving a third to rip away the left side of his neck and lay bare the flesh and arteries underneath. Bright red blood fountained from his neck and painted a brilliant crimson rooster tail on the wall as he toppled onto the floor. Shrill, discordant brass and strings filled Zoe's head as she stifled a scream.

Then from the stairway above them, the urgent voices of strangers filled the stairway above. More voices in Russian signaled an ambush. Stratton hesitated just an instant.

"Here!" He thrust a Mini-Uzi into her hands. "Safety's off. Hunker down and blast anybody who comes up the steps." Then he pulled an automatic pistol from his shoulder holster and leaped up the steps two at a time. Stratton gained the top of the stairs and instants later the air was filled with more gunshots, long sustained jackhammerings from two or three different-sounding guns, Zoe couldn't tell how many. Then, suddenly, it was silent save for the low desperate cries of wounded men in mortal pain.

Fear choked off the words in Zoe's throat. Who had died up there? If it was Stratton, she was again all alone. She felt herself tremble.

"Back in your room or I'll blow your head off too!" Zoe recognized Molotov's voice from the corridor below, obviously barking at a curious hotel guest. A door slammed, followed by loud locking sounds. An instant later, Molotov stepped so quickly into her view that he stunned Zoe into a moment of indecision. Stratton's Mini-Uzi hung loosely in her hand next to her thigh, hidden in the shadows and the folds of her coat.

"Don't move," he said in English.

"You!" Zoe said bitterly. Her heart quickened as, in the dimness of the hallway, she made out the features of one of the men from the warehouse. Damn! She was too slow, she cursed silently as her hand closed tightly on the Mini-Uzi, her finger loosely curled around the trigger. Zoe made eye contact and tried to hold his gaze while she raised the gun's muzzle ever so slowly.

Molotov smiled as his eyes locked on hers. "Yes. Me. I've come to collect you."

He walked casually toward her, his pistol hanging loosely in his hand.

At the top of the stairs, Zoe heard more footfalls. Would it be George? Or would it be one of this man's associates? Molotov gained another step while Zoe slowly raised the Mini-Uzi's muzzle, millimeter by slow millimeter.

"You will come with me," Molotov said. Then her movement caught his eye and he spotted the gun. He began to raise his own weapon.

God, please help me, she prayed.

Zoe brought the muzzle up swiftly and squeezed the trigger. The Mini-Uzi exploded into a full-automatic death dance. It bucked and danced and rattled. In front of her, Molotov's torso split open like a smashed melon, disgorging blood and entrails and the smell of fresh warm meat. He collapsed. Instants later, a shadow crawled down the stairwell and reached out for her. Zoe whirled with the gun. George Stratton flattened himself on one side of the stairs.

"Don't," he shouted. "It's me." There was a red stain at the thigh of his trousers. She rushed up the stairs.

"You've been hurt," she said, as she watched him struggle to his feet.

"Nothing serious." He stood for a moment then began to climb the stairs.

"Come on," he said, looking back at her. "We've got to get out of here. No telling if reinforcements are on the way."

They headed back up the stairs. At the top, they passed two dead men on the floor as they rushed back to the suite. Zoe lost no time throwing her newly acquired clothes into a suitcase. She heard Stratton in the next room talking on the telephone in subdued tones. She couldn't understand most of the conversation, but made out Rich's name and the name of the hotel. Stratton hung up the telephone and minutes later they descended to the basement via the service elevator at the end of the hall.

Heaviness filtered into Zoe's heart. She thought of Rich Cartiere and remembered Molotov and how she had prayed for his death. She remembered the two men she had killed at the warehouse, another answer to her prayers. When, she wondered, would God give her a chance to pray for something that didn't cause death and suffering?

Seth Ridgeway pressed himself deeply in the shadows of a darkened doorway and watched the Volvo pull slowly into Großmünsterplatz. His tongue dragged roughly across the bone-dry roof of his mouth. Police cars had already swept past the area twice. Both were marked cars with their sirens wailing.

This Volvo, though, was different. Two people inside, cruising slowly. They were looking for someone. Him? He felt his heart beating loudly. The Volvo's brake lights flashed. The car slowed to a stop across the square, too far away to make out the people inside: they were gray silhouettes behind dark windows.

A moment later Seth watched as the driver's door of the Volvo opened. The man who got out moved like a cop: he bristled with caution, his head moving like a hungry hawk's. Seth could see a weapon in his right hand. The man walked slowly ten or twenty yards behind the car, and then an equal distance in front of it. The man—a cop? Had they found him?—walked over to the passenger's side and leaned down to say something to the person seated there. He then opened the door and stood back to allow the passenger to get out.

Seth felt his heart stop when Zoe got out of the car. The door closed with a solid thunk and she and the man who looked like a cop walked back toward the front of the car and looked around.

Still, Seth did nothing as his heart raced anew. Was it *really* Zoe? The dim streetlights painted her face with shadows, yet . . . yet he saw how she moved, how she stood, how she moved her head when she talked and waved her hands in the air. Suddenly, he felt as if someone had rolled a great rock from his heart. He stepped from the shadows and took the steps one by one, as if he didn't entirely trust his legs anymore. He saw their faces fix on him as he crossed the square. The man who looked like a cop brought his weapon to bear.

"Zoe," cried Seth, no longer able to contain his joy. He began to run.

"Seth?" Zoe said at first, not quite believing it was really he. Then she knew. They met in the middle of the cobbled darkness of Großmünsterplatz.

"Oh God," Zoe cried as she wrapped her arms around him. "Oh God, oh God, I didn't think I'd ever . . . we'd ever . . . that—" Her voice shattered into sobs of elation. "This is a miracle. God's miracle."

Seth looked at her, and felt his heart breaking for all she must have been through. He pulled her close and held her tight against him.

"Zoe, oh, Zoe . . ." Seth's voice cracked. "I'm so glad to see you. I love you so much, so much." His eyes filled with tears.

Unheard now were the sounds of the city: the mournings of sirens, the crashing surf of automotive traffic down on the Limmat Quai, the distant scratching roar of a jet overhead. They all disappeared along with the Großmünster and its Platz and the Volvo and all the police and spies and killers and dead old men. They were alone.

Then the moment was gone. The glare of oncoming headlights galvanized Stratton into action. He rushed to the driver's door of the Volvo and opened it.

"Get in," he yelled. "Hurry." He sat down behind the steering wheel and started the engine. The oncoming headlights grew brighter. Seth and Zoe ran toward the Volvo hand in hand. Stratton felt a pang of envy as he watched them slide into the backseat. He drove away as Seth shut the door.

The approaching car entered the Großmünsterplatz just as the Volvo reached the square's other end at the Oberdorfstrasse. Stratton braked briefly at the corner. He glanced in the rearview mirror, and as be turned right on the Kirche Gasse, noted that the car that had entered the square had emblazoned on its side the insignia of the Zurich police.

TWENTY-EIGHT

Seth Ridgeway awoke, suddenly and disoriented. The strange room frightened him until he reached out with his right hand and found Zoe sleeping next to him. She slept as trustingly as a child, curled up next to him with her head buried in the pillows. He could feel her soft breaths against his bare shoulder.

He relaxed and took in the strange surroundings: the knotty wood on the walls, the open ceiling with its exposed beams, the gray stone fireplace across the room, and the rustic furniture hand painted in the alpine country tradition. Bright morning light, still rosy with the dawn, glowed beyond the fir trees he could see through the window.

His mind raced frantically. Where were they? He remembered their escape from Zurich and Stratton's insistence that they not go near the Eden au Lac, for it was sure to be crawling with police.

They had driven south of Zurich. He remembered passing Zug, then a turn off the main road before getting to Lucerne. The road had gotten mountainous after that, and he remembered a lot of signs directing people to ski slopes and lodges. There was a lake nearby; he remembered that much, a small lake.

The thoughts came more clearly to him now as he woke up. It was a safe house, a chalet near one of the ski slopes. Seth felt his muscles relax as it all came back to him.

Zoe made a small mewing sound in her sleep and snuggled closer to him. He looked at her face and wondered what she was dreaming about. It didn't matter, he thought, as long as it wasn't a nightmare.

She looked so vulnerable, he thought. So fragile. Yet he knew how tough she had had to be to survive her ordeal. Had it changed her? Of course it had, he told himself. Would it change them?

He thought about that one for a long while and finally conceded that the experiences of the past six months couldn't fail to have changed their relationship. He consoled himself with the thought that changes didn't have to be bad.

Gently he touched her; he caressed the outlines of her face, softly ran his hand along her shoulder and up the soft vulnerable curve of her neck where wisps of hair curled in provocative disarray. It was as if by touching her he could retrace the memories and put himself back into the past. He heard her voice from the previous night:

It's a miracle!

Was it? He wondered. Did God have some purpose here, or was there just no damn God and they were being jerked around by chance in a random world? He wanted to thank God, but the sentiment wouldn't come.

Zoe awakened slowly.

She drifted upward through layers of sleep like a diver in no hurry to reach the surface. She caught the world a fragment at a time: first the light gentle touches like kisses on her shoulders and neck, then the bright morning light of the new day.

She stirred and threw her leg across Seth's flat belly, nuzzling closer to him. She felt his hands along her back, caressing, exploring. His touch lingered at the small of her back and then moved lower. She felt herself growing moist. And she felt him growing hard against the back of the leg she had thrown across his belly.

She opened her eyes when he kissed her just behind her left ear. And in her left ear. She quivered.

"Good morning," she said, her voice fuzzy with sleep.

"It sure is," he said.

They kissed, exploring with their tongues like first-time lovers. And then all control vanished.

They made love as if it were the first time . . . or the last. The sun rose in the sky and turned its faint rosy tint into the glaring brilliance of a clear alpine day. But neither of them noticed the passage of time. They were in a place where time could not touch them. It was a place where people never grew old, never suffered, never died. Only a fool would ever trade this place for heaven.

And finally, they slept again, warmed and exhausted and refreshed. Zoe slept as she always had, with her head on Seth's right shoulder, her body pressed into the hard angles of his body. He held her with his right arm and fell asleep with his head resting against hers.

George Stratton's knock at the door sounded like thunder, startling them, wrenching them from a rest they had missed for more than six months.

"Eight o'clock," Stratton said as he rapped gently at the door. "Banks open in two hours. Water's hot for a shower. Breakfast in half an hour."

Seth stretched as he listened to Stratton's footsteps fade down the hallway.

"Cruel bastard," he muttered in a good-natured way. She mumbled a reply into the pillow. He leaned over to kiss her once more before getting up.

"Interpol has an advisory out on you," Stratton said, as the chalet's caretaker cleared away the remains of the extravagant breakfast he had prepared for them.

Stratton looked at Seth. "You're wanted for murder."

Zoe gasped.

"Somebody's pulling strings," Stratton said. "They want you out of circulation."

Seth nodded slowly. It wasn't surprising. He had been too near too many murders to remain unnoticed. He thought of the murders on his boat, Rebecca Weinstock and her chauffeur, Tony Bradford, the massacre in Amsterdam, the killers at Yost's apartment, and the hapless crane operator. Death had scorched a wide, dark path behind him.

"Any details?" Seth asked finally.

"Seems that you were seen near the body of a UCLA professor, Tony Bradford."

"Oh my God," Zoe exclaimed. "How did Tony get tied in with all this?"

"It's a long story," Seth began. "I'd better start at the beginning." He took a deep draught from his coffee mug and then began: "I was sleeping on the boat—" He turned to Zoe. "I couldn't sleep in our house . . . not with you gone. Everything there reminded me of you. It was as if it was haunted." He took a deep breath.

"It was raining like hell one morning and I get this frantic knocking on the companionway."

He told her about Rebecca Weinstock and the killers and the chauffeur and George Stratton.

"The *Valkyrie's* gone, then?" Zoe asked sadly. Seth nodded slowly.

Then he told her about the rest of it: the mysterious motel that was a safe house, the recovery of the painting, and the discovery of Bradford's body. His flight to Amsterdam and the killers who found him there.

"And this priest used the word 'brown'?" Stratton asked. "Are you sure that's what he said?"

Seth nodded. Stratton said he would sure like to know more about this mysterious group of priests in the Vatican.

Except for the occasional interjection or question, Zoe and Stratton remained silent for nearly two hours as Seth related the story of a string of murders that had begun in Marina Del Rey and continued to follow him through the streets of Zurich.

They sat in silence for a long time, listening to the caretaker rattle dishes and pans in the kitchen, watching the shadows grow shorter as noontime approached.

"Well, I think we need to get moving," Stratton said. "I assume that this Father Morgen that Yost told you about isn't likely to remain in Alt Aussee forever."

Seth nodded.

"Okay, then," Seth said as he stood up. "Rock 'n' roll!"

TWENTY-NINE

The Bahnhofstrasse was as crowded as ever. The Mercedeses were jammed hood to trunk along the street. Limos were double-parked. Crowds of well-dressed Zurichers rushed past the window of the small restaurant, their arms bulging with packages. From a great distance, the sounds of carolers reached their cars. They were having trouble staying on key. Across the Bahnhofstrasse a Salvation Army van pulled to the curb and disgorged a quartet of soberly dressed men carrying musical instruments. They were accompanied by a woman who struggled with a tripod, making sure it was stable enough to support the donations pot that hung from it. Her bell slipped from her coat pocket and clanged loudly as it struck the sidewalk, rolling almost into the gutter before a passerby retrieved it. The group arranged itself just to the right of the entrance to the Thule Gesellschaft Bank.

In front, Stratton pulled the Volvo to the curb.

"Make sure you have some spare change," Zoe said. "Or they'll give us dirty looks when we go into the bank."

"Yes, but they'll probably give us one anyway if it's not large enough," Seth joked.

A young boy of eleven or twelve passed by selling newspapers, and Seth fixed his eyes on the paper's bold headlines. FOUR DEAD IN APARTMENT BOMBING, read the biggest headline. Below that was a smaller story: LINK TO WAREHOUSE MURDERS?

Ridgeway held his breath. Would he find his own picture there? The paperboy and his papers moved out of his range of vision, leaving the question hanging.

He held on to the priceless package wrapped in brown kraft paper and string.

"What are your instructions, again?" Stratton quizzed them.

"To present this to the clerk inside."

"Remember, if the painting really is the key to a box at that bank, it's illegal. The only reason they'll give you access is because the arrangements were set up before the banking laws outlawed anonymous accounts."

Seth was suddenly worried. "Are you saying they won't honor the painting as proof of access to the box?"

Stratton shook his head. "No. The Swiss are nothing if not reliable. But they won't act if things look suspicious. Just go in there as if you own the place. Act a bit like an arrogant rich—very rich—American. They expect that, even prefer it. They won't risk offending you."

"Right," Seth said. Then to Zoe: "You ready?" She nodded reluctantly.

"You'll wait here, then?" Seth asked Stratton.

"Here, or maybe close by," Stratton responded. "Since this isn't a Mercedes limo, I'll probably have to keep moving. If something . . . bad happens and I can't hang around, there's a parking garage on the Sihlstrasse." He pointed. "Through the old town. I'll park on the highest level."

With that, Ridgeway and Zoe got out of the car. The Bahnhofstrasse was filled to overflowing with bright sunshine and crisp biting breezes.

"He makes me nervous," Zoe said as they walked toward the door.

"I know what you mean," Seth said as he looked warily about him. Death had come out of nowhere before. This time he wouldn't let it take him by surprise. "He struck me the same way when I first met him. But you have to admit he's come through every time. Neither of us would be alive if not for him."

"Still . . ." Zoe's voice trailed off. "He has the connections to get you on the Interpol watch list."

"Why in hell would he want to do that?"

"To make you dependent on him. Keep you from seeking help anywhere else."

"Well, it's the only hand we've got. Might as well play it."

They passed the Salvation Army band, which was playing a rigid tune that sounded as if it had been written by a Calvinist who felt that musical notes were a work of the Devil. Seth dropped a ten-franc note in the donation pot as they passed.

"Danke schön," the woman called after them.

Ridgeway stopped and looked up at the building, his heart thudding in his chest. The eye of the former policeman probed deeper than the grillwork and the secure-looking stone and found what he expected: the discreet and nearly invisible metallic glintings that betrayed a variety of modern security devices behind the facade of old elegance. Ridgeway had heard talk of these banks, how they employed scanners built into doorjambs, lobbies, and elevators to check for weapons. Each anteroom, office, and elevator in the building was built to be automatically sealed off from the others, to isolate possible thieves, terrorists, or the merely suspicious.

Swiss banks were too discreet to allow publicity concerning their security systems, but it was known in law enforcement circles and—Seth presumed in the underworld—that once sealed off, each of the compartments was as secure as the best prison cells ever devised. Soundproof, bulletproof, able to resist substantial explosive charges, they could hold a fugitive for police without his disturbing the daily business conducted by the bank's other, legitimate, customers.

Seth looked at the door. He rubbed his moist palms against each other and then reached for the knob. Would the door be one that led ultimately to their freedom? Or would the people inside see them as the fugitives that they really were and trap them in some impenetrable room to await the arrival of the Swiss police? He had the uncomfortable feeling that this was not a place he wanted to go inside. He swallowed against the fear in his throat and pushed the door open for Zoe.

The room was not at all like a bank. To one side were a sofa and two armchairs separated by a cocktail table. A brass lamp burned on an end table next to the sofa. They stood on midnight-blue carpeting that seemed ankle deep. The walls were paneled in dark wood hung with hunting prints. A large man with blond hair sat behind a massive wooden desk at the far end of the room. He rose to greet them. It would all have been very corporate or ordinary had it not been for the fact that other than the door through which they had entered, there seemed to be no other way in or out of the room.

"You have business with us, sir?" the man said as he rose. He wore a dark, conservatively cut business suit, and as he came toward them, Seth noted that the suit had been expertly tailored to conceal the weapon the man carried under his left arm. The use of English was explained by the casual dress of the two visitors. Swiss bankers knew that people dressed like that were usually American and usually curiosity seekers who wanted to tell their friends back home they had visited the gnomes in Zurich. But the man's voice was deferential. For Swiss bankers also knew that for every score of curiosity seekers there was an extremely wealthy American who simply dressed inappropriately for the conduct of financial business.

"I have confidential business to discuss," Seth said imperiously. "And I have very little time. I must see an officer immediately."

"Of course, sir," the man said as his eyes took in the cheaply wrapped parcel and Zoe's new—and obviously expensive—running shoes. He returned to his desk, plucked a telephone receiver from a hidden access, and spoke into it so softly that his words were unintelligible.

The man replaced the telephone and turned his attention to the couple. The Americans stood, apparently at ease in the middle of the reception room.

"The receptionist will see you now," the man said. And as he spoke, a door, camouflaged by the joints in the room's dark paneling and hidden further by subdued lighting, opened behind the desk. A tall, ascetically thin man with a Lenin beard and navy pinstripes stepped from the door.

"Good afternoon," he said, with a polite but reserved voice. "I am Gunter Abels. How may I be of assistance?" He shook first Zoe's hand and then Seth's.

"We have an account," Seth said, determined to brazen his way through. "A box whose access is determined by certain . . . arrangements." Ridgeway looked about him. "I'd prefer to say no more until we're in more . . . private accommodations."

Abels raised his eyebrows. "Of course," he replied obsequiously. "Pardon me, but . . . but we really have to be careful to screen out those who have no bona fide business here. Please. Follow me."

Abels led them back through the door he had used to enter the reception room. It led to an elevator Abels entered last, closing the paneled door that faced the reception area, then punched a button for the eighth floor. The doors slid smoothly shut and the car moved upward. Seth avoided the receptionist's glance and said nothing during the ride. Rich and powerful people, especially those who maintained accounts and boxes in Swiss banks, didn't usually fraternize with the help. Besides, they had been accepted, at least this far. Anything he might say could not help them, and could possibly raise suspicions. Rich people were quiet people and he decided to see if he could play that part of the role.

Zoe followed Seth's lead and kept silent.

"To your left, please," Abels said, as the elevator slid open on the eighth floor. He held the elevator door while they exited. They were in another darkly paneled reception area, twin of the one on the ground floor. Another heavyset guard sat behind another massive wooden desk. Only this room had two corridors leading off both sides.

The guard respectfully returned Seth's glance as the trio got off the elevator.

Abels led them to a door at the end of the hall and unlocked it with a key he took from his pocket. The room, which occupied a corner of the building that overlooked the Bahnhofstrasse and the lake, was decorated in a tasteful opulence as if designed to please those who had a great deal of money but didn't want to spent it frivolously.

"Please make yourselves comfortable," Abels said, "while I notify one of our officers that you are here." Then, without waiting for a reply, he turned, executing a perfect military about-face, and left the room. The door slid shut as firmly and solidly as a vault door. Seth tried the knob. It was locked.

He and Zoe looked silently about them. The room was the size of a luxury hotel room and furnished in much the same way. Besides the sofa and chairs, there was a television set, a rack of current magazines, a small computer terminal displaying financial quotes, and a wet bar stocked with liquor. Seth went to the wet bar, set the wrapped painting down on the counter, and filled a tumbler with water from a chilled bottle of Perrier.

"Some bank, huh?" Zoe said with a false cheerfulness. "The fascist droids at NationsBanc could learn a few things from these people."

Seth walked over to the window and looked down at the street. The Salvation Army was playing its heart out, competing for the odd franc here and there. "Maybe," he said tersely. "They're all the same, bankers—the big ones anyway." He turned to look at her. "Honest people rarely profit from dealing with them."

"My, we're touchy this afternoon," she said, half joking. She walked over to him.

"I'm sorry," he said, putting his hands on her shoulders. "I was just thinking about how this fellow Abels is falling all over himself in a half swoon. But then he locks us in this room just to make sure. Bank procedure. They all have procedures. Bankers are all like a bunch of Nazis strutting around saying: "*Ve haf our orders, und you* vill *like it!*" And when they screw you, accidentally or on purpose, it's always because they were just following orders." He paused. "It's just business. Anytime you hear somebody say that, you can be sure they checked their sense of morality at the door."

He looked at her and saw the depth of patience in her eyes. She said: "It's good to know you haven't changed in the past six months."

Seth looked at her for a long moment, then laughed.

"Sorry," he said. "I'm a little nervous."

"I know," she said.

Just then, they heard a key grumble into the lock. It clicked open and a distinguished man with gray hair and a tightly clipped mustache entered the room. His face was patrician, his suit Savile Row. He spoke English with the terribly proper accent of one who had studied at the best of schools.

"Please forgive the delay," he said as he walked toward them. The door closed behind him. "I am Josef Mutters." He extended his hand. Ridgeway took it and shook its warm firm grip. "I am a vice president here at the Thule Gesellschaft Bank." He repeated the full name of the bank as if to help his two visitors make sure they were in the right bank. "What may I do for you?"

Seth retrieved the package from the wet bar.

"We wish access to our box," he said as he handed the package to Mutters.

For an instant, the vice president looked at the roughly wrapped parcel as if it might contain some new American disease. Just as swiftly, though, his professionally obsequious face reassembled itself.

"May we sit for a moment?" he asked. Seth nodded and the three arranged themselves around the sofa. Mutters placed the parcel on the coffee table and began to unwrap it.

He almost stifled a short gasp of surprise when he saw the painting. He looked at it silently for a long time. When he looked up again, the obsequious look in his eyes had turned to fear.

"After these many years," Mutters said, as much to himself as to his guests. He nodded to himself, confirming the inevitability of the painting as one confirms death when it finally arrives.

"My father made arrangements for this," Mutters said. "Back when such procedures were still legal. It was unusual, but he saw nothing illegal, and thus accommodated the customer." He looked at them sharply. "But then you must know all about that, don't you? After all, you have the painting."

Seth felt the hand of fear clutching at his intestines. Did the man suspect them? Would he ask them questions they couldn't answer? The police wouldn't be long.

"Of course we know all that," Seth snapped. "We didn't come here for a history lesson. We came to collect the contents of our box."

Mutters's gaze was intense. Seth could see the man's thoughts shifting in his eyes, evaluating, measuring, deciding.

"Of course," Mutters finally said. "Please forgive my lapse of manners. It's just that . . ." He looked at Seth. This time his eyes had the soft, compliant texture of the servant. "This is the last of an era." His voice was nostalgic. "All of the other accounts with . . . unusual arrangements have all been converted to standard procedures. And Swiss law forbids us from reinstituting the practice." Mutters looked like a mourner lamenting the passing of a dear friend. He was silent for a moment. Then, abruptly, he stood.

"By your leave," he said formally. "I must gather a number of items to proceed." Seth nodded curtly and Mutters quickly left the room.

The vaultlike thud the door made each time it closed had begun to play on Seth's nerves. He cracked open a bottle of Grange at the bar and poured glasses for Zoe and himself. They drank mostly in silence.

Mutters returned just as Seth had filled their glasses the second time. Mutters held the door open as Abels pushed in a small wheeled metal cabinet with a counter-height work surface. In one hand, the vice president held a sheet of paper and a torn envelope from which the paper had obviously come. He followed Abels into the room and had him position the cart next to the window overlooking the lake.

Abels left and the door made its irritating vault sound again.

Still holding the paper and envelope, Mutters walked over to where Seth and Zoe still sat. He glanced at the bottle. "An excellent choice," Mutters said. "One of the finest wines available."

"Not bad," Seth replied, trying to sound unimpressed. "But I do think it is not aging gracefully."

Mutters raised an eyebrow, then without comment picked up the painting from the table. "Shall we proceed with the arrangements?" he said.

Ridgeway nodded, placed his glass on the coffee table, then joined Mutters at the cart Abels had brought. Zoe came up beside him.

They watched as Mutters looked at the paper, placed it and the painting on the work surface of the cart, then unlocked the cabinet doors. He studied the paper again.

From a shelf in the cabinet he pulled a bottle of turpentine, a rag, and a gray metal safe deposit box. It, too, had a small padlock securing its opening.

Without rolling up his sleeves or even taking off his coat, Mutters opened the bottle of turpentine, drenched the rag with it, and began wiping at the surface of the painting.

Zoe's breath caught at the back of her throat. Seth's eyes widened, but he gripped her forearm gently to warn her to be silent.

The decades-old paint softened slowly. It had been applied in some places with a spatula and Mutters had to use cloth after cloth to remove the stubborn pigments. The colors ran and smeared to a streaky brown. But finally, after nearly twenty minutes of work, the surface began to change.

"Ah!" Mutters said cryptically, and kept on rubbing.

First one shiny gold spot and then another appeared in the middle of the painting.

Ten minutes later, Mutters was through. He had exposed a very small gold ingot fixed into a recess of the wood substrate on which the paint had been applied. The ingot was the size of the broad side of a pack of cigarettes. Mutters held it up for them both to see. The ingot was embossed with a series of letters and numbers: the stamp of the foundry certifying the gold as .99999 fine, the weight of the ingot, and the swastika, eagle, and lightning bolts of the SS. Zoe gasped.

"I believe this is what you were expecting, is it not?" Mutters directed his question at Seth.

"What? . . . Ah . . . yes. Yes!" Seth said, trying to hide his surprise. "Precisely what I was expecting."

Mutters held the block of wood out for Seth to hold. "Careful," Mutters said. "It might still have some soft paint around the edges."

Seth took the object from Mutters and held it up to the light. He held his breath, a sharp pain forming in his stomach as he gazed at the swastika pressed into the gold. The tangible symbol of evil brought home to him the awful web that had ensnared them.

He handed the object back to Mutters. The bank vice president picked up the paper he had carried into the room. As he did, the envelope fell to the carpeting. Seth reached down and picked it up. He noticed then the name on the return address. It was that of Hermann Goering. Below the Berlin address, there was a single word: "Instructions." Ridgeway's hand trembled as he placed the paper back on the table.

Mutters looked at the paper that had come out of the envelope once again, and then, taking a short-bladed knife, pried the ingot from its recess in the wood. Beneath it was a key. He pried the key from its slot and handed it to Seth.

"This is your key to the box," Mutters said. "And this," he handed Seth the gold ingot with the numbers and letter showing, "is your account number. It matches exactly the number as presented in the instructions we were given by the"—he cast a searching glance at Seth—"gentleman who opened the account and left a trust for its maintenance in perpetuity."

Seth accepted the ingot and key hesitantly. He could not picture so evil a figure as Hermann Goering holding the very same items that he now touched.

"Well, let's proceed," Seth said impatiently.

"Of course," Mutters said. "I'm afraid, though, that the access numbers embossed in the gold indicate a Priority One account."

Seth felt his heart wrench, "Which means what?"

"It means that we are not allowed to remove the box from the vault without your presence." Seth relaxed as Mutters continued. "It's highly unusual. Normally we would bring your box to you here"—he looked around the room—"or in one of the other examination rooms. But with a Priority One account, you must be there to actually witness the unlocking of the box space."

Seth nodded. "Let's not waste any more time."

Mutters grabbed his page of instructions, then led them back to the elevator and pressed an unmarked button.

"This takes us to our deepest vault level. The most secure."

Seth nodded, trying to affect the self-centered disinterest in which the rich usually enshrouded themselves. Somehow it seemed to comfort Mutters.

From the elevator, they walked along a brown marble floor, past corridor after corridor lined with safe deposit boxes of varying sizes.

After descending a flight of stairs, they found themselves facing a bank of large safe deposit boxes, some as large as office file drawers. Mutters stepped back from the bank of boxes and bent backwards, hands placed in the small of his back as he scanned the numbers from ceiling to floor. He spotted the right number immediately.

"There," he said, pointing with his finger. He indicated a box, about four feet off the floor, whose door looked more than a foot wide and six inches high. Zoe and Seth stepped closer to examine the box. Both locks were sealed with a thin gold foil.

"Please examine them closely to be assured that no key has ever penetrated the locks since the seal was applied," Mutters said.

The seals were intact.

"Shall we proceed?" Mutters asked. Seth nodded and handed Mutters the key that had been hidden for forty years under the gold ingot. The ingot rested uneasily against his thigh, tugging at the fabric of his trousers pocket.

Seth held his breath as Mutters inserted first the bank's key and then the one from the painting through the foil seals and into the locks. He turned both simultaneously and the lock clicked open. Mutters opened the door to reveal a standard metal safe deposit box container. He reached in, slid the box from the recess where it had lain undisturbed for more than four decades, then held it out for them to see. The lid was secured with four thick gold seals; these, like the gold ingot, embossed with the seal of the SS. Mutters looked at the seals and at Seth. His face remained expressionless; it bore the look of a man who has seen everything once and is waiting for a second time.

"Would you like me to take it back to the viewing room for you?"

Seth nodded his assent. As he and Zoe followed Mutters back out of the vaults, Seth looked at the rows on rows of boxes and wondered what other evils were stored within. Were there people being killed right now for the boxes' contents? The thought made him shiver.

THIRTY

The viewing room still smelled faintly of turpentine. Mutters had brought them the contents of the safe deposit box and left them alone. Impatiently they had torn at the seals of the box, and found, inside, a metal briefcase of the sort used to protect cameras and electronic instruments. It had an elaborate combination lock that yielded when the numbers were set in accordance with the numbers in the bank account number.

The contents of the briefcase now covered the coffee table: papers—many with seals—documents from the Reichschancellery and the Vatican; bound instruction books relating to a fortified installation; the blueprint of that installation identified only as "Habersam Facility," microfilm labeled "historic testimony originals at Habersam Facility," and photographs, scores of photographs.

Seth nervously handed one of the photographs to Zoe. "No wonder they are still willing to kill for the painting," he said.

Zoe took the photograph. Printed on expensive sulfur-free paper, a fine-grained image of a face stared back at her. The face was the shadowy image of a young woman or girl in death, the expression a peaceful one of relief, as if a great suffering had just ended.

"I can't believe it," Zoe said. "Hitler blackmailed the Pope into silence on the Nazi atrocities."

"Believe it," Seth said. "Here's the document that proves it."

He fished through the mess on the table and pulled out a document, the agreement that guaranteed the Catholic Church's silence, in exchange for which Hitler guaranteed the safety of the Vatican and agreed not to make public any of the evidence relating to Sophia's Shroud. At the bottom, verified by the seals of the Vatican and the Third Reich, were the signatures of Pope Pius XII and Adolf Hitler.

Zoe laid the photograph back on the table on top of the other images of the shroud.

They both stared at the material on the table. It seemed overwhelming: the cover-up of a female Messiah by an emperor and a Pope, the discovery of the shroud and all the supporting documents—the Sophia Passion—by Hermann Goering. Hundreds had died in the original cover-up; millions more had been killed in the resulting silence.

"What do we do now?" Zoe asked.

"Go to Alt Aussee, I suppose," Seth said "That's what Yost said we should do. Go see Morgen. Besides, we can't stay here for very long. The police would like to nail us. Maybe a little town in Austria is a good place to hide out until we can figure out exactly how to get out of this mess."

"It would also give us a chance to look at this material more closely. We've only scratched the surface."

Seth nodded, bent over the table, and started to sweep the piles of papers into his briefcase.

The entire business had taken more than two hours. Stratton would be impatient and worried by now. They would find him and take the Volvo to Alt Aussee. There, an old priest named Hans Morgen would help them find some answers. And in those answers there had to be solutions; a way to stop the killing that followed the shroud, a way to exonerate Ridgeway of the murder charges. There had to be a way. There had to be.

Seth held Zoe's hand as they followed Mutters to the elevator. From the corner of his eye Seth saw two men at the end of the hallway walking toward them. He looked at them closely. One of them looked familiar, but Seth couldn't remember from where. Cops and professors—and hunted men—see a lot of faces in their lives.

Mutters nodded at the men and smiled as the elevator doors began to open. He seemed to know the men. The man on the right stuck his hand into his coat, and when it appeared again, it was holding an automatic pistol with a long tubular cylinder attached to its muzzle. Seth felt his insides grow cold; a small gasp of surprise escaped from Zoe's mouth. The man with the gun stopped suddenly about twenty feet from them and raised the weapon.

"No—" was all Mutters could say before the man shot him. The killer then trained his gun on Seth.

Operating on instinct, Seth shoved Zoe into the elevator car and frantically punched the button marked ZUMACHEN. From the hallway came the sounds of running feet muted by the tasteful plush carpeting. Still the door failed to close.

Seth grabbed Zoe by the upper arm and pushed her into the corner of the elevator by the control panel. Zoe watched as he gripped the handle of the black metal briefcase with both hands and hefted it like an Olympic hammer thrower. "Don't move," he said. He swung the case tentatively at first, then planted his feet firmly and put his entire weight behind it just as the gunman's head entered.

The metal briefcase was heavy with the papers and documents inside. One sharp corner caught the killer just above his left ear, the metal edge easily penetrating the thin soft flesh. The next instant, a soggy cracking sound filled the interior of the car as the momentum split open the side of the man's head like a rotten melon.

The silenced automatic flew out of the killer's hand and clattered against the elevator wall. Seth kept his grip on the briefcase as the man's body sagged, then fell heavily, torso in the car and legs in the corridor. The elevator doors finally began to close, slamming repeatedly against the body.

Seth tossed the bloodied briefcase toward Zoe as he lunged for the killer's weapon. As the elevator doors slammed into the man's kidneys again, then retracted, Seth saw the second man speaking into a small handheld radio. There were more of them. But where?

The man saw Seth's gun and quickly stepped close to the wall, out of the line of fire. The elevator closed again against the fallen killer and Seth stooped to get a grip on the body. As he hauled it into the car, the doors slammed against the man's ankles and again retracted.

When the doors opened fully, the second man was standing there, and instead of the radio, he was holding a pistol, the twin of the one Seth now held. For an instant the two men stared at each other, dumb and surprised. Then each raised his weapon and brought it to bear. Seth was a split second faster and a hair more accurate. He felt the pistol recoil firmly in his hand once, twice, and then dived to safety. As the doors closed firmly this time, Seth caught a glimpse of the man as he fell to his knees and then went face first onto the carpet.

Inside the descending elevator, Seth rolled the dead killer's body over and found two additional clips for the automatic. He stuffed them into his trouser pockets.

"Who . . ." Zoe's voice cracked. She cleared her throat and tried again. "Who were they?"

Seth shook his head and continued his search of the dead man's body. He pulled out the man's wallet and flipped it open. There was a thick wad of currency: Swiss francs, Austrian shillings, a scattering of German marks. Among the stack of credit cards, Seth found a photo ID that identified him as Bernhard Saltzer, an employee of the Thule Gesellschaft Bank.

He held the card up for Zoe to see. "Herr Mutters wasn't the only person here prepared to service those who came for the contents of that box."

The elevator began to slow at the ground floor. "Here, keep this," he said, handing her the man's wallet. The elevator stopped and the doors slid open. Seth picked up the metal briefcase and pushed at the door that would detach itself from the paneled wall in the reception room. He stepped from the elevator. Next to him the guard was slumped over his massive wooden desk, blood streaming from a small round hole in his temple.

Sitting at the sofa was a man dressed in a black uniform with red piping. It took Seth a second to recognize one of the Salvation Army band members. Another stood by the front door to the reception room. Both men looked surprised to see Seth. They froze for an instant.

The Salvation Army band member sitting on the sofa raised a lumpy device that Ridgeway recognized as a H&K MP5A. Ridgeway stepped quickly back into the recesses of the elevator, stumbling over Zoe as he did. They tangled feet and fell to the floor just as slugs from the H&K thudded dully into the paneled walls of the elevator car.

"*Schnell! Schnell!*" Quickly! Quickly! Seth heard his assailant shout. Seth untangled himself from Zoe and, aiming from his knees, fired a shot at the onrushing killer with the machine pistol. The shot slapped into the man's belly and straightened him up, his face a mask of wide-eyed surprise. Apparently no one had told him Ridgeway would be armed. Seth took advantage of the man's surprise and fired again. Most of the man's right eye vanished in a spray of red and pink.

Zoe climbed to her feet and punched every button on the elevator's control panel. As the elevator doors started to close, Seth fired again and again at the second Salvation Army band member. The automatic ran out of ammunition as the doors closed. Seth sighed as the car began to ascend.

"Where are we headed?" he asked her, as he turned the pistol over in his hand and tried to locate the clip release.

"Up," Zoe said. Seth slammed a fresh ammunition clip into the grip of the pistol. "Some of the lower floors have to be offices," she explained. "And where there are offices, there have to be fire escapes."

The elevator doors opened into a large cavernous room punctuated by glass-topped dividers. The room was filled with the quiet busy chatter of computers, calculators, printers, and the business of money. Seth quickly concealed the gun in the waistband of his trousers.

Zoe took in the scene, then stepped past him into the room. She walked over to a red fire alarm on the wall and pulled it. A bell began to ring. She screamed, "*Feuer! Feuer! Feuer!*" Fire! Fire! Fire!

An anxious murmur rumbled across the vast room. People began to rise from their seats. Seth grabbed the briefcase and joined Zoe. "Fire! We must get out! Fire!" The murmur rose to a loud excited babble. Some of the workers began to gather things from their desks. Women went for their purses. A tall man with authority engraved in his face stalked up to them.

"Look here," he said angrily. "What's the meaning of this?"

"Fire on the first floor," Seth yelled. "Herr Mutters told me to come and evacuate the floor." The man stiffened at the name of his superior.

"This is highly irregular," the man replied. "I really must speak with Vice President Mutters himself." He moved purposefully toward a telephone. The room, however, had erupted into chaos as people pushed and jostled toward an open door in a far corner. An alarm bell, no doubt actuated when the emergency exit had been opened, infected the room with a virulent sense of urgency. Zoe and Seth joined the masses of people, who were now near panic.

At the bottom of the fire escape stairs, the crowd milled about in a broad courtyard connected by alleys to other streets. The people were confused and hung about, talking in small groups. Many among the group complained loudly that they couldn't see any smoke, some speculated that it must be another fire drill.

Seth and Zoe detached themselves from the crowd and walked slowly down one of the alleyways leading away from the Bahnhofstrasse. Wailing sirens grew louder—fire trucks no doubt, and perhaps police cars as well—if the bodies had been discovered.

The alley led them to a quiet street in the heart of Zurich's old medieval quarter. They walked silently, each too stunned to talk. A half hour later they reached the underground parking garage on the Sihlstrasse, and minutes later, Zoe spotted the Volvo. Stratton waved.

THIRTY-ONE

They arrived in Alt Aussee on the morning before Christmas Eve. A heavy snow had begun just before dawn and had grown heavier as the day wore on.

The road from Bad Aussee was narrow and followed every twist and turn of a small creek that flowed toward the lake. By the time they reached Alt Aussee they had slowed to less than ten miles per hour. Snow caked on the windshield and turned to ice where the ends of the wipers couldn't reach.

The three checked into two rooms at the Kohlbacherhof, a small Gasthaus at the edge of town adjacent to a small church.

Finally, huddling under an umbrella against the wet snow, Zoe and Seth walked the quarter of a mile from the Gasthaus to the center of town. Yost had been specific, only the two of them would be expected.

"By whom?" Zoe and Stratton had asked almost simultaneously.

Seth had shrugged. "He said they would recognize us."

On the way into town, the only vehicle that passed them was a single tractor pulling a wagon loaded with hay. The farmer, bundled against the cold, waved at them as he passed.

Otherwise, they saw no one else until they arrived at the center of Alt Aussee. They passed several small stores: hardware, clothing, and a shop that sold toys, books, and sundries. All of the stores were housed in individual one-story frame or stone buildings set along the road and separated from one another by narrow alleys or driveways. All of the stores were closed. Christmas had begun for the gentle villagers at Alt Aussee.

About fifty yards past the toy/bookstore, they found a combination police station and post office set in a two-story building made of rough gray stone. When Seth tried the door of the building, however, he found it was locked.

"Where now?" Seth wondered aloud.

They stood in front of the building for a moment and turned to look about them. More stores lined the main street on both sides. But like the three stores they had already passed, most of them looked closed, their windows dark and gloomy. A farm truck, its cab rusted and patched with pieces of metal cut from cans, rattled down the main street past them, etching fresh tire tracks in the snow-covered roadway. Its driver, too, waved at them. They waved back and watched as the truck began to disappear into the thick shroud of snow. But before it vanished its one working brake light burned brightly as it pulled over to the curb. Seth and Zoe squinted into the cotton fluff blanket that covered the town and saw, just beyond the truck, light coming from the windows of a building.

They watched as the driver got out of his truck and walked into the building.

"Shall we?" Zoe said, taking a tentative step toward the truck.

"Might as well," Seth agreed, following her. "It looks like the only inhabited place in town." As they got closer, they could discern the outlines of a small café and beer hall. They pushed on across the street.

By the time they got to the farmer's truck, the tracks it had left in the snow were already obliterated. Parked in front of the truck at the curb were a battered Mercedes and a brand-new Fiat.

They stopped in front of a restaurant with a steep peaked roof and windows composed of scores of small diamond-shaped panes set in a dark wood lattice. Snow had gathered in the lower portions of the diamond shapes and left them with the natural decorations that Americans tried so hard to imitate with aerosol cans of fake plastic snow.

Through the window, they watched the farmer greeting the people inside. Two uniformed policemen sat at one table nursing cups of coffee and shot glasses filled with a clear liquid, probably schnapps. They accounted for the locked door of the police station across the street. Three more people—rough, heavy types with red faces and the green loden clothes of the Alps—sat at a large picnic-type table with benches along either side. They drank from nearly empty beer steins.

The innkeeper and a dumpling-shaped woman who had to be his wife stood behind the bar and greeted the new arrivals with broad smiles and waves of their hands.

Seth and Zoe went through the door and traded the crisp cold world of snow for a warm one, redolent with the yeasty aroma of beer, the spicy, slightly sulfurous aroma of cabbage, wursts in all their many permutations, and the humid, earthy odors of human beings warming up, drying out after a bout with inclement weather. All heads turned as they walked through the door. The looks they got were not unfriendly, Seth noted. Just curious. Alt Aussee was a place where the roads came to an end before dwindling into footpaths that led into the rugged hills and mountains beyond. Strangers didn't often come to such a place on Christmas Eve.

"Gruss Gott," Seth said, offering them the traditional Austrian greeting.

"Gruss Gott," came a ragged chorus of replies. Seth and Zoe walked to the bar behind which the proprietor and his wife stood. As they crossed the floor, Seth noticed a wizened old man sitting by himself in the corner of the café, nursing a half-liter mug of beer.

"May I help you?" The proprietor offered in the soft accents of the Austrian countryside that made German sound almost lyrical.

"Yes, please," Seth replied. "I hope you can help. We're looking for a man. Father Morgen." He saw the proprietor's face stiffen almost imperceptibly. "Do you know him?"

"Yes." The proprietor's answer was slow. "I know him . . . I know of him." The man said nothing more.

Seth felt the eyes of the people behind him boring into his back. When he finally spoke, his voice was shaky. "Have . . . have you seen him?"

The proprietor looked at him seriously for several moments and then laughed cheerlessly.

"Yes, I have seen him." He paused. "I was a small child the last time I saw him. I do not believe I have seen him since then." He paused again. "That would have been in the last weeks of the war."

Seth nodded slowly and turned.

The two policemen sat at their table silently and eyed him with the suspicion that guardians of law and order everywhere have for the unusual.

"Officers," Seth began, his voice even more unsteady "Have you any idea where I might find Father Morgen?" Both men shook their heads wordlessly. Again Seth nodded.

"But where would he stay if he were to visit here?" Zoe had turned back to the proprietor and his wife.

They shook their heads in unison before the man answered: "At the Kohlbacherhof perhaps," he replied. "Or perhaps at the old inn." He looked at the wall of his café that faced north. "It's a few miles from here. Up the road."

Zoe waited, but the man was apparently finished talking. "Well," she said tentatively. "Thank you for your . . . information."

They left the café and began walking slowly back toward the Kohlbacherhof.

The snow fell finer and heavier now.

"I can't believe it's so hard to find one old man in a place this tiny," Zoe said.

"They know where he is," Seth said quietly.

"Why do you say that?"

"Didn't you see the looks on their faces? They were friendly when we walked in and as soon as we said we were looking for Father Morgen, a wall dropped. Their faces turned to stone."

"But why?" Zoe asked.

"They're protecting him."

"Pardon me." A voice came unexpectedly from behind them. Seth and Zoe whirled to face the old man who had been nursing his beer in the corner of the café.

"I know Father Morgen," the old man said. "Perhaps I can help you."

The old man was stooped and bent, but even so, his head was nearly level with Seth's. He had apparently been quite tall in his prime. His unruly shock of gray hair made him resemble Einstein in his Princeton days.

"My name is Gunther," the old man said. He held his bare hand out. Seth took the hand and shook it.

"I'm Seth Ridgeway. And this is my wife, Zoe."

The man who called himself Gunther bowed and took Zoe's hand. For a moment she thought he was going to kiss it, but he merely shook it and then let it drop. "I can introduce you to Father Morgen," he said. "I will call you. You wait at the Kohlbacherhof . . . alone . . . in the bar."

He turned then, and with surprising speed for an old man, walked back toward the café.

Hours passed for Zoe and Seth as they sat in the basement restaurant and *bierstube* of the Kohlbacherhof nursing their *gluhwein*—hot mulled red wine. Up in his room, Stratton fumed silently, chafing at the instructions that Seth and Zoe had been given.

As they waited for the afternoon rendezvous with the old man to pay off, Zoe tried to explain what she had seen in the warehouse and how she had engineered her escape. Seth sat silently, marveling at her strength and ingenuity.

"I have to say that the only thing that surprises me is why you didn't think of your escape plan sooner."

Zoe took a sip of her *gluhwein* and nodded. "Maybe it was psychological. Maybe I didn't want to leave until I had seen all the art. Or maybe . . ." She stared into the distance for a long moment.

"Or maybe?" Seth prompted.

"I know you're going to find this hard to believe," Zoe said hesitantly. She stared up at the ceiling and then back to Seth. "But I think maybe God wanted me there. I think I was *meant* to remain until I had gotten her message. Then she gave me the plan for how to escape."

"Oh sure. You're telling me that there's a God—you pick the gender, either, or, both neither—who's so screwed up that we almost have to die before we believe?"

Zoe just looked at him.

Seth shook his head. "Zoe, that's not faith. That's the desperation of mortal fear looking for anything at all to hang on to." He turned to her. "Look, you had everything you needed to know in your head."

"I'm not all that sure I did," she said uncertainly.

"Of course you did," Seth persisted. "All it took is remembering all that stuff your dad taught you and putting it into action."

"I'm not really sure of that," Zoe began slowly. "Now that I think back, there's so much that I'm just not aware of knowing before."

"*Of course* you knew all that stuff. You just haven't thought about it for years because you haven't had to."

"So why did it all come back to me so clearly," Zoe asked. "It was almost as if I could see blueprints."

"*Because* the pressure of impending death focuses your thoughts . . . trust me, I've been there, thought that."

"Your recent encounters with death seem to have had the opposite effect on you."

"Yeah, one time and the experience is mystical, but when people keep trying to kill you time after time, you just start to think that God's either twisted and sadistic or isn't there at all."

Zoe shook her head. "That doesn't wash. I was in grave, constant danger the entire time. Death was always just around the corner every day that passed. So why did the specter of dying not focus my mind before I really started learning about the Great Goddess, before I started believing in a God that embraced the female?"

"I am not believing this," Seth said as he drained his wine. "You, Ms. confirm-it-to-believe-it, who never trusts anything you can't touch with your own hands, see with your own eyes."

"And I am not believing what I hear from you, Seth. You're the believer until things get rocky and you ditch your faith? How strong was—"

The telephone behind the bar rang at precisely seven P.M. The owner's teenage son picked up the receiver, listened, and then said: "It is for you, Mein Herr."

Seth walked behind the bar and put the receiver to his ear.

"Yes?"

"Herr Ridgeway? It's me, Gunther. I believe I can help you. That is, some friends of mine may be able to help you meet with Father Morgen."

"He's here in Alt Aussee then?"

Gunther remained silent. "They may be able to help you. Would you be willing to meet them?"

"Of course."

"Wonderful," said Gunther. "Leave the Kohlbacherhof and walk down the main road, toward town. Before you get to town, at the point where the road splits, there is a small shop that sells toys, books—"

"I know the one."

"Good," Gunther said. "Meet me outside that store."

"When?"

"Now."

"Now?"

"Have you better ways to spend your evening in Alt Aussee?" The man's voice was suddenly laced with impatient sarcasm.

"No. No, of course not."

"Good," Gunther replied. "My friends are eager to meet with you. Come right away."

Seth hung up, paid for the gluhwein he and Zoe had been drinking, then explained the conversation to her as they returned to their room to fetch their coats. Stratton listened to Seth repeat the conversation.

Seth and Zoe walked outside. The snow had slacked off to a fine powder sifting down from the sky. The temperature had dropped and the snow squeaked underfoot as they walked the rest of the way in silence, hand in hand, reaching the toy/bookstore about five minutes later. They stood about stamping their feet as if the cold were an insect that could be tramped to death under the soles of their boots.

A few moments later, something hard jabbed into Seth's ribs from behind. The sound of a car engine starting filled the night.

"Don't make any quick movements, Mr. and Mrs. Ridgeway." He didn't recognize the voice. It was not Gunther's. The battered Mercedes they had seen parked in front of the café earlier pulled to the curb. Seth turned his head to catch a glimpse of the license plates, but could see nothing through the glare of the headlights.

"Get into the backseat," said a voice in his ear. The back door swung open. Seth looked as Zoe opened her mouth as if to scream. Swiftly, a gloved hand clamped itself over her mouth. She began to struggle. Seth moved to help her and a blunt heavy blow slammed into the back of his head.

The blow cut his legs out from under him.

"That was unwise," a voice said as they were hustled into the back of the car. "There's no need for alarm." There was no threat in the voice. As soon as Seth and Zoe were inside the car, the doors slammed and it began to move forward.

"I am going to cover your eyes," said a voice. Seth tried to turn his head to the source of the voice but the splitting pain in his head arrested his movement. Moments later, hands pulled what seemed to be a thick black sock over his head. The cloth was opaque, yet thin enough to breathe through without difficulty.

"Please relax," the voice told them. "We don't intend to harm you."

The ache in Seth's head made the words hard to believe. He remembered the killers he had encountered in Zurich, in Amsterdam, in Marina Del Rey. He tried to console himself with the thought that, unlike those men, these had merely tried to capture him, not kill him. It didn't offer him much consolation.

The car made its way on paved road for about five minutes, then began to pitch and rattle as it slowed for a rough surface. They were thrown about in the backseat and somehow Seth found Zoe's hand. He squeezed and she squeezed back. Strength, comfort, hope, love. They communicated all these things wordlessly as the old Mercedes banged its way slowly into the darkness.

After what seemed like half an hour the Mercedes stopped. They were led out of the car and placed, still blindfolded, into another seat, this one hard and cold. An instant later, the sounds of a small engine roared to life in front of them. Seth recognized it as a snowmobile engine.

They started to move and, still holding Zoe's hand, Seth imagined that they were in some sort of sled being towed by the snowmobile.

They went for another half hour, mostly slowly through brush that plucked at their clothes.

"Duck your heads," they were warned once as they obviously went under some low-hanging objects.

Finally they stopped on a level area and the snowmobile engine died in the night. They were led through the snow. A door opened. Warm air enveloped them as they were led into a room. They heard the door close behind them.

A voice said: "Take off their blindfolds," and the sock was pulled off his head. Seth didn't have to squint to adjust his eyes, for the only light in the room came from a kerosene lantern and a wood fire burning in a crude stone fireplace. The room looked like the alpine huts that dotted the countryside throughout the Tyrol. It had a rough bunk and an assortment of rough-hewn furniture. The room smelled of burning wax and coffee.

Zoe put her arm around Seth's waist. They turned. By the fireplace, each with a tin mug in his hands, were two men. They recognized Gunther. A thinner, more aristocratic man stood beside Gunther. He looked at Zoe and Seth for a moment and then walked toward them.

"Welcome," he said as he extended his hand. "I am Hans Morgen."

THIRTY-TWO

orgen didn't look like a priest. In his heavy cable-knit sweater, wool blazer, and wool slacks, he seemed more a professor or research scientist. He did not wear a clerical collar. He shook their hands, Zoe's first, then Seth's. "I must apologize for the bizarre way you were brought here," Morgen said. "But there are many people who would like to find me now. I had to be sure you were who you said you were."

Seth rubbed the back of his neck. "I am truly sorry, Mr. Ridgeway," Morgen apologized again, "about your head. But Richard . . ." He glanced at a man by the door. Seth turned to look at him. Richard Stehr had a gentle, almost baby-round face with soft blue eyes, set on top of a defensive tackle's body. "Richard is fortunately an expert. You have been done no lasting harm."

"Easy for you to say," Ridgeway replied, but his anger was only skin deep.

"Of course," Morgen said gently. "Would you like to sit down? I have some fresh coffee brewing." He indicated two ladder-backed chairs next to a rough-hewn table on which sat a stack of cups, bottles, hard sausages, and a partially sliced loaf of dark bread.

They seated themselves at the table and watched silently as Morgen used a padded mitt to pluck a battered coffeepot with chipped enamel from a grate in the fireplace. He selected chipped crockery cups for Zoe and Seth and poured them cups full of the steaming black liquid. He then replenished his own cup and sat down at the table with them. The other men—the two who had brought them to the cabin and Gunther, who had been with Morgen when they entered—all remained standing. Periodically, they would part the curtains and peer out of the cabin. There were apparently people outside, sentries, for one of the men inside the cabin would periodically motion outside to acknowledge some communication.

"I understand you have gone to some extraordinary lengths to recover the Sophia Passion." Zoe and Seth nodded in unison. "Why don't you tell me how it all came to be?"

"I don't want to be an ungrateful guest," Seth replied. "But since you've brought us here in such a . . . bizarre manner, I'd feel a lot more comfortable if you told us about yourself and"—he looked around the room at the men standing there—"your group."

Morgen's eyes softened. "Of course," he said. "Forgive me for being both too anxious and such a poor host. I understand your reluctance completely." He looked over at Gunther and motioned with his head for the man to join them. Gunther shambled over and took a chair next to Seth.

"Gunther may be able to add the colorful details I leave out."

"I gather my late friend Jacob Yost filled you in on the beginning of all this." He looked around him as if the alpine hut were the symbol of all that had afflicted him for more than four decades.

"Let me begin where Yost undoubtedly left off," Morgen said. "The past decades have been hard to believe, but they will be more comprehensible if you have some context within which to put them." He took a sip from his coffee mug, made a sour face, and leaned back in his chair.

George Stratton squinted over the light snow that fell through his headlights. The snow had nearly stopped. He drove the Volvo slowly over the uneven, rocky path that headed steeply up the hillside. Boughs caked with snow reached out from either side and slapped against the side of the car.

Stratton had followed Seth and Zoe's footsteps, only barely obscured by the slackening snow up to the meeting spot. His practiced eye took in the tire treads, the scuff marks in the snow, and the tire tracks leading away from the store. There were no footprints leading away from the site, so Stratton assumed that Ridgeway and his wife had gone—willingly or unwillingly with the people in the car.

So he followed the tire tracks, a simple job thanks to the sparse traffic and the slackening of the heavy snow.

The undercarriage of the Volvo scraped hard against a rock now. Stratton stopped and, taking a flashlight with him, continued up the slope on foot.

"Then I kept looking for the sergeant after the war," Morgen continued his story. "But the sergeant, like many of his comrades, had successfully disappeared."

Morgen slowly got up and went for the coffeepot that he had set back in the fireplace to keep warm. "In addition, I tried as best I could to verify the sergeant's contention that Hitler had blackmailed the Pope. That had two results." He bent over and fetched the pot with the padded mitt. "The first," he said as he walked back to the table, "was a meeting with a small group of people in the Curia who were dedicated to making sure that no other Pope ever had to yield to such moral or theological blackmail."

"The priest in the park," Seth said. "In Amsterdam." He looked questioningly up at Morgen.

Morgen nodded sadly. "Father Smith. I had sent him to follow you. To protect you."

"Just before he died he said something about 'brown.' What could that mean?"

Morgen looked as though he had been slapped.

"He used that name?" Morgen said.

"Then it is a name?"

Morgen paused for a moment, as if allowing the impact to sink in. "I suspected," Morgen said, "but I didn't know, not for absolutely sure." His face was dark and his lips trembled almost imperceptibly.

Seth and Zoe looked at him, waiting for an explanation of his cryptic remarks. For a moment, Morgen's eyes wore a distant, misty veil. Then the veil suddenly cleared, replaced by a sparkling anger.

"I'll tell you about that in a moment," he said as he sat down. He stared briefly at the thick veins on the backs of his hands, as if he were a public speaker who had lost his place and knew the notes would be inscribed on his hands.

He looked up at them and continued. "The second thing that happened is that I became the object of intense scrutiny by other members of the Curia, people who seemed content to let me go on looking for the painting and the sergeant, but who seemed determined to keep me from ever making use of my information if I succeeded.

"They are a shadowy group," Morgen said. "I found out who they were at the lower levels . . . fellow priests, the occasional bishop." He paused. "My abbot in Munich was one of them. I would give a great deal to determine whom he talks to when he relays information about me to Rome."

Morgen paused, his eyes distant and vague, as if he were seeing in his mind exactly what he would do if he found the men in Rome. With a little shake of his head, he continued.

"They have left me pretty much alone except for the close surveillance. I assume they are content to let me roam as long as they can somehow benefit from my information, my efforts. I've been a sort of Judas Goat for them. Sent out into the jungle to attract the tigers while they conceal themselves in the bushes waiting for the tiger with the right pelt to come along. I've been careful, extremely careful over these last years, not to give them any indications that I was aware of their efforts. They make more mistakes that way. Even the most professional, the most fanatical, can be lulled into sloppiness."

Seth thought of Stratton's man and how he had let Seth leave the UCLA library the night Tony Bradford was murdered.

"So over all these years since the war," Morgen continued, "I made sure to post my important letters to Jacob Yost and make telephone calls to him in secret. Of course, the Vatican knew I was working with him to try and locate looted works of art. All of our letters and calls regarding the art were done in the normal manner and I'm certain were intercepted by whoever in the Curia is having me watched.

"But the situation changed drastically about a year ago. Last . . ."—Morgen closed his eyes for a moment—"last January, Yost and I managed to recover a semifamous painting. It was one of the early works of Pissarro, and had been discreetly offered for sale by a former SS colonel living under a new identity in Portugal. We led the police to his villa on the coast near Lisbon, where they took the painting and the colonel into custody. The incident received quite a lot of attention from the journalists.

"As the result of all the publicity, a man I had known forty years before as Franz Bohles von Halbach called me from Kreuzlingen. He was the SS sergeant who came to me that night forty years ago and asked forgiveness for the shooting of the village boy. He was also the one who had shown me the shroud and the Sophia Passion in their protective vault in the mine.

"Well, von Halbach was now very wealthy and calling himself Willi Max," Morgen said, as he pushed his chair back and crossed his legs, trying to get comfortable on the hard wooden seat. "Max—von Halbach—was also dying and the moral issues he had managed to ignore or repress for forty years had begun to catch up with him. The guilt-wracked young sergeant had become a remorseful dying old man, afraid for his mortal soul.

"He had grown a bit more sophisticated in the forty years since he had come to my home in Alt Aussee for confession. He knew the significance of the painting, knew it held the keys to recovering the shroud and the Sophia Passion. And so he didn't show up on my doorstep with painting in hand. And a good thing, for the painting would probably now be in the hands of my enemies in the Curia.

"No, realizing that secrecy was important, he decided to act discreetly. He contacted Yost, who immediately called me."

Gunther interrupted to suggest that they eat. The men outside kept watch in shifts, coming in one by one to wolf down cold sausages and bread before continuing their watches. The men were mostly in their fifties and sixties and deferred to Morgen.

"They used to be priests," Morgen interrupted his story to explain the men outside. "They took all they could of treachery and deceit from the church.

But even after leaving the church, they felt the call to serve God. They live like priests now, but in service to God, not the church. They help a dwindling number of us within the church to fight its dishonesty and abuses."

"With the shroud and the Sophia Passion, we may even be able to win a few of our battles," Gunther added, then receded in his chair. "Now, I believe it is your turn."

Over the simple cold meal, Seth and Zoe once again recited the tales of their ordeals. The stories had grown shorter with each telling, as they chose an economy of words to rush past the pain and fear.

Morgen, in turn, explained that the nucleus of reformers in the Vatican had steadily dwindled over the years. They were seen as a threat to those who had vested their lives in the power struggles and Byzantine bureaucracy. And even those who agreed that Vatican corruption was fundamental and had to be re- formed looked upon the reformers as a potential source of embarrassment.

"That is why we were not able to protect either of you so well." Morgen said regretfully.

Ridgeway nodded understandingly before he spoke. "What you've said clears up a lot of things, but it still doesn't explain why the KGB killed your man in the park in Amsterdam. You've been talking about the danger from the church. But all the danger Zoe and I have faced has been from the Russians, I don't see where the two—the church and the KGB—are connected."

"You have really asked several questions," Morgen began. "First of all, the KGB wasn't responsible for the killing in Amsterdam." He paused as if what he had to say next hurt even to think about. "The Congregation killed him. The Congregation for the Doctrine of the Faith—the new name for the Holy Inquisition."

Ridgeway and Zoe fixed Morgen with an incredulous look.

"Believe me," he said. "And it wasn't the first time. The Church has money and it has influence. Both of these can be used to hire men, to influence them to kill. They have been killing for almost a millennium now."

"I thought that went out with the Borgias," Ridgeway said.

Morgen shook his head sadly. "It didn't end with the Borgias and it didn't start with them. They just took it to its greatest extremes. Governments—all governments have found it necessary to kill people for one reason or another. The killing is sometimes written about in brave and noble terms, but then, history is always rewritten to justify the winners.

"And that's where the KGB and the church are linked—they are both governments, and as such, act like governments. The church fears and loathes Zhirinovsky. He and his supporters—including much of the KGB—

But even after leaving the church, they felt the call to serve God. They live like priests now, but in service to God, not the church. They help a dwindling number of us within the church to fight its dishonesty and abuses."

"With the shroud and the Sophia Passion, we may even be able to win a few of our battles," Gunther added, then receded in his chair. "Now, I believe it is your turn."

Over the simple cold meal, Seth and Zoe once again recited the tales of their ordeals. The stories had grown shorter with each telling, as they chose an economy of words to rush past the pain and fear.

Morgen, in turn, explained that the nucleus of reformers in the Vatican had steadily dwindled over the years. They were seen as a threat to those who had vested their lives in the power struggles and Byzantine bureaucracy. And even those who agreed that Vatican corruption was fundamental and had to be re-formed looked upon the reformers as a potential source of embarrassment.

"That is why we were not able to protect either of you so well." Morgen said regretfully.

Ridgeway nodded understandingly before he spoke. "What you've said clears up a lot of things, but it still doesn't explain why the KGB killed your man in the park in Amsterdam. You've been talking about the danger from the church. But all the danger Zoe and I have faced has been from the Russians, I don't see where the two—the church and the KGB—are connected."

"You have really asked several questions," Morgen began. "First of all, the KGB wasn't responsible for the killing in Amsterdam." He paused as if what he had to say next hurt even to think about. "The Congregation killed him. The Congregation for the Doctrine of the Faith—the new name for the Holy Inquisition."

Ridgeway and Zoe fixed Morgen with an incredulous look.

"Believe me," he said. "And it wasn't the first time. The Church has money and it has influence. Both of these can be used to hire men, to influence them to kill. They have been killing for almost a millennium now."

"I thought that went out with the Borgias," Ridgeway said.

Morgen shook his head sadly. "It didn't end with the Borgias and it didn't start with them. They just took it to its greatest extremes. Governments—all governments have found it necessary to kill people for one reason or another. The killing is sometimes written about in brave and noble terms, but then, history is always rewritten to justify the winners.

"And that's where the KGB and the church are linked—they are both governments, and as such, act like governments. The church fears and loathes Zhirinovsky. He and his supporters—including much of the KGB—

"I don't want to be an ungrateful guest," Seth replied. "But since you've brought us here in such a . . . bizarre manner, I'd feel a lot more comfortable if you told us about yourself and"—he looked around the room at the men standing there—"your group."

Morgen's eyes softened. "Of course," he said. "Forgive me for being both too anxious and such a poor host. I understand your reluctance completely." He looked over at Gunther and motioned with his head for the man to join them. Gunther shambled over and took a chair next to Seth.

"Gunther may be able to add the colorful details I leave out."

"I gather my late friend Jacob Yost filled you in on the beginning of all this." He looked around him as if the alpine hut were the symbol of all that had afflicted him for more than four decades.

"Let me begin where Yost undoubtedly left off," Morgen said. "The past decades have been hard to believe, but they will be more comprehensible if you have some context within which to put them." He took a sip from his coffee mug, made a sour face, and leaned back in his chair.

George Stratton squinted over the light snow that fell through his headlights. The snow had nearly stopped. He drove the Volvo slowly over the uneven, rocky path that headed steeply up the hillside. Boughs caked with snow reached out from either side and slapped against the side of the car.

Stratton had followed Seth and Zoe's footsteps, only barely obscured by the slackening snow up to the meeting spot. His practiced eye took in the tire treads, the scuff marks in the snow, and the tire tracks leading away from the store. There were no footprints leading away from the site, so Stratton assumed that Ridgeway and his wife had gone—willingly or unwillingly with the people in the car.

So he followed the tire tracks, a simple job thanks to the sparse traffic and the slackening of the heavy snow.

The undercarriage of the Volvo scraped hard against a rock now. Stratton stopped and, taking a flashlight with him, continued up the slope on foot.

"Then I kept looking for the sergeant after the war," Morgen continued his story. "But the sergeant, like many of his comrades, had successfully disappeared."

Morgen slowly got up and went for the coffeepot that he had set back in the fireplace to keep warm. "In addition, I tried as best I could to verify the sergeant's contention that Hitler had blackmailed the Pope. That had two results." He bent over and fetched the pot with the padded mitt. "The first," he said as he walked back to the table, "was a meeting with a small group of people

in the Curia who were dedicated to making sure that no other Pope ever had
to yield to such moral or theological blackmail."

"The priest in the park," Seth said. "In Amsterdam." He looked questioningly up at Morgen.

Morgen nodded sadly. "Father Smith. I had sent him to follow you. To
protect you."

"Just before he died he said something about 'brown.' What could that
mean?"

Morgen looked as though he had been slapped.

"He used that name?" Morgen said.

"Then it is a name?"

Morgen paused for a moment, as if allowing the impact to sink in. "I
suspected," Morgen said, "but I didn't know, not for absolutely sure." His face
was dark and his lips trembled almost imperceptibly.

Seth and Zoe looked at him, waiting for an explanation of his cryptic
remarks. For a moment, Morgen's eyes wore a distant, misty veil. Then the veil
suddenly cleared, replaced by a sparkling anger.

"I'll tell you about that in a moment," he said as he sat down. He stared
briefly at the thick veins on the backs of his hands, as if he were a public speaker
who had lost his place and knew the notes would be inscribed on his hands.

He looked up at them and continued. "The second thing that happened is
that I became the object of intense scrutiny by other members of the Curia,
people who seemed content to let me go on looking for the painting and the
sergeant, but who seemed determined to keep me from ever making use of my
information if I succeeded.

"They are a shadowy group," Morgen said. "I found out who they were
at the lower levels . . . fellow priests, the occasional bishop." He paused. "My
abbot in Munich was one of them. I would give a great deal to determine
whom he talks to when he relays information about me to Rome."

Morgen paused, his eyes distant and vague, as if he were seeing in his mind
exactly what he would do if he found the men in Rome. With a little shake of
his head, he continued.

"They have left me pretty much alone except for the close surveillance. I
assume they are content to let me roam as long as they can somehow benefit
from my information, my efforts. I've been a sort of Judas Goat for them. Sent
out into the jungle to attract the tigers while they conceal themselves in the
bushes waiting for the tiger with the right pelt to come along. I've been careful,
extremely careful over these last years, not to give them any indications that I
was aware of their efforts. They make more mistakes that way. Even the most
professional, the most fanatical, can be lulled into sloppiness."

Seth thought of Stratton's man and how he had let Seth leave t
library the night Tony Bradford was murdered.

"So over all these years since the war," Morgen continued, "I
to post my important letters to Jacob Yost and make telephone calls
secret. Of course, the Vatican knew I was working with him to try
looted works of art. All of our letters and calls regarding the art we
the normal manner and I'm certain were intercepted by whoever in
is having me watched.

"But the situation changed drastically about a year ago. Last . . .".
closed his eyes for a moment—"last January, Yost and I managed to
semifamous painting. It was one of the early works of Pissarro, and
discreetly offered for sale by a former SS colonel living under a new
Portugal. We led the police to his villa on the coast near Lisbon, v
took the painting and the colonel into custody. The incident receiv
lot of attention from the journalists.

"As the result of all the publicity, a man I had known forty year
Franz Bohles von Halbach called me from Kreuzlingen. He was the
who came to me that night forty years ago and asked forgiveness for th
of the village boy. He was also the one who had shown me the shro
Sophia Passion in their protective vault in the mine.

"Well, von Halbach was now very wealthy and calling himself V
Morgen said, as he pushed his chair back and crossed his legs, tr
comfortable on the hard wooden seat. "Max—von Halbach—was
and the moral issues he had managed to ignore or repress for fort
begun to catch up with him. The guilt-wracked young sergeant ha
remorseful dying old man, afraid for his mortal soul.

"He had grown a bit more sophisticated in the forty years si
come to my home in Alt Aussee for confession. He knew the sig
the painting, knew it held the keys to recovering the shroud and
Passion. And so he didn't show up on my doorstep with painting in
a good thing, for the painting would probably now be in the h
enemies in the Curia.

"No, realizing that secrecy was important, he decided to act dis
contacted Yost, who immediately called me."

Gunther interrupted to suggest that they eat. The men outside
in shifts, coming in one by one to wolf down cold sausages and b
continuing their watches. The men were mostly in their fifties and
deferred to Morgen.

"They used to be priests," Morgen interrupted his story to expl
outside. "They took all they could of treachery and deceit from

fear and hate the church. And in this joint fear and hatred, there is a broth-
erhood of violence."

"But what's in it for the KGB?" Seth persisted. "Why do they want it so
badly? It can't just be because the church wants it badly and therefore they
should want it too."

"That's partly it," Morgen said. "But mostly, they want it for the same
reasons Hitler wanted it."

Ridgeway and Zoe looked at him questioningly.

"The Sophia Passion is power. Power to use however you wish, whomever
you are. In this case, Zhirinovsky—or if he dies, the people just like him—
want to use the Sophia Passion to blackmail the church—all churches—into
silence on his atrocities and his new Russian expansionism and the genocide
that will certainly follow. Churches have been a great influence in rallying
people against unjust regimes. Zhirinovsky knows, just as Hitler did, that a
government is secure where it is not in conflict with the people's religions.
People everywhere still vote their religious beliefs.

"Hitler, the KGB, the kill-an-abortionist-for-Jesus groups, violent animal
rights activists—religious fanatics and political terrorists are all brothers under
the skin," Morgen said. "The differences among them are trivial. It doesn't matter whether it's a Zhirinovsky or anyone else. If not him, then some other tyrant.
We must not allow a tyrant to again use the truth to tie the moral hands of the
church." Morgen's words were steeled with the strength of his convictions.

"But how can you do that without throwing the church into turmoil?"
Seth asked. "The Christian churches, in whatever guise, are all based on a belief
in Christ as the Messiah. Aren't you in a position of destroying the church's
unity if you make public the existence of another Messiah? One whose existence
could be proven without doubt? Especially a woman? Wouldn't some people
abandon their own religions to worship this new Messiah? Think of the antag-
onism between the new believers and the old. I mean, the violence in Ireland
is over differences in how to worship the same Messiah. The split would be as
bad as . . ." He stopped to collect his thoughts.

"As bad as the differences between Islam and Christianity," Zoe said.

"Exactly," Ridgeway agreed.

Morgen looked at them quietly with eyes that told them that he had considered their arguments for decades.

"You're talking like the Vatican leadership," he said finally. "That's the
same line of reasoning Constantine and his handpicked Pope used to kill Sophia
and her followers in the first place. The church has always been in danger—
from Romans, Huns and Visigoths, ambitious kings, fascists, Nazis, and from

those ambitious to run it—and that will always be so. I firmly believe that." He paused, and when he spoke his voice was lower, steadier, surer: "But God is never endangered, especially not by the truth.

"Don't you see that it was a lie that created this situation in the first place? Constantine and the church bureaucracy were more concerned with the bureaucratic survival of the institution than they were about the faith and souls of the believers. So when they killed Sophia and covered up the truth in pursuit of preserving their own power, they sowed the seeds of destruction that are coming to flower now. And when you tell one lie, you later have to tell another lie and another and another until you've plastered the truth so far away that the pattern of lies destroys faith all by itself. Because of this every Pope has born false witness against the most important articles of faith, but they have had no choice but to defend the orthodoxy with more lies and false witness. Those who have tried to break with this shameful tradition have met untimely deaths."

Morgen leaned forward, his eyes bright with commitment. "But what we have to worry about is the spiritual faith of the people, not the church. What is important is not the survival of one of the world's oldest surviving bureaucracies and its petty human strivings and failures, but the inner religious faith of those the church is supposed to serve. Whom the people worship is not nearly so important as that they worship. Believing is important, whether it's in Buddha, Christ, Muhammad, Vishnu, or the gods that carry the sun across the sky every day."

"My dad believed that," Zoe said softly. "He told me to think of all the world's religions and faiths as a stained glass window glowing with every color in the spectrum. Many colors, but only one sun. God made us all different colors and God speaks to us in many tongues."

"Your father was a wise man," Morgen said. "We are finite creatures grappling with the infinite. Our questions are what matter. Questions and not answers matter because the answers are never whole, always limited by our physical senses. And they're never all true since human 'answers' to the secrets of the divine are always colored by culture, society, expediency, prejudice, greed, and every other deadly sin.

"Despite all this, people must believe. Faith in things we do not see is what feeds our creativity, lifts us to feats that cannot be explained by natural phenomena, and enables us to transcend our physical world." He leaned closer now, elbows planted solidly in the middle of the table. "People must believe, and they must believe in the truth. We can be the instrument to bring that truth to them."

Morgen wiped away the beads of perspiration that had broken out on his forehead. "The church today is founded in great part on a lie. In the long view—in the length of time that can only be measured by historians who won't be born for perhaps another century or more—in that long view, the truth will make for a stronger faith. But we and those who come after us will suffer for the sins and indiscretions and fears of those men back in 325 A.D. The alternative is to continue to let fascists and dictators and ambitious men use the truth to blackmail the future."

He slumped in his chair, visibly exhausted.

After a minute or so Seth got up, walked to the fireplace, and used the padded mitts to bring the coffeepot to the table. He asked Morgen, "Would you like some?" Morgen nodded weakly and Ridgeway filled his cup. After filling Zoe's cup and his own, Seth returned the pot to its warming shelf.

Morgen had rejuvenated his flagging energy enough to sit up to the table, although he leaned on it like a man clinging to the last piece of floating debris from a sunken ship. They listened to the wind whistle, to the wood knots snapping in the fireplace, to the almost impalpable sounds of human beings breathing, moving.

Seth finally broke Father Morgen's silence.

"I just don't understand how you can know all of this . . . go through all of this and still remain a Catholic, much less a priest."

Morgen studied Seth's face, then gave him a rueful smile. "I have been through many crises of my faith, as I sense you are now experiencing," the old priest began. "But I believe faith in God supports us, sustains us—"

"But the notion we have of God is so corrupted by the politics and expediency of organized religion," Seth replied contentiously. "The notion is corrupt and the existence is totally suspect."

"Yes," Morgen said patiently. "Yes it is. Faith sustains us; religion divides. But answer this. If you are climbing a mountain and find that the rope keeping you safe has rotten fibers, do you cast off the entire rope? Will you abandon your entire faith because of the rotten fibers?"

Seth frowned.

"Faith binds us to the spiritual," Morgen continued. "But faith and religion have become intertwined in the same rope. In every organized religion true faith and blasphemy lie next to each other like strands in a rope. I despair of being able to tease away the evil without destroying the whole. I am mortal and limited and don't always have the vision to truly know which fibers should remain and which should go."

"So you just accept the church as it is, warts and all."

Morgen nodded slowly. "Mostly." He paused. "As best I can. You see, instead of the stained glass example, I look at every religion as a different doorway to God. As finite creatures, we can never comprehend more than one small part of the infinite. So it's no wonder that different people, cultures see just their own small true part of God."

"Like the blind men describing an elephant?" Zoe prompted.

"Precisely. We are all blind in our own ways," Morgen said. "I believe that every religion has its own true glimpse of God."

"But how can they all claim to be the one true way?" Zoe asked.

"They can't really. Not honestly. Not in true good faith," Morgen said. "The exclusion, the rejection and reviling of other views of God are the evil that men do."

"And women," Zoe added.

Morgen smiled. "And women. God is male. God is female . . . both and neither. We try to catch a glimpse of God and we want so badly to believe in someone like ourselves."

"So faith is our connection with the divine, and religion is our attempt to impose our vision of God on other people?"

The old priest nodded.

"But don't you think it's wrong to hold up one vision of God over another or to try and make God male or female exclusively?" Zoe asked. "Isn't that some sort of intellectual idolatry: to limit the limitless, to put a face on the faceless? Perhaps the commandment against graven images was an attempt to have us focus on the abstract, the infinite, the all-encompassing rather than on the concrete embodiment of the theology of the moment."

"You are right," Morgen agreed. "Limiting God in whatever way or only believing in a God that looks like you is blasphemy, pure and simple. I believe—" He stopped abruptly as they heard shouts from outside the cabin.

"Quick," Morgen said to Gunther. "The Passion." Seth's eyes followed Gunther's bent physique as he shambled to the corner of the hut occupied by a mattressless bunk bed.

"How did you get that!" Seth exclaimed when he saw Gunther bend low to pick up the black metal briefcase they had taken from the Thule Gesellschaft bank the previous day.

"Those who work with me are extremely talented," Morgen said.

Seth watched speechlessly as Gunther brought the briefcase to the hearth. The third man in the room, a stocky man in his mid-fifties with a skin-close haircut, joined Morgen and Gunther. Together they lifted one of the rock slabs that composed the hearth.

As the shouting outside grew louder, the three men put the briefcase in a recess in the hearth, then struggled to replace the stone. Seth shook off his momentary indecision and joined them, his healthy strong back making the chore easier.

They had barely finished when the door burst open with an explosion of sharp biting wind and a flurry of snowflakes. Two of Morgen's men hesitated in the doorway for a moment, holding a semiconscious man by his arms. Morgen nodded to them and they walked forward, half dragging, half carrying the man, who was dressed in a warm down parka much like Seth's, thick twill pants, and sturdy lug-soled hiking boots.

"We found him sneaking around outside," one of the men said as they dropped the man at Morgen's feet. The man groaned.

"Turn him over," Morgen ordered.

When they turned him over, Zoe gasped. The man was George Stratton.

THIRTY-THREE

The Habersam mine is a large one," explained Gunther. "I should know. I was the superintendent there until the SS arrived." He had taken the plan of the mine and spread it out on the table in the hut. Sitting around the table were Morgen, Ridgeway, Zoe, two of Morgen's men, and George Stratton, his head patched in half a dozen places with bandages covering the wounds received in his battle with Morgen's three men. All three of the men who had captured Stratton also wore bandages. None was happy about the American joining their effort.

The three men would have killed Stratton had not Zoe and Seth vouched for him. "He saved our lives," Seth told Morgen, and recounted in detail the incident in the limousine in Marina Del Rey. Zoe followed with her own rescue in Zurich.

"You seem to be suspiciously handy, Mr. Stratton," Morgen said. Reluctantly he agreed to allow the American to join the team.

They sat around the table now, planning their assault on the mine. They would go after the shroud and the Sophia Passion on Christmas Day. "Our sacrifice shall be our celebration," Morgen had said.

Gunther explained in detail how he and the others, not including Morgen, had labored for several years to cut a passage from an adjoining abandoned mine into the Habersam mine.

"The entrance to the Habersam mine is so thoroughly blocked that it would take a major effort . . . heavy equipment, explosives, to clear it." Gunther said. "For obvious reasons we didn't want to attract the attention that major effort would require."

"Not to mention the expense," Morgen said. "It would be prohibitively expensive."

Gunther nodded his agreement. "I have lived here all my life and have worked at some time or other in just about every mine from here to Bad Ischl.

The hills are honeycombed with mines. There are so many of them that a substantial number are not even mapped."

It took less than a year for Gunther to find the right mine. It had to be abandoned so they could work in it without notice, and it had to be close enough for a handful of men working part time to dig a passage from it into the Habersam mine. It took Gunther and his coworkers more than nine years to dig the passage.

"But if you've already cut a passage into the mine, why haven't you hired a safecracker or something to get the shroud out before now?" Seth asked.

Wordlessly, Gunther reached into the black metal briefcase and pulled from it a small bound booklet. He displayed it for all to see.

"The good Sergeant von Halbach told Father Morgen about an extensive system of safeguards, mines, and traps that lined every approach to the vault," Gunther said.

"And in addition," Morgen said, "not only is the vault itself designed to be dangerous to any unauthorized entry, but also von Halbach told me that as an ultimate safeguard there were mechanisms to destroy the shroud and the Passion to keep them from falling into the wrong hands."

"And this is the key," Gunther said, eagerly thumbing through the book's pages. "Page after page after page on how to avoid, disarm, dismantle the defenses." He paused as he scanned one page in the back. "Including the procedure for entering the vault." He bent the book's binding back to the page and held it up for all to see.

"But surely the explosives or poisons . . . whatever, will have deteriorated over the last forty years," Zoe said.

Seth shook his head, "People are still being killed by World War Two grenades and bombs that some farmer plows up in his fields or that some gas company worker slams a shovel into."

Gunther looked at her and nodded his agreement. "He's right, Mrs. Ridgeway. And there are poison gases the Nazis produced, nerve gases like tabun, anthrax bombs, that are still just as potent today and probably thousands of times as dangerous now that their metal casings and containers have deteriorated." He shook his head. "No, the Nazis made good weapons. We can expect most of them still to pose a danger."

Zoe shivered.

"I assume, then, that one of you"—Seth looked at Gunther—"is an expert in the sorts of explosives or devices from the World War Two era?"

There was a pregnant pause as Gunther looked to Morgen.

Morgen cleared his throat. "I'm afraid he was killed in Amsterdam," Morgen said. "He died in the park next to you—"

"I've learned a bit about explosives," Gunther said, "in the course of being a mine superintendent. But an expert? Hardly, Mr. Ridgeway."

"That's why we'd like you to accompany us into the mine tomorrow," Morgen said to Seth. "I understand your law enforcement experience includes some expertise in explosives. That, and because you have a young, strong back."

"No, Seth!" Zoe cried. "We've already done enough. Let them handle this part."

Morgen looked at her with troubled eyes, and then said: "We will—we can—help you clear your names, help you deal with the criminal charges that are pending against you, regardless of our success here tomorrow."

He swallowed, looked briefly at Seth, and then back at Zoe. "I have no doubt that you will be exonerated if we can offer the proof that sits now inside that mine." He paused again, a debater giving the judges time to absorb the information. "However, without the shroud and the Sophia Passion, your story—the facts in the matter—will be dismissed as lies, as fantasies. They are too fantastic to believe . . . without some sort of proof. You will either spend the rest of your lives in a prison or in hiding."

He got up and walked around the table to where Seth and Zoe sat. "Your help tomorrow makes our chances of success much greater and improves the chances that you will be cleared of all these charges. On the other hand, should we fail . . ." He shrugged as if trying to rid his shoulders of the implications. Seth suddenly felt the weight of the decision fall on his own shoulders.

"May I think about it until morning?" He asked.

"Of course," Morgen nodded. "But you must sit up with us tonight as we study the plans. Preparation is all that will save our lives tomorrow. Preparation, luck, and prayer."

THIRTY-FOUR

They arrived at the mouth of the abandoned mine about noon on Christmas Day. The weather had taken a turn for the worse. The wind whipped up off the valley with a vengeance, driving with it hard, sand-sized grains of snow that stung like cold needles when they found exposed skin. Visibility had dropped to nearly nothing as a whiteout threatened to close in around them. The sun was a vague gray disk against a uniformly gray sky. Seth and Zoe were grateful for the goggles Gunther had provided.

The snowmobiles crawled through the bright stinging murk as Gunther led them from landmark to landmark, relying on his uncanny knowledge of the area to keep them from getting lost.

Morgen sat behind Gunther on the lead snowmobile, which towed behind it a small tarp-covered sled filled with the tools, explosives, and other items he thought would be necessary. Behind him was a second machine, ridden by Stratton and piloted by one of the three men who had captured him the night before. Bringing up the rear of the procession was a third snowmobile, driven by Seth Ridgeway. Zoe sat behind him with her arms around his waist. He had tried to convince her to stay at the hut with Morgen's other men, but she refused. "I told you in Zurich. I've found you and no matter what happens, no matter how dangerous things get, we're not going to be separated again." She could not be persuaded otherwise.

Seth doggedly kept the tail lights of the second snowmobile in sight. He could not see the lead machine, and to lose the second one would mean being instantly lost.

Just as the gray disk that was the sun climbed to the day's zenith, Seth heard the pitch of Gunther's snowmobile drop suddenly. The sound was followed immediately by the brake lights of the second machine. Seth gripped the brakes on his own snowmobile's handlebars and squeezed them to a stop.

Wordlessly, they dismounted and helped to pull the supply sled toward the mouth of the mine.

In a matter of minutes they dragged the sled into the shelter of a rock overhang. Ahead of them an iron gate barred their entrance to the mine. Gunther pulled the tarpaulin from the sled and began to pass around the equipment. To Seth, Zoe, and Stratton, he handed backpacks that weighed about twenty-five or thirty pounds. He handed all of them flashlights and whistles with a lanyard. "Wear these around your necks at all times," he told them. "If you get separated, stay in one place and blow on the whistle."

He slung a large coil of climbing rope diagonally over one shoulder, then buckled a beltload of carabiners and pitons, as well as a hammer to drive the pitons, around his waist.

"The rock entrance to this mine is very unstable," he told them. "Once we hit the salt, everything will be fine. But the rocks and the shorings that compose the first four hundred feet of the tunnel are in danger of collapse." And, as if to confirm Gunther's gloomy diagnosis, a scattering of rocks clattered somewhere in the darkness beyond.

"There is a vent hole cut vertically into the upper portion of salt. If the entrance is blocked, we can work our way out using the climbing gear." He walked up to the iron gate, unlocked a remarkably battered padlock, and swung the gate open. They followed him in.

The impoverished light penetrated only the first fifty feet or so of the mine entrance. Everyone had turned on their flashlights. Still, the going was treacherous, with ice underfoot and great stiletto-like stalactites of ice suspended from the ceiling.

Seth and Zoe walked cautiously along the icy floor, daring to take only small steps as the floor of the mine sloped inexorably downward. Remnants of the pitiful daylight vanished entirely now in the great blackness of the tunnel. To conserve batteries, Gunther ordered everyone but him to turn off their flashlights. His light picked out rotten wooden shorings and the rusty remains of metal ones. It was apparent that the rock faces above and to either side of them hung there against gravity with no support at all. Seth wanted to ask Gunther about that, but didn't. He didn't really want to know the answer.

Suddenly the sounds of falling rocks filled the tunnel. Somewhere in the darkness, not too far beyond the bright cone Gunther's flashlight carved out of the darkness, came the dull hollow clattering of stone against stone.

"Wait," Gunther said in a hushed voice. He had warned them earlier not to make loud noises. The rocks in this portion of the mine were so poised for a cave-in, he said, that any loud noise might be enough to trigger a collapse. His warning had a chilling effect on any conversation, loud or otherwise. He, after all, was the man who had worked in the mines all his life. The sound of falling rocks continued for several seconds. The tunnel floor vibrated under their feet, and instants later small rock fragments began to fall around them from the tunnel ceiling.

Zoe said a silent prayer.

In a minute the rocks had stopped falling, and once again they were alone in the tunnel with the sounds of their own breathing. Gunther hesitated for several more seconds, then moved forward without talking.

Over and over in his mind, Seth ticked off the things they would have to deal with once they crossed over into the Habersam mine. They had gone over the plans and the instructions from the safe deposit box half a dozen times. The Nazi maps of the mine marked with the locations of the planted explosives and other devices were compared with the mine company maps Gunther had been able to obtain locally.

Not surprisingly, the two maps were not in total agreement. The mining company maps showed tunnels where the Nazi map showed none. Just as cartographers—before the days of aerial and satellite mapping—used to differ on the shapes of the continents, mining engineers of forty years past used comparatively crude methods, a fact that guaranteed that no two mining maps, particularly those of small backwoods mines, would be the same.

Today, though, even minor differences could prove to be dangerous, since it was necessary to know exactly where the Nazi traps were located. A foot the wrong way, or even a few inches, could mean disaster.

"And of course we have no way of knowing if everything is properly charted," Gunther had told them the night before. "The commandant of the SS unit could have ordered other protective measures in the last days of the war and not bothered to update the materials in the box."

The ice in the tunnel gradually thawed as they walked deeper into the mine. Filling the tunnel now was the sound of running water.

"The hills are riddled with underground streams and rivers," Gunther had said. "The greatest danger that a miner faces, next to cave-ins, of course, is the disaster that results from blasting through a rock wall only to find an underground stream."

He explained that rain and melting snow seeped into water—re-taining layers of rock, which gradually migrated downward. Some of it flowed naturally into fresh water springs that fed mountain streams. But much of it ran along the cracks and fissures in the rock of the mountains, and eventually into the ubiquitous salt deposits buried underneath. The salt, some of it containing sulfur and other minerals, dissolved in the water and was carried down with it toward the warmer layers of rock that lay at the base of the mountains. Eventually, many of these warm, mineral-laden streams of water emerged at the surface again, in the guise of the warm mineral springs around which the great spas were built.

Seth recalled Gunther's words now as he walked through the tunnel the walls of rock on either side seeming to press malevolently inward, reaching out for him as if they wanted his life. He had an urge to walk faster, but Gunther set the pace. Seth tried to pass off his anxiety as mild claustrophobia. The real danger lay ahead.

The documents from the black metal briefcase described a series of ingenious killing devices set by the Nazis to protect their prize. There were machine guns whose triggers had been connected to trip wires.

"Just like the former East Germans used to employ in the border zone that separated them from the old West Germany before unification," Zoe had said.

Then there were covered pits with stakes at the bottom.

"Just like the North Vietnamese," Ridgeway had added.

Containers of napalm were rigged to incinerate those who triggered the mechanism. Those who escaped being immolated would probably die as the flames consumed the oxygen in the tunnel. In the larger chambers of the salt mine, where the formation was stable, antipersonnel mines had been buried beneath the salt.

All of these were marked clearly on the charts, along with procedures to avoid or disarm the devices.

But the presence of booby traps possibly added at the last minute nagged at Seth, as did a single handwritten notation inside the back cover of the booklet.

"What does 'Pfeil' mean?" Ridgeway had asked Gunther.

"Arrow," the Austrian had replied.

But they found no further reference to arrows. Seth had forgotten it until just now, as he ran down the list of things that squatted in the distant darkness, defying them to enter.

Gunther's light seemed to grow brighter in the tunnel now, and Seth quickly realized it was because the man had walked into an area where the tunnel walls were white. The column quickened its pace, anxious to leave the uncertain stability of the rack-walled tunnel for the more reliable salt formation. Moments later, Gunther's flashlight seemed to extinguish itself as they entered a giant chamber the size and dimensions of an auditorium.

Gunther stopped. "Switch on your lights for a moment, all of you," he said. The gasps of awe came from Seth, Zoe, and Stratton as they looked about the vast white room.

"Salt formations are considered extremely stable," Gunther said. "In addition to using them to store looted art and treasures, the Nazis actually moved entire factories into mines such as these, where they could continue to operate, safe from the Allied bombings. The hills around us are filled with chambers like this one."

Morgen spoke next. "Some of them had been used by Jews and others as hiding places from the Nazis. On the other side of the valley there are mine chambers that are sealed off as graves. They contain the bodies of people executed by the Nazis when they surveyed the mines for storehouses and found entire families living in them."

He turned sadly and nodded to Gunther, who ordered them once again to extinguish their flashlights. As Seth moved forward, he noticed that there was a faint brown path in the salt, created no doubt by the scuffling of Gunther and his helpers as they cut the entrance into the Habersam mine.

They followed the path around a pile of boards, rusty metal scaffolding, and a conical pile of salt that had collapsed from the ceiling of the great salt chamber.

"If you don't dig your mine in the right places, water can do that over time," Gunther explained.

Minutes later they passed out of the huge white chamber and into a spacious corridor. Its white salt walls took the light from Gunther's flashlight and diffused and reflected it so that the passageway seemed to be lit indirectly from within the walls.

About fifty yards into the corridor, it began to narrow, obstructed by piles of salt that stretched most of the way across the floor and halfway to the ceiling.

"These are the tailings we took from the passageway," Gunther remarked.

They walked another fifty yards before coming to a rough opening in the corridor walls. The column stopped in single file. A long trail of salt obstructed the corridor in the other direction for as far as the light penetrated.

"This is it," Gunther said with as much pride in his voice as Michelangelo might once have used to announce the completion of his statue of David. They crowded around the opening, Seth climbing the loose talus of salt to get a good look. Zoe clambered up alongside him.

The opening was about six feet high and a bit less than three feet wide. It reminded Seth of the open face of a coffin. When Gunther shined his light into the opening, the beam revealed a long, straight passageway that continued beyond the ability of the light to illuminate. Seth looked at his watch and noted it was nearly 1 P.M.

"I'd like to go over a few last-minute things before we enter the tunnel, just so we remember the important items we went over last night," Gunther said. "First of all, remember that there are antipersonnel mines buried in the floors everywhere. The plans indicate a random placement except near the chamber where the vault is. There they are clustered very densely." He looked at the large, close-cropped man in his fifties who had helped to capture Stratton the night before. "For this reason, Richard will precede us with a metal detector. I hope the moisture will have rusted the detonators, but we can't be sure.

"Remember," Gunther cautioned, "we have not actually been in the Habersam mine. We needed the chart you obtained from the bank vault so we could make sure that we didn't take any action that might result in our injury or, more importantly, damage to the Passion. So as soon as we set foot on the other side of this passage, we will be on completely new ground. And because of the discrepancies between the Nazi mining charts and the company charts of this mine, we don't know precisely where in the Habersam mine our little passageway leads to."

"That means our prediction on which booby traps we'll face might not be right?" Zoe asked.

Gunther nodded. "I think I know where we'll turn out."

"I pray you are right," Father Morgen said. And then, addressing the group, he said: "Would you like to pray before we enter the passage?"

Heads bowed in unison. Seth was reminded of the old saying that there are no atheists in foxholes. He stood apart from the group, head unbowed.

Morgen began with the Twenty-third Psalm: "The Lord is my Shepherd; I shall not want. He maketh me to lie down in green pastures; He leadeth me beside the still waters. He restoreth my soul; He leadeth me in the paths of righteousness for His name's sake."

She maketh, Zoe thought silently. *She leadeth; She restoreth; She leadeth; for Her name's sake.*

The priest's voice grew in intensity as he recited the psalm. "Yea, though I walk through the valley of the shadow of death, I will fear no evil: for Thou art with me; Thy rod and Thy staff they comfort me. Thou preparest a table before me in the presence of mine enemies; Thou anointest my head with oil; my cup runneth over. Surely goodness and mercy shall follow me all the days of my life; and I will dwell in the house of the Lord forever."

In the dimly lit corridor beneath the mountain, there was a murmuring of quiet "amens" from all but Seth, who remained silent.

Then, taking the rough, dark mountain bread and a canteen of water, Morgen broke bread and said the Eucharist. Seth stood aloof. Afterward they all silently consumed the remaining bread and water. Then, like paratroopers nearing the drop zone, they wrapped themselves in personal thoughts of their own mortality.

Seth and Zoe stood with their arms around each other. He felt her warmth and her love and wished that he could recapture the spiritual certainty that had now failed him.

Finally, without prompting, for they had discussed things many times and to do so again would be to procrastinate, Richard Stehr stepped into the passageway, followed by Gunther, then Seth, Zoe, Father Morgen, and finally, George Stratton.

"I love you," Zoe told Seth as he stepped into the passageway.

"I love you too, kid," he said, then kissed her. Reluctantly, he turned and followed Gunther's gnarled but strong body down the narrow corridor.

They had been walking for less than a minute when the sounds of running water filled the passageway.

"What's that?" Seth asked Gunther.

"An underground stream," Gunther replied without breaking stride. "I've listened to it for years now. It used to scare me." He paused as if searching for the words to describe his feelings. "Now, it's like an old friend."

Seth felt less sanguine about the noise and the rumbling beneath his feet, both of which increased as they continued. The tunnel crackled with an ozone of emotions—mostly fear—that bound them all and seemed to propel them faster and faster.

They had walked for another ten minutes when finally Richard's flashlight illuminated a white wall at the end of the passageway. There seemed to be a fist-sized hole in the middle of it.

"That is the very end," Gunther yelled. The roaring of the water was now so loud he had to shout to be heard for more than a few feet. "It's only about six inches thick." As the rest of the party approached, Gunther asked Seth to hand him the shovel that was tied to the back of the Austrian's pack.

Seth was leaning forward to untie the strap that bound the spadelike shovel when Richard screamed.

Seth lifted his gaze. Richard seemed to have shrunk. He had turned to face them, his arms outstretched for help.

"Help me!" Richard screamed desperately. Gunther shed his pack in an instant, fell on his belly, and began to crawl toward Richard, who had now shrunk to the size of a large stuffed bear.

It took Seth several moments before he realized that Richard had not shrunk at all, but had sunk into the floor of the tunnel. He flailed his arms and shrieked as he sank deeper and deeper. Around him, the hard-packed salt floor had turned dark with water. Condensation from the warm water formed a modest fog in the cool air of the corridor.

Gunther approached him cautiously now, his arms and legs spread to distribute his weight more evenly. There was no telling how far the floor had been undermined. Seth quickly shed his own pack and crawling on his belly moved forward to grab Gunther's ankle.

Seth looked up. Only Richard's head could be seen now. The man was grasping for Gunther's outstretched hand. Pieces of the tunnel floor broke off around him and disappeared. Seth felt Gunther stretch out and grabbed the old Austrian. The next instant, Gunther shouted to Seth, "Pull! Pull us both. Now!"

Pulling with all his might, Seth edged backward, tugging against the grasp of the underground currents. Progress came by the inch.

"Here." He felt strong arms pulling at his belt. Stratton had wedged his way around Morgen and Zoe to help.

They progressed a foot, a foot and a half, when the tunnel filled with a high-pitched scream. Seth and Stratton fell backward suddenly as the tension was abruptly released. Richard shrieked one last time, then disappeared into the wet sucking hole.

They sat there, too stunned to move. Zoe rushed to Seth and held him. Moments later, Gunther's agonized weeping filled the air. Hans Morgen squeezed past to comfort him.

"It was not your fault, Gunther," Morgen said, as he put an arm around his old friend's shoulder.

"But I let him go," Gunther protested. "I held him and I let him go." He began to sob softly.

"You did all you could," Morgen countered.

Seth, Zoe, and Stratton sat quietly for perhaps ten minutes before Stratton motioned them to follow him back toward the auditorium-sized chamber through which they had passed.

Gunther and Morgen were waiting for them when they returned, dragging two long boards the size of a two-by-twelve. Stratton and Seth jockeyed the boards into the narrow passageway while Zoe led Morgen and Gunther back to the stack of timbers they had separated from the pile of debris they had skirted on the way in.

It took them more than an hour, but when they finished, the hole in the floor of the passage was bridged with boards.

"We must hurry," Gunther said. "Now that the water has broken through, we do not know how long it will take to eat away at the edges. It could swallow up our little bridge."

Gunther led them across the bridge and made short work of the thin salt wall he had left at the end of the corridor. He worked with the vengeance of a man punishing himself. When the hole was large enough, Gunther leaned through it, like a sailor leaning through a porthole, swinging his flashlight through long broad arcs as he surveyed the tunnel beyond. He paused long enough to examine the plan, which he had pulled from the black metal briefcase. He looked at the plan, then stuck his head through the hole, comparing reality to the map. Finally, he turned to the others and spread the map on the floor of the corridor. Seth, Zoe, Morgen, and Stratton crowded against each other, trying to see.

"We're here." Gunther pointed to a spot on the map near the conjunction of two tunnels. "I thought we'd come out . . ." He moved a finger grimy with work to another spot less than an inch away, "right here." There was pride in his voice now, leavening his sorrow. "We're about fifty feet off. But that doesn't matter as long as we know exactly where we are at all times."

He folded up the plan and finished widening the hole, so that they could easily gain entrance to the tunnel in the Habersam mine.

On the other side, he insisted that they walk single file, each distanced from the other by at least twenty feet. Only Seth and Zoe violated the rule.

The metal detector had been lost with Richard. So Gunther used the page-by-page details of the mine to find the antipersonnel mines. He measured their progress accurately, using a hundred-foot tape measure that he let play out behind him as he walked. He gave the task of holding the other end of the tape to Father Morgen, who protested being given such a relatively safe task. But he yielded to Gunther's insistence. To Zoe he gave the task of sprinkling small amounts of carbon black on the floor to mark their path, so that it would be easier to find their way out safely.

The carbon black came in containers the size of soft drink cans. Zoe quickly discovered that Ridgeway's pack contained nothing but can after can of the inky black powder.

They all had their flashlights on now, scanning the corridor for signs of booby traps that might not have found their way onto the plans taken from the safe deposit box in Zurich.

They came to the first trip-wired machine gun at half past two.

"Wait!" Gunther shouted. They were approaching the intersection with another tunnel when they stopped. Gunther lowered his flashlight. "Look here," he called. There, in the middle of the intersection, was a thin wire stretched taut from one side of the corridor to another. Gunther motioned them on slowly. They followed his lead right up to the wire and then stopped. Gunther shone his light into the intersecting tunnel to his right. There was nothing but the post to which one end of the wire was attached.

In the other direction, however, was a machine gun on a tripod. It had a square body with a long barrel that ended in a sort of flare. Around the barrel was a perforated metal sleeve, the air-cooling jacket. They stared at the gun for a moment, half expecting it to open fire.

Gunther motioned them back to the safety of the tunnel from which they had come. Seth peered around the corner as Gunther walked up to the machine gun and swiveled it toward the bright white salt wall. Next, he took a pair of wire cutters and clipped the tripwire. It fell slack in the middle of the tunnel intersection.

Gunther started to walk back toward them, then stopped and went back to the machine gun. He bent over the gun and pulled the trigger.

The gun leaped to life, filling the tunnels with fire and noise for perhaps a dozen rounds, and then fell silent as the hammer fell on a dud.

A smell that reeked of cordite and the ghosts of ancient enemies come to life accompanied Gunther back to where the group had gathered.

"That's why we must be careful," he said, then ordered the tape brought up and planted firmly at the edge of the intersecting corridor. He then took the other end and began walking again. As he got to the intervals indicated on the plans, he would turn one way or another to circumvent the mines.

A hundred yards on, he bent to rip the camouflage from a deep pit. A clattering of boards filled the mine, accompanied by a rolling cloud of dust as the materials dropped into the hole. Like the others, Zoe shone her light into the pit as she walked the narrow ledge between it and the tunnel wall. Barbed metal spikes that looked to be three feet long grinned back up at her.

The mines grew closer together, and the number of booby traps they had to disarm increased as they neared the chamber containing the shroud's vault.

Their first surprise came as they stepped into a huge chamber nearly as large as the auditorium-sized one in the other mine. They had moved inch by inch, skirting a field of mines that had been placed side by side, with barely room for a footprint between the triggers. Gunther took a can of the carbon black from Zoe and sprinkled it, not in a path, but in the specific places where they should put their feet. Placement had to be precise. To slip or lose one's balance could mean being ripped apart by the explosives buried beneath the salt.

This last minefield was nearly forty feet wide. Gunther had them all wait nearly fifty yards behind as he picked his way through the mines. In the dimly lit distance, he seemed to move at a stop-frame pace.

They all stood silently, holding their breaths. Zoe looked at Father Morgen and saw his lips moving in a silent prayer.

Finally Gunther straightened to his full height and shouted, "It's all clean. Come one at a time."

Zoe watched, terrified, as Seth picked his way through. Finally he turned around. "Why don't you wait on that side, Zoe?"

"No way," she said, with a bravery she didn't feel.

Ridgeway's fingertips tingled as he watched her begin picking her way through. To him, she looked like a ballerina dancing a lethal solo. The cave seemed to drop away from around him as he watched her step by agonizing step. She seemed to walk forever and not get any closer. Then she was there in his arms. He led her to the side while Father Morgen and George Stratton made their way across.

Finally they were all assembled.

"This is the main vault room," Gunther said, looking first at the plan of the mine and then around him. "The plans show no booby traps here." The chamber was perhaps seventy-five yards square and thirty or forty feet high. The floor was uneven, covered with dimly lit debris, looking like packing crates or irregular piles of rubbish.

"Yes, I know," Father Morgen said dreamily. He looked about him, a sleepwalker suddenly awakened from his trance. "I was here," he said, as if he didn't entirely believe it. "I was here more than half a century ago . . . a lifetime ago." He played his flashlight around the room, "We walked in . . . We walked in there." His flashlight beam fixed on the entrance to a corridor on the other side of the chamber. "And the entrance to the vault is right over . . ." He swung the flashlight beam to the right. "There."

The metal vault door was set into an outcropping of gray rock. It was large, unrusted, and from the distance at which they stood, looked remarkably like the door to the Thule Gesellschaft Bank's safe deposit box vault.

"There wouldn't be booby traps here," Morgen said, still in his dreamy tone of voice, "because there were men here, many of them. Walking about. The sergeant showed me. The main entrance was heavily guarded, and the rest of the approaches booby-trapped and mined to guard against people like us."

Ridgeway led them toward the vault door. He had made it halfway across the chamber when he felt a section of the floor move slightly downward. From across the room came the metallic clacking and snicking of a mechanical apparatus.

"Hit the dirt!" Ridgeway yelled as he dived to the ground, pulling Zoe along with him. A single shot echoed in the room, followed by the dull clanking sound the dud ammunition had made in the other machine gun. Seth swore he heard the bullet parting the air above him

Moments later, they all got to their feet and continued. As they approached the vault door, Seth shined his flashlight on one of the piles of debris scattered around the chamber. The piles were the skeletons of men dressed in the uniforms of the SS. There were a score of them scattered about the chamber. But with nerves burned and numbed by the horrors that had already played themselves out that day, neither Seth nor Zoe nor the others reacted to the bony hands and skulls sticking out of olive-drab uniforms.

Instead, they walked like weary gladiators, crossing an arena littered with the bodies of their slain enemies. They crossed to greet the emperor and to receive their reward. It seemed to Seth that they had finally come back to write the ending chapter to a war that had begun in another era and which had waited for them all along. The enemy still fought back at them over time, as if destiny were still waiting to be decided.

The first vault door had two combination dials that had to be turned simultaneously. Zoe read the numbers aloud as Seth on the right dial and Gunther on the left turned the mechanisms.

"Left dial to the left to twenty-seven," she read from the documents, as Stratton held the light for her, "and right dial to the left to fifty-nine. Get ready. Go." Seth and Gunther moved the dials in unison, then waited for their next instruction.

"That's it," Zoe said. "That's all the numbers."

Seth and Gunther looked at each other and then, as if a communication had passed between them, turned and gestured to Morgen.

"Father," Gunther said. "Will you do the honor?"

Morgen walked reverently to the door with the hesitancy of a man approaching the fulfillment of his life's work. He took the handle on the vault door and wrenched it clockwise. Somewhere inside the massive door the mechanism clacked solidly, moving its well-oiled parts for the first time in more than four decades. This sound, too, seemed to solidify this vault's relationship with the one beneath the streets of Zurich, as if they had both been designed by the same man for the same act of destiny.

Morgen strained at the door. It wouldn't move.

Alarmed that they had come so far for nothing, Seth placed his right hand beside the priest's and heaved. Still nothing.

The joy and reverence had fallen into ruins on Morgen's face.

"Seth?" Zoe asked. "What's the matter?"

"Door won't open," Seth said. "The mechanism moved inside, but it won't swing open." He paused. "Let me see the instructions."

She handed him the papers from which she had been reading. Ridgeway examined the papers with Gunther looking over his shoulder. After a pause he handed them to Gunther.

"We did everything right," Ridgeway said. "It must be the hinges or something."

Morgen's face looked blank, as if his thoughts were focused in another era. "They had some sort of automatic mechanism, I believe." Morgen said finally. "I remember the door almost opening by itself when the sergeant brought me here."

"Perhaps something the camp commandant added?" Gunther suggested.

Ridgeway shrugged, his face dark with thought. Then, a moment later, he said to Gunther, "Take off your rope. Tie one end to the handle of the vault door."

Gunther complied, and when the knot was secure, Seth arranged them along the rope like members of a tug-of-war team. Seth gave himself the anchor position at the tail of the lineup.

"Pull!" he yelled. The rope tightened and swayed as they arranged themselves in a straight line. They took a step back as the nylon climbing rope stretched. But the door remained stationary.

"Harder," Seth urged. "Pull harder,"

The sounds of boot soles scrabbling for purchase on the gritty salt floor mixed with puffing and heavy breathing. Finally, a complaint creaked from the vault door, and it swung open.

"All right!" Stratton yelled.

"Thank God," Morgen muttered.

Inside the vault was a room from another age. It was a good twelve or fifteen feet wide and at least twice that in length. It was arranged like an office, with a desk, chair, lamp, and long conference table. The floor was carpeted. The two long walls were covered with wood. The end wall was concrete, and set into it was another safe.

They walked in slowly. Morgen looked like a man exploring an almost forgotten dream.

They played their flashlights around the walls.

"There," Morgen said, pointing toward the middle of the right-hand wall. Ridgeway looked, but failed to see what the priest had been pointing at. Morgen walked up to the spot and pointed toward a nail. "This is where the picture hung," Morgen said. "Sergeant von Halbach took it from here. He must have. I saw it that time. I saw it." He turned to them as if he didn't expect them to believe him.

But Gunther and Seth moved quickly past him, anxious to get the last phase of the job done. They reached the end of the vault and spread out the papers on the table.

"The combination is a standard one," Gunther said, as they looked at the papers. "But once the door's open, we have only ten seconds to insert the gold ingot from the picture in the slot, here." He pointed first to a drawing of the safe door, then at the slot on the door in the wall beside them. The slot was blocked by a piece of metal. Ridgeway produced the ingot from his pack.

"There must be some sort of counterbalance mechanism inside," Gunther said. "It is probably activated by an object of the correct size and weight." Seth nodded. "Will you hold the light for me?" Gunther asked. Seth nodded as the Austrian turned to the safe and began to twirl the dial.

There were sixteen numbers in all, and Gunther dialed them slowly and precisely. Finally, with the last digit in place, there was a clicking and momentary whir as the slot was suddenly free. The second hand on Seth's watch hit 3:13:26 and kept moving.

"Quickly," Gunther said. "Give me the ingot." Seth handed the ingot to Gunther.

3.13:29.

Gunther turned to face the safe. His hands shook as he brought the ingot to the slot.

3:13:30

Gunther cursed as he bobbled the ingot.

3:13:31.

The ingot thudded quietly on the carpet.

"Oh, God! Quickly!" Gunther and Seth dropped to their knees simultaneously as the mechanism in the safe ground on.

3.13:34.

"Here," Gunther handed the ingot to Seth. "You do it."

Seth stood up.

3:13:37.

Seth rammed the ingot into the slot. It quickly passed out of sight, swallowed in the mechanism of the door. The whirring stopped.

"Did we make it?" Gunther asked.

Seth looked at his watch. "A second or two late," he said, reaching for the handle. "Let's see if it still works."

He started to turn the handle when Zoe screamed.

"The door! Seth! The door's closing!"

Seth whirled in place and saw the vault door slowly moving on its hinges.

"George!" Seth barked. "You and Zoe and the Father get out and hold on to the rope and see if you can slow it up. I'll help Gunther."

But before any of them could move, Gunther reached up and turned the handle of the safe. There was the hissing sound of springs uncoiling. Instants later, half a dozen harpoon-like arrows shafted through the wood paneling next to the safe and through the air. One impaled Gunther through his right breast and slammed him against the opposite wall The rest thudded harmlessly into the wall around him.

"*Pfeil!*" Gunther shouted. The word came back to Seth now with the fullest impact. They had found the arrows.

"Gunther!" Morgen started toward him. Seth grabbed Morgen and stopped him.

"Father, get outside," Seth said as he watched the door continue to close.

"Take him out of here," he said to Stratton and Zoe. "I'll help Gunther." Seth physically turned Morgen around and shoved him toward the narrowing gap in the door. "Go on. All of you," he barked. Stratton grabbed Morgen and headed for the door. Zoe stood her ground.

Seth turned and ran toward Gunther. He looked dazed, his mouth working now like a fish out of water. A large quantity of blood had gushed from his wound, staining the carpet under his feet. The end of the arrow protruded about four inches from the upper part of his chest, almost to his shoulder There was no froth from the wound, which meant the shaft had missed the lung. He might survive if they got him medical care soon.

Seth looked at him, glanced back at the door, which was half closed now, then back at Gunther. He reached out and grabbed the old Austrian by his shoulders.

"This is going to hurt like hell, Gunther."

The old man looked at Seth through eyes hazed with pain and nodded.

Seth took a deep breath and pulled Gunther off the spear that had nailed him to the wall. Gunther shrieked horribly and then, amazingly, pushed Seth away, staggering toward the safe.

"Gunther, what . . ." Seth couldn't believe the man was still standing.

"Back," Gunther said, in a voice suddenly grown feeble. He backed against the wall and held there for a moment.

Seth cast an anxious glance at the closing door. When he looked back around Gunther had leaned into the safe and was struggling with its contents. He slid something heavy from the safe and turned.

Seth's mouth dropped open. In his hands, Gunther held a box, a golden box encrusted with jewels that burned green and red and white and seemed to amplify the beam from Seth's flashlight. Suddenly, a horrible remembered sound whispered again in the silence of the vault. Seth felt his body tense as a second volley of spears, undoubtedly triggered by lifting the box off its pedestal in the safe, snaked through the darkness. One of the spears entered Gunther's face just to one side of his nose. The impact lifted him from his feet and slammed him back against the wall. Two more spears slammed dull and wet through his midsection, but his open dead eyes didn't flinch. The bejeweled gold box thudded to the floor, spilling its contents.

"Seth. Hurry. The door."

Seth shot a panicked look at the door, then looked back at the contents of the box spread out on the floor: a bolt of cloth and ancient yellowed pages. If he left now, all of the dying would be for nothing. And the killing would continue.

Fighting the panic that swirled in his chest, Seth dropped to his knees and scrambled for the contents of the box. He put them in the box and closed the lid.

"Get out now," he yelled to Zoe as he lunged toward the door. It was inches wide. Zoe slipped through easily.

"Here," he shouted as he jammed the box through the opening. She took it. Seth jammed himself in sideways as the gap continued to narrow.

He couldn't fit through! He could feel the steel edges of the door closing on him, pressing his back into the frame. Panic consumed him now. He felt like screaming. Not this close, he wanted to yell. *It's not fair.* He fought the panic and shoved with all his strength against the edge of the door. He seemed motionless for a moment, then finally slipped through the opening, falling face first onto the salty floor.

THIRTY-FIVE

and me the box."

Stratton's voice was arrogant and demanding.

Zoe ignored him as she knelt beside Seth on the hard gritty floor of the salt chamber. He was winded and shaken from his narrow escape, slipping out with the Sophia Passion just instants before the massive vault door slammed shut. He tumbled out head over heels, half a heartbeat away from being crushed like an insect and landed facedown beside the fully uniformed skeleton of a long-dead SS trooper.

He fell on top of the box, panting from the exertion, from the pain, and from the horror of seeing Gunther pinned to the wall, not once, but twice. He would always remember the way the old Austrian's eyes bulged open even after he died, and the way his right arm continued to twitch.

"Give me the box now!" Stratton ordered.

"Piss off, Stratton!" Zoe snapped back as she leaned over Seth.

Tears of relief and gratitude shimmered in both their eyes.

"Thank God you're safe."

"The box! Now!" Stratton's voice was strident.

Zoe turned, furious, but her angry words died in her throat when she saw the muzzle of his gun pointed at her. In his other hand he held a flashlight, which he pointed into her face. She squinted into the glaring light.

"What—?" She could not comprehend what she saw.

"Hand me the box," Stratton repeated himself. "Now!"

In the darkness, they heard a scraping sound, shoes against the salt floor.

"You, Father!" Stratton pointed the flashlight at Morgen. "Hold still or I'll shoot her." Morgen stopped.

Seth sat up.

"Hold it!" Stratton commanded. "Don't do anything foolish."

Seth looked up, dazed for a moment, but the new threat rapidly cleared his head.

"Now," Stratton said with the impatience of a man trying to sound patient. "Hand me the box."

Zoe looked at Seth. He nodded.

As she reached over to grab the box Seth noticed, out of the corner of his eye, a holstered revolver lying on the floor, still attached to the dead SS trooper's belt.

Stratton took the box from Zoe, who sat down on the floor after handing it to him. It was heavy, at least thirty or forty pounds.

Stratton backed away from them until he was a good twenty feet away, close enough for them to be at point-blank range, but far enough so they could not rush him.

"Now turn off your flashlights and throw them over to me." They complied. Stratton gathered the lights and put them in a pile at his feet.

"Walk over to them, Father," Stratton said, indicating Seth and Zoe. "And sit down next to them."

Morgen walked over to where Seth and Zoe sat. He looked at Seth who, with a nod of his head, motioned for the priest to sit down.

"I—" Stratton cleared his throat. "I wish things didn't have to come to this," he said as he set his flashlight on the floor of the chamber and pointed it at the trio. He unburdened himself of his pack looking down briefly as he did. Seth moved slightly toward the trooper's gun.

"But what we are dealing with is an awesome spiritual matter that affects the souls of millions." Stratton spoke as he knelt beside the pack and with one hand unbuckled its straps. "A handful of lives—mine included—matter little when balanced against that." He opened the top flap of the pack, and with his free hand began to unload its contents: first-aid supplies, a blanket, canned water, dehydrated food, a small butane stove with a cover that doubled as a pot.

"But isn't the truth more important?" Morgen asked, his voice steady as it can be only in a man who was long done fearing death. "Ye shall know the truth and the truth shall make you free."

"Truth? I am not sure what the truth is or even whether it matters anymore," Stratton responded, his voice growing in pitch as he spoke. "I know that believing in a creed, in a certain steadfast faith, matters to a lot of people and it would be terrible to deprive them of that comfort just so we could give the world another exciting spiritual equivocation."

Seth inched closer to the holster and grabbed it by the narrow end. He began to pull it toward him. Seth was amazed at how easy it was. He had somehow imagined that the uniform full of bones would be heavy, as if there should be weight in death.

Morgen opened his mouth to speak, but Stratton angrily waved the gun at him.

"Don't, Father!" Stratton said. "Let's not delay the inevitable. I can't just leave you here to starve to death like the rest of these miserable souls." He paused to swing his arm in a broad arc to take in the skeletons in the chamber.

"I'm not a sadistic man," Stratton told them sadly. "Starving to death is a long and painful way to go." He paused. "Don't worry," he said as he bent to try and get a grip on the box. It was unwieldy. "I'll give you each two shots at the base of the skull. There won't be any pain."

"Thou shalt not kill," Morgen said, his voice booming like an Old Testament prophet in the cave.

"Don't!" Stratton ordered. His voice was ragged with the raw edges of hysteria. "I will not be the first to kill in defense of the faith."

Seth got his fingers around the snap closure of the holster and gently pried it open. It made the barest of clicks. Stratton was occupied now with trying to maneuver the box into the empty pack. Seth slid the revolver from the holster. He felt the grip firm and cold in his hand.

Stratton had succeeded in getting the box in the pack. On top of the box he had thrown the flashlights. Now he was trying to refasten the straps. Seth nudged first Morgen and then Zoe with the muzzle of the gun. As they looked at him, he cast his eyes down at the revolver. There was no way to tell them, but he hoped they'd scatter in the darkness when the time came.

The time came very soon. Stratton finished with the straps, hoisted the pack, and slipped one arm through a strap. He would have to switch his gun to his left hand for just a moment in order to get his right arm through the second strap.

Seth watched, waited. Timing was all. Timing and whether or not the ammunition in the old pistol would fire. Stratton adjusted the left strap, shifted it to make the right one hang open. His hands started to come together. The left hand closed around the gun; for an instant, neither finger was on the trigger.

Now! Seth thought as he brought the revolver up. He nudged Zoe with his shoulder so that she sprawled on her side out of the light.

Stratton's face changed from one of annoyance with the petty details of the pack to one of surprise as his hostages began to move. His eyes bulged with fear as he saw the revolver in Seth's hand.

Stratton fired first with his left hand, but the aim was jerky and went wild. Morgen sprang to his feet and joined Zoe in the darkness. Together they ran toward yet another lump of bones on the floor, hoping to find another weapon.

Seth pulled back the hammer of the revolver, aimed for Stratton's chest, and pulled the trigger. The dull thudding mechanical sound made by the hammer falling on a dud round fell like a mortal pain on Seth's ears. He rolled out of the light of Stratton's flashlight as the NSA man switched hands and fired again. The slug plowed a deep trench in the floor at Seth's feet.

Seth fired again on the roll. This time the revolver roared in the darkness. But the shot missed Stratton. Instead, it kicked up the salt at one end of the flashlight and sent it skittering across the chamber, casting wild strobing lights. In the surreal light, Seth caught a glimpse of Stratton running toward the exit from the chamber. The flashlight came to rest with its beam pointing directly into a corridor that led from the chamber. Light illuminated the sides of the corridor, but the chamber itself was cast into the deep formless darkness of nightmares.

Suddenly from his left Seth heard the roar of another gun. In the light from the muzzle flash, they saw a white geyser of salt erupt from the chamber wall behind Stratton as he made the safety of the corridor and disappeared into the darkness.

"Seth?" It was Zoe's voice.

"Over here," he called. Moments later, the three were once again together.

"Ridgeway." This time it was Stratton's voice. It had the hollow echoing tones of sound bouncing through underground distances. "Ridgeway, I have spare ammunition. And it's all live and reliable. If you come after me, I'll be waiting for you in the darkness. You'll never see me in time. I know where you have to walk to get out."

"Stratton," Seth called. But there was no reply.

They huddled in the claustrophobic, clinging darkness, fearful of making their position known. Was Stratton waiting for them to go after the flashlight? They squatted for what seemed like hours as the flashlight's bright blue beam began to fade toward yellow. Without the light, there was no hope of following their carbon-black trail out of the mine.

Finally, Seth stood up in the darkness, revolver in one hand, the other trembling with indecision. Was the flashlight bait? Was the starved rat finally forced to have a go at the cheese in the trap? Finally, he tucked the revolver into his pants, sprinted toward the light, grabbed it, and dived away from the spot, trying to turn off the switch as he waited for the roar of bullets and the impact of slugs.

But the roar never came. The only sounds in the darkness came from his own heavy breathing. Had Stratton left? They might die if he was there waiting for them to try and make their way out of the mine. But they'd surely die if they didn't try. To conserve the flashlight's flagging batteries, he flashed it once to determine where Zoe and Father Morgen were, then turned it off and walked slowly toward them.

Darkness was their friend. It would hide them. Darkness was their enemy; it could lead them into traps and ambushes left by foes both old and new.

They gathered the water, gas stove, Gunther's climbing rope, which was still attached to the vault room door, and one of the blankets that Stratton had dumped from his pack. The blanket was made of an aluminized plastic, and reinforced with some sort of fibers. It was of the sort motorists and campers carry for emergencies. This was definitely an emergency.

Seth lit the small gas stove, and in the gentle blue light it cast, they made their way along the trail of carbon black that Zoe had so carefully laid down on the way in.

The anemic light of the gas stove took them as far as the massive minefield that guarded the immediate entrance to the chamber. Ridgeway pulled out the flashlight then and used its remaining minutes of light to guide them through the minefield step by step.

The rest of the going was made easy by the dark trail that snaked around mines and booby traps. In several places they could see where Stratton had tried to obliterate the carbon black. But his efforts only smudged the trail.

Stratton had also tried to isolate them by pulling the bridge boards from the roiling underground stream in Gunther's tunnel. But after only a dozen or so tosses, Seth was able to entangle the far end of one of the boards with the climbing rope and pull it to them. With the rope tied around his waist, he crossed the single shaky board while Zoe and Morgen hung tight onto the rope's other end.

Once on the other side, he replaced all of the boards so the others could cross.

It was dark by the time they reached the entrance to the abandoned mine. The snowstorm had cleared completely, leaving a dark moonless sky filled with stars. A sharp wind keened up from the valley.

One of the snowmobiles was gone and Stratton had removed the distributor wires from the other two. He had either taken the wires with him or thrown them into the snow, where they would remain hidden until the spring thaw.

Ridgeway looked first at one of the snowmobiles and then the other. He removed a sparkplug wire from one, and, taking it over to the other vehicle, fastened it first to the distributor and then to the high-voltage coil. The engine roared with the try of the starter.

The three of them mounted the snowmobile with Ridgeway at the controls.

"He has gone to Innsbruck," Morgen said flatly, breaking out of a nearly catatonic silence. "Stratton has gone to Innsbruck."

"How do you know?" Seth asked, raising his voice above the roar of the snowmobile engine.

"Brown," Morgen said.

"What?" Seth asked. "I don't understand."

"I told you I would tell you what that meant, didn't I?" Morgen said.

Seth nodded slowly, afraid that the events of the day had unhinged the old priest's mind.

"It was not brown, the color," Morgen said quietly. Seth turned off the snowmobile engine to hear him better. "No, it was Braun." He paused, looking off into a place where neither Seth nor Zoe could go. "Braun. He mentioned the name just before he died as if Braun were to blame. I prayed it would not be him. But it must be."

Morgen fixed Seth with pain-filled eyes.

"Braun lives in Innsbruck," Morgen said. "Stratton has taken the Sophia Passion to him. We must go there."

Seth waited for more information, but Morgen had fallen silent. Seth started the snowmobile engine once again and steered the machine down the mountain.

THIRTY-SIX

Dawn had barely begun to model the shadows in Bernini's colonnade around Saint Peter's Square when police began setting up the crowd-control barriers in preparation for the Pope's weekly audience.

For a very long time, Wednesday had been the day when the Pope granted audiences to people "without rank or name" from anywhere in the world. Even though this Wednesday fell on the day after Christmas, the Pope saw no reason to postpone the weekly audience.

The Pope walked thoughtfully from his private chapel, fortified by more than ninety minutes of matins, lauds, and the prime of his daily audience.

He paused at a window of his apartment in the Apostolic Palace and looked out at the activity below. At the very periphery he saw the beginnings of the crowd that later would parade through the auditorium that Paul VI had built solely for the convenience of the public audience. He particularly enjoyed the public audiences. These were the real people, the flock that God had chosen him to administer to. No one could take that away from him, not even Braun.

The Pope tried to quench the rage rising within him. He had trusted Braun with the most sensitive issues of the church, had defended him from those who felt the Cardinal from Vienna was too combative, too lacking in charity and forgiveness. Standing there, looking down at people who had gotten up in the middle of the night to get here before the sun rose, the Pope felt tears of frustration, anger, and sadness welling up in his eyes. If Braun had his way—and the bold cardinal had almost always succeeded—these public audiences would very soon pass into the ambitious Austrian's hands.

The Pope took a long shuddering breath, held it, and let it out in a sigh that could have encompassed the universal sorrow of the world but that this morning only included the unearthing of the shroud and the Sophia Passion.

Braun had awakened him late last night with the news, and the demand that the College of Cardinals be convened immediately. Braun emphasized that he wanted an orderly transition.

Orderly transition. The Pope snorted to himself as he turned away from the window with his uncharitable thoughts. He walked toward the dining room. Despite the crisis, he was hungry.

Immediately after Braun's telephone call, the Pope had sent his secretary of state, Richard Borden, and a team of Vatican archivists to Innsbruck to authenticate Braun's claim. The Pope looked at the old clock with the wooden cogs hanging on the wall. When would Borden call? It had been a sleepless night for all of them. When would he call?

He walked into the dining room and greeted his staff. They bade him good morning with sad, searching eyes. Did they know? How?

The call the Pope had been waiting for came as he scanned the front page of the *Rome Daily American*.

In his private study he took the call.

"Yes, Richard?" The Pope said, trying to sound cheerful. "What have you found?"

The Pope's face crumpled like paper. His erect carriage sagged, and his strong square shoulders slumped. He searched jerkily for several moments before he found a chair to sit in.

"Yes," the Pope said in the voice of an old man. "I understand."

He listened for perhaps half a minute. "Is there anything—anything at all we can do?"

Shaking his head as if his secretary of state were in the room with him, the Pope's voice was emphatic when he spoke. "No! You mustn't. That would make us as morally bankrupt as he. Leave there as soon as you can. I need you here."

Slowly the Pope replaced the telephone on its receiver and got to his feet. He passed by the window again on his way back to the chapel. Dawn had colored the square a rosy pink. The crowd had thickened. He looked on them now with the bitter fondness of someone saying good-bye to a loved one.

And then he went to his private chapel to pray for a miracle.

"It's magnificent, George, simply magnificent." Braun walked around the conference table in the ecumenical council meeting room once again. The Shroud of Sophia lay stretched flat, covering most of the massive wooden table. The bejeweled gold box and the bound volume of the Sophia Passion rested on a small table brought in from the reception foyer.

The shroud was nearly twelve feet long, woven of linen, and bore two head-to-head images, one anterior, one posterior, of a young girl entering puberty. The faint straw-colored outlines of her wounds were visible in the bright light of early morning.

Beyond the closed door to the council room came the muted voices of the men the Pope had sent from the Vatican to authenticate the shroud. Braun had enjoyed watching them work. As professionals they had been excited to examine such an obviously genuine part of history. But as people loyal to the current Pope and his doctrines, they went about their task with heavy frowns, knowing what their authentication would mean.

The most troubled of all was Richard Borden. It didn't really matter, Braun thought. Like Constantine's scribe who had interviewed all of Sophia's townspeople, Borden and the others had all outlived their usefulness to him. And like the scribe, their days and their lives were finite.

A knock sounded on the door.

"Get that, please, George," Braun said as he leaned over the table to stare into the face of the image.

Stratton's shoes thudded dully on the bare wooden floor as he walked to the door and opened it. Richard Borden, soon to become ex–secretary of state, was standing on the other side.

"Please tell the cardinal that we will be going now," Borden said.

Braun lifted his head. "How is the Pope this morning, Borden?"

The secretary of state struggled to control his temper. "He's quite well, Your Eminence, and has agreed to your . . . request. When may we expect you in Rome?"

Braun looked at him for several moments as if carefully considering the question. "When I'm ready," Braun said, then turned his attention back to the shroud.

Just then, a mild vibration shook the floor. The gondola had arrived to collect the Vatican party. Stratton closed the door on Richard Borden's face and returned to Braun's side.

"Would you like to be head of my personal security detail?" Braun asked, still gazing down at the shroud.

"Yes, sir," Stratton said eagerly. "Of course, Your Eminence."

Stratton stood protectively beside Braun for several moments.

"Ah, Your Eminence?"

Braun looked up at him and raised his eyebrows.

"What about Rolf? He's been your personal bodyguard for so many years now."

"Rolf is getting old," Brain said quickly. "And he lacks a certain . . . a certain finesse that the new job requires."

"Will you tell him? Soon?"

"Just as soon as he returns." Braun stood up straight. "Meanwhile, repack all this." He waved his hand over the conference table. "I have to pack. We've got a charter flight to Rome at noon. I'd like to be out of here by eleven." He turned and walked toward the door. "Would you inform the staff?"

"Of course, Your Eminence," Stratton replied eagerly.

Seth came out of the doorway of the Hotel Central just before 10 A.M. He held the door open for Zoe and for Father Morgen. The brightness of the day made them all squint as they walked down the Gilmstrasse toward the parking lot where they had left Gunther's old Audi. Seth carried bags for them all.

"It's way up there." Morgen pointed toward the north, his long thin finger describing a group of jagged peaks. "I was there once, nearly thirty years ago, before Braun was made a cardinal."

They had reached the corner of the Erlerstrasse and turned right, toward the university.

They found the car five minutes later. Ridgeway first unlocked the doors, then started the engine to warm it up while Zoe settled herself in the passenger seat and Morgen arranged himself in back. Ridgeway threw the bags in the trunk and brushed away the light dusting of snow that the wind had deposited during the night.

Finally he slipped back behind the wheel, put the transmission into gear, and drove out of the parking structure.

The roads in Innsbruck were slick with snow and patchy with ice where the extreme cold had overcome the ability of the road salt to melt. The roads cleared, however, once they reached the autobahn and headed for the airport, where Seth had booked a helicopter flight from a company that offered sight-seeing tours of the ski slopes.

"The helipad's on the roof toward the rear of the chalet," Morgen said. "According to Braun's housekeeper—who has been working with us for nearly twenty years now—the entrance to the house from the helipad is never locked. It connects with an elevator and a staircase that leads down the center of the main chalet. The guards are stationed at the perimeter of the grounds and have their own quarters separate from the main chalet. Braun doesn't like to be reminded of his need for security, so the main chalet is off limits to the guards except in an emergency. The only security man allowed in the chalet under normal conditions is Braun's chief bodyguard, Rolf Engels. He's a big man and loyal. You will have to kill him if he confronts you. He may be getting on in years, but he's still formidable."

"Terrific," Seth mumbled. "The best we can expect is for half the rounds in these old revolvers to work." He thought of the revolvers and the extra ammunition they had taken from the skeletons of the SS troopers in the Ha-bersam mine.

"With any luck, we can use the revolvers to bluff our way out." Zoe said hopefully. Neither Morgen nor Seth made any reply.

They arrived at the airport less than thirty minutes later and were directed to the proper terminal. Seth introduced them to the helicopter pilot, who expressed surprise when Seth told him where they wanted to go.

"It's a busy day for the Cardinal's Nest," the pilot said.

Seth asked him what he meant.

"I have a request to pick up the cardinal at eleven and bring him back here. He's chartered a jet to Rome. Some emergency, I guess." He paused and added, "The cardinal doesn't like to be visited unexpectedly. I'll have to give him a call first, if you don't mind."

Seth looked at Morgen, who quickly unzipped his down parka to reveal his clerical collar. The effect on the pilot was immediate.

"I'm carrying important information to the cardinal," Morgen said, which was not entirely a lie. "He is expecting me and will be angry if I'm delayed. You may call him, but I assure you that he is expecting us."

The pilot looked at Morgen with respect in his eyes. "Of course, Father," he said. "Just follow me." He reached for a wool knit hat, pulled it on over his bald head, and headed for the door.

They fastened their seat belts as the Jet Ranger's turbine engines whined to their idling pitch. After running through his preflight checklist, the pilot turned to them and nodded. With a sudden start, the engine's pitch increased and suddenly the ground fell away from them as they drifted forward, nose down.

The pilot leaned the stick sharply over, forcing them against the window. The copter banked steeply now and climbed rapidly enough into the sky to leave butterflies in their stomachs.

THIRTY-SEVEN

Neils Braun had just finished packing his bags when he heard the *thwack-thwack-thwack* of the helicopter blades in the distance. He glanced at the elegantly expensive Piaget watch on his wrist to make sure that he was not late. The helicopter was early. That was fine, he thought. The sooner he could get to Rome, the sooner he could assume control.

Braun took a last look around his quarters and smiled. It would be the last time he would view it through the eyes of a cardinal. In seventy-two hours, give or take a handful, he would be Pope. He looked forward to the abdication ceremonies.

He used the telephone by his bed to call his manservant and told him to take the packed bags up to the helipad and wait for the helicopter. Then Braun walked briskly down the stairs to the conference room.

The Cardinal's Nest was situated at the very top of the peak on a ragged, uneven, roughly square plateau about a quarter of a mile from sheer cliff to sheer cliff. The buildings perched on one cliff overlooking the Inn Valley and the Olympic ski slopes of the Axamer Lizum.

About a hundred yards from the Cardinal's Nest, and connected to it by a covered, heated passage, was a small cottage designed to house a dozen men, the men who, in shifts of four, patrolled the area around the Cardinal's Nest twenty-four hours a day.

Like their counterparts who maintained security at the Palace of the Archbishops in Vienna, they were all seasoned men, veterans chosen from the ranks of the world's best military units. The twelve men were under the direction of Rolf Engels, a former member of Hitler's elite Mountain Corps. He had been recommended early on by a member of the ecumenical council as a suitable bodyguard for the then-up-and-coming bishop who spoke so eloquently against communism and who had very quickly become a target for its agents of violence.

Rolf Engels was at the gondola house drinking hot tea with the gondola operator and his security man when he heard the blades of the helicopter. Quickly, he glanced at his watch. His eyebrows rose slightly when he noted the time.

"Bernhard," Engels said to his soldier. "Step outside and tell me what you see."

Bernhard, a ruggedly built man in a white alpine camouflage suit, stepped outside. He was back in a moment.

"A yellow helicopter," Bernhard reported. "With black writing. It's too far off to make out the words on the side, but it looks like the same one the cardinal usually flies."

Engels nodded. "Thank you, sergeant." He took another sip from his tea, looked in his cup to see how much, was left and sighed.

"Better crank up the gondola," Engels said to the lift operator.

"Would you like me to come with you?" Bernhard asked.

Engels shook his head. "Strictly routine," he said, draining the rest of the liquid from the plastic cup. He tossed the cup into a trash can, followed the gondola operator into the motor shed, and watched while he started up the smoothly oiled mechanism that carried the gondola car up the almost sheer cliff to the Cardinal's Nest.

The helicopter's skids had barely touched the snow on the chalet's helipad when the door opened. Ridgeway jumped out first and helped both Zoe and Morgen out. A set of stairs led down from the pad to a railed catwalk that led across the roof to a door set into an outhouse-sized structure.

"I'll wait here," the pilot spoke to Morgen. "No need for me to go back to the airport and then return for the cardinal's trip. Tell him to take his time. I'll be here."

Morgen nodded and joined Seth and Zoe, who waited for him on the catwalk.

As Morgen had promised, the door was not locked. Seth pulled out the heavy old revolver as he stepped through the door. There was nothing but a set of stairs leading downward.

"Come on," he whispered, and began padding softly down the steps. The stairs were made of welded metal and covered with a rubbery nonskid material. They descended in silence.

At the first landing, they heard a door into the stairway open, followed by what sounded like the grunts and thuds of a man struggling with a heavy object. The sounds grew louder.

Seth went to the landing door and turned the knob. The door was locked. Below them, in the stairwell, the noises grew closer. Seth reached into his rear pocket and pulled a credit card from his wallet. Then, tucking the revolver in his belt, he knelt before the doorknob and inserted the card between the door and its jamb. Moments later, he was rewarded with a satisfying click. The door came open when he pulled on it.

Beyond the door was a stretch of attic, its flooring covered with a scattering of cardboard boxes and wooden crates.

Seth motioned Zoe and Morgen to get inside. They complied as the noises from below grew louder. As Seth closed the door, they could hear clearly the breathless efforts of the man making the noises.

Seth pressed his eye to the narrow crack between the door and jamb, and moments later watched as a thin man staggered up the stairs with two massive hard-sided valises. The man paused on the landing long enough to wipe the perspiration from his face, and then continued on up the final flight. A few seconds later the stairwell was flooded with brilliant white light.

When the stairwell had once again fallen into the yellow dimness made by the low-wattage lightbulbs, Seth opened the door and led the two others downward.

Stratton was replacing the shroud and the last of its documentation in the jeweled gold box when Braun walked in.

"The helicopter's early," Braun said as he walked to Stratton's side and inspected his work. "I want you to—"

Suddenly the door to the council meeting room flew open and slammed back against the wall with a bang.

Braun stopped so quickly he almost stumbled. Stratton dropped the lid to the box as he whirled to confront the noise. The lid clattered dully on the wood of the table.

"Ridgeway." Stratton spoke with the stunned incredulity of a man confronted by a ghost.

Pressing his advantage of surprise, Seth stepped quickly forward and motioned Zoe into the room.

"Cover him," Seth pointed at Braun. Zoe stepped forward and leveled the old revolver at him. She pulled back the hammer.

At the sound of the revolver's mechanism, something flickered in Braun's eyes. But his steely self-control kept his face hard and straight.

"What is the meaning of this outrage," Braun blustered. "How dare you invade my privacy like this."

"Shut up!" Zoe said with authority. Braun tried to back away. "Stay still."

Braun mustered a dignified pose, but behind his composed exterior his mind whirred. He had talked his way out of worse situations in his life. He looked at the angry but attractive woman approaching him.

Stratton had backed away from Seth, trying to put the table between him and the old revolver that might or might not be capable of tearing a terrible hole through him.

"Don't be fooled, Your Eminence," Stratton said. "Those guns are relics. The ammunition's forty years old."

"Hold it, Stratton!" Seth ordered. "Stop right where you are." Seth smiled. "Just look over here, Your Disgrace," he said harshly. Braun's head turned. "Your stooge here has stopped because he knows that the gun just might blow his head off." Seth grinned at Stratton. He paused. "Are you willing to chance the odds that the gun might not fire?"

"No." Braun swallowed trying to restrain his anger. "No, of course not. You've obviously got us at a disadvantage." As he faced Zoe's gun, Braun tried to figure out where Rolf would be. The old soldier was a man of routine and he made his inspections of the grounds on a schedule that kept better time than most watches. His mind raced, trying to remember. Then the floor beneath his feet rumbled faintly. The gondola lift motor had started.

Inwardly, Braun smiled. It took the gondola about three minutes to climb the precipitous slope. Three minutes. He had to keep them talking long enough for Rolf to finish making his rounds.

Seth stepped back until both Stratton and Braun were in his field of vision. "Put your gun on the table," Seth told Stratton. The NSA man hesitated as if he was calculating the chances that Seth's revolver wouldn't fire. Seth stepped toward him. "On the table, friend." Stratton reached inside his coat. "Easy," Seth said. "Bring it out by the grip with thumb and forefinger. If I see a finger near the trigger you're a dead man."

Stratton nodded and pulled his gun out from under his armpit and laid it on the conference table. It was a heavy U.S. Army Colt .45 automatic.

"You were clever, Stratton," Seth said. "And convincing. You certainly made a fool out of me."

"Now don't be angry, Mr. Ridgeway," Braun said, his confidence rising with the knowledge that Rolf would be along shortly. "We're reasonable men. Why don't we talk."

"Reasonable?" Seth thundered. "You call killing people reasonable? You self-righteous, hypocritical bastard. We ought to kill you right now. You've got the nerve to try and call yourself reasonable? You've betrayed everyone and everything you've come in contact with." He looked toward the box. "Or lock it up so no one will know what it really is. You want to hide Hitler's blackmail, hide the shame." Seth paused. "Or maybe you want to blackmail somebody yourself." Seth looked at the flicker of recognition in the cardinal's eyes.

"Who do you want to blackmail, Mr. Cardinal Archbishop? What are you going to do with the shroud?"

"You misunderstand me, Mr. Ridgeway," Braun said.

"Yeah," said Seth. "Hitler and Eichmann were misunderstood too."

Braun raised his hand slowly. "Please let me say something, if you will?" Seth nodded. "What I want to do with the shroud is nothing more than save the Christian world."

Seth looked at him in shocked silence for a moment. "You're joking," Seth said, then coughed a small cynical laugh. "I know people like you, Braun. You're out for yourself. You don't give a good goddamn for saving anything or doing anything that doesn't benefit yourself. You don't care how you get the power or which side you have to be on to get it. You're interchangeable, people like you. Just unplug you from one side and plug you in on the other. Well, whatever you've got in mind for the shroud isn't going to come through for you."

Seth walked toward the box on the long conference table. "We're taking the box with us." He glanced up at the ceiling. "We've got transportation waiting. So I want you and Stratton here to lie down on the floor." Seth waved the muzzle of the gun at both men. "Down here in the middle of the floor. Facedown, legs spread."

Neither Braun nor Stratton complied. "Now." Zoe prodded Braun with the muzzle of her gun. He jumped as if shocked by an electric wire, then glared at her.

"Go on," Zoe said. "You heard him."

"We can kill you now," Seth said. "Just like you had people killed. Or you can lie down on the floor and let us take the box peacefully."

"You must let me explain," Braun wheedled. "You just don't understand."

"Perhaps not, but I do." Morgen's voice boomed through the room. "Perhaps Mr. Ridgeway and his wife don't understand, but I certainly do. I should. I've spent enough years studying you."

"Damn you, you foolish old man!" Braun cursed as Morgen approached.

"Yes," Morgen said blandly. "I probably am damned. But what does that make you?"

The two men stared silently at each other for several moments.

"Why have you done it?" Braun said. "There was no good reason. Why have you done these things, you meddlesome, senile old fool?"

"I've had two things that kept me alive all these years," Morgen said. "After that day in Alt Aussee. One of them was to recover this box. The other was my pride in you."

"What are you saying?" Braun said. "You're talking nonsense."

"They tried to tell me," Morgen said, his eyes focused on a memory. "They tried to tell me you were the man responsible for this madness, but I wouldn't believe them. I couldn't believe them."

Braun turned to Seth. "Would you try to get this old fool to make some sense?"

Morgen fished about in the deep pocket of his parka and pulled from it a wrinkled and much-folded envelope. His hands shook as he unfolded the flap of the envelope and pulled out a crinkled piece of paper. He walked up to Braun and held the paper out in his hand.

"Look at this," Morgen said.

Braun stared at Morgen as one looks at an asylum inmate. He hesitated for a moment, then snatched the paper from the priest's hands. The cardinal's eyes scanned the page quickly, then he handed it back to Morgen.

"So?" Braun said.

Without answering, Morgen pulled another piece of paper from the envelope and offered that. Braun rolled his eyes but took the piece of paper. Moments later, he handed that back to Morgen. The performance was repeated for yet a third piece of paper.

"My patience has its limits, old man," Braun said. "And your riddle here has just about reached that limit."

"What do those pieces of paper mean to you?" Morgen asked.

Braun gave Morgen an exasperated look. "They mean nothing, not together at least," he said. "You gave me a copy of a letter from my father to my mother, a copy of my birth certificate, and a copy of the Wehrmacht's notification of my father's death on the Polish front."

Morgen nodded slowly without taking his steady, sad gaze from Braun's face. Morgen handed the papers back to Braun. "Look at them again. Look at the dates."

Braun looked toward Ridgeway. "Why must I—"

"Take the papers," Ridgeway ordered.

Scowling, Braun snatched the papers from Morgen's hand and examined them again.

"Look at the dates," Morgen said.

Seth watched the interplay of the two men with increasing fascination. There was tension between them, that was for sure. But it wasn't the tension of two old enemies. It was something more . . . personal than that.

Stratton, too, watched the drama played out between the two clergymen, but not with any regard to the issues between the two men. Rather, Stratton was waiting for Seth's attention to be completely directed to Braun and Morgen.

The scowl on Braun's face gradually gave way to a look of astonishment as he examined the papers Morgen had given him.

Morgen read Braun's face: "So the dates do mean something?" Morgen said.

"I . . . I don't understand," Braun said, looking first at Morgen and then with confusion at the papers.

"It's quite simple, actually," Morgen said. "The letter to your mother from her husband was written by a brave Oberleutnant from Radom, about sixty miles south of Warsaw, on September 7, 1939. That same brave Oberleutnant—"

"My father," Braun interrupted.

Morgen ignored him as he continued. "That brave Oberleutnant died in the battle on September 9 in the German assault on Warsaw." The old priest paused, licked his lips, then resumed. "You were born August 6, 1940, nearly eleven months after this brave Oberleutnant died."

"I still don't understand," Braun said softly, genuinely confused. "You've gone to great lengths to prove that I'm illegitimate. So, I'm illegitimate? I wouldn't be the first Pope who was born a bastard. But that hardly justifies your behavior for the past forty years."

"No, ordinarily you'd be right," Morgen said. "But you're not just any bastard. You're my bastard."

Braun's face drained of color as if a plug had been pulled. His mouth flew open. "You . . . you're my father?

Morgen nodded.

Attention focused on Morgen and Braun. Stratton lunged for his pistol.

"Seth!" Zoe's scream dragged Ridgeway's attention away from Morgen and Braun.

Seth leveled the revolver at Stratton and pulled the trigger. The hammer made a self-important click as it fell on a dud round. Seth felt his stomach drop through the floor. Stratton's hand was inches away from the Colt. Seth followed him with the muzzle of the revolver, brought the hammer back, and pulled the trigger again. And again the revolver's hammer fell on a dud round.

Stratton grabbed the Colt and let his lunge carry him in a roll off the other side of the table and onto the floor.

"Get back," Seth yelled to Zoe, but she stood her ground and aimed her revolver toward where Stratton had disappeared behind the table.

In an instant Stratton jumped up, firing wildly with the Colt. Stratton trained his gun on Seth. Seth fired at him again, but for the third time, the revolver failed to fire. Stratton tugged smoothly on the Colt's trigger.

Please, God, Zoe prayed. *Let my aim be true. Save us.*

She aimed her revolver at Stratton's chest and pulled the trigger. The gun rewarded her with a deafening roar and a flare of flame that reached halfway across the room. The slug slammed into Stratton's shoulder just as he fired the Colt, causing his shot at Seth to go wild. He dropped the Colt on the floor as the bullet's impact spun him around. Zoe fired again. Her second shot struck Stratton in the back with enough force to slam him against the broad expanse of glass that overlooked the Inn Valley.

As they looked on in stunned silence, the window buckled under the impact of Stratton's body. The shattering glass sounded like crackling thunder, but its intensity paled under Stratton's screams as he teetered against the sill for a second, then toppled from the window in a hail of glass fragments. They heard his steady wailing scream for several seconds.

THIRTY-EIGHT

W hen he got out of the gondola car at the top of the cliff Rolf looked up at the helipad, puzzled that the cardinal hadn't already taken off. He was usually out like a flash. Never liked to wait. Rolf shook his head slowly and started up the steps to the chalet, listening to the lazy *shwoop-shwoop* of the idling helicopter blades.

The next thing Rolf Engels heard was the crashing of glass and the screams. As sturdy as the chalet was, with its stone walls and thick wood, it was not surprising that he failed to hear the shots fired in the council meeting room.

But the screams and the glass; something was definitely amiss. As he stealthily let himself into the chalet, he checked off the available men he could summon. Three men were taking their shift off by going into Innsbruck. One was by the gondola shed. That left him with two men on duty up here plus three more sleeping in the barracks.

It would be enough, he thought, as he slipped quietly into the grand foyer that had once been the lobby back in the days when the chalet had been a resort. From within the building, Rolf heard the excited murmurings of the domestic staff. The housekeeper came running down the hall.

"Oh, Herr Engels," she cried, "I am so glad you're here. Something has happened in the council meeting room. I heard breaking glass, and a loud noise. It could have been a gunshot or perhaps an explosion of some kind."

Explosion? That surprised him. He had heard no explosion. Immediately, he thought of the new natural gas logs the cardinal archbishop had recently installed in the huge fireplace in the council meeting room. Rolf had been against it from the start. It was unsafe, he had argued unsuccessfully. Hadn't the cardinal read of all the stories about homes and office buildings—sometimes entire blocks of buildings—that had been destroyed because some undetected gas leak had been allowed to build up and then had exploded from a minuscule spark? Rolf had lost that battle.

But now, the fact that he might have been right was not uppermost in his mind as he raced up the stairs toward the council meeting room.

"Stop him," Seth shouted to Zoe. In the confusion, Braun had grabbed the box with the shroud and the Sophia Passion. He was halfway to the door when Zoe turned and fired her revolver. It was her turn to be rewarded with a dull click.

Braun bolted through the door with the box under his arm and ran left down the corridor toward the stairwell. He passed the entrance to the dining room and rushed past the doors to the kitchen. Near the end of the hallway, he stumbled momentarily on the carpeting and resumed his headlong rush toward the stairwell door at the end of the hall.

Zoe fired again. This time the revolver jumped in her hand, but too late. Seth rushed past her, sprinting down the hall. She and Morgen followed him. Seth was halfway down the hall when Braun jerked open the door to the stairwell and dashed into the kitchen.

Most of the vast kitchen was unused except when the Cardinal's Nest hosted large dinner parties. It was a huge room, perhaps forty feet square, with a gleaming stove, freezers, and food processing machines lining the stainless steel counters. Pots hung from racks dangling from the ceiling. It was a kitchen that could handle a state dinner for any president or dictator in the world. But on this morning it was deserted except for the cook, who was preparing a large pot of stew for the guard staff.

Seth raced through the doors of the kitchen, followed closely by Zoe; far behind her, Morgen made his way slowly toward the door.

"Stop!" Seth shouted at Braun, who was only a few paces in front of him "Stop or I'll shoot."

From the corner of his eye, Seth saw the cook drop to the floor, Braun ran, heedless of Ridgeway's threat.

On the run, Seth aimed the revolver and pulled the trigger. The gun roared, striking a thick skillet next to Braun's head just as he turned the corner of a counter. The intense gonglike sound startled Braun and he lost his balance, crashing to the floor, still holding on to the jeweled box. Seth was on top of him in an instant.

"Give me that," Seth said. When the cardinal refused to relinquish the box, Seth tucked the revolver in his belt, bent over, and tried to wrest it from Braun's hands.

"Call Rolf!" Braun screamed at his terrified cook. "Call him now."

Zoe rushed over to the cook and covered him with her pistol.

From the outside entryway, Rolf padded quietly toward the kitchen, his .44 Magnum drawn and ready. As he approached the door to the kitchen, he heard the shot and the sounds of a scuffle.

Seth grappled with Braun for the box, trying to loosen the man's almost deathlike grip on it. Suddenly Braun lashed out with his free fist, catching Seth on his forehead and stunning him for an instant. Braun was nearly standing when Seth recovered. Carrying the box under one arm, Braun tried to stagger to the stairwell. Seth stepped quickly over to him and leaned into a right hook that caught Braun on the left side of his head and knocked his feet out from under him.

The jeweled box and its contents flew out of Braun's hands and scattered on the kitchen floor as the cardinal landed heavily and lay very still on the black-and-white tiles.

It was silent for an instant save for Seth's heavy breathing and the vigorous bubbling of a stew that needed to be stirred.

Then Rolf Engels burst into the kitchen. He raised the Magnum to shoot when, suddenly, out of the corner of his eye, he saw another person, this one with a gun leveled at the cook. Years of military and bodyguard experience had equipped Rolf to make instant assessments. He decided quickly that the woman with the gun was a secondary target to the man who stood over the cardinal. It didn't much matter to him if she shot the cook. Engels was hired to protect the cardinal at all costs.

So Engels returned the Magnum's aim toward the man, centered the sights so the slug would hit him in the small of the back. Rolf had seen the power of the .44 Magnum. He had once fired one at the rear of a fleeing car. The slug had passed through the trunk, through the person in the backseat, through the driver, through the dashboard, and into the engine compartment, with enough force to stall the engine. At the very least, this man's spinal cord would be shattered, his heart pulverized, and the entire front of his chest ripped away with the insides exposed. He squeezed the trigger.

Just then, Seth bent over to gather the box and its contents, and the .44 Magnum's slug passed through the space his chest had occupied just instants before.

"Get down, Zoe!" Seth yelled when he heard the Magnum's cannonlike report. He dropped to his knees next to Braun as a second shot boomed through the kitchen. Somewhere behind him Seth heard a hiss, and moments later smelled natural gas.

"Turn off the stove, Heinrich!" Rolf cursed at himself. His second shot had smashed into the pastry ovens and had undoubtedly shattered a gas valve or pipe. Rolf looked over and saw that Heinrich was still huddled on the floor next to the woman. The former mountain trooper hurdled the counter and turned off the gas under the stew pot, almost ripping the cowling from the stove and throwing the hot stew on the floor.

Zoe saw the huge man vault over the counter and as she crouched on the floor, pointed her revolver at him and pulled the trigger. When nothing happened, she felt like crying.

Braun began to stir. Seth pulled the revolver from his waistband and knelt beside the fallen cardinal.

"You're taking orders from me, understand?" Seth growled as he stuck the muzzle of the revolver under Braun's chin. Braun nodded.

"Good," Seth said grimly. "Now tell your man to hold his fire. If he shoots Zoe, you're dead."

Seth waited a moment and then jammed the revolver muzzle harshly into the cardinal's throat. "Tell him or I'll blow your fucking head off!"

"Rolf?" Braun said weakly. "Rolf, is that you?"

Engels turned from the stove and trained the .44 Magnum on the woman. He had begun to pull the trigger when Braun called out to him.

"Yes, Your Eminence," Rolf said, relaxing the tension on the trigger.

"Rolf, hold your fire," Braun said. "I'll be killed if you don't. Do you understand?"

Rolf looked down at Zoe with hatred in his eyes. He hated above all being kept from doing his job properly. "Yes, Your Eminence," Rolf replied.

"And above all," Braun said, "don't harm the girl."

The smell of gas grew intense in the kitchen. Morgen reached the doorway and paused as he tried to determine what was happening.

"Stand up," Rolf said, looking at the woman on the floor. Zoe complied. Rolf stood behind her, holding the muzzle of the Magnum to her head.

"I want to see the cardinal," Rolf announced. "Have him stand up so I know he's all right or I'll shoot the girl."

Holding the revolver steady under Braun's throat, Seth got to his feet, pulling his hostage up with him. Seth's heart skipped when he saw Zoe across the kitchen standing in front of one of the largest men he had ever seen.

Rolf and Seth stared at each other. "We are either going to gas ourselves or blow this place up if we don't act soon, Amerikaner," Rolf said.

"It's up to you," Seth replied. "Let her go, and I let your precious cardinal go."

Rolf smiled a broad evil grin. "You think I am dumb? You are wrong."

Suddenly there was a clattering at the hallway door. Rolf Engels was lightning fast. He looked over, saw a man he didn't recognize, and in an instant, fired the Magnum. Morgen dropped to his face as the slug chewed into the wall behind him.

THIRTY-NINE

Rolf's bullet missed Hans Morgen as he approached the kitchen door on his return from the conference room. The old priest dropped painfully to his knees holding Stratton's Colt .45 and saying a prayer of thanks for deliverance from yet another bullet. Beyond the kitchen door, Braun was coughing and choking violently from the gas now. Morgen felt the love for his son at war with the sins the man had committed. There was no way to win this. Regardless of how the day ended, the pain in his heart would torture him the rest of his life. The dark realization nurtured a sudden reckless disregard for his own safety.

Seth Ridgeway's voice echoed in the kitchen: "Look, Ralph, or whatever your name is, you're going to kill your beloved cardinal if we don't get out of here soon. Why don't we continue our Mexican standoff outside and maybe get someone to switch off the gas at the main valve?"

"A Mexican vaht, you say?" Rolf asked.

"Never mind," Seth shook his head. "We have to get out of here before we're all killed." Rolf shook his head.

"Okay," Seth said, then coughed. "You stay here. We're leaving." Dragging Braun with him, Seth began to move toward the swinging doors through which Rolf had entered.

"Stay there." Rolf's voice rose in pitch; Seth could see the beginning of panic in the man's eyes. "Stay there or I will shoot her."

Seth continued to move slowly toward the door, his eyes flickering from the big man's face to his trigger finger and back. If there was any movement from the man's trigger finger, Seth would stop immediately. He tried not to look at Zoe's face. He knew it would unnerve him. Stay calm. He told himself. Stay calm. You're playing a dangerous game with all the lives here.

As Seth and Braun neared the door, there was no tensing of Rolf's trigger finger. Instead, he started to move toward them. The loyal bodyguard was not about to let his charge out of his sight. Rolf moved quickly to close the distance between them. Instants later, Seth knew something was wrong, terribly wrong.

Rolf began to smile. Then he dumped Zoe on the floor and stood there grinning. Instants later, steely muscled hands and arms clamped themselves around Seth's neck and arms and twisted the revolver from his hand. The rest of the garrison had arrived. Hands pushed Seth face first onto the floor. The last glimpse he had before hitting was of the cook, staring timidly around the doorway into the hall.

For an instant, Seth felt old and used up. He had lost—they had lost. He thought of his last look at Zoe, so beautiful, so . . . so not ready to die. Then summoning all his strength, he lashed out at his captors, but they were very young and very strong. He felt the toe of a boot slamming into the side of his head, and for a long moment, the world turned fuzzy.

"Good shot, David," Seth heard Rolf's victorious laughter through the fuzz. After a short while, he heard Rolf's voice again, this time in a more respectful tone.

"How are you feeling, Your Eminence?"

Braun's comment was unintelligible. Then Seth heard Zoe's gentle strong voice calling for him. "Seth?" she said.

"Over here," Seth said. Someone, maybe the man called David, kicked Seth in the head again.

"Shut up, swine," the man said.

"Are you all right, Your Eminence?" Seth heard Rolf say.

This time, the cardinal replied, "Yes, a bit shaken." There was a pause. "I see you've proved yourself once again. I have never lost faith in your abilities."

"Thank you, sir," Rolf said proudly.

"Take me up to the helicopter now," Braun said. "Help me up."

Seth heard the rustling and grunts.

"What shall we do with them?" Rolf asked.

The tone of Braun's reply made Ridgeway's blood run cold. "Whatever you wish, Rolf. Whatever you wish." There was a pause, then Seth heard Braun's voice again, this time closer. "Turn him over."

The three men pinning Seth to the floor complied. Seth blinked and looked up; Braun spun dizzily above him. Seth had barely focused his eyes when he saw the cardinal lean over him and spit. Seth tried to turn his head, but strong hands held it. He closed his eyes as the spittle struck him on his forehead.

"Go gather the box and its contents," Braun said to Rolf. "And then let's leave. I have an appointment to keep in Rome."

Holding George Stratton's Colt .45 in his right hand, Morgen crept through the kitchen toward the gathering, staying out of sight behind the counters. He looked up just in time to see Braun spit on Seth's face. Rolf had turned toward the kitchen to fetch the shroud and the Sophia Passion.

Morgen took in the scene instantly. In front of him was Rolf. The rest of them were to his left, near the door that led into the corridor. Seth was pinned to the floor by three men, Braun still standing over him; Zoe was on her knees, struggling with two other men on top of her, trying to wrestle her down.

Morgen stood there in the open door, a stinking tide of gas pouring past him. His eyes locked with Zoe's for just a moment. Rolf raised his weapon and pointed it at Morgen. Morgen raised the .45, smelled the gas again, but instead of shooting, he dropped to the floor just as Rolf pulled the trigger.

There was the roar from Rolf's gun and then a larger, bright flaming *whump*! Rolf Engels' last view of this world was how the fire from his gun seemed to continue on back and behind Morgen. As the kitchen ignited, Rolf knew they should never have installed gas anywhere in the chalet.

The fireball ricocheted through the kitchen, setting it aflame in a thousand places. Pinned to the floor, Ridgeway felt the weight on him vanish. Instants later, he sat up and viewed a scene from the *Inferno*. Rolf and two of Braun's other men were burning like torches. Their mouths were open as if they were screaming, but Seth heard nothing over the roar of the flames. The dried wood and furnishings of the old, old building burned eagerly.

Seth got to his feet and rushed to Zoe. Braun crouched nearby, frozen like marble. Kitchen counters had shielded both of them from the initial ignition. Seconds later the surviving security men rushed back into the kitchen. Seth was prepared for a struggle, but the men were dragging a fire hose from a corridor box and paid no attention to anything but the fire.

"Zoe, get up." He slipped his hands under her armpits. "We've got to get out." She stood up shakily. Moments later, Morgen reached their side.

Then suddenly, like a statue coming to life, Braun was all over them.

"The shroud, you must help me get the shroud." His eyes glinted from fires that burned within. He pulled and tugged at Seth, nearly causing him to lose his balance. Seth lashed out and caught the cardinal with the back of his fist. Braun fell to his knees.

"Get your own fucking shroud," Seth screamed over the roar of the flames.

Morgen looked at the Cardinal equivocally. "Come with us, son," he yelled.

"Go to hell old man!" Braun yelled as he scrambled toward the scattered relics.

Morgen stood stock still for a moment, his shoulders slumped, his head hung low as the flames roared louder around them. Morgen was transfixed by the sight of his son, his only child scrambling in the flames, oblivious to his safety. Seth went to Morgen and placed his hand on the priest's shoulder.

"Quick, Father," Seth said. "Let's get out of here."

Morgen wrestled with the instincts that impelled him toward his son. He saw the energy of the maniacally driven man in the flames and something seemed to speak to the priest, to tell him that perhaps only flame could heal, could quench the insanity that had taken over the son he had never really known. Morgen's heart lurched in his chest and then he turned toward Seth. His tear-streaked face wore the pain of a father's ultimate rejection by his only son, his only child, whom he had loved for a lifetime, but only from a painful distance. Lear. For an instant he knew the heart of that king and the darkness that had filled it.

A screaming commotion erupted behind them and they turned as four of the uniformed security men wrestled with Cardinal Braun, who was trying his best to walk into the flames.

"No, let me go," Braun cried. "Let me go. Let me go."

Suddenly, Braun loosed an inhuman scream as he turned on the security men until, finally, with the superhuman strength people are capable of only when all they hold dear is at stake, the cardinal broke free and lunged into the flames. The security men tried to follow the cardinal, but the flames beat them back. Morgen took half a step forward and then stopped himself.

They all stood transfixed staring at the wall of flames, not believing what they had just witnessed. Then, instants later, they heard Braun's shrieks rising above the roar of the flames. The shrieks began low and rose through the full range of the human voice into a range that seemed to border on the edge of hearing. The sound continued for what seemed like a very long time, but which was probably only a few seconds. The shrieks seemed too loud, too powerful to come from a human being. But the thing that would chill Seth and Zoe for the rest of their lives was the tone of the shriek. It didn't sound like pain; it sounded like a man in ecstasy.

"God be with you," Morgen said.

As the shriek ended, Seth, Zoe, and Hans Morgen raced for the stairwell and to the helicopter they prayed would still be waiting on the roof.

EPILOGUE

The first of the cardinals had begun to arrive at the Vatican in response to the Pope's summons. He had begun chatting with them when he was interrupted by Richard Borden, the Vatican's secretary of state.

As he walked into the room, Borden wore an expression on his face the Pope could not decipher.

"I apologize for disturbing you, Your Holiness, but I felt you would want to receive this as soon as possible." Borden handed him a yellow telex, then left the room.

The Pope read the message three times. It took him that long for the true import to sink in. The telex was from the bishop of Innsbruck.

He read the telex a fourth time, and then turned to his visitors, who by now were consumed with curiosity.

Filtering the joy from his voice, the Pope announced solemnly that: "Cardinal Archbishop Neils Braun has died."

Gasps filled the room.

"How?" said the archbishop from Paris.

"Where?" asked the archbishop from Milan.

The Pope proffered the telex and tried again to keep his inner joy from seeping through to his face and voice. For the first time since he was a small boy, he truly believed in miracles.

"Shall we say a word of prayer for our departed brother?"

The Pope delivered a prayer of condolence and intercession. And in his heart he sang a prayer of thanksgiving.

The chalet was a modern A-frame normally used by the local Bavarian parish as a spiritual retreat. The head of the parish was a close friend of Hans Morgen's. The building was filled with varnished wood everywhere and had a freestanding metal fireplace now filled with the pop and flash of burning logs. Seth Ridgeway added another split oak log from the stack he had just carried in. Then he closed the metal cinder curtain and walked over to Zoe, who stood by a vast window overlooking the evergreen-clad slopes of the secluded alpine valley. She snuggled close as he put his arm around her.

"I could get used to this," Zoe said.

"Yeah. I know what you mean," Seth replied.

"I know its only been a couple of days, but it seems like a lifetime."

"The Cardinal's Nest *was* a lifetime ago."

They stood silently for a long time watching the sun spill through cracks in the clouds and play across the trees like green fire.

"God has been good to us," Zoe said.

"If you say so." Seth's voice was dark. "I hope you're right. I'd really like to believe that, but I just can't anymore."

Zoe gave his hand a squeeze. "You will," she said. "Just give it time."

"It's going to take a lot more than time."

They were silent again for a long while, watching the wind sweep up the valley, passing a frosted brush through the tops of the trees. Then they both saw the movement at the same time. Down below, following a serpentine path between the trees that was a hiking path in the summer, they could make out the red speck of Hans Morgen's down parka. He sat astride the snowmobile he had ridden into town more than two hours before. A small sled tagged behind piled high with its tarpaulin-shrouded cargo. Sounds of the snowmobile's engine grew barely audible above the crackling of the fire.

"Maybe getting back to teaching will help," Zoe suggested.

"Maybe," Seth replied, shaking his head. "But I don't think so. After all this—after all I've learned from the Sophia Passion and all the rest—I'd have to throw away the syllabus and start over."

Zoe turned to him. "Maybe that's your answer."

"Huh?"

"Throw away all your old ways of believing and start over." She paused. "I did. I couldn't just hold on to a faith that was riddled with rotten fibers. I needed something new that spoke to my soul. Maybe you do too."

He gave her an admiring smile. "You're something else." He was silent for a moment. "I don't know . . . I've never felt so rudderless in my entire life . . . so untethered inside."

"I felt that way when I finally realized what a sham my mother's church was," she said.

"But I don't want to spend years like you did before the certainty returns."

"Maybe you had a false certainty that's gone now," Zoe said. She felt her heart twist as she looked at the pain in his eyes. "Maybe all certainty is an illusion."

"Thanks, professor," he said.

"No, I didn't mean—"

He gave her a broad smile. "It's okay. Really." He took her in his arms and they kissed.

Behind them, logs shifted with a dull thud. The snowmobile grew louder.

"Maybe getting rid of a false certainty is God's way of telling you it wasn't the truth to begin with," Zoe said finally. "A new syllabus means you'd have to start looking at new ideas, searching for the truth. I think that God delights in our searching. Maybe the ultimate truth is that there is no ultimate truth— that what we're supposed to do is to keep on searching all our lives."

"That's a real comfort."

The snowmobile engine grew very loud outside the chalet and then fell silent.

"You have a better idea?" Zoe asked.

Seth shook his head.

"Thalia has done a lot of research, has a lot of source materials and notes. She can help when she gets here," Zoe said. "Not to mention the alabaster wheel."

"If you can get it back."

"Count on it," Zoe said. "The art and database material I downloaded off the server has everything: dates, names, prices, bills of lading, shipping numbers. Everything I need to prove the art was stolen—twice—and to prove I have the right to get it back."

"You're going to piss off a lot of people," Seth said. "All those prominent museum curators, those powerful buyers. That's not going to do your business any good."

Morgen's footsteps made dull thuds on the outside deck behind them. They both turned.

"I really don't care." Zoe said. "They deserve what they get. They're the spineless ones that sell their souls to the devil to get the art at any cost. I don't care about the business as much as I do getting the art back to the people and the heirs to whom it rightfully belongs. If I have to close the business to do that, fine."

"I still don't know if I want to go back to teaching," Seth said. "I was a pretty good detective once. Maybe I could just help you with your work."

"So what do *you* know about art?" Zoe joked.

"About as much as *you* know about religion!" he retorted.

They were both laughing when a snow-caked Hans Morgen stormed through the door like an iceman born on a cloud of frigid air and blown snow. He held an olive canvas rucksack in one hand.

"Good afternoon!" He said heartily as he pulled off his goggles with his free hand. "Nothing like alpine snow to make me feel thirty years younger." He reached into the rucksack as he walked toward them. "Word from the parish priest is that your friend Thalia will be arriving tomorrow. She's flying out right after her father's funeral."

"Bastards," Seth mumbled.

Morgen nodded. "The dear girl had no idea that he had died quietly in his sleep just weeks after she arrived in Zurich." He pulled a copy of the *International Herald Tribune* from the rucksack and handed it to Zoe.

"What was it?" Seth asked as Zoe unfolded the paper.

"A stroke," Morgen said. "He died instantly. They put his body in a meat freezer."

Seth shook his head slowly.

"Oh!" she said when she looked at the front page.

She read silently for a moment, then handed the paper to Seth. The front page carried the story of the burning of a Vatican-owned retreat outside Innsbruck. There was an aerial photograph of the structure in flames that the helicopter pilot had taken with a small pocket camera just after lifting off. Next to the aerial shot was an official Vatican photograph of Braun with the caption: "Killed in fire."

Seth read the story closely.

"Here," he said finally, pointing to a paragraph toward the end of the article.

"Police are still searching for two survivors of the fire who were rescued by a helicopter waiting to take the cardinal to the Innsbruck Airport."

"That's us. They must know our names. Why aren't we named?" Seth asked Morgen. "Aren't we being hunted? Isn't Interpol still scouring the earth for us?"

"I told you our allies in the Vatican had their friends." Morgen smiled. "Your help has earned us even more gratitude, among the good members of the Curia and with the Holy Father himself. Otherwise, I am quite certain he would not have blessed our sojourn at this wonderful retreat."

Then Morgen turned toward the door. "You two read that." He pointed toward the newspaper. "I have the computers you ordered and I need to get them inside."

"Let me help you," Zoe and Seth said almost simultaneously.

Morgen shook his head. "I feel like a lion today."

"Really?" Zoe said doubtfully.

"Absolutely!" Morgen replied and swiftly made his way outside.

Seth moved toward the door. Zoe grabbed his arm. "Don't. You'll hurt his pride." Seth looked at her doubtfully for a moment, but allowed her to drag him over to a pair of rustic chairs by the window. In the distance, a pair of cross-country skiers made their way through a broad meadow.

After they settled into the chairs, Zoe read aloud from a sidebar article inside the paper.

" 'VILLAGERS SEE RELIGIOUS LINK IN RUINS' is the headline . . . it's a sidebar to Braun's obituary. 'Workers who arrived at the scene after the fire said the entire structure had been completely burned except for a patch of linoleum that had been identified as having covered the kitchen floor. The linoleum, some said, was in the shape of a woman.

" ' "It had eyes, hands," one worker was reported to have declared. "I swear I could see it. It's a miracle, a sign from God." ' "

The image was dismissed by most as just one more instance of people seeing what they wanted to see in the random images on the side of a building or a warehouse, in shadows, stains, and light patterns shining through frosted glass. The Innsbruck fire chief was quoted by the paper as saying, "Fires can do some strange things. We've seen many instances where burned structures seem to have pictures of faces in them. But it's like finding ships in the clouds or a face on the moon. It's just a matter of human imagination."

The bishop of Innsbruck issued a statement agreeing with the Innsbruck fire chief.

In later years, another Pope would have to contend with a small but zealous cadre of Innsbruck churchgoers demanding that the Vatican declare the site of the image a holy shrine. That Pope would make the same reply that had been given by the man who was Pope when the Cardinal's Nest burned down: "Faith in the unseen is stronger than faith in things we can touch or see. The truest test of our faith in a supreme being is the willingness to believe without seeing. And in the long run, the Christian churches—all religions of all faiths, for that matter—are better off without such visible signs. Because there will always be those who will see and never believe. But God will especially bless those who believe without seeing."

The Pope never directly told anyone whether or not he believed in the sign.

AUTHOR'S NOTE

This is a work of fiction based on fact.

Hitler did set up an organization called the Sonderauftrag Linz, whose purpose was to loot the finest public and private collections of Europe. He planned to exhibit the stolen art in a magnificent museum he would construct in his hometown of Linz, Austria. Plans for the Fuhrermuseum were drawn up by an architect, but the structure was never built.

Hitler's liaison with the Sonderauftrag Linz was a man called Heinrich Heim, with whom I spoke in Munich in December 1983. There was then a close-knit community of unrepentant Nazis still residing in Munich, a group that included two of Hitler's former secretaries and his personal pilot. At the time of my visit, they met with each other occasionally to console themselves on their losses, which they have never quite accepted.

Heim lived in an old World War II bomb shelter in the Schwabing section of the city, a few blocks from the Staatsbibliothek, the Bavarian equivalent of the Library of Congress. In addition to the meager royalties he collected from a book he wrote (that discussed his spying on Hitler for Hermann Goering), Heim generated a small amount of revenue by answering requests for information sent to him from all over the world. Most of his research was conducted at the Staatsbibliothek. Werner Meyer, the chief reporter at the time for Munich's evening newspaper *Abend Zeitung,* introduced me to Heim one night just before Christmas.

Snow, sleet, and freezing rain poured down on us that evening as we parked Werner's car in a dark unpaved lot and made our way down a cluttered alley littered with paper and illuminated by a naked streetlight bulb.

Werner knocked at the metal blast shield that served as Heim's front door. I noticed that the other two windows set into the concrete wall of the structure were covered by blast shields also. Werner told me that Heim lived in constant terror of retribution from the Israelis because—even though he did serve some time in an Allied prison—there are many who believe he was involved in activities far more heinous than merely being Hitler's main adjutant for coordinating art thefts.

After several minutes, Heim came to the door and after some difficulty pushed back the protective barrier and welcomed us.

The phrase "stooped but unbowed" characterized Heim precisely. At first glance, he looked like a street derelict, dressed as he was in two overcoats and a layered succession of sweaters and shirts. But Heim's eyes still shone a bright pale icy blue that could have served as a poster child for Hitler's virile Aryan superman.

He showed us into the room where he conducted his research, and, once we were seated amid the prodigious clutter of papers, solicitously placed threadbare blankets over our knees lest we get cold. The bomb shelter was not heated. Meyer began to talk with Heim as I, with a novice's grasp of the German language, listened. Heim and Werner spoke for a few minutes about their progress in trying to locate some of the original scores of the composer Wagner, which had disappeared during the war. This search is Werner's passion. They talked for a while about the authenticity of Hitler's diaries, which had just surfaced. Heim said that he had read parts and felt they were genuine.

The conversation then turned to me and my attempts to track down missing pieces of art. As part of my research, I had put my talents as a former investigative reporter to work, not only in gathering material for the novel, but also in keeping my eyes open for some find that might serve as the basis for a good magazine article or even a nonfiction book.

We talked only a few minutes before Heim began to speak fondly of Frederick Stahl, the painter favored by Hitler and other Nazis mentioned in this book. Heim quickly grew misty-eyed as he remembered Stahl and, I suppose, the old days. He spoke of the beauty of Stahl's work and of how Hitler treated the artist as if he were a brother, or perhaps a surrogate father.

By now, he had begun to include all of us in the room each time he used the word *unser*, the German familiar form for "us," but which meant more: something that could be roughly translated as "our circle." I grew increasingly uncomfortable as he expanded his use of the word to refer to his Nazi comrades and even to the Fuhrer himself. This was not part of a crowd to which I wanted to belong.

Heim, incidentally, refused to refer to Hitler by name, as if he were afraid to take his name in vain—in much the same way that very religious people will not pronounce the name of their god. Instead, he referred to Hitler as "A. H.," pronounced in German, "Ah-hah!"

After a time, the old Nazi produced a sheaf of papers and an envelope of small photographs. He showed the photographs to us. They were all small black-and-whites, about two inches on a side and each depicting a painting. All the paintings were Stahl's and all were inventoried on a sheet of paper Heim handed to me. The paintings, he said, had disappeared, having last been seen in Zurich just before the fall of the Third Reich. He wouldn't say exactly when they had last been seen or by whom.

He gave me one of the photographs and the inventory after I promised to look for the paintings and let him know through Werner if I had made any progress.

From Munich, I went to Zurich to learn if there were any remaining traces of the Stahl paintings. After checking into my hotel room, I made inquiries and obtained the names of several art galleries that had been in existence during the period of the paintings' disappearance.

I went to the oldest of the galleries and spoke with the owner. I showed him the picture Heim had given me and said that I represented a wealthy collector who was interested in acquiring the Stahl painting.

The man threw me out of his gallery and threatened to call the police if I did not leave the neighborhood quickly.

He said he had nothing to do with the paintings of which I spoke and furthermore did not want anything to do with them or with the people who might be interested in them. I had a difficult time determining whether he was frightened or angry. Probably both. I was certainly frightened.

In the course of my investigative reporting, I had had my life threatened before and had managed to press on, undeterred until I had gotten my story. But that was in the past and I was now committed to staying healthy and hearty; ending up missing in Zurich was not my idea of how to spend the holiday season.

Thus it was that I washed down a *rosti* with a liter of beer that night, went to bed, and took the first train back to Munich the next morning. To this day I remain ignorant of where the Stahl paintings are, and what's more, I don't think it would be healthy to know.

There are many other things in this book that are true. For example, the stories of how escaping SS troops used looted art to buy their freedom. You can rest firm in the knowledge that many of the artworks lost during the war are hanging on the walls of chateaux in the Alps. Many more rest beneath the streets of Zurich. As I learned firsthand, many of these artworks are fantastically valuable, worth much more—in the estimation of some—than the life of someone asking the wrong questions.

The last years of the twentieth century have also been filled with long-overdue attempts to locate looted art and return it to its rightful owners. Also overdue was the public exposure of Nazi collaborators: Swiss banks and a number of American and European corporations. Demands for reparations from surviving victims of the Holocaust and their families were met with arrogant derision and stonewalling on the part of Swiss banks until recently when international pressure has led to a modest effort to compensate owners or heirs of the accounts.

There was also an Emperor Henry IV who was kidnapped. All of the other historical shenanigans involving Popes (three claiming the spot at one time) and emperors is true. And of course, there was an Emperor Constantine who put an end to spiritual squabbling with bureaucratic decrees enforced by the blade of a sword. It has been true throughout religious history—regardless of religion—that matters of faith are decided by political expediency rather than affairs of the spirit. The sections of this book dealing with the Nicean Conference and the events and religious controversies leading up to it are true and far better documented than any of the scriptures in the Hebrew or Christian Bible or the Muslim Koran.

I'm fairly sure that the parts about Sophia as a flesh-and-blood woman are my imagination, created as they were from fragments of intriguing research about the early Christian church and the seminal roles that women played in it; roles that the male-dominated spiritual revisionists have tried to excise. They have been largely successful, but significant references remain—just read Proverbs or the Song of Solomon—where Wisdom is given her due.

To this day, the Catholic Church and other faiths—especially the Greek and Russian Orthodox Churches—are still ambivalent about a mythical Sophia. Some, particularly those who follow Gnosticism, say she is the prime creator of all the universe. Others believe in her as the feminine part of an androgynous God. And still others identify her as the embodiment of Wisdom or even the Logos of the Christian Trinity before it was thoroughly masculinized. There is no question that for the vast part of human existence, God was viewed as a woman.

Sophia has a place in history, but where is still to be determined.

The Catholic Church is not alone among modern religions in its abject fear of women and rejection of them in spiritual or dominant roles. Most of the Roman Catholic characters in this book could have easily been cast from among the leaders of Judaism, most Protestant religions, and Islam. All of these (save an unfortunately very few) would kill before admitting that a woman could be an equal, much less a savior.

It is also a matter of public record that Pope Pius XII turned a blind eye and a deaf ear to the atrocities of the Third Reich. As to the Pope's motives, one can only speculate, but certainly his silence at the time does seem at odds with his perceived role as a moral authority. His unwillingness to raise his voice in protest against Nazi policies is, and no doubt shall remain, a mystery. With its millennial apologia, the Catholic Church has confessed and apologized for a few of the mortal sins it has committed in the name of God and Christ. While only a small step, it does set a good example that the rest of Christendom as well as Judaism and Islam should emulate.

Students of history, theology, geography, and political science will find many, many more things in this book that are true. But in the end, the book as a whole is, after all, a work of fiction. At least, I believe it is.

But if we can find truth in fiction, the truth I have tried to write is the spiritual imperative to question and to search for a relationship with God. And further, to know that this relationship does not exclude different relationships that others have established. No faith has a monopoly on God any more than the color red has a more favored position in the spectrum of light from the sun.

Finally, the Golden Rule rests at the spiritual heart of all major religions, a heart frequently ignored by those who preach and claim to practice it. The timeless command to love others as you love yourself, to treat others as you would have them treat you, is something that even our limited human minds can grasp, understand, and practice. As the Jewish sage Hillel said, you should love your neighbor as yourself. The rest is just commentary.

Lewis Perdue
Sonoma, California
September 1999